The Khmer Connection

By

Braxton DeGarmo

Christen Haus Publishing

COPYRIGHT

DEDICATION

This book is dedicated to all of those parents whose lives and families have been forever changed by vaccine injuries or the death of a child due to a vaccination.

AUTHOR'S NOTE

Several years ago, while still practicing as a physician, I was a stalwart supporter of the need and use of vaccines in public health. Shortly after retiring, while researching a different topic for an earlier book, I stumbled across a medical article that challenged my entire thinking about vaccinations. The subsequent research into the topic led me to realize that it was a topic worthy of presenting as a social justice issue in the MedAir Series. After witnessing firsthand the people and the country of Cambodia on a missions trip in 2017, and learning the horrors of their history during the Pol Pot regime, I saw the perfect opportunity to marry both topics into one story, *The Khmer Connection*. (By the way, for those who don't know, Khmer is pronounced like our slang for 'come here'—c'mere.) I hope you enjoy the book.

CHAPTER ONE

The woman deserved death for what she had done to him. Now he would repay her, but not with so quick an end.

Abdullah Said Abdi glanced about the bay as the moon reflected off its calm waters. There was a serenity about it that he found disturbing, as if it could distract him from his mission. Life, for him, had never been calm. Calm had only predicted another rising storm.

The son of a warlord in Somalia, he had risen to that position after his father had died, but not without opposition. The man who dared to challenge him had never seen the knife coming. Still, the man had inflicted his own mark upon Abdi. He traced the scar that marked his face with his left index finger—forever a reminder that distractions could be dangerous, if not fatal.

It was the distraction of a woman when he was a younger man that had almost cost him his life before dispatching his opponent to Paradise. From that he had learned that women were to remain chattel—easily bought and sold for pleasure—and meant to be subservient. A woman's place was to serve her husband, or her master if she was a concubine within the harem. Cooking. Cleaning.

Preparing her children for their appropriate roles in life. Those things were expected. Not feminism, the workplace, or equality with men. Dressing indecently. Talking back to men. Bringing humiliation to a man.

Not what one Amy Gibbs had done to him.

The young girls of his tribe, both in Somalia and the U.S., must never see that she got away with dishonoring him. The members of his tribe would never assimilate into America and those values. It would be their pleasure to join their Islamic brethren in bringing down the American Satan. To regain face, he would have to deal with Amy Gibbs—even if it required going to the other side of the world to do so. There was more at stake than his small faction in America.

Thanks to his men working as baggage handlers at the airport in St. Louis, he had discovered the destination of that woman. Now he would see to it that she could no longer humiliate a man. She would soon discover the real destiny that awaited her for her impudence.

He sensed the trawler slowing. They did not want to be discovered by the local authorities, and he would transfer to a smaller boat for the rest of the trip. The captain approached him.

"We are at the transfer coordinates. You have fifteen minutes before we must depart. I cannot be caught in these waters."

"I have been assured that I have a boat to move to shore." He handed the captain an envelope. "Here is your payment."

The man took the envelope and nodded. "Fifteen minutes."

Abdi scanned the waters to the north. On his second pass, he saw three flashes of light. He returned the signal with four flashes.

His twenty-hour ordeal was about to end. It paid to have money and connections, even if those connections were more likely to be seen on Interpol wanted lists than on social media. His trip back into Mexico followed the same path along the open southern border as had his entry into the U.S. years earlier. A wall back then would have kept him out, while a wall now might have corralled him in for authorities to round up. Once in Mexico, his cartel associates there assured him they had a way to confuse the U.S. authorities that sought him—a drone that could land and take off from water and also transmit a false radar signature. If it worked, the U.S. agents would see a Somali ship "parked" off their western coast and anticipate the potential of his escaping on it.

Instead, he transferred to a larger aircraft for the trans-Pacific flight, landed at another private airstrip in Indonesia, and bought passage on a small plane to the island where the Somali fishing trawler met him for the trip into the bay. No commercial flight schedules to meet. No airports and their security checkpoints. No customs or immigration hassles.

A man, to whom he had provided a steady stream of children and young girls, had a connection inside this country. That connection, in turn, had clients with expressed interests in a tall, attractive American woman for their harems. Upon seeing a picture of Amy Gibbs, he had become more than amenable to helping Abdi find this woman, whom they would capture and auction to the highest bidder. That suited Abdi's purpose. Death was too quick. Years of drugged imprisonment and sadistic abuse was the more appropriate lesson for this woman who must learn her place.

Abdi checked the clock on his phone. With allowances for the International Date Line, he estimated that he was nearly a full day ahead of her. He would be ready.

CHAPTER TWO

"Where is she, Macy?"

Lynch Cully confronted Macy Johnson as she exited her car to go to work at the Mercy Medical Center Emergency Department. He knew she'd never answer the phone if he'd called her. Macy was Amy Gibbs' BFF, having gone to nursing school and finding jobs together at Mercy before Amy became a med-evac flight nurse. He had seen her driving away from the airport after dropping off Amy. If anyone knew where Amy was going, she would.

The woman ducked back into the car to retrieve her gear but stopped and turned to face him, her hands on her hips.

"Well, look at you, all high and mighty. Don't you get all mister policeman on me, Lynch Cully."

Lynch was no longer a detective. Following a serious injury a few years earlier, he had chosen not to return to active police work in hope of proving to Amy that he'd changed. Fully recovered, his most recent position had been as chief of security for the Bradley Graham presidential campaign. But, now, President-elect Graham had a full Secret Service detail, and Lynch served on the transition team.

Make that *had* served. He had been granted a leave-of-absence to deal with Amy's situation. He *had* to track her down.

He softened his stance and took a deep breath.

"Macy, look, I know you don't like me. I know you don't think I've changed, but I have. And I know you'll do anything you can to protect Amy, but I'm not the enemy here."

She glowered at him, looking unconvinced.

"Seriously? I watched her mope around for months after you dumped her. My shoulder was damp for a year from her tears. And you want to convince me you're not the enemy. No sirree. It'll be a tropical day in Greenland before that happens."

He had no counter-argument for that. He had left Amy . . . and regretted it every day. They were finally making some progress in reconciliation when he had his accident and was off the grid for months, assumed dead.

"Yes, I'm serious, Macy. She needs support right now, not running away. She needs you. She needs her brothers. And I want to prove to her that she can trust me to be there, too."

From the change in her face he could see that she agreed with at least part of what he'd said.

"But it's more than that. It's more than her father's recent murder—"

"And Richard's, too."

He nodded. "Yes, and Richard's, too."

Over the past month, Amy's life had been caught up in maelstrom. After Lynch had gone missing nearly four years earlier, she had met an Army veteran named Richard Nichols. They'd become engaged. Lynch didn't hold that against the man. He liked Richard. They ended up both working for Bradley Graham. He knew Richard would protect and care for Amy, and that's what really counted— her happiness.

But Richard had commitment issues, and from what Lynch had learned, Amy finally got tired of waiting and broke off the engagement. Within a week of that, his realtor allegedly murdered him. Lynch had his doubts about that scenario; too many things didn't add up. But that investigation belonged to someone else. What mattered to Lynch was that during that time, Amy crossed paths with a terrorist cell and by pure serendipity foiled the group's plot for mayhem. Her father had caught the bullet meant for Amy.

Lynch reached out toward Macy, but she backed away.

"Macy, listen to me. Amy's still in danger. A new friend of mine in the intelligence community has told me that Abdullah Said Abdi, the Somali warlord who killed her father, has left the country. And recent chatter says he's going after Amy."

Amy stared ahead into the darkened cabin. As an Army brat, she had done her fair share of overseas flights, but never had she encountered a ride this long—16 hours in the air. It would have been two hours longer if she'd taken the flight out of Chicago.

She tried to adjust her five-foot, 11-inch frame in the

cramped seat, but after two hours in the air she couldn't find any comfortable angle. She had managed to snag an aisle seat, but that hadn't stopped the beefy businessman in the middle seat from invading her space. His laptop sat halfway in front of her, and his hefty arms bumped her continually as he typed. At least he was friendly, had recently showered, and used breath mints. She couldn't say that of her neighbor on her last long flight, to the Middle East.

She leaned forward and grabbed her purse from under the seat in front of her. She retrieved a set of small headphones from within and proceeded to investigate the selection of recent movies offered by the in-flight entertainment system. She had watched all but three. Tears filled her eyes. She had seen them with Richard before . . . before . . .

Her thoughts switched to her father and the tears began to flow. She hid her face. She didn't want anyone to see her crying.

Richard's death hit her harder than she had anticipated. She had, after all, been the one to break their engagement. That didn't mean she didn't love him anymore. She couldn't help but think that he'd still be alive had she been there. He would not have been in a position of being alone with that realtor accused of his murder if she had been with him. The whole situation surrounding his death confused her. Something just didn't ring true about the evidence presented to her by the detectives.

However, she *had* been there with her father, and he still died.

Why, God? That was a question she asked over and over.

She had been the target, not her dad. Why had she bent over to pick something up at that precise moment? Why had he decided to stand behind her when he always sat in one of her cushioned barstools at the counter when she cooked? Why had she let her curiosity get the better of her and make her stumble onto that stupid explosives cache in the first place?

For both of the men in her life, the chain of events seemed to go back to one incident—her following Richard to that house and getting mad enough to break off the engagement. Had she not done that, Richard would still be alive. Had she not broken up with him she would never have been walking at Busch Wildlife and would not have stumbled upon those Somalis near bunker 64. And, in turn, her father would still be alive.

Why, God? Why?

"Hey, lovely lady. My name's Jake Riddout, and I'd love to buy you a drink."

She had noticed the guy across the aisle eyeing her since the plane's departure. He appeared well-groomed and successful. Clearly, he felt confident enough in himself to approach her, but . . .

"Thanks, but I'm not thirsty."

He leaned further into the aisle, closer to her. "Well, we've got another 14 hours to this flight. I hate to drink alone. So, where you headed? I've got business in Singapore this next week and then it's on to Taiwan."

Amy shook her head, looked toward her entertainment system screen, and readjusted her headphones, hoping the man would take that subtle sign and leave her alone.

"So, again, my name's Jake. What's yours? Maybe we could get together for dinner in Singapore. I've been there dozens of times and know several nice places to eat. If you're going to be there for a day or so, I'd love to show you around the city."

Amy took a deep breath and focused on finding a movie to watch. She didn't want to answer verbally for fear that her doing so might be misconstrued as a willingness to talk, or worse, share a drink with him. Besides, her sleaze warning system had begun its steady beat. It was the same uneasiness she had felt around Darko Komarčić, a sex trafficker who had kidnapped and held her briefly at his home outside St. Louis, before Richard, and Lynch, had come to her rescue.

"So, have you ever been to Singapore?"

She felt his hand on her shoulder and flinched. She was about to forcefully remove it, and his arm from his body, when the stewardess approached. The man pulled his hand back to his side of the aisle.

"Miss, is this man bothering you?"

Amy looked up to see the woman glaring at the man. Once upon a time, she would have brushed it aside and said "No, we're fine." But in the day and age of #MeToo, she no longer tolerated such brashness.

"Yes, he won't leave me alone."

"I see. Would you please collect your belongings and come with me? That includes your carry-on piece, too."

Amy was about to protest. Why was she being moved when *he* was the troublemaker? But then she saw a subtle smile directed her way from the stewardess. She decided not to make a row.

With her gear both in hand and in tow, she followed the woman forward in the cabin. A moment later, they crossed into the business class area, and the stewardess pointed to an empty seat.

"We have a couple of empty seats here. Hope you don't mind." She grinned. "Your carry-on can go in there. Here, let me take it for you."

Amy watched the woman stow her bag for her, as she herself put her small backpack "purse" in its place and sat down in the spacious seat with ample room for her legs and feet . . . and no one's laptop invading her space.

"Thank you so much. The guy was starting to creep me out."

"I know. I've been on this flight four or five times with that guy. I remember him because we've had complaints about him before. He creeps me out, too. Anyway, you'll depart through a different door, so you shouldn't run into him again. Now, can I get you a drink? It comes with the seat." She smiled again.

Amy laughed. "Sure. A glass of white wine sounds nice. Thanks."

She settled back into the seat and relaxed as she'd never been able to do in economy class. Plus, she wouldn't have to fight off the guy's advances for the next 14 hours. As she thought about it, she realized she wouldn't have to worry about that at all where she was heading. She would be working with Christian missionary friends at their children's home and feeding programs. She hoped it would be the diversion she needed, as she grieved the loss of her father.

* * *

"Cully, I don't know where she went."

Lynch scrutinized Macy's face but couldn't tell if she was telling the truth or not.

"Well, Abdullah Said Abdi sure seems to know where she's headed. How would he know and her best friend doesn't?"

This time the nurse's face told him everything—hurt and anguish. She didn't know. Amy had not shared that with her best friend. Why?

"I, I'm telling you the truth. I asked a thousand times, and she refused to tell me."

Tears welled up in Macy's eyes.

"I'm sorry, Macy. I didn't mean to hurt your feelings. I'm sure she had a reason for not telling you."

Lynch sought to control his own feelings. He had come to accept the fact that he loved Amy Gibbs, with all her quirks and penchant for getting into trouble. But she now had a twelve-hour lead on him—wherever her travels were taking her. Maybe she was holed up in some spa in the Rockies, or on a beach in Southern California. If so, he could probably catch up with her by the next day . . . if he could find out where she was.

Macy wiped the tears from her face and collected her things from the car.

"Cully, I need to clock in, or I'm going to get a lecture. Let me do that and explain to my charge nurse what's going on. I'll meet you outside the ambulance entrance in 15 minutes."

Without waiting for his reply, she turned and rushed toward the hospital. Lynch watched her walk away and debated what to do next. He had already "misused" his position with the President-elect to ask Homeland Security if they could help him track her. After a lot of hems and haws, his contact gave him a conditional 'yes' but said it could take a day. He didn't have a day. Amy was over half a day ahead of him, and Abdi was at least six hours ahead as well.

As he walked toward the ambulance entrance, he pulled out his cell phone and made a call.

"Grant Gibbs."

Finally, thought Lynch. He had tried to reach all three of Amy's brothers without success.

"Grant, it's Lynch Cully. Hey, I'm—"

"Lynch, I . . . um, thank you for coming to Dad's funeral. I know that meant a lot to Amy. Greg, Garrett and I appreciated it, too."

"Man, that's the least I could do. Your dad was special."

"Thanks. I, uh, well, what's up?"

"Grant, I'm trying to track down Amy. Something has come up, and I need to get ahold of her."

He hesitated in telling Grant the true nature of his concern. The man had just lost his father. He didn't need to worry about losing his sister, too. That wasn't going to happen on Lynch's watch.

Lynch heard a deep sigh from the other end.

"Wish I could help, but you know how she can be sometimes. She refused to tell any of us. She just gave me power of attorney to sell her house and everything she left in it, and told me she'd check in when she got back."

When she got back. The words registered, but gave Lynch no hint as to how long she planned on being gone.

"Did she say when she'd be back?"

"Sorry. No clue, but it didn't seem like she planned a short trip. Why else would she want someone to sell her house for her?"

That was one possible explanation for having Grant do that for her. Yet, Lynch suspected it was a more emotional reason—not wanting anything to do with the house where she had been targeted and her father had been murdered. As he thought about it, he realized why she hadn't told her destination to anyone close to her. She thought their not knowing protected them. The less they knew the better. Lynch knew it often didn't work that way.

"Grant, it's really important that I find her. If she calls any of you, please call me right away, any time of day."

There was a hesitation on the other end.

"Uh, sure. Is . . . is there something we should know about?"

"Not at the moment," Lynch lied. "Just rumor, but I'll let you know if something concrete comes up. Thanks."

"Um, sure. Keep in touch."

The call ended on a cordial note, but Lynch could hear the questions in Grant's tone. Maybe he should have been upfront with the man.

He heard the automatic doors open behind him, and Macy appeared, now dressed in scrubs and ready for anything . . . except maybe for what Lynch asked of her.

As she approached, he could see she had her cell phone

to her ear.

"Macy, I—"

She held up a finger and shook her head to quiet him. "Yes, Michael. That's all I have, her name and the approximate time of her departure . . . Sure, hon, you know I'll wait. And I'll have a double batch of your favorite cookies at your door before the weekend . . . Thanks, hon."

She put her hand over the phone and said, "I'm talking with my cousin Michael. He works at the airport. I probably would have called him eventually 'cause it really bothers me that I don't know where she's headed."

Amy had told Lynch about Macy's untold number of quirky cousins, many of whom seemed to work at places that never failed to come in handy, like the meter maid who always looked the other way when Macy and Amy went clubbing on Washington Avenue and parked conveniently, although illegally, close to their favorite club.

"Well, you're not alone. Her brothers don't know either."

"Not surprised. She would have told her father but not her brothers. I-I still can't believe he's gone."

Lynch noticed a difference in Macy. She was no longer antagonistic toward him. Had he won her over? Finally?

She held up her finger again. "Yeah, hon, I'm still here . . . She went *where*?" The woman's eyes bulged in shock. "Cousin, thank you. I'm gonna make you those cookies sometime next month, too. You coming to the family reunion? . . . Yeah, me, too. See you then."

She shook her head. "Cully, you are not going to believe this one. My girl has outdone herself this time. And if you think you've won my approval, don't. But if you keep her safe and get her home without trouble, then maybe I'll consider it."

The woman kept shaking her head. "Yes indeed. She has outdone herself on this one. My, my, my."

"Macy!"

She looked at him. "Man, you sounded just like her the way you said that."

"Macy?"

"Our girl Amy is headin' to . . ."

CHAPTER THREE

Lynch paced the concourse adjacent to gate A16 at Lambert International Airport. Upon learning Amy's destination, he had driven home, packed for the overseas trip, and contacted the President-elect's transition team to update his boss on his status.

Intent on creating an action plan for his mission, he missed the overhead announcement about his flight to Houston. His focus caught the tail end of that message and he thought, *Please, say that again.*

He glanced about and saw a few people doing the same, heads looking up wondering what had just been said. Admittedly, he was early. The flight didn't leave for over two hours and no one attended the gate at that moment. He simply couldn't wait around at home, doing nothing. Instead, he was at the airport . . . doing nothing . . . except stressing out about not being in the air en route to finding Amy.

"This announcement is for all travelers on Flight 3668 to Houston. Severe thunderstorms across the south have delayed dozens of flights and Flight 3668 is now canceled. Please see the nearest gate agent for assistance."

Lynch grabbed his carry-on case and hurried down

Concourse A looking for the first open gate with that airline's agents present. Four others beat him to the line that had already formed there. He scurried past, hoping to find a shorter line at an open gate farther along.

His persistence paid off. An open gate with only one person being assisted loomed ahead to his left. He stepped up behind that person, a plump older woman who appeared to be in her seventies. She had her purse strapped across the shoulder opposite to where it hung, with a leopard-print neck pillow wrapped around her neck, an umbrella dangling from her left forearm, and her right hand resting on the extended handle of her carry-on case, which had zippers that appeared ready to burst from the overstuffed contents inside.

He couldn't help but overhear the conversation.

"I'm sorry ma'am, but you're too late."

"Too late? But this is gate A4, isn't it?"

"Yes, ma'am. You have the right gate, but you're late. You missed that flight."

"Missed the flight? How could I have missed the flight? It leaves at six-o-five and it's only four-thirty. And it says right here, Gate A4." She held up her itinerary for the agent.

He saw the woman becoming a bit agitated, and gave the gate agent kudos for maintaining her calm.

"Yes, ma'am, but look at the date. This ticket was for yesterday's flight."

There ensued a small argument about the date and day of the week. The attendant was professional, but firm, and yet, the older woman didn't want to back down. Lynch wanted to butt in and support the gate agent—anything to get the woman moving—but held his tongue. He'd been working on his patience and didn't want to backslide. Particularly now, as he wanted nothing to happen faster than to be on his way, soaring through the friendly skies.

"Sir?"

Lynch looked up and raised his brow to silently ask, *Who? Me?*

"Yes, sir. Could you straighten out this young woman and tell us what day it is today?"

He saw the gate agent sigh and roll her eyes. He hoped he wasn't about to get smacked with that umbrella.

"Ma'am, the gate agent is correct." He retrieved and displayed his cell phone to the older woman. "Sorry."

The woman looked defeated. "Oh no. What am I going to do? I-I . . . Oh my. I need to get to Washington. What can I do?"

The gate agent took control. "Let's see what we can do."

Lynch began to wonder if the other gate's long line still existed. But then, his own plans might tie up an agent just as long. He reminded himself that patience was a virtue.

As he started to put his phone back, it rang.

"Cully," he answered.

"Mr. Cully, this is Special Agent Liam O'Brien. I'm with the FBI Terrorism Task Force. I understand you're looking for information on an Abdullah Said Abdi."

Lynch turned away from the desk but refused to step away and lose his place as next in line.

"Thank you for calling. I'm not in a secure area to speak openly. Were you briefed on the reason for my request?" He lowered his voice, but remained acutely aware of the people around him.

"I was, and I understand. Look, we're trying to track down this guy. He doesn't appear to have gone through any airports, and he's on the 'No Fly' list here and in Canada. What I can tell you is that a suspicious Somali ship was detected off the West Coast early yesterday. It seems to be keeping its position about twenty miles off the coast, where the Coast Guard is tracking it. In the meantime, I've notified the captain of the Coast Guard cutter that's tracking it about your interest, and we've also sent word to the U.S. Embassy at your destination to be available to Miss Gibbs should she reach out to them for help. They are also expecting you."

"Hey, thanks. That's more than I asked for. I really appreciate it."

"No problem. I looked a bit at your record, and I'm glad to help out a former law enforcement officer, especially one who's helped us as much as you have in the past. I hope you find your friend quickly."

Lynch nodded. So did he. But first, he had to get there.

He glanced at his watch. Going on five p.m. That meant five a.m. the next day in Cambodia. What in the world had led Amy to travel halfway around the world? She had nearly a full day's head start on him, but she wouldn't arrive there for at least another day. Maybe someone from the embassy would meet her upon arrival. And how long would it take a ship to travel there? A couple of weeks at least, he figured. As he attempted to find the transit time by ship, his turn arrived to discuss his options with the gate agent.

Twenty minutes later, his entire flight schedule rearranged, he had to hustle to a different concourse and gate. He would now be flying to San Francisco for a connecting flight to Hong Kong, and then Singapore. Following an eight-hour layover there, he would catch the first flight to Phnom Penh. But the plane to San Fran was boarding now.

He really wanted to try yet again to phone Amy, but he had no time. His first dozen calls had gone to voicemail. And his half dozen texts had gone unanswered. That alone had his concern at red alert. At home, her phone had been surgically attached to her. This was totally out of character. But then, so was leaving everything and everyone to go to Cambodia.

Captain William Chase, USCG, grew up knowing that one day he'd be a seafaring man. His parents had thought that funny and his brothers had teased him relentlessly about it, seeing as they lived on a wheat farm in the middle of Nebraska. They laughed when he told them that their amber waves of grain reminded him of ocean waves. He'd never seen the ocean.

Yet, he was so persistent in his dream of heading to sea, that his parents saved up for a family vacation to Destin, Florida, the year he turned 14, so he could see it firsthand. While the rest of the family couldn't wait to head home, he became more insistent and began to read up on marine biology, oceanography, underwater oil exploration, and any and all other occupations that would take him to the water. The summer following his junior year in high school gave him his first opportunity to experience the ocean beyond the shoreline. That summer's fellowship at the Woods Hole Oceanographic Institution in Woods Hole, Massachusetts, was the first major milestone in his quest to go to sea.

The second milestone began with the onset of the first Gulf War and his realization that his destiny was to serve his country. Three years later came his acceptance at the Coast Guard Academy in New London, Connecticut. He had not had the funds or scholarships to even consider a place like Woods Hole, Duke, or Sanford with their marine sciences programs, so, with his congressman's support, he applied to both the CGA and the Naval Academy. He figured whichever accepted him first was meant to be . . . and the CGA won.

The military lifestyle, with its regimentation, came hard at first, but he excelled during his plebe year and rose in the ranks of cadets. He set his sights on ocean cutter duty, which he considered the creme de la creme of the corps.

Upon graduation he found his dream fulfilled with his assignment as an ensign aboard a small coastal cutter. He set his mind on bigger and better duty stations, but his promotion to Lieutenant JG gave him his first, and only, setback—in his mind anyway—being assigned to Saint Louis and the Upper Mississippi River. Not the ocean, a river. As a marine inspections officer checking out barges and other big boats. That was like signing on to a 5-star restaurant as a waiter only to find yourself bussing tables. Whom had he pissed off?

But now, 19 years later? He commanded the USCGC Bertholf, home based in Alameda, California, and his past caught up to his present. He hadn't heard the name Lynch Cully in nearly 16 years.

How had a rookie cop found his way to the President-elect's inner circle? And what in the world was his interest in a Somali ship?

"What's the latest position of that Somali fishing vessel?" He looked about the bridge and realized he had a decision to make.

"Still 30-degrees off starboard and holding about 20 miles offshore, sir."

The fact that their course now took them due south and that the ship remained 30-degrees off their starboard side meant that it, too, cruised south at roughly the same speed.

"Chief, I think it's time we intercept and inspect that vessel. Set course and proceed at full speed. Estimated time of intercept?"

"Twenty-five minutes, sir."

With easy seas, they could make 30 knots, or a little better. He had time to satisfy his curiosity about one Lynch Cully.

"Chief, I'll be in my quarters. Let me know when we're five minutes away."

"Yes, sir."

The captain smiled as he felt the engines pick up speed. Inside his quarters, he awakened his laptop and entered "Lynch Cully" into the search bar of his browser. He owed Cully one. The man had just applied to become a fledgling detective, but already had the smarts that had saved Will's butt. A drug ring had been operating on the river right under his nose, and he had missed the signs. While true that such activity fell on the turf of the DEA, Cully had pointed him in the right direction just in time for Will to stop a major deal that resulted in the removal of hundreds of pounds of crack cocaine from streets throughout the Midwest. That bust caught the attention of several superiors and helped fast track Will toward his next promotion.

So, what was his old friend up to these days? Just as the first page of results filled the screen, his intercom squawked.

"Captain, you might want to come see this."

He secured his computer and made his way back to the bridge.

"Sir, within a minute of changing course, the radar signature on that fishing trawler changed and it picked up speed. It's approaching 50 knots. We can't catch it. Should we take to the air?"

Chase reviewed the new radar signature. He'd not seen anything similar in over two decades in the guard. And its speed? Sure wasn't some fishing trawler. Only hydrofoils were known to reach such speeds on water, but design constraints—the weight limitations of the bow foils, the cavitation problems of running on high seas, and the engine requirements—made ocean-going hydrofoils more of a dream than an affordable, realizable option.

The Bertholf's MH-65C Dolphin was a search-and-rescue helicopter, not an armed intercept aircraft. That "trawler" seemed intent on not being boarded, which meant his aircrew would likely be fired upon. Their VT-UAVs, on the other hand, could take a closer look and keep a close eye on this mystery vessel.

"Send out one of the UAVs."

The vertical takeoff-unmanned aerial vehicle with its 225-mph max speed would soon catch up with the ship, and its high-def cameras could spy on the crew picking their noses. They would soon know what and whom they were dealing with.

"Will Chase One, prepare to launch," barked a crew member into his mic.

The captain smiled. It never got old. Little had he known upon joining the corps that his reputation for chasing down drug boats and others loaded with contraband would become a legend of its own. That legend had been sealed by their takedown and ultimate sinking of a semi-submersible narco-submarine loaded with six tons of cocaine off Panama a few years back. His name itself had become code for "let's get 'em, boys!" and his crew took delight in naming their UAVs the Will Chase One and Two.

"Coordinates programmed in, sir. Ready to launch on your command."

"Launch!"

As they watched the UAV pass their starboard bow, the radar tech yelled, "Sir, it's gone! No radar signature. Whatever it was, it's gone."

CHAPTER FOUR

The slight man drove his silver Mercedes E300 sedan carefully along the rutted dirt road bordered by family rice paddies, lotus ponds, and the occasional coconut grove. The monsoons had ended, the rivers were retreating back within their banks, and the foliage grew lush, aided by the hot, humid climate. He was but an hour away from the capital, toward the Vietnam border almost due east of the city, and had turned off National Highway 1. He had passed through the village of Me Sang and now followed directions given him by an associate from the area. The home he sought should not be much farther.

He came to a stop as a farmer drove his cattle along the road. The man wore a traditional *sampot* and Khmer scarf, or *kroma*. He kept the cattle moving with a long, slender bamboo switch and appeared in no hurry.

Khay Oudom gave a short toot of the car's horn to let the man know he was there. He knew better than to lay into the horn, as it would not speed things along. Besides he needed the goodwill of these people, not their animosity.

Everything about him was planned to favorably impress those he visited. His clothing had been chosen to speak of education and refinement. The same with his grooming. In a country where permits to own a car cost more than $10,000 U.S. and the vehicle itself cost much, much more, his car spoke of money. And money spoke to these people whose livelihoods depended on the few dollars a week they might earn selling eggs, chickens, or perhaps rice.

He had been to America once, the land of opportunity. He had not been impressed. He had seen it as a nation of excess and greed. He laughed at the "poor" in the U.S. who protested for $15-an-hour wages. In his land, such jobs were lucky to pay one to two dollars a day. The poor in the U.S. had televisions and cell phones. The poor Khmer had mats to sleep on and enough food for one meal a day . . . on most days.

And yet, his short stay in America had made one impression on him. He would do whatever was required to avoid living in poverty.

As he waited upon the farmer and his herd, Oudom rechecked his directions. The home he sought was just ahead. Half a dozen young children ran from its yard to greet the farmer, whom Oudom now recognized as a teenage boy, likely the oldest sibling of that cabal of children. The children weaved through the herd and soon surrounded his car. He waved them away and inched toward the house, parking in the front yard once the cattle had cleared it.

As he exited the vehicle, the children stood, huddled together, a short distance away and watched him. He retrieved a small leather briefcase from the back seat and turned toward the dwelling. He saw a typical village home—

a single room sitting ten to twelve feet above ground on stilts, with a roof of galvanized metal sheets, and rough lumber enclosing the building. The area under the structure held the open fire "kitchen," a handful of net hammocks suspended from above, and two dilapidated aluminum lawn chairs. While many such homes had real staircases—with or without railings—to climb to the room above, this one had but a ladder made of sticks. At its base was a bright, colorful spirit house, a place for roaming spirits to stay so they would not enter the abode.

His associate would appear to have been correct. This was a family of little means and too many mouths to feed.

He approached the home and a man left one of the hammocks and walked toward him. Oudom set his briefcase on the ground and placed his hands together at chest level and bowed slightly. The other man responded with the same *som pas.*

"*Choum reap sur, Lok Raksmei.*" Hello, *Mr.* Raksmei, using the man's given name, not his family name, as was customary. According to his associate, Chey Raksmei had already been approached and knew to expect Khay Oudom.

"*Choum reap sur, Lok Oudom.*"

Raksmei turned and pointed to the shade beneath his home. Oudom followed. As Raksmei pointed to one of the chairs, a woman emerged from nearby and bowed in *som pas.* Oudom noted that her bow was deeper, as the appropriate sign of respect that a woman should show any man. She did not speak, and he did not expect her to do so unless asked.

As he sat down, she extended to him a short, clean

plank on which sat a cup of tea and a small plate of *chek pong moan*, chicken egg banana—the national fruit, plus a small piece of bread. He nodded in acceptance and took it from her. To do otherwise would be rude.

As she retreated from the men and stood aloof within earshot, he saw the children gather about her. She placed her arms around the young twin boys and held them tightly to her small frame. Would she risk a beating from her husband by contesting what was about to happen? He doubted it from the look of resignation on her face. The children, too, looked hopeless.

As a sign of respect, he took a piece of banana, followed by a sip of tea, and smiled.

"So, *Lok* Raksmei, I've been told that a man from my organization has already talked with you." The man nodded. "Good. I would like to repeat one test before we continue."

He reached down for his briefcase, sat it upon his lap, and opened it. He retrieved what was considered a toy in more developed countries. A toy, and yet one that played a role in development of small children.

He saw recognition in the man's eyes just before the father snapped his fingers and said, "Ponleak."

One of the twins bowed his head and approached. The "test" was different than those previously shown the child, so as to prevent the child's success purely from rote memory of the earlier encounter.

Oudom laid the board on his lap, glanced at his watch, and handed Ponleak a wooden shape. The boy looked at it, then gazed at the board on Oudom's lap, and hesitated only a brief moment before placing the shape into its respective hole in the board. He did so with all eight shapes. The boy finished within three minutes. "Very good."

The father snapped his fingers again and Ponleak joined him by his side. "Phirum."

The other twin came to Oudom and stood in front of him. Oudom repeated the test with this six-year-old. He completed the task in just over two minutes.

"Excellent."

The boy moved to stand on the other side of their father.

"*Lok* Raksmei, your boys show great intelligence and potential for their age." Oudom knew better. Their time was average—for a four-year-old—but the truth would not advance his cause, his reason for being there. "We would like to give your boys an education, a chance to learn English, and a place to live while they learn. In addition, we would reimburse you for the loss of their service on your farm."

The father looked at his wife. Oudom followed his gaze and saw tears in her eyes. He knew from his observations so far that she was a good Buddhist wife, deferring to her husband's decisions. A thought came to mind, and he glanced about quickly. He saw no crucifix, no cross. Yes, a good Buddhist family untouched by those meddlesome Christians and that Jesus person's teaching of equality, love, and repentance from sin, whatever that was.

"How much? They are already a big help with our chickens. They will work harder as they get older."

Oudom had no doubt that they were and that they would. He also had no doubt that the man would jump at their offer.

"I am sure of that, but let me show you what we offer them." Oudom pulled two colorful brochures from his briefcase as he placed the toy inside. He handed one to Raksmei and pointed the other at his wife, before handing it to Raksmei, too. It was not proper for him to hand it to her himself. The father held out the paper to her, and she hurried over to take it.

Oudom saw her eyes widen at the sight of the beautiful children's home and school sitting on manicured grounds, with children in immaculate school uniforms. Likewise, Raksmei appeared impressed. The text of the brochure told of the purpose of their organization—to educate the poorest of the country's children—and of the amenities of the school beyond a basic education—the food, sports, and language skills. The back of the brochure showed two attractive graduates of their program, with testimonies of the colleges that had accepted them and the jobs they ultimately secured. Oudom verbally stressed their purpose and the amenities, assuming that neither parent had learned to read. Raksmei's lack of questions seemed to confirm that.

"We are prepared to offer you $500 US to compensate you for their lost service." The eyes of both parents widened further. "For each boy," added Oudom. The wife's hand flew to her mouth.

Five hundred dollars amounted to at least two years of income for the entire family, enough to feed their family of ten. With two fewer mouths to feed, the money became even more valuable. Plus, it was money they could use on top of what they would continue to earn with or without the boys.

Oudom doubted that Raksmei had the ability to think beyond the short term in which $1,000 seemed a fortune.

"It is not enough," blurted out the wife.

Oudom sat back in surprise. He had underestimated the woman. Raksmei glared at her, and she backed away in obeisance. Raksmei stood and walked over to her. Oudom expected him to strike her for her rudeness and disrespect. Instead, he leaned over to listen as she whispered in his ear. He then returned to his seat.

"It is not enough," he repeated. "They are strong boys and smart, like you said. In a few years, they could bring that much to our family each year."

Oudom recovered from his surprise. He had encountered resistance before.

"You are no doubt correct. But think what they could do for your family if they get an excellent education and great jobs. You have many mouths to feed and . . . " He paused. "Tell you what. I wish to help my fellow countrymen. I am willing to raise our offer to $750 each. But no more. This education I offer costs money to provide."

Oudom saw Raksmei glance at his wife, who returned with a subtle shaking of her head to the negative. He had indeed underestimated this woman.

"We have much need. We will agree to $1,000 for each boy."

Now Oudom's eyes widened. Something beyond his comprehension had emboldened this family. Not once had he paid more than $750 for a child.

He stood. "A moment please." With that he walked toward his car, pulling his cell phone from his pocket and pretending to talk on it. That was a ruse. He needed time to think. Perhaps he could wrangle more money from those who paid him. These were twins, after all, at the perfect age for their work. Twins, whether boys or girls, were not commonly available and for a farm family to give up a boy was even more unusual. Boys had value on a farm. Girls and their dowries were seen as a future expense.

He mulled over his prospects for another minute or so and decided that, yes, he could get more money for six-year-old twin boys. As he returned to the father, prepared to agree with their price, his phone rang.

"Break off whatever you are doing. You are required in Srae Ambel as soon as you can get there. We have a foreign friend arriving who needs your assistance. Meet Seoung there. He will give you the details."

The man on the other end of the call was not one Oudom cared to cross, even with a simple request such as delaying the trip so Oudom could complete the deal with these parents and transport the boys to their new home. And the fact that he was to meet Seoung, a man whose temper he never wished to face, added to the gravity of this "command."

Yet, as he thought about it, this might work in his favor. A delay in consummating the transfer of these children might make the parents reconsider their exorbitant fee. If they were to think the deal might fall through altogether, they might jump at his lower offer.

He returned to the father, who now appeared a bit anxious. "*Lok* Raksmei, I am sorry, but I must leave urgently. I am needed at . . . at the school. The headmaster is considering your offer, and I hope for your sons' sakes that he will agree. I will return within the week and we will resume our discussion."

As he turned toward the car, he saw the crestfallen looks in both parents' eyes, despite the smiles on their faces. He smiled as he walked toward the car. Yes, that phone call was perfectly timed. As he reached for the door handle, he heard hurried footsteps behind him.

"*Lok* Oudom, my apology. We wish the best for our sons. We will accept your offer of $750 U.S. for each."

Oudom looked at, but past, the man. Unlike in the West, looking directly into another's eyes was disrespectful. "Very good, *Lok* Raksmei. I will return for them within the week."

Why did air travel have to become so difficult? It was once considered a major time saver. Now, with repeated security checks, passenger screenings, and the like, Lynch felt as if he could have *driven* to San Francisco in the time it took him to fly there. Sure. He knew better, but it felt that way all the same.

It was only after he'd gone out of the domestic flights' Terminal 3 and back through the security checkpoint for International Terminal G that he learned there was a secure connecting pathway between the two terminals on Level 2. That would have saved him 45 minutes. He had hoped to make several calls before leaving the States, but now his remaining time was limited.

He checked into the international gate where his flight to Hong King would be leaving and learned there would be a slight delay due to some minor mechanical issue. Boarding would begin in 30 minutes, unless the delay was extended. The last thing he needed was to miss his connection in Hong Kong.

He made his first call at that gate to Amy's cell phone. That was far from his first call to her, however. Again, his call was directed to her voicemail, which he felt surprised to hear had not been filled up with all of his previous calls. He left yet one more message to call him. He did *not* want to leave a message warning her about Abdi. He wanted to tell her directly—not through some messaging system—so he could gauge her reaction. Actually, he preferred telling her face-to-face, to be able to see her body language, too, but the delay in being able to do so made that a less than likely scenario.

Next on his list: her brother, Grant. He needed to know what was transpiring. The man answered on the second ring.

"Lynch, hello again. Twice in two days. Now you really have me concerned."

"Sorry, Grant. I take it you've not heard from her."

"Not a peep."

"Well, I can tell you now that I've discovered where she's headed. She's probably there by now. She's in Cambodia."

"Cambodia?"

The man sounded even more incredulous than Lynch had been when he found out.

"Yep. Any idea why she might have gone there? Did she ever voice a desire to take a trip there, maybe to see the ruins of Angkor Watt?"

"What in the world is in Cambodia? I simply don't see her . . . um, no, she's never voiced a desire to go there that I'm aware of." The man paused. "But you know, she once mentioned an older couple at a church she attended for a while. They're missionaries there, but that's all I know. I can't even give you their names."

A missions trip? Now that resonated with Lynch as something she would do. And to do so on the complete opposite side of the world. Maybe. That's as far away from her house and the memory of her father dying there as she could go, except perhaps to Australia. This trip began to make a little sense.

"Grant, I'm in San Francisco heading to Cambodia after her. If you and your family are praying people, keep her in your prayers. We have reason to believe Abdullah Said Abdi is already after her, to finish what he wasn't able to do in St. Louis. She needs prayer warriors right now more than anything else."

The words he heard on the other end were not exactly acceptable in church. After a short pause, he added, "I-I will pass that info on to my brothers and her church. Thank you for being up front with me. I was worried and didn't know why I should be."

And now you're worried and know why, thought Lynch. He wasn't sure if that was better or not. They signed off after Grant extracted a promise from Lynch to keep him posted. Lynch did so with the caveat that any communications with him wouldn't be on a regular basis.

One more higher-priority call to make before

boarding—his parents. They needed to know where he was going and why. He called their house phone, hoping no one would answer and he could leave a message. Instead, his mom answered on the first ring. He wondered if the call would finish in time to board the plane. She would want every little detail.

"Why Carson, so sweet of you to call."

Lynch noted a hint of sarcasm in her voice, particularly when using his given name—as only she was permitted to do. He wondered why. His last call hadn't been *that* long ago, had it?

"Mom, I hear it in your voice. Dad's never home, so I don't get to talk with him much. But you and I talked, um, when? A couple weeks ago?"

"Hmmm, let me check my calendar."

There it was, more sarcasm. Maybe it had been a while.

"Okay. I get it. Look, I don't have much time. I'm about to board a plane for Cambodia."

"Cambodia? I thought you were working on Mr. Graham's transition team."

The sarcasm had turned to a mix of curiosity and concern. He went on to explain the reason for his trip.

"Sweetie, I don't like this. At all. Going after the girl I understand. But, hunting an internationally wanted terrorist? There are people paid to do that, and you're not one of them."

"Mom, I'm not *hunting* Abdi. I just want to make sure Amy isn't in his cross-hairs again. I'll be fine."

"I've heard *that* before. Don't you get caught up in something that makes me think you're dead, like that one time. Worst months of my life."

He could hear the faucet of tears open on the other end. He knew his parents had gone through hell when he went missing and was presumed dead a number of years back. It wasn't like he did that on purpose. He hadn't planned on nearly dying and having amnesia.

"Mom, please. It won't be like that. I promise."

"Carson, terrorists could blow up your plane. The communist government in Cambodia could declare martial law. Drug lords could go after Americans there. Crime there is . . ."

"Mom, Mom, please don't go there. I'll be fine. Nothing's going to happen."

"First call for boarding for flight . . ." came over the P.A. system. *Why do they always mumble the last part of an announcement?* he wondered. Lynch saw people around him getting up and moving into their respective queues. That confirmed that it was his flight.

"Mom. I'll be fine. Gotta go. They're starting to board."

"Carson, are you sure—"

"Mom, sorry. I really have to go. I'll be safe. Love you. Bye."

He heard her say "Goodbye" as he disconnected the call. He then proceeded to turn off his phone. He wouldn't need it for the next 12 hours.

CHAPTER FIVE

Amy glanced at her watch and deduced the time back home. That part was easy. She was halfway around the world, 12 hours ahead of St. Louis. That made it just after eight a.m. in Missouri.

Remembering which day it was proved more difficult. After a four-hour flight to San Francisco, a two-hour layover, 16 hours to Singapore, a 12-hour layover, and another two-hour flight to Phnom Penh, and compounding that by having crossed the International Date Line, she had lost track of the day.

She retrieved her luggage and made her way to Immigration and Customs. The line was long and she yawned frequently as she waited. A six-hour sleep at the transit hotel in Singapore's Changi Airport had helped move her body clock forward. It hadn't made up for much of her sleep deficit from weeks of sleepless nights after her father's death, however.

"Amy Gibb!"

She heard her name from the last of eight clerks at the Immigration windows. She approached the window and the man handed her passport, with its visa secured inside, back to her. She glanced at it and frowned. Only a 30-day tourist visa.

It would have to do. Without a job, she could not justify a longer stay, although there was a chance of getting one extension. Only one.

With her passport in one hand and her bags rolling behind her, controlled by the other, she followed the crowd toward Customs. She almost laughed as she rolled right past the single man standing at a podium, smiling and nodding, as everyone passed by.

Cambodia's oppressive heat and humidity blasted through the open doorway at the end of the customs area. She thought she had been prepared for it. Still, it hit her like a moist blanket smothering her body and covering her mouth. For someone who rarely broke a bead of sweat at home, she could feel her skin begin to ooze that salty fluid.

She glanced about and acknowledged she was "not in Kansas anymore, Toto." She stood head and shoulders taller than all of the women around her, as well as most of the men. And if her height didn't single her out, her dirty blond hair with month-old highlights shone like a headlight on a dark country road compared to the coal black hair of the native Cambodians.

The sudden need for a bathroom pointed her toward the public "restrooms" just outside the building's exit. However, two factors prompted her to wait—the lack of someone to watch her luggage and the stench of sweat and urine that wafted from the grimy latrines whose doors were propped open for ventilation.

She had been warned about the culture shock she

would encounter. Yet, only her visit to Cairo came close to what she saw all about her—the filth, the crowd, the rapid-fire speech in a language so very different from her own, and the chaos in the street and adjacent parking lot as vehicles of many descriptions jockeyed to meet arriving passengers.

As her bladder and her desire for cleanliness debated, a man pushed into her and grabbed her arm. Her heart began to race and she prepared to fight him off if he did not let go. After a previous run-in with human traffickers, she had embarked on training in self-defense and had earned her way to a brown belt in Taekwondo and early lessons in Krav Maga. She did not want to cause problems or risk deportation having just arrived, but . . .

He started to pull her one way when a man's voice called her from the other. The man let go and hurried away. She tried to get a glimpse of his face beneath the Khmer scarf he wore, but he disappeared quickly into the crowd. She glanced about her. Both of her bags were still there, as was her backpack that doubled as her purse. She lowered the pack and saw that it had been undisturbed. If the man had been after her passport or money, he had not succeeded.

"Miss Amy Gibb!"

She looked toward the sound of her name being called a second time and saw a slim man of her own height waving at her across the crowd. He was a handsome man with glistening black hair. Her first thought was one of wondering what hair products he used to achieve such shine, but then she questioned herself. The majority of heads she saw held similar lustrous locks.

She took a deep breath and worked her way toward the man, as he did likewise toward her. As they approached each other, he pressed his palms together, as if praying, and bowed his head down and back up quickly. Amy's hands were full, so she bowed her head as he had. She had read that this was called a *som pas.* She would have to get accustomed to it, as shaking hands was not at all customary as a greeting.

"Miss Amy Gibb, I am Charya. Pastor Jim tell me to meet you here. I also have Christian name, Paul, if that is your wish to call me."

"Thank you, Charya. Did I say that correctly?"

He nodded. "Yes, you say correct. Pastor Jim is at hotel to meet you. Come, come. Car is there."

He pointed to the parking lot where she saw cars parked in every possible space and many double-parked in front of those in proper slots. Disorder ruled. He grabbed the handle of her large suitcase and led the way.

"Charya, did you see the man who grabbed me just as you called my name the first time?"

He shook his head. "No, Miss Amy Gibb, I do not see that. Here you must be careful for pickpocket. Come. We get to van and away from them."

In the van, Charya patiently waited five minutes for the lane where his van was parked to open up long enough to let him pull out. He worked his way into the line waiting to pay the parking fee, and they inched toward the main road. The chaos she had witnessed upon exiting the building now surrounded her.

"Miss Amy Gibb, Pastor Jim say to please use seatbelt."

She began to sense the need to comply and fumbled around the side of the seat to find the end of the belt. They neared the attendant's booth as she found it, and moments later they were driving along a main road. She had no idea where they now headed and had to trust this total stranger.

And within a few minutes, she realized how total that trust had to be . . . and why Pastor Jim insisted on the seatbelt. Driving here was a free-for-all. The main road had lines on it, as in the U.S., but clearly, they were only suggestions. She flinched as a car on their right pulled ahead and turned left directly in front of them. A moment later, a car coming the other way turned in front of them as well. Hundreds of small motorbikes wove in and out of all lanes of traffic. Appearing to be no larger than 100cc bikes, some carried a single rider while others carried two or three people. She even saw one motorbike carrying a family of six.

Yet, Charya drove on nonplussed. As she began to "appreciate" the seemingly unchoreographed ballet on the road, she realized the man required the broken-field navigation skills of an NFL running back combined with the courage of two drunks playing chicken.

Half an hour later, she saw that they had entered the heart of Phnom Penh. The Tonle Sap River, at its confluence with the broad Mekong River, coursed to the east of the boulevard they now traveled. A different form of transportation now seemed as common as the motorbikes.

"Charya, what are those?" They appeared to be rickshaws powered by the same style motorbike.

"They are tuk-tuks, Miss Amy Gibb."

"Please, just call me Amy."

"Yes, Miss Amy."

They turned down another street and then another. Tuk-tuks lined the roads. Small shops filled the storefronts. Some motorbikes pulled trailers filled with fruits and vegetables she had never seen. Above, hundreds of electrical wires and cables running between poles and buildings formed an electrician's nightmare.

A moment later, Charya stopped and laid on his horn. He yelled something out the window at two tuk-tuk drivers. Slowly, they responded, and one moved a meter or so farther along the curb, while the second driver pulled out and double-parked next to the first tuk-tuk. Charya squeezed his van into the empty space and jumped out. He ran around the front of the vehicle and opened her door.

"Here is hotel. I call Pastor Jim and tell him you are here."

Abdi pulled the scarf tighter around his head and merged into the crowd milling about the exit from the Phnom Penh International Airport. His man at St. Louis' Lambert International Airport had provided the woman's flight number. Those passengers would be working their way through Immigration and Customs now.

His contact in the country had come through with first-class flair. The cigarette boat, also known as a rum-runner in the U.S., had taken him in record time to a landing near the town of Srae Ambel, which sat inland from the Bay of Kampong Saom along a small river. The boat flew across the water, much faster than the skiffs his people used in the waters off Somalia to seize tankers and other lumbering container vessels during their prime piracy days.

At the landing, a man awaited him with his Mercedes E300, ready to take him wherever he wished to go. Following a period of rest at a brothel owned by his contact, he had changed clothes to better disguise himself and headed toward the airport. If all went well, he would have his revenge this day and be on his way to Mogadishu. He would not return to the U.S. while still a suspect for the murder of the woman's father.

His driver emerged from the building and found him in the crowd.

"She is walking through Customs now. I will get the car."

Abdi nodded. "Very good, *Lok* Oudom. I will meet you there."

As the man walked toward the parking lot, Abdi prepared a syringe of midazolam. His plan was to come up behind her and inject it through her clothing into her buttock. Then, as she began to feel its effects and become sedated, he would "assist" her to the car. Her luggage was of no concern to him. Unattended, it would disappear in seconds anyway.

He hid the syringe in his sleeve and scrutinized the door. Two minutes later, she emerged. He had been correct in assuming that she would not be difficult to spot. He hastened to fall in behind her.

As he approached, he saw that his plan would fall short without revision. She wore a backpack that covered part of her backside and her trailing luggage on wheels prevented him from coming in close. He grabbed her arm to turn her aside and expose her rear area. As he did so, he heard her name being called.

Someone is meeting her, he realized. He, or they, would see him leading her away, see that something was wrong as she left her luggage behind, and would not hesitate to call for police. To continue would put him in extreme jeopardy, as he was in the country without a visa. The small Somali community in Cambodia faced great prejudice and were treated as slaves even when there legally. They would lock him up and let him die.

He let go of her arm and rushed back into the anonymity of the crowd, hoping that she had not seen his face. As soon as he cleared the area, he doubled back to the parking lot and found Khay Oudom. Before getting into the car, he spotted the woman with a Cambodian man as they loaded her things into an older Mercedes van, although older was a relative term. He had learned that no vehicles older than ten years were allowed to operate in the country.

"They are there . . . in that van three rows over." He spoke in English, as that was a mutually spoken language between them.

Khay Oudom nodded. "Yes, I see them."

Good. Maybe they would get the woman after all. The man was expendable.

As the driver pulled out of his spot, Khay Oudom did the same, only to get stopped by another vehicle backing out in front of them.

"Go around, go around," yelled Abdi.

There was no room as the car kept backing up and

blocking the entire lane. At that instant another car sped around the corner and appeared to come straight at them, before cutting off the car that had left its spot in order to take the now empty space.

Abdi slammed his fist on the dash. Even if they managed to clear the car in front of them, the Mercedes van was a good ten cars ahead in the lane to the exit. They would never catch up to them, and he had no way of knowing which direction they headed.

As he stewed in anger, he noticed that Khay Oudom appeared unconcerned. That made his anger intensify. The man had a job to do—help Abdi capture this woman—and he had failed.

"We have lost our chance. Now we have no way of knowing where to find her." His rage rang clearly in his tone.

Khay Oudom smiled. "Not true. I have my ways. I will know where she is by morning."

CHAPTER SIX

Walter Tillson, MD, PhD, sat at the lab table staring past his computer monitor through the window to the jungle outside their compound. A pair of macaque monkeys, with a baby on the back of the female, sat in a papaya tree just outside the fence. They first appeared to be watching *him* through the window, but he decided they were watching the kitchen staff in the canteen building between the main lab and the compound's living quarters. The cooks were known from time to time to throw fruit and vegetable scraps to the simians, to appease the mischievous Sun Wu Kong, the Monkey King cast to earth by Buddha to learn humility.

The story of Buddha getting the best of the Monkey King was one of many tales about the mythical monkey born from a rock. After five years of doing research in the mountains of Cambodia, Tillson remained amazed at the superstitions of the people. The only thing that continued to surprise him more was how he ended up in his current position.

Had someone told him as a medical student at Georgetown that he would be doing vaccine research in the Khmer highlands, watching monkeys play outside his window, he would have thought that person crazy. His goal in also getting a PhD in Virology had been the top scientific position at the Centers for Infection Control followed by the directorship itself. He hadn't read the fine print when he accepted the position they offered him. And here he was, thanks to the fine print, as well as a minor misunderstanding between himself and another staff member back in Atlanta. Why they had taken her word over his, he still did not fathom.

A knock at the doorway pulled his attention from the macaque family. Sok Darany, using the traditional name structure in which the surname came before the given name, had been hired as a lead technician. The man's education and experience left much to be desired, but Tillson knew that he would lose the man altogether if he sent him to the U.S. for further training. He had learned that the hard way. The last two techs he had sponsored Stateside never returned. He couldn't blame them. The opportunities and lifestyle of the western world were too great a lure. Who, in his right mind, would want to come back to this torrid, impoverished, third-world nation once they experienced the possibilities of the West and had a marketable skill?

But, Cambodia? Filthy. Poor sanitation. Dirt roads and impossible traffic. Mosquito-borne infectious diseases. High heat and humidity. Monsoon rains that inundated much of the countryside and required homes to be built on stilts. He had learned that difficult lesson, too. Flooding had destroyed their first facility and forced them to higher ground.

He yearned to return home. Even now, just a splash of "tap" water in his mouth could make him ill. True, they had purified water in the canteen, but not yet for the living quarters. Having to use bottled water for everything, even brushing your teeth, had gotten old.

"Doctor, here is new result you ask for."

The tech handed him the papers and bowed in *som pas* before exiting the room. The man seemed a bit too anxious to leave. Tillson took the papers with some trepidation.

The last DNA sequence had shown a mutation in the viral strain that had developed during the process of creating a vaccine. They used both eggs and human fetal cell cultures to grow the virus which was to be "crippled" and used in the attenuated-virus immunization. But, in both cases, the mutated virus did not match the source virus, making the vaccine less than 15% effective. This had been reported with the most recent flu vaccines by two different research teams in separate countries. The current flu shot was only considered 10% effective, and his bosses in the U.S. had tasked him with, first, invalidating the findings of those teams, and second, finding a way to make the vaccine more effective.

He pounded his fist on the table as he scanned the latest data. Three runs, three sets of data proving those research teams to be correct. And he couldn't blame Darany. He personally set up each run, and the tech simply babysat the equipment and printed the results.

"Darany!" The tech appeared at the door in an instant and bowed. "Where are the other results? The antibody titers."

"Not done yet. Five minute more."

"Okay. I need them right away. As soon as they are

ready."

"Yes, doctor." He made *som pas* again and left.

"And stop doing that!" yelled Tillson after him.

The man's bowing every time he entered and left Tillson's presence had become an annoyance. Time and time again, that curt little bow, whether or not he put his hands together. Tillson had lectured his staff regularly that such courtesies were not needed while at work. In the back of his mind, he knew the *som pas* was meant as a sign of respect. But in the Khmer culture, you were expected to return the gesture or be considered rude. After his first month there he felt like a Drinking Bird toy, repeatedly bowing up and down as its wet beak dried and the evaporative cooling effect changed the vapor pressures of the dichloromethane inside. After the sixth month he wondered if he would require lumbar disk surgery. By now he must be considered the rudest American these Cambodians had ever met.

He returned to his computer and focused upon the software he used to develop new chemical models. He hoped for an innovation in the preservatives used to stabilize vaccines for extended storage. He hadn't yet succeeded.

He heard footsteps behind him. He turned to see Darany as his head began to bow but stopped short.

"The other result, doctor."

"អរគុណ, Darany." The Khmer word for "thank you" was pronounced 'aw-koon.'

This time as he perused the data he smiled. The antibody titers were higher than he had predicted. Perhaps they now had a way to make the vaccines more effective, even though incubating the virus in eggs and human cells had a negative effect. He had doubled the amount of aluminum hydroxide—used as an adjuvant to bolster the immune response—and it had worked.

Of course, the anti-vaxxers would protest. Aluminum, like the preservative thimerosal, was linked to autism and other neuropsychiatric disorders. He would let his bosses at the CIC decide how to handle that community of protesters, should they decide to increase the metal's content in their vaccines. After all, they were the sole source for $5.4 billion worth of vaccines. Every state's health departments bought from the CIC. Hospitals bought from the CIC. The CIC held the patents on numerous vaccines. Vaccines were a, if not *the*, primary source of non-government revenue for the centers. He had to give the anti-vaxxers credit for being truthful on this fact. The CIC truly was, first and foremost, a vaccine company, earning billions of dollars in sales and millions in royalties for many private and corporate patent holders.

CHAPTER SEVEN

"Good morning, Amy. I hope you slept well." Pastor Jim gave her a broad smile as he stood up from the table where he sat drinking coffee.

Amy glanced around the lobby of the small hotel after she had passed the small reception counter in the hallway next to the elevator. To her right was a short bar with glasses and maybe a dozen bottles of liquor behind it, as well as the door to the kitchen. Jim sat at one of the two larger tables that occupied the space in front of the bar. Three tables for two lined the middle of the room, while a couch and two upholstered chairs filled the other side of the lobby. Two sets of oversized double doors stood open onto the sidewalk and street. The room was a small island of calm compared to the frenzy of motorbikes and tuk-tuks outside.

"Good morning. I slept very well, thank you. The room is nicer than I expected."

"Good. Glad it suits you. This place is owned by a British ex-pat who understands how to cater to westerners. They serve a decent English breakfast, too." He pulled out a chair for her. "I was waiting for you before ordering. There's a menu." He pointed to the end of the table next to the wall.

"The missus should be down in a moment."

Amy barely knew Jim's wife, Pat, but from their brief interactions back in the States, in preparation for Amy's trip, as well as from their meeting the previous evening, she had become fond of the woman. And she often chuckled at how the woman's realism countered Jim's optimism. The two were certainly well-suited for each other.

A young woman approached the table and made *som pas*. Amy placed her hands together and bowed her head in return.

"Coffee?"

"I think I would like hot tea, instead. Do you have Earl Grey?"

"We do." The woman bowed her head and returned to the bar.

Moments later she returned with the tea and asked for their orders. Amy ordered eggs, bacon, and toast, along with orange juice, while Jim ordered for himself and his wife.

"By the way, don't ever order iced tea, even in the restaurants I take you to because I consider them safer. You'll get sick. Hot tea should be okay because they boil the water."

Amy had taken to heart all of the food warnings the pair had offered her. Only bottled water was truly safe, as well as commercially produced ice, soft drinks, and beer. No lettuce, tomatoes, or other veggies that required washing. Only fruits that could be peeled. And never, ever, buy food at the local or roadside markets. Even properly cooked meats might have been cut with a knife washed in a river or local water. Amy had listened intently to those instructions, among others. She had no desire to spend time praying at the porcelain altar.

Pat joined them as they waited on their food, and the two women exchanged hugs.

"So, has Jim given you our itinerary for the day? We figured to give you a day or so to acclimate to the time change."

Jim nodded. "That's right. Today will be sightseeing, to give you a glimpse into the culture and their past."

As Jim spoke, Amy saw a young boy with what appeared to be a poorly healed broken leg that caused him to limp and use a crude crutch. He reminded her of Bob Cratchit's Tiny Tim from Dickens' *A Christmas Carol*. He hobbled his way to a place just outside the building and stood leaning on his crutch while holding a small box for donations. Just as quickly, the waitress rushed to shoo him away.

"Excuse me, Jim. That little boy on the crutch." She pointed with her entire hand because she had already learned that pointing with one's index finger was considered crude. "What do you think might have happened to him? Should I give him something?"

Her heart went out to the youngster. As a nurse, she had researched the levels of medical care available in Cambodia. While Thailand next door offered top-tier medical care and was now considered a medical destination for people from all over the globe seeking quality care at a third of the cost in the U.S., Cambodia lacked even basic healthcare services. Most people relied on the *kru-khmer*, traditional herbalists, or the *aa-jaar*, laymen practicing

Buddhist healing ceremonies, for their care.

The child was a clear example of that. In the U.S. it would have been basic care to set a broken leg for proper healing. It appeared to her that this boy had received no care, not even a simple splint that any Boy Scout back home would know how to do.

She began to stand, but Jim placed a hand on her forearm to stop her.

"Don't. It's best not to give any money to these kids, no matter how bad they look."

Amy sat there stunned. She couldn't believe that this man, whose life centered on helping people, particularly children, now turned away from a crippled child.

"Amy, these kids have been trafficked, and they're crippled, maimed, blinded, and worse, on purpose, for the sole purpose of begging. To give them money is to support the human traffickers. It won't help *them*. And worse, the kids learn nothing but begging, so that when they are older and no longer cute, no longer able to tug at westerners' heartstrings, they know no other way to support themselves. At that point, when they no longer bring in the dollars, the traffickers throw them out the door, and they starve."

Pat added, "You will see these kids all over the country, but mostly at popular tourist spots where they work the visitors for their pimps. As sad as it is, there's only so much we can do. The Buddhist culture sees this as the child paying for something he did in a past life. He was bad in his past life, so he was reincarnated to be a beggar. Buddha taught nothing about sin or repentance. They have no concept of sin, as we know it in Judeo-Christianity. There is no Golden Rule in Buddhism."

Amy mulled that over for a minute. She disliked that she might have to harden her heart to these unfortunate children, but she hated the thought of supporting those who would prey upon these kids.

"We try to get to some of these kids *before* the traffickers do, but our resources are limited," Pat continued. "You'll be staying at the children's home we operate. You'll get to know some of these children quite well."

"Where do these kids come from? Are they all orphans?"

"Not orphans as we understand the word. Some have no parents, but most have *a* living parent who's unable to care for them. Sadly, a fair number of the trafficked children are bought from the parents, parents who have too many kids to feed and the money paid them can help support the family for a long time."

Amy sat there aghast at the thought of parents selling their children.

"You mean there are parents who are willing to sell a child to become a beggar?"

Jim's head bobbed back. "Oh, no, no. The parents don't know what their children are about to become. The traffickers promise the parents that the child will be educated, taught English, given a good place to stay and food to eat. The traffickers prey on the poorest of families and women who have been kicked out of their homes along with their children. In this culture, a man needs only to say he's divorcing his wife, and it's done. She *and* her children are then kicked out to fend for themselves. Particularly if there's a new wife in the picture, she doesn't want to take care of another woman's children."

Amy didn't know what to say. She knew that women's rights were a foreign concept in much of the world, but now she was about to see it up close.

"But Amy," said Pat, "what most recognize as a travesty, we see as opportunity. The women are open to teaching about the love of God. As they begin to understand that the God of all creation loves them, each of them, they begin to change. When they see us feeding and caring for their children, they see that love demonstrated firsthand."

The couple's work with children was what had attracted Amy to join them. Their ministry fed nearly 3,000 children daily—for many that was their only meal—and their preschools taught close to 600 children. The children's home, where Amy would stay, housed 32 school-aged children, feeding and educating them. Some remained through the American equivalent of high school and several graduates had progressed to attend college.

Jim looked her in the eye. "In fact, Amy, we're hoping you might be willing to work on a project for us. Cambodia has never had a women's conference, one where hundreds of women are invited to meet at one time. We'd like to do that. Charya and his wife help lead our main church in Kampong Thom, and they say they could bring a thousand women together. We think you could help coordinate that . . . and maybe even speak at it. We have a fantastic translator who could work with you."

Amy's mouth went dry. Helping to coordinate a meeting

was one thing. She had put on teaching conferences for MedAir. She had even taught at them. She knew pre-hospital medical care and emergency medicine topics backward and forward. But God's Word? Was He really calling on her . . . to preach?

Lynch hadn't felt this stiff since his Police Academy days where the grueling physical training could sometimes leave his body sore for days. This time all that was required was sitting in a cramped airplane seat for 12 hours. He needed to get back to a regular workout schedule.

The cancellation of his flight to Houston had resulted in being rerouted to San Francisco where he was supposed to pick up a 12-hour flight to Narita International Airport outside of Tokyo, with a direct connection to Phnom Penh. But a cyclone off Japan's eastern shore had delayed the flight by an estimated six hours. Rather than delay that long, Lynch went to Plan C and found a flight to Singapore through a connection in Hong Kong.

Due to the last-minute nature of that change, he had been "rewarded" with that dreaded middle seat—between a steroid enthusiast competing in the Mr. Universe competition on his left and a sumo wrestler on his right. Okay. So, he planned to exaggerate a bit when retelling his adventure. The flight just *felt* like he'd been wedged between two heavyweights, and he wasn't exactly a lightweight himself.

The deplaning process seemed to take forever, partly due to the fact that his seat sat near the rear of the plane and partly due to no one appearing to be in a hurry. Once finally off the plane, he followed the herd ahead of him. He had expected the gate to open onto the international concourse where he could head directly to the gate for his Singapore flight. Instead, the crowd seemed to follow signs in English and Chinese leading them to "International Flights."

After a few minutes, the crowd suddenly stopped, and Lynch found himself at the back of the line for another security checkpoint. He checked the time on his phone. He had a little leeway in time before having to get to his next flight.

But that time margin dwindled as the agents scrutinized every passenger. When Lynch's turn came, he showed the first agent his ticket and boarding pass, and then placed his carry-on onto the belt to go through the scanner. He went through the metal detector and was about to pick up his bag when a second agent took it and said, "Follow me, please."

In an area off to the side, the agent demonstrated a spread-eagle stance with arms straight out to both sides. Lynch complied, and the agent used a hand wand to scan each extremity and his torso. Nothing, as Lynch expected.

"Open, please." The agent pointed to the carry-on case. Lynch complied. He knew the drill but time was running short.

"Yes, sir, but will this take long? My next flight starts boarding in 15 minutes."

The man's face showed no recognition, as he took his time to root through the bag. After what seemed like five minutes, he produced Lynch's small worn-leather dopp kit.

From inside the kit he retrieved a smaller leather kit and unzipped it to reveal Lynch's razor, nail clippers, tweezers, small scissors for nasal hairs, and a metal nail file about four inches long. One end of the file was round, while the other barely came to a point. It had passed through two separate security screenings in the U.S. without red flags and armed agents taking Lynch into custody. But here?

The man held up the file.

"Sorry, it's just a nail file. Had I known it might be a problem I would have tossed it into my check-in luggage. Security in the U.S. had no problem with it."

The man continued to hold the item up for Lynch to absorb the full impact of the weapon of mass destruction he had in his belongings. After a minute, the man threw it into a nearby garbage receptacle and waved Lynch on. Not once through the encounter had the man's affect changed. Lynch now understood the term 'inscrutable' as applied to the Chinese.

He repacked his bag in a rush and checked his phone for the time. If he hurried, he would be in time for the start of boarding.

CHAPTER EIGHT

Abdi paced the street outside the flea-ridden excuse for a hotel waiting for Khay Oudom. The man had reiterated his promise of knowing the woman's whereabouts by morning. He simply had not mentioned what time of morning that would be. Abdi glanced at his phone for the time. Only ten minutes had passed since his last check.

He noticed the locals staring at him and pulled the *kroma* up and over to hide his face. The last thing he needed was for someone to contact the police. Where was Khay?

A moment later, the Mercedes careened around a corner and headed his way. As it stopped next to him, he saw the driver urging him to enter . . . quickly.

No sooner had he sat down, Khay raced away and turned down the first intersecting street.

"That was close, *Lok* Abdullah. Someone must have called the police on you. I was but two blocks ahead of them. I thought I told you to stay inside until I arrived."

"I could not stay inside that rat-infested, cockroach-filled hovel any further. That place should be burned."

"I, I am sorry. We had little choice since you have no visa."

Abdi knew there was more to the story than that. He was, after all, Somali. That left them with fewer choices in accommodations. In Somalia, there were family rivalries and feuds, but they all shared the same race, religion, and language. In the U.S., minorities decried racism, but as with their claims of poverty, they had little experience with *true* racism. This was Abdi's first taste of such in the Khmer kingdom. As much as he wanted the experience of capturing the woman himself and seeing the look on her face when he auctioned her off to become a sex slave for one of his local benefactor's clients, he now recognized that perhaps he should have contracted her capture to locals.

Khay handed him a plastic bag.

"Here, I thought you might be hungry."

Abdi had been so angry at the morning's delay, he hadn't acknowledged his gut's grumbling for food. In the bag he found a small loaf of French bread, a container holding fried eggs, and another with two sliced bananas.

"That coffee is for you, too." Khay pointed to one of two cups in the vehicle's cupholder. "If you prefer tea, I can stop to get you a cup."

Abdi waved at the man to continue, as he chewed on a large bite of egg. "No, no. Drive. We are behind schedule and must get to the woman before she disappears again. You *do* know where she is, yes?"

"Yes. We are three kilometers away."

With the traffic he saw about them, Abdi estimated their driving time to be under five minutes. He inhaled his food, determined to be prepared to act upon arrival.

*   *   *

Amy finished her meal and washed it down with the last of the tea. She had watched the young beggar as she ate, struggling with the inhumanity of the traffickers who would maim a child for profit. No one offered the child money while she watched, although Jim relented and provided some fruit for the boy. That, he said, would help the child directly and not enrich the traffickers.

"Well, I think it's time to get moving. We have a lot to do today," said Jim. "Are you pretty much packed and ready?"

Amy nodded. "I want to brush my teeth and freshen up a bit, but otherwise, I'm ready and can be back down here in 15 minutes."

"Sounds good. Our first stop opens in ten minutes and I'd like to get there early, to beat the crowds."

Pat widened her eyes and shook her head. "Un-uh, bud. *I* can't be ready in 15 minutes. Maybe 25."

Jim pointed with his entire hand toward the street. Amy followed with her eyes and saw that the van had pulled up at the curb. But it was not Charya driving.

"That's not Charya."

"That's Atith. Charya had to drive back to our main base at his church in Kampong Thom. We'll meet up with him in three days, and you'll get to meet his lovely wife, Daevy, and children. Atith is an excellent driver, which I know you'll come to appreciate shortly." He grinned. "If you thought the roads were chaotic coming from the airport, you ain't seen nothing yet."

Jim softly clapped his hands together and rubbed them. "Okay. Meet you back here as soon as I can get Pat moving."

Pat rolled her eyes and headed toward to the small

elevator. Amy smiled and chuckled to herself. Many had called Amy the champion eye-roller. She now recognized that Pat was seasoned and worthy competition in that arena.

"Oh, and your room is already paid for. You just need to leave the key at the desk."

Jim turned and caught up with his wife. As the elevator door opened, he held it, and said, "You coming?"

Amy hurried to the lift and accompanied them to the floor where their rooms awaited.

Minutes later, Amy descended to the main floor with luggage in tow, handed her key to the clerk, and headed toward the van. She approached the driver, who greeted her in the customary way. Releasing her luggage, she returned the gesture.

"Good morning. I am Amy. I am told you are an excellent driver."

The young man smiled and nodded. "I am Atith. *Aw-koon,* um, thank you. My English not so good, but I learn."

"Well, Atith, my Cambodian is worse. If you will teach me your language, I will help you with English."

The man beamed. Amy had been told that learning English was a privilege to many in Cambodia, and that those with a good command of the language were highly prized in business and government. She would no doubt find herself teaching English to many. She only hoped she might gain a rudimentary level of Khmer in return.

Atith insisted on taking her luggage and loading it into the van.

"*Aw-koon.* See, you've taught me some Khmer already."

Amy wandered across the narrow street to what

appeared to be a market. Bins of fresh fruits and vegetables sat in front of the store windows. The appearance brought to mind images of 19th-century general stores in the U.S. Behind the windows, she saw packages of crackers, cookies, and candy—all of the treats that might lure a westerner from the hotel across the street into the store. She was surprised that she recognized many of the products just from the labels. She had envisioned discovering all sorts of foreign goods only to find the usual U.S. brands she could find in any grocery or convenient mart back home.

In fact, as she looked about the street, she felt a sense of disappointment. Everything was so "Western." The men wore jeans and tee-shirts. Many of the young women, too. She saw no clothing she had expected of the Southeast Asian culture.

She turned her attention to the produce in the bins. While she recognized pineapples, apples, and bananas, they were much smaller than those at home. But it was the other fruits that caught her attention—a red one the size of a tennis ball that looked like it had hair, a smaller knobby purple thing with a thick green "hat," and a large, yellow-green thing that looked like the old weapon swung on a chain, a mace. Now she felt like she was really in a different land.

"Amy, we're ready to leave. Pat's in the van."

She pointed to the fruits. "These are different. What's this one?" She pointed to the red, hairy one.

"Rambutan. That actually translates to red, hairy fruit. It's a lot like lychee, which you might have heard of. The purple one with the green top is purple mangosteen—one of my favorites. That other purple one with the simple stem is passion fruit. But, hey, let's get going. You'll have plenty of time to sample all of these, plus my favorite, durian."

"Durian?"

He gave that mischievous grin again. "Oh, you'll find out. Don't worry. Let's go."

As they pulled away from the curb and eased past several tuk-tuks, cars and motorbikes appeared to come out of nowhere, surrounding them, passing them, seeming about to hit them head-on before veering away. Amy would have been holding the steering wheel in a white-knuckle death grip had she been asked to drive. Atith looked as if it was another day relaxing in a recliner.

She saw a silver Mercedes sedan pass them going the other way and did a double-take. Clearly, she had to have imagined the person she saw in the front passenger seat. The face seemed to follow her as they passed. Those eyes. That long scar. She shook her head to remove the image from her mind. She looked back but could no longer see the man—*if* there had actually been a man in that seat.

Abdullah Said Abdi. The man who murdered her father. But that would be impossible. No one, absolutely no one, at home knew where she was. She hadn't told Macy or her brothers. Certainly not her boss or co-workers. Not Lynch. She hadn't told them so she could keep them safe from that Somali terror cell.

No, she had imagined him. But the thought of him brought back the image of her father bleeding on her kitchen floor. She began to cry and tried to keep the others from noticing, but she felt Pat's hand give her a gentle squeeze on the forearm.

That van! That was her, the woman. Abdi was sure of it, despite the glare of sunlight on the van's glass. And they were headed in opposite directions.

"There! That van! That was her! Turn around and follow them." Abdi became animated in his seat. He had been given another chance.

"Turn around? Where? We are lucky to be moving in the direction we are heading." Khay shook his head in seeming disbelief.

"But she is going the other way."

As Khay looked for a place to turn around, Abdi noticed two more white Mercedes vans pass by. He realized that such a commonplace vehicle would be difficult to track after even the brief lapse of time that had passed. They required a license plate number or other distinguishing marks to help them find the correct van.

Khay slowed down and began to make the turn.

"No, no. We are too late. We will never catch up to them in this traffic."

Abdi felt lost now. How would they find her? Unless perhaps she would be staying at the same hotel tonight. Yes. Tonight would be his opportunity.

"Go on to the hotel. I will wait for her there, for when she returns."

Khay shrugged, but drove on. Minutes later, they pulled up outside the City Centre Hotel.

"*Lok* Abdullah, please stay in car. I will check inside."

Minutes later, Khay Oudom emerged from the hotel.

"I must make a call."

Abdi listened to the man's foreign tongue, understanding nothing that was said. His patience wore thin. He had expected to have accomplished his task and started his trip to Somalia by now. Instead, the woman eluded him and every additional minute in the country increased his personal risks.

Khay ended his call and turned to Abdi. "The bad news is she checked out. The good news is the waitress inside heard the woman and her friends talk about their plans for sightseeing here in Phnom Penh. We will head to the closest location. I have a contact at the other location the waitress heard them mention. She will be looking for them and call me when they show up."

Oudom glanced at his passenger as he pulled away from the hotel. Had he done something to dishonor or offend the boss, Tep Rithisak? How was it that he had to babysit this African? Was he being punished for something?

And yet, he dared not to question his assignment to the task. He enjoyed a certain freedom as a freelancer for what Americans would call a "top crime syndicate." He did not want to upset the papaya cart, so to speak.

Yet, he had a payday waiting for him when he delivered those twin boys and this disrespectful creature, this Somalian, kept him from it. Worse, the man was *costing* him money. Finding a place to lodge the man had been time consuming and expensive. His usual connections wanted nothing to do with an African. And now he played wild buffalo chase with some American woman. More time. More gas. Additional informants wanting dollars for their services. Even the waitress at the hotel balked until she saw a five-dollar bill. And then she held out for twenty. That was more than her week's wage.

Oudom needed to get this macaque off his back, the sooner the better.

CHAPTER NINE

If Amy had thought the human traffickers cruel for their treatment of the children, she faced even worse as they walked through the Tuol Sleng Genocide Museum, the infamous Security Prison 21, or S-21, from Pol Pot's reign of terror. Formerly a high school, the classrooms had been divided into three-by-five-foot brick cells with no water or sanitation short of wooden buckets. The administrative offices had become rooms for torture, and its victims faced the terror of the sadists whether they gave up names or not. The second and third floor terraces outside the classrooms had been covered with a mesh of barbed-wire fencing to prevent prisoners from jumping to their deaths as they sought a quick end to their terror. The horror of what she saw now usurped the image of the young beggar in her mind.

"Amy," said Jim, "I have someone I'd like you to meet. He's outside at the end of this building."

Amy followed Jim and Pat to a spot where a pleasant-looking man nearing 50 appeared to hold court with a tour group. After the tour guide prompted the group to move on, Jim approached the man and made *som pas*. They talked as if they knew each other and Jim beckoned Amy to join them.

The man's smile never left his face. As Amy neared, he made *som pas,* and she returned the gesture.

"Norng Chan Phal, this is Amy Gibbs. Amy, this is Norng Chan Phal. I have gotten to know this man a little from our many visits here with others like yourself, but I will let him tell his story."

Norng Chan Phal proceeded to tell his story, clearly a tale he had told thousands of times before. "My English not good, so excuse please. I was nine year . . ."

As Amy listened with rapt attention to the man, she soon learned he was one of five children who survived this place by finding refuge under a pile of prisoners' clothing as the Khmer Rouge fled from the advancing Vietnamese Army. He had found the spot and sequestered his two younger brothers and sister, and a one-year-old child from his village there, to avoid being taken away by the guards. He recalled running past dead bodies covered with flies, looking for his mother, as the guards left. He never found her and assumed she, too, had been killed. His youngest brother and the other child died from starvation shortly after their liberation. His sister and other brother were adopted from an orphanage, and he had not seen or heard from them since.

Another tour group waited off to their side, so Amy thanked him and moved away with Jim and Pat.

"Jim, I can't imagine the horrors that this place saw. And it's considered one of the top tourist attractions in the country? Why?"

Jim nodded. "They don't want history to repeat itself. Schoolchildren are brought here to learn to avoid this kind of tyranny. It has become a place of national healing because families that were once at civil war with each other still live side-by-side and work together. I wanted you to understand this because we work with such families, and we do *not* talk about this. We don't know which families were on which side of the war and do not want to inadvertently stir anything up. We want to be part of the healing."

Pat added, "You will also see that they lost an entire generation to that war and to Pol Pot's Killing Fields. Many young adults have no parenting skills because they had no one to teach them. I had one family bring me their infant which had been crying for days. Their village healer couldn't help. They didn't know where to turn but had heard once that Christians believed in a God who did miracles. I put the child up to my shoulder and began to pat his back, to try to calm him. He let out the biggest burp I've ever heard, short of Jim here, and stopped crying. They had never been taught to burp a child."

They had nearly finished their tour of the grounds and approached the exit. Atith stood just outside waiting for them. As they approached him, he pointed toward the van.

"Park this way."

Amy turned to follow and saw a silver Mercedes E300 parked just beyond their vehicle. Seeing it brought a mental flashback to the car they had passed after leaving the hotel. *There must be lots of silver Mercedes in this country*, she thought. *This is just a coincidence.*

But the man outside the car gave her look of recognition that surprised her. She hadn't imagined it. The man looked at her as if expecting her. He appeared excited as he rushed away toward the grounds' exit. She glanced back to see him bobbing back and forth as if looking for someone.

Abdi had heard of Prison S-21. Some of the torture techniques employed there had also been used in Somalia. He had found it curious that an American tourist would go there as her first stop in this country.

They had pulled into the small parking area and discovered three white vans similar to the one they sought. Khay parked as close to the first one as possible. That also put them as close to the facility's common entrance and exit as possible.

"I think we should both wait here for them to exit," said Abdi.

Khay shook his head and pointed to a uniformed man nearby. "The parking is limited. If they see that we are tying up a parking spot, they will force us to leave. One of us must buy a ticket and go inside."

Abdi could read between the lines. *He* should buy a ticket and go inside. Yet, as he thought about it, that made sense. One person to go in, find, and follow the woman, while the other stayed behind as a safeguard.

"Yes, I will go look for the woman. I cannot communicate well with the guard, if it would come to that, so you should stay outside in case they leave before I find her. We cannot take her here, so we must follow and find the right opportunity."

Khay nodded. "I agree fully. They are accustomed to

Khmer drivers staying with their vehicles, so I must stay here."

Abdi mentally debated using the *kroma* to hide his face, but this was a tourist spot and the traditional scarf seemed out of place. And yet, to go without it would risk the woman's spotting and identifying him. He watched as people exited cars and buses and lined up for tickets. Except for some western-style ball caps, he saw few head coverings of any kind.

He removed the scarf and adjusted his appearance to look more like a tourist. As he stood in line for a ticket, he noticed a few people staring at him, but that was nothing new. The scar on his face *was* noteworthy, and despite the attention it sometimes drew, he wore it as a badge of honor for defeating his enemy.

Once inside, he glanced about and realized his task would be more difficult than he had imagined. There were three large main buildings, each with more than a dozen rooms opening off open-air terraces that faced the central courtyard. She could be in any one of those rooms, and if he were to enter one room, she could exit another, so that they would never cross paths.

But there were two more complications. The place was filling with tourists, many of them western. No longer would her height and light hair features be easy to spot in a sea of people. The second hindrance was the foliage. While it gave the compound a pleasant, park-like setting, it prevented him from seeing anything or anyone on the opposite side.

No, he needed an advantage, a place where he could watch for her yet remain enough out of view so that she would not see him. He looked about and saw the perfect spot—the second-floor terrace of Building A. It gave him a clear vantage of those coming and leaving the museum, while being easily accessible. People did not tend to look up. The odds were in his favor that she would never see him.

He climbed the stairs, found a perch next to a pillar for added obscurity, and waited. And waited. And waited. Twice he thought he saw her, but neither of those women were his target. He glanced at his watch and saw that he'd been there over 90 minutes. Could there be that much to see here? Had they been incorrect in selecting this location first? Maybe she wasn't here. Maybe he should return to the car to see if Khay had heard from his contact. He disliked the uncertainty and rued missing his chance of taking her at the airport.

He gave it another 15 minutes and decided he should check with Khay. As he gazed along the walkway leading to and from the exit, he saw another tall, light-haired woman hidden somewhat by the foliage. An older man and woman accompanied her, and they were walking toward the exit. His heart rate accelerated in anticipation, as he waited for the trio to clear the greenery.

It was her!

He resisted the temptation to rush to the ground level. If he emerged from the stairwell at the wrong time, she would see him. He timed their pace and prepared to move to the stairs.

At the right time, he made his move . . . only to be confronted with a tour group climbing the stairs. Five, ten . . . fifteen people. He had no space to get past them. Ten more people passed him before he could descend.

As he rushed toward the exit, he saw Khay pacing frantically outside, looking for him.

"Quickly, *Lok* Oudom. We must follow them."

"I have been waiting for you. We were parked just two cars away."

As they turned the corner toward the car, Abdi saw that the van had vanished. Again, they had missed her!

"What do you mean, you don't have a seat reserved for me? Here's my itinerary. I'm supposed to be on this plane."

Lynch was fatigued, hungry, anxious to get on with his search for Amy, and in no mood to be told he had no seat on the plane. He was fit to be tied, but he knew no amount of arguing would help his cause.

"Look, miss, storms in the U.S. and off Japan forced me to change my itinerary twice. The agent assured me that my connections were all booked."

The gate agent waved to a man off to the side, who joined them.

"Good morning, sir. I'm Geoffrey Williams, the gate manager. How can I be of assistance?"

Lynch repeated his story, while the agent told her boss her side of it. The man began to type on the keyboard and query the computer.

"I'm sorry, Mr., uh, Cully, is it?"

Lynch nodded.

"The computer shows that your reservation was canceled."

"But it wasn't supposed to be, and they told me back in

the U.S. that it wasn't."

"Evidently, they were wrong. The computer shows we have one open seat."

Lynch wanted to slap his forehead, or maybe Mr. Geoffrey Williams' forehead.

"Of course, you do. That's my seat."

Lynch pointed to the computer screen where it revealed the open seat to be the same one showing on his printed itinerary.

"See, it's the same seat number."

The manager inspected Lynch's paperwork.

"But that seat has no reservation for it."

"Can't I just take it? I'm supposed to be in it anyway."

The man typed some more.

"Yes, you could reserve it. The ticket cost would be $250 U.S."

"But I've already paid for it." Lynch shook his head in disbelief. This trip had become the stuff of nightmares. He worked to keep his cool. The only thing worse would be getting arrested and jailed in this foreign country for creating a disturbance.

"We can't give you this seat. It was booked through your original carrier. They would have to correct the problem. We're a separate airline out of Australia, and not one of their affiliated companies. We have no direct access to their computer system, but here's their toll-free number, if you wish to call them."

With the number in hand, Lynch stalked away from the counter and placed the call. An hour later, he was still talking with the reservation clerk in the U.S. Their computers showed the empty seat as still taken. Until the smaller airline's computer system fully processed the cancellation and opened the seat again, they couldn't rebook it for Lynch.

With phone in hand, Lynch returned to the desk and reengaged the manager. The manager took the phone and discussed the issue with the U.S. reservation agent. Despite his best effort to free up the seat, the issue remained unresolved 30 minutes later.

At that point, the gate manager looked at Lynch apologetically. "Mr. Cully, I'm so sorry this has happened to you, but the boarding for that flight has ended, and they're taxiing onto the runway right now."

CHAPTER TEN

Oudom's frustration kept rising. He had his own business to attend and grew tired of catering to this man. He had been told that Abdi was a ruthless warlord in Somalia. Here, he appeared to be a flailing incompetent. Perhaps he should make the suggestion that Abdi find local "talent" to take care of the problem.

Abdi sulked in the passenger seat. "We have lost her."

Once again, Oudom knew he would rise to the occasion and "save the day."

"All is not lost, *Lok* Abdullah. I can contact the right men to take care of this problem for you. They are *very* efficient in finding people."

Abdi glared at him. "No. That would not bring me satisfaction. I wish to be the one to capture her, to see the look on her face when I do. If you cannot assist me, then I will call Tep Rithisak to ask for someone who can."

No, no. That would not be good, thought Oudom. He started the car and drove away from Tuol Sleng.

"From the information given me by the waitress, they are heading next to Choeung Ek, the Killing Field. It is only six kilometers from here and I know a shortcut. My contact there is already on the alert for them."

Abdi seemed assuaged. Still, Oudom wanted a backup plan. His experience with the man so far had proven to him that he *needed* one.

As he drove, he pulled out his cell phone and made another call. *Another contact who would want payment*, he thought. What choice did he have?

Abdi did not like that they had missed their mark once again. However, he had come to dislike Khay Oudom more. The man functioned only as a driver and interpreter and had been no help in taking the woman. One of his own men would have delayed her somehow—flattened a tire on the van, created a diversion, pulled his car behind to block the van. Something.

Instead, he found the man pacing at the entrance to the museum, waiting for *him* to act. And as he waited, the woman got away. Perhaps he should call the chief of their syndicate and ask for new help, although when he voiced that option, he could see fear in the man's eyes. Maybe the simple mention of making a complaint would motivate Khay.

Abdi began to rethink his position when taking Khay's "short-cut" proved to be a mistake. New construction led to one hold-up after another. The 15-minute trip became 45.

"I am sorry, *Lok* Abdullah. I did not know about this construction. But do not worry, we will be there with plenty of time. And unlike Tuol Sleng, parking is abundant and there are no police guarding the lot. We can both wait and watch together. We will be ready to follow. We might even be able to take the woman right there."

Abdi's mood brightened at that comment.

As they headed west toward Choeung Ek, Jim's phone rang. Amy saw Jim's countenance grow grim, but from his limited replies to the other party, she could glean nothing about the conversation. It was none of her business, of course, but the change in Jim gave her cause for concern.

As he ended the call, he turned toward Amy and Pat. "Amy, I'm sorry, but we need to cut short our sightseeing. We can return to Choeung Ek some other time."

"Or not. It's more of the same nasty stuff as the prison. Some of it even worse," said Pat. "What's up?"

Amy had enough of "man's inhumanity to man" for the day. Maybe skipping the Killing Field wasn't such a bad idea. She, too, was curious as to what was happening.

"That was Felix," he said to Pat. He then looked at Amy and continued. "Felix Abrego Castañeda is a missionary friend who works out of Battambang. That's the second largest city in Cambodia and capital of the province of the same name. Looks like we might have to stay the night there. Not my first choice."

Amy gave him a look, wondering what he meant by that.

Pat rolled her eyes. "Jim did not have a good experience there a few years back when we were just getting started here."

"You think? I had a self-proclaimed Christian pastor threaten to kill me. I found out later he was ex-Khmer Rouge and thought I was trying to steal his turf instead of just assisting him. Still, threaten to kill me? A pastor? Really?

That province was the home of the Khmer Rouge, and there are still a lot of men there holding a grudge. I tend to avoid the area."

"Which is why Felix is such a blessing there. He's a fireball. As Hispanic in ancestry as his name says, he doesn't come across as the typical white, American missionary, and the people he works with love him. His work focuses on Battambang, Pailin, and Pursat Provinces, south and west of Tonle Sap, the big lake. We focus on Kampong Thom and Kampong Cham Provinces, to the north and east of the lake, and we work together in Siem Reap Province." Pat tried to use her hands to demonstrate where each province sat with respect to the others.

Jim nodded. "And he's perfectly suited for Battambang. He's ex-Special Forces and rumored to have been part of Delta Force. He can hold his own, and those Khmer Rouge rowdies respect him."

"Yeah, after two of them tried to roust him. When it came to their threats to him, personally, he turned the other cheek. When he caught them trying to steal a child, they ended up in the hospital for a week."

Jim frowned. "Unfortunately, that's what he called about. Two children from a village where he has a small church planted have gone missing. Fraternal twins, boy and girl, age five. The family started attending the church six months ago."

Pat looked sad. "That's the fifth and sixth child to go missing this month, all from families that recently converted to Christ. Two of the other families lost twins as well."

Amy thought of Lynch and his game of "what if." But

she didn't want to play, not after what she had learned today about Cambodia's past. Besides, this seemed obvious.

"Are the traffickers targeting Christian children?"

Oudom left his car and walked up to the ticket pavilion at the entrance to Choeung Ek. He needed to get away from that toxic charge of his. The man was spitting cobra venom, and Oudom had personal experience with all three species of cobra living in Cambodia. He had no doubt that this man's copious saliva, as he spewed invectives toward him, could be just as painful as that of the Thai spitting cobra, *Naja siamensis*.

At the counter he asked for Pich, one of the groundskeepers, who appeared about five minutes later. He noted that it felt good to again speak his native Khmer. He and Abdi both struggled with the English they had as a common language, a fact he recognized as adding to their difficulties working together.

"*Lok* Oudom, it is good to see you again." The two exchanged *som pas.*

"*Lok* Pich, have you seen the tall, light-haired American woman I called you about earlier? The African I must babysit has become more than I can bear."

Pich shook his head. "I made a point of working the grounds near here, to be able to see everyone who came and went. No one matching your description has been here today."

For confirmation, Oudom pulled out his phone and showed the gardener a photo of the woman they sought.

Pich shook his head again. "No. I would remember a woman like that."

Oudom thanked him for watching out for her, and returned to the car. He had suspected trouble when they first entered the parking lot and saw no white vans. Hoping that the woman and her friends had simply stopped somewhere to eat, they waited. Over the next two hours, only one white van had arrived, and it transported Cambodian schoolchildren.

"*Lok* Abdullah, it is as I feared. The woman has not been here. Either the waitress heard incorrectly, or their plans changed. My contact here will continue to watch for her, but I am not optimistic, given the time of day."

The African glared at him.

"I do not know what you expect of me. You missed your best opportunity at the airport, not me. Now we are just one team looking for one woman in all of Cambodia. I have provided leads, but I do not have an inside line to her plans. You must recruit help. We must have eyes in every city, but that is not free."

Oudom sensed a change in the man. Something he had said must have hit home with the man.

"Take me to Battambang. I must talk with Tep Rithisak in person."

Oudom took a deep breath. That was *not* where he wanted to go. Battambang was on the opposite side of the country, over seven hours away from the children he was to pick up and deliver. He did not want to delay obtaining those children much longer and give the parents time to reconsider.

He did the math in his head. He was currently three hours from the children and almost six hours from Tep Rithisak's building, with the two being in opposite directions. But the children were to be delivered outside Krakor, on the way to Battambang. He decided to make a stand and stop catering to every whim of this man.

"I can take you to Battambang, but it is too late today. I also have business to do on the other side of Phnom Penh. Tep Rithisak expects that to be completed by week's end." That last part was a lie. Tep Rithisak knew little about Oudom's side jobs, but he hoped it would keep Abdi quiet. "Completing that job requires stopping on the way to Battambang."

Abdi said nothing.

"I will find you different lodging for tonight, and do the first part of my job before dark. Then we can leave early in the morning, make my quick stop along the way, and be in Battambang by midafternoon."

Abdi did not look happy, but nodded. "Very well."

Oudom started his car and pulled away from the Killing Field. He smiled as a thought crossed his mind. He would also suggest to Tep Rithisak that the African pay a large reward to whoever finds the woman for Abdi. If agreed upon, he had a good chance of reaping that reward. He had another card up his sleeve, to use an American idiom he had learned while in the U.S. He had taken the license number of the white van and currently had another of his connections finding the registered owner. Unless this was a rental, he would soon know where the van was based, and that knowledge would give him an edge in finding the woman.

CHAPTER ELEVEN

Lynch looked as though a water buffalo had dragged him through a rice paddy. He felt like that, too. Had he only been traveling for 44 hours? It felt like he'd spent the past week in airports and planes.

The final resolution of the problem in Singapore resulted in booking him on the last flight from Singapore to Bangkok, where he had just 30 minutes to connect with the final leg to Phnom Penh—on Thai Airways' last flight of the day. The flight in to Bangkok deplaned on the tarmac with the passengers being required to board buses for a ride to the international terminal. Once there, Lynch didn't just have to hurry, he had to *run* to the gate. He was the last to board, but then they couldn't take off due to bad weather and sat on the tarmac for another hour.

But he made it. He wanted to kiss the ground upon leaving the plane in Phnom Penh. To his surprise, however, despite the late hour, a staffer from the embassy waited for him as he entered the terminal. How they had followed him and learned of his arrival flight confounded him. He wasn't sure *he* could actually retrace all of his steps at that point.

"Mr. Cully, I'm Reggie Crutchfield." The man extended

his hand. "I'm first secretary at the embassy."

And not simply a staff member, but the number four—or was it five? —guy at the embassy. Lynch shook his hand.

"Thanks for greeting me. I didn't expect that."

"Yes, well, we were asked to assist you by the President-elect himself. I understand that an Amy Gibbs recently arrived here and might be in danger."

They headed for the baggage claim.

Lynch nodded. "She was involved in exposing a terrorist group in Missouri and her father ended up paying for it with a bullet aimed at her. The leader of that group is out to get her, and we think he's here or coming here. At a minimum, I need to find her to warn her. I've tried calling and texting her nearly 30 times now, from every airport I could on the way. She must not have her phone on . . . or even with her. Ideally, I'd like to convince her to go home where we can protect her better."

The diplomat nodded and retrieved his cell phone from his coat pocket. "Let's see what I can do to help while we wait on your bag." He walked away from the claim area.

Fifteen minutes later, Lynch grabbed his bag and approached the man.

The first secretary smiled. "We have her. She listed the City Centre Hotel on her immigration form as her address while in country. Ends up it's just four minutes from the embassy, and even better, they have a vacancy for you. I'll take you there, and you can see her in the morning."

A Cambodian police officer came up to them and made *som pas.* Crutchfield returned the gesture.

"*Lok* Reggie, here is visa for Lynch Cully. Is this he?"

"Yes, sir. I'm Lynch Cully. Thank you." He repeated the *som pas*.

"I need copy of passport, please."

Lynch nodded, handing over the copy he had expected to use at the immigration window. The officer attached the visa to Lynch's passport and escorted the men out of the building to an official embassy car that waited for them.

The hassles of the flight and the burden of worry that had weighed down Lynch's shoulders melted like shaved ice in the southeast Asian heat. The embassy had come through. He would surprise Amy in the morning at the hotel.

Thirty-five minutes later, they pulled up to a tall, narrow building crammed in among other narrow buildings. Two sets of high, double doors opened to the street where rickshaw-like vehicles lined up along the gutters. A variety of people of multiple nationalities milled about the lobby area, and several people sat at an outdoor table laughing and drinking.

Crutchfield preceded him to the reception desk and spoke to the clerk. Lynch dragged his bag behind him and caught up.

"Well, Mr. Cully, they have your room ready. I think you'll find this place quite comfortable, and after your long flights, I'm sure you're ready for a good night's sleep. Please let me know how things turn out after you talk with Ms. Gibbs." He handed Lynch a business card. "That's my direct number on the back."

Lynch nodded. "Thank you, Mr. Crutchfield. You have been extremely helpful, and, yes, I will keep you informed."

He watched the diplomat return to his car and turned

back to the reception clerk, who pointed to a form he needed to complete. Lynch completed the registration sheet and handed it back with a copy of his passport. He fished out his credit card.

"How many night you plan stay?"

Lynch thought about that for a moment. He had come this far. Maybe he could convince Amy to join him sightseeing and spend some time in the country before returning—assuming he could convince her to do so.

"I am not sure. I am to meet my friend here in the morning, and I'll have to make that decision after talking with her."

The man gave him a puzzled look.

"Your friend, she come here to meet you?"

"I was told she is staying here. Her name is Amy Gibbs."

The man shook his head. "No. No woman name Amy Gibb here. American?"

"Yes, American."

"No Americans except you stay here tonight."

Lynch hoped his extreme fatigue was responsible for his not hearing the man correctly. Amy had listed this hotel on her immigration form. He knew he had heard Crutchfield say that. He pulled out his phone and found a picture of Amy in his photo gallery, which he showed the clerk.

The man smiled. "Yes, very nice woman. Staff here welcome her generosity and friendliness."

"You saw her then. She's here, yes?"

The man shook his head. "Sorry, she leave this morning. I not know where she go."

CHAPTER TWELVE

Despite his worry about Amy, Lynch had barely pulled up the sheet of his bed before he "died" for the night. He hadn't slept since departing St. Louis, which might have been his best move anyway to combat the potential jet lag. He didn't hear the alarm on his phone, and started fully awake when, half asleep, he saw that it was almost nine a.m.

Yet, as he sat up in bed, he realized he had no reason to hurry. He had no idea how to proceed, knowing that Amy had left the previous morning. How would he even begin to find her in a country that was nearly as large as his home state of Missouri, with almost three times as many people?

He dressed and went downstairs, where he ordered breakfast and coffee. As he sat watching the crowded street through the large double doors, he mulled over his options. The waitress reappeared with his coffee. He decided to fall back on what he knew best, being a detective.

"Did you work here yesterday morning?"

She nodded. "I work all morning, seven day a week."

Lynch grabbed his phone from the table top. "Do you remember this woman? Did she eat breakfast here yesterday?"

The waitress gave him a broad smile and nodded again. "Yes, she very nice. She eat with Pastor Jim and wife Pat. They stay here many time. She leave with them."

"She's a very special friend of mine, and I need to find her. Did they say where they were going?"

The young woman shuffled a bit in place. "You pay? Man yesterday ask about her and pay $20."

"A man yesterday?" Lynch felt his heart accelerate. "What man?"

"Cambodian. But I see him get into car, silver Mercedes, with African man."

Lynch's heart now dropped into his gut. An African man! That could only mean one thing. Abdullah Said Abdi was already here and ahead of him. He became frantic and stood to face her.

"Th-that African man wants to kill her. I flew here from the United States to warn her, to protect her. Please, if you know anything more, I *need* to find her."

Her eyes widened in understanding. "They go Tuol Sleng and Killing Field yesterday. I not know where they go after."

Lynch had one other clue to work with. "This Pastor Jim, do you know his full name? Do you know where he works when he is here in Cambodia?"

A voice called her from the kitchen. She turned her head toward that person and responded. She then faced Lynch and pointed to the table with her extended hand.

"Please, sit. I be right back."

She rushed into the kitchen and returned with his breakfast. He had no appetite. Did she really expect him to eat?

"You eat. Keep up strength. I find more on Pastor Jim."

She dashed from the table toward the reception clerk. Lynch began to wolf down his meal as he watched the two people in animated conversation. The clerk appeared resistant to revealing any information, while she seemed determined to get it. And she won. The clerk handed her a piece of paper.

She smiled as she offered Lynch the paper—a copy of Pastor Jim's registration form. Lynch now had a name and a Cambodian address, but curiously the line for a phone number was blank. What he needed now was a way to get there ASAP.

He pulled out his wallet and took a $50 bill from it. He handed it to the waitress. "Here. To pay for breakfast. You keep the rest and give some to your co-worker over there."

Her eyes bulged at the sight of the money, but Lynch didn't wait for a thank-you. He ran to the elevator and grew impatient at its slow speed. He found the first secretary's card and after entering his room a few minutes later, dialed the number.

"Crutchfield."

"Morning, this is Lynch Cully. You asked to be kept up-to-date." Lynch proceeded to brief the diplomat. "You can let your CIA station chief and Interpol know that Abdullah Said Abdi is in the country. I might need the help of local authorities if I find him first."

"Well, that's a given. I don't think I have to remind you that you have no authority in this country, and they don't exactly play by our rules. But, in the meantime, it sounds like your first priority is a car and driver. I could use a break from the office. I'll be there in ten minutes."

Lynch finished packing and headed downstairs to clear his bill. As he approached the desk with his key, both the clerk and the waitress waited for him there. Both gave him a deep *som pas* and thanked him repeatedly. Lynch recalled from his online research that the lower the bow, the more respect was being offered. He returned the gesture. "No, thank *you*. Because of you I have a chance to save my friend."

Lynch moved outside to the table and awaited the car. At first, Lynch felt elated that Crutchfield had offered to drive, but the more he thought about it, the more he wondered about it. Why would the head of the office staff of the U.S. Embassy here want to chauffeur him around the country? Surely, the guy must keep busy. Something about it just didn't smell right.

True to his word, Oudom had found lodgings for Abdi and then drove to Me Sang where he completed the transaction with Chey Raksmei. With the twin boys in tow, he, too, had found a place to spend the night not far from Abdi. He desperately needed to fulfill his end of the deal for the children and get paid. His cash supply dwindled with all of the added expenses.

Before picking up Abdi, he went to a nearby market and found clothing for both boys, buying a set of clean shorts and a shirt for both. He could not command top dollar for them if he presented them in the rags they wore. Shoes would not be necessary.

Following yet another stop for food, he drove to the boarding house where Abdi had spent the night. The man had learned his lesson the day before with his near run-in with the police. Oudom found him just inside the dwelling's entrance with his usual impatient scowl etched across his face. The man took the food Oudom offered him without protest and devoured it as they walked to the car.

But as Abdi opened the passenger door, he reared back.

"What is this? You bring children? We have no time for children."

Oudom stood his ground and did not yield to the man. "I told you I had another job to complete. These boys have to be delivered today and it is on our way to Battambang. If you do not like it, then I can leave you here one more night and return for you tomorrow morning."

"Do not—"

Abdi cut short his protest, but Oudom could hear the guttural growl that replaced the words. The African seemed to be learning. He was on Oudom's turf. He could not afford to alienate his sole resource within the country. Even more, he could not risk turning Oudom's role as assistant into one of betrayer. Such betrayal could occur with a single word, in a language Abdi did not understand. The man wouldn't know what hit him.

After three hours of driving in near silence—short of the boys whispering to each other in the back seat—Oudom entered the boundaries of Krakor shortly after noon. Along National Highway 5, there was little to show of the community. But three and a half kilometers to the north lay the main part of town, one of Cambodia's famed floating villages. There, dozens of homes sat high on 30-foot stilts, with rickety stairs descending to the ground during the dry season. During the peak of monsoon season, however, the water of the lake, Tonle Sap, lapped at their doorways making it appear as if the homes floated upon the lake. Krakor, along with the other two floating villages, Kampong Phluk and Mechrey, were favorite tourist destinations.

Oudom turned south, not north, onto route 53B. Several kilometers down the gravel road, he found the sign for the "U.S. CIC-Cambodia," with a paved road to the left. That was his signal to turn soon. However, he turned right onto a smaller gravel road, almost hidden by brush. This road led to a large, enclosed compound hidden behind a lotus pond, a grove of banana trees, and palms. In truth, the place had been a military barracks that had been abandoned 15 years earlier. Six one-story rectangular buildings sat lined up opposite a larger two-story building that had once been the facility's offices and training center. That would explain the compound's being surrounded by a 10-foot-tall chain-link fence with several strands of razor-wire across the top, designed to keep intruders out but now intended to keep "students" in.

"*Lok* Abdullah, I suggest you stay in the car here. I will be right back." He switched to Khmer and said, "Ponleak, Phirum, come with me."

The boys looked scared but did not hold back. They followed Oudom into the office building. He opened a door for them and followed them into a room with spare furnishings other than a large, worn wooden desk that dominated the center of the office. The other table and chair, as well as the single filing cabinet could have been abandoned and left there by the military. A photo of the prime minister adorned the wall. That, too, could have been left behind. After all, the man had held the office for over three decades.

Oudom made *som pas* to the man seated there. "*Choum reap sur*, *Lok* Chea. Here are the twin boys I talked with you about. They proved to be more expensive than I am used to."

The man stood and walked around his desk to inspect the boys. Oudom smiled as the boys made deep *som pas* to the man. He had not coached them to do so. *Good, good*, he thought. *A show of respect should help my price.*

"They look healthy and strong."

"They are, *Lok* Chea. And, as twins, they have more use to you."

The man nodded. "That they have. Very good, I will pay the price we agreed to earlier, $1500 each."

Oudom let a gentle sigh escape. He had expected more bartering.

"Take them to building one. Samang will meet you there."

Chea handed him an envelope.

"*Aw-koon, Lok* Chea. I have leads on more twins near Cheay Sbay."

The man gave a nonchalant toss of his head. "Will it cost me as much? If I can pay little for Christian children, why should I pay your price for Buddhist children?"

Oudom did not like what he heard. Rumors floated within his circle of men kidnapping Christian children to avoid payment to Buddhist families. With the increasing

Christian population, such stealing of children had become easier and more tempting. Oudom would not bow to such practice. It wasn't just that kidnappers could face a death penalty if caught. He honestly believed he was helping families with the "traditional" payments.

"We will discuss it, *Lok* Chea."

Oudom herded the boys to building one. Here, the boys balked. He couldn't blame them. The hallway had a strong disinfectant smell. In the first room to his left, four young boys sat on the floor staring into empty space and rocking back and forth. Even though those boys could see Oudom and the twins in the hall, there was no acknowledgment of their presence. In another room, one child cried like a cat shrieking. Boys of varying ages in other rooms appeared normal and ran to the doorways to see who was there, but no words were spoken.

A gnarled old man met them halfway down the hall. The twins looked at Oudom with fear in their eyes.

"Excellent, *Lok* Chea. "Two more sets of twins is great. Are they settled into the home yet?"

"*Jah, Lok* Walter. The second twin arrive minute ago. We feed and watch them, as you instruct us to do."

Tillson nodded, still holding the phone to his ear. The twins would have the day to learn their new surroundings, and then tomorrow they would undergo neuropsychiatric tests, along with some basic blood work. They would be assessed for intelligence the next day, to properly place them in the private school run by Duong Chea. Tillson would then work them into his test groups based on age and physical attributes.

In return for his financial support, Duong Chea gave Tillson access to the students . . . and turned a blind eye to any ethics involved. In fact, Tillson had been somewhat surprised upon first starting at the CIC lab that the medical ethics of the West held little sway here. Money talked and the people around him listened, including the government official in charge of monitoring the private school. He had made great strides in exploring workable preservatives and adjuvants for their vaccines, in turn surprising his peers in Atlanta.

They didn't need to know he ran an end run around their ethics guidelines. They also had no need to know he again had started testing thimerosal, as a preservative, and increasing doses of aluminum hydroxide, as an adjuvant to boost the immune response, in twins. He would prove the anti-vaxxers wrong about both. But he faced an uphill battle. Dozens of studies so far had shown direct links between both the ethyl mercury of thimerosal, as well as aluminum, and various neuropsychiatric disorders, including autism, while not a single study confirmed the safety of these metals in the micro-doses delivered by their vaccines. He would make his name by presenting that first safety study.

CHAPTER THIRTEEN

Amy's culture shock continued on their drive toward Battambang the day before. National Highway 5 was best compared to little more than a rural two-lane road back home, if you crowded dozens of tuk-tuks and hundreds of motorbikes onto it. She also saw the first of another common vehicle—the hand tractor—as it hauled a trailer holding three cows along the edge of the road. That, however, didn't hold a candle to the small motorbike with a live pig draped and tied across the back.

She marveled more at the traffic than the scenery, a monotonous trail of pastures, rice paddies, and lotus ponds interspersed by typical rural Cambodian homes on stilts—homes that were little more than unpainted shacks. As the day darkened, however, one thing caught her attention. Out in a number of fields, sheets of plastic appeared draped over rods suspended between two poles with a light on one side. Jim had informed her that they were cricket traps. The insects were attracted by the light and jumped onto the plastic, where they slid down into a bucket of water and drowned. The buckets were cleared of their "harvest" each morning, but the bugs weren't used as bait for something else. They were a staple in the typical villager's diet. Amy's stomach turned at the thought.

Another discovery had surprised her. All of the road signs were in both English and Khmer script. She asked Jim about that.

"Yes, you'll find almost all signs here in both languages—hospitals, stores, hotels. A knowledge of English is prized here."

In line with his comment, she then noticed that, indeed, the signs she saw were in both. Often the English text was larger and above the native text.

True to Jim's wish not to spend the night in Battambang, they had stopped two hours short of the city to spend the night in Krong Pursat, a town of 25,600 residents on the Pursat River. The hotel was luxurious compared to that of the previous night—new, spacious, and air conditioned—all for $19, with Jim's discount as an NGO—non-government relief organization. They finished a delicious breakfast and now headed back toward Krakor where they were to meet Felix.

"Jim, I meant to ask you yesterday when we passed by, what's the Krakor Floating Village?"

Jim explained the floating villages to her, and finished by stating, "If we get done with Felix in time, maybe we'll head there for a tour. Since this isn't the monsoon season, it won't be nearly as impressive, but it's still something to see."

"So, explain again what Felix is worried about."

"We teamed up with him to plant a small church and feeding program in a village a couple dozen kilometers south of Krakor. They have maybe a dozen families now attending the church, and one of those families reported two of their children as missing, the twins I mentioned yesterday. He wants to talk with me about the problem."

"The problem? Don't the police take care of missing children?"

Jim shook his head. "Unfortunately, not so much. Human traffickers bribe officials who then squash the investigations. He has concerns about a new trend he's noticed. I have to admit, we've not seen it in Kampong Thom province, but it's likely to show up soon."

"What trend?"

Pat replied, "Jim told you how traffickers buy children under false pretenses. Well, in the past month, three Christian families have had children kidnapped. You see, Christian families won't part with their kids, like the Buddhist parents will do. The extended church family helps out those in need."

Amy thought about the problem, and the fact that twins were involved stuck out. Why twins?

"Were there twins involved in the other two families?"

Jim's countenance took on a look of new concern. Pat took a deep breath. They answered in unison, "Yes."

Pat continued, "The one family for sure, with the fraternal twins. Another family, I, uh, think—"

"Yes. The second family, too. Twin boys. The third family I don't recall the details on, except that their twins were taken. All of the kids involved are under age seven."

Amy gave them a questioning look. "So, why twins? Have you ever seen twins begging together?"

The spouses both shook their heads.

Pat said, "You know, I never have seen two kids at one spot, twins or otherwise. I guess it'd be like sending two people to do one job and get paid for one job. Not wise use of their resources. So that's a good question. Why twins?"

An annoying thought tugged at Amy's brain, but she refused to voice it. *The odds of such a thing happening here are astronomical, aren't they?* she thought.

At Krakor, Atith turned south onto a road marked 53B. The gravel road was barely two lanes wide, but the traffic was markedly less, consisting of motorbikes, hand tractors and bicycles. Amy noticed only one tuk-tuk as they drove along.

After what seemed like miles of churning dust, Amy asked Atith, "How much farther?"

"Three kilometer, Miss Amy."

Amy sat back and watched the monotony of fields and palms pass by. Suddenly the background began to change. Hills dotted the horizon beyond the fields on both sides of the road. A dusty, faded sign announced the village of Kamraeng, 6.5 km ahead, and Bamnak, 16 km ahead. *Three kilometers, eh?*

Minutes later, a new sign appeared—"U.S. CIC-Cambodia"—with an arrow pointing to the east onto a paved road that was clearly in better condition than their current "highway." Amy gazed down the road, hoping to see whatever was there. It appeared to cross the broad plain they were on and head into the hills.

"Jim, did you know the CIC had a facility in Cambodia? Do you know what they do there?"

Jim turned around in the front passenger seat to face her. "I know they've been here helping to start vaccination programs for the children, but I wasn't aware of any facility in country."

Amy furrowed her brow and thought about it. Why have a remote facility in this country? Biohazards were the first thing to pop into her mind. "Curious. Must be a research facility of some kind, to be out in the boonies like this. I would think an administrative office for assisting the Cambodian health authorities would be in the capital."

"Makes sense."

As they continued the drive, it didn't take long for the hills to disappear and the flat terrain to dominate again. Ten minutes later, Atith slowed and turned onto a side road. A moment after that, he pulled into the front "yard" of a simple concrete building with a small cross attached to the center above a wide-open doorway. Through the door, Amy could see the simple furnishings—folding chairs facing a small platform at the other end, and two narrow tables just inside, one on each side of the opening.

As they exited the van, three young couples emerged from the building, along with a slightly built, middle-aged Cambodian male who walked with an exaggerated limp. Clearly, he had been in some kind of accident and received poor medical care of the resultant leg injury. He walked with difficulty, and yet a broad smile crossed his face. Several small children wearing only oversized tee-shirts followed the young couples, and each woman carried an infant on her hip.

Pastor Jim walked up to the older man and made *som pas.* The man as well as the couples returned the gesture.

"James, it is good to see you again."

The man gave another quick bow. "Pas-tor Jim. *Aw-koon.*"

Atith hurried to Jim's side and began to talk with James, translating for Jim. Amy heard bits and pieces as Pat pulled her aside: Pastor Felix on his way, the one couple had their children stolen, the others were family.

"What happened to James?" asked Amy.

"He was a victim of the traffickers as a boy. They crippled him for life, but once he hit fifteen, they tossed him aside. One of Felix's predecessors found him clinging to life from starvation. He was about twenty then. Their group nursed him back to health and he gave his life to the Lord, studied, and became a pastor about three years ago." Pat nodded her head toward the church. "C'mon, let me show you around. You'll be working at places like this."

Amy held a new respect for the man. The Bible talked about overcomers, and this man exemplified them. Pat pointed to the church building, but Amy's attention was elsewhere. She would have plenty of time to see the simple structures.

"This is a typical village church that we build, and we try to dig a deep well with each church we plant, if we have the money." She pointed to a hand-pump wellhead sitting on a small pad of concrete not far from the buildings. "It brings everyone in the village here, to the church. Then, when funds become available, we also start a feeding program for the younger and school-age kids."

Pat insisted on showing her around, but Amy wanted to hear what was going on with the couple. She also wanted to know if James knew about the CIC facility. Something nagged at her.

"At some of the villages, you'll also see a larger, separate, two-story . . ."

Amy inched herself away from Pat and back toward Jim. More of the story about the couple waking up and finding the children missing. The reply of the police when they reported it. Their frustration. Their fear. The translation was spotty and halting as Atith searched for the correct English words.

At that moment an old, dirty Land Rover pulled up next to the van. A man in his late-thirties, early forties emerged from the passenger seat, while another young Cambodian man exited on the driver's side.

"Oh good, he brought Sokham," said Pat. "He's a better translator."

The man, whom Amy assumed to be Felix, waved to them as he approached, gave *som pas* to the older man with Jim and shook Jim's hand. Pat grabbed Amy by the arm and pulled her next to the men.

"Jim, thank you for coming. I see you brought lovely reinforcements."

"Flattery can get you somewhere . . . sometimes . . . Felix," Pat replied with a smirk on her face. "Amy, this is Felix, Felix; this is Amy Gibbs. She's here for a month to help us."

Amy smiled. "Or longer. Nice to meet you."

"The honor's all mine."

He took her hand and kissed the back of it. She wasn't quite sure what to make of that gesture. Off to her side, she saw the three women giggling and saying something to each other. The husbands remained stone-faced.

"Is that also a Cambodian custom I should know about?" she asked.

"Not that I know of, but it should be," he answered.

Jim interrupted the man's flirting. "James, with Atith's help, was telling me what has happened. What's your take on it?"

Felix turned back to the men. "Pretty much the same. He and I have talked about it at length. After the third occurrence, I put out some feelers to contacts I've made in country. There's a sense that someone is *taking* Christian kids because he, or they, know the Christians won't send their kids away like many Buddhists do, no matter how enticing the offer, unless it's to one of the Christian children's homes that they know and trust."

"But no one knows who's doing it. Word is that the known traffickers are denying involvement. Twenty years ago, there were three major kidnapping gangs, the Asian Boyz, gangsters from Macao, and a corrupt group of police and military officers. There was a major crackdown, and now they know that kidnapping will be shown no leniency and no one will look the other way. The government understands that poverty drives some parents to sell their kids, but even parents can get in trouble if caught selling their children. However, this is outright kidnapping without money being involved."

"The government's crackdown hasn't really stopped the problem," said Pat.

"No, it hasn't," Jim added in confirmation.

"True. Which brings me to my main concerns. One, they're taking mostly boys. 70% of child trafficking involves girls. And two, they're taking twins. Why?"

Amy had an idea, but she was an outsider here. Not just a stranger, but the *new* stranger, having just arrived. She wasn't ready to add her opinion to the mix. Plus, she had a hard time believing that her idea could have validity. She needed more information.

"Have you asked around to see if any families have *sold* twins?" she asked. "I recognize that these families have had their kids *taken*, but what if others are selling them? What if being twins is the real key factor here?"

All three Americans looked at her quizzically, while the Cambodian pastor, James, started nodding his head after Sokham finished translating. Sokham looked conflicted, as if he wanted to say something but did not wish to be rude and interrupt. Amy used her hand to point to Sokham and James. The others followed her gesture.

"Yes, Sokham, you know of others?"

"Not I, Pastor Jim, but Pastor James say he hear of one family near Battambang that sell twin and that men go around country ask about twin."

"If someone is looking for twins, there are probably other families across the country who have given up their children." Felix looked concerned. "But again, why twins?"

"Some kinky fetish trend we haven't heard about?" asked Pat.

"If there is, I *don't* want to hear about it," said Jim.

Amy could sense that the others were curious about her thoughts. But she wasn't ready to share them, for fear they might sound like accusations—accusations she could not back up. Yet, she realized she would need to be bolder if she wanted to get the information she needed.

"Sokham, does Pastor James know anything about the U.S. CIC facility down the road? Do you know the place I mean?"

He nodded, and she watched as the two men conversed. Khmer sure was a different language from those she had experienced before during her travels when her dad was in the Army. Thinking of him threatened to wrap her in a shroud of sadness, which she fought. She focused on what James was about to tell her.

James stopped talking and looked at her. Sokham began to speak.

"He not know what they do there. It is new buildings, three, maybe four years. Big place compare to most he see. Big fence all around." He used his hands to show that it was high. "Guards at gate. That is all he know."

She battled with the idea that kept floating through her consciousness, but anyone with a lick of medical knowledge knew that twins were a "holy grail" for medical research subjects.

CHAPTER FOURTEEN

Lynch stared out the window as Crutchfield drove along National Highway 6, first north along the Mekong River and then turning northwest into flat, wet countryside. His mind registered the rare, concrete, three-to-five-story homes mixed in with shacks on stilts, ponds filled with lotus pads, palm and banana groves, rice paddies, and barren fields with emaciated cattle dotting them, but he didn't dwell on them. He had no interest in the occasional travel monologue provided by the embassy staffer.

His police training, however, cringed at the lack of order among the drivers and the mix of vehicles, mostly motorbikes, that invited accidents and major injuries. He shook his head in disbelief when he saw a family of six on one 100cc motorbike, with the young mother nursing the infant in her arms.

He was most impressed with Crutchfield's driving skill. It attested to years of in-country experience.

"How in the world did you learn to drive here?"

The first secretary smiled. "It's not really that hard. You just have to pay attention to *everyone* around you and expect them to do something crazy."

Just then a motorbike with two riders passed them on the left and immediately turned right, almost being hit by the car that attempted to pass them on the right shoulder.

"See what I mean? Unlike home, we rarely exceed 50 miles per hour, 35 in the cities, so your reflex time is a bit more forgiving."

Lynch shook his head. "Man, driving back in the States must be boring for you."

Crutchfield laughed. "True. When I'm home visiting family, I'm more worried about the speeds folks travel than traffic."

Lynch saw increasing signs of civilization at the same time as his stomach growled audibly.

"Hungry?"

"I guess so," replied Lynch. "To be honest, my mind is focused on finding Amy."

"Well, we're almost there. Kampong Thom city is the provincial capital and something like the 12th or 13th largest city. It's also called Stueng Saen, and sits on the Stueng, or Snake, River. It marks the halfway point between Phnom Penh and Siem Reap . . . where the Angkor Wat World Heritage Site is located."

They entered a large roundabout circling a statue of a large elephant fighting two tigers and proceeded into a small city not much larger than University City, Missouri, a St. Louis suburb. Small shops fronted equally small homes. A few minutes later, they pulled up to a six-story building on the south side of the main road.

"I thought we could stay here for the night. There are a couple of other hotels that have bigger rooms and beautiful grounds, even a pool, but they also have major mosquito issues and so-so food. The restaurant here is good, and the food is safe."

Lynch looked up at the building and then scanned the area around it. For the first time, the culture shock of being in a third-world country hit him. Small food carts covered by colorful umbrellas lined the street selling foods Lynch could not identify from the distance. No method of refrigeration was evident, and the merchants kept busy fanning flies away from the foods when not dealing with a customer.

He must have been staring, because Crutchfield caught him by stating, "If you want to take a closer look, go ahead. I can check to see if they have two rooms. But do yourself a favor, don't get adventuresome and try something. You have no idea how they were prepared, and I don't want to enlighten you. I also don't want to have to nurse you back to health over the next few days."

Lynch nodded and walked to the closest row of vendors. He saw a variety of fruits and vegetables he had never seen before, but what got his interest was the fare of TV shows like *Bizarre Foods* on the *Travel Channel*—crickets, roaches, beetles, tarantulas, and small snakes, all of which appeared fried. No thanks. He would leave eating those things to Andrew Zimmern.

He caught up with Crutchfield in the small lobby of the Arunras Hotel, where the smell of food from the adjacent restaurant on the ground floor got his stomach grumbling. Whatever they were cooking smelled much more appetizing than how the foods outside appeared.

"We're in luck. They have two rooms on the fifth floor,

which was recently remodeled and is quite nice. The rooms aren't huge, but the beds are comfortable and the AC works. Oh, another tip, don't drink the tap water. Don't even use it to rinse a toothbrush or get it in your mouth when showering. It's bottled water *only* most everywhere in this country. Same thing with the ice. Make sure it's commercially produced ice. I like the restaurant here because the food is safe." He tossed a key to Lynch and nodded toward the car. "Let's get our bags, stow them in the rooms, and grab a bite to eat. Then we can search out this church we need to find."

After grabbing their gear, they waited for what seemed like forever for the small elevator. On the way up, Crutchfield filled him in on the history of the hotel.

"The new owners have taken this place in the right direction, catering to westerners. Ten years ago, the floor we're staying on was a brothel and the floor above was a karaoke bar that stayed open all night."

Lynch was not sure what to expect.

Despite Crutchfield's assurance that the water used at the restaurant for tea, both hot and iced, as well as for coffee was boiled and harmless, Lynch played it safe with a can of Coke™. He found the lemon grass chicken soup delicious and the French bread among the best he'd ever had—which said a lot considering he and Amy used to frequent her favorite place, *La Bonne Bouche*, a French bistro and bakery in a suburb of St. Louis. He did take up Crutchfield's challenge for something exotic for dessert—translated to "baby bees," the honeycomb dripped of honey but also included the bee larvae inside.

The culture shock this time was a favorable one, not just the food but also the price. His share of the bill came to six dollars. The can of soda alone at home would have been two dollars, or more.

"I can't believe the price, and the waitstaff practically hovered near us to make sure we were taken care of."

Crutchfield nodded. "Most tourists would be cynical and say they see two Americans, and since all Americans are rich in their eyes, they make sure to take care of us. But they take pride in their service. You might not have noticed that all of the customers received the same level of attention. That's even more amazing when you learn they make maybe $4 a day, which is considered a good wage in rural Cambodia."

Lynch counted out five $1 bills and left it as a tip on the table.

His companion smiled. "They'll remember you for sure at the next meal. Probably fight over who gets to serve us." He laughed.

The drive to the church that this Pastor Jim guy listed on the NGO forms filed with the embassy was a short one down two side streets that became rutted mud lanes just a block off the main road. From the road it was clear that this was a building under construction. Scaffolding, if you could call it that, surrounded the structure and consisted of sticks tied together with rope and supported by sticks that actually went through holes in the walls. Rough cut, warped planks of wood formed the platforms on which the builders stood as they worked on the walls.

They exited the car and walked into an enclosure which had a narrow, single-story building to one side and a covered open area on the other. That space was filled with motorbikes, which Lynch presumed to belong to the workers. The main building was three stories tall, with a two-story open area that Lynch envisioned might become the main sanctuary. Free-floating, concrete stairs, minus any railing, ascended in two flights to the third floor. A smaller room behind the open space was enclosed behind glass doors and windows and appeared to be set up for meetings with a small stage, chairs, and ceiling fans.

All in all, the place was a building code inspector's worst nightmare and guaranteed to bring OSHA a windfall in fines, had it been in the States.

They glanced into the enclosed room and saw no one. A worker saw them looking around and pointed up. Lynch and the first secretary looked at each other and shrugged. Lynch figured they'd be checking out the integrity of those stairs behind them in a moment.

At the top of the stairway they discovered more rooms like the one behind the windows below. The first room appeared to be a small, rudimentary computer lab holding older model desktop systems cabled into a network of sorts leading to a hub supported by a cable modem. An old blackboard at the front of the room held what appeared to be instructions written in the native language.

The next room was larger . . . and occupied. Lynch knocked on the doorway, and all heads turned toward him. He noticed a blackboard in this room that held Khmer letters followed by English. Inwardly, he thanked God. They had stumbled onto an English class. No translator needed.

The man at the head of the class appeared to be in his late thirties, looked scholarly in black-rimmed glasses, and was well dressed. He smiled at them.

"May I help you?" he asked.

"We're looking for Pastor Jim and Amy Gibbs. She just arrived from the U.S. to help here, I guess." He wasn't really sure of that last part. Was she here to help, to work? Or did she simply know this Pastor Jim as a friend.

The man said something to the class in Khmer and then led Lynch and his companion back into the hallway. Lynch made *som pas* to the man, who reciprocated.

"I'm sorry to interrupt. Looks like you have a full class. I'm trying to find Amy Gibbs. I followed her here from the U.S., and it's important that I locate her."

"I am Sokhon, the pastor of this church. She has arrive safe. I talk with Pastor Jim two day ago, and they were to do sightseeing before coming here. I have not yet seen them, and I have not talk with him since."

Lynch was impressed with the young pastor's command of English. He was clearly prepared to teach this class.

"Your English is excellent."

"Thank you, or *aw-koon*, as we would say. I spent a year in the U.S. for Bible training. Miss Gibbs will stay at our children's home in Tnolbail village, about twenty minute from here. Let me call my wife and see if they have arrive."

The man turned aside and retrieved a cell phone from his pocket. Moments later, he was talking with someone, although Lynch couldn't understand a single word on this end. As the call ended, the pastor turned back to them.

"I am sorry. They have not arrive at children's home. Pastor Felix from Battambang also call two day ago, look for Pastor Jim. He need help, but did not say for what. Pastor Jim, Mama Pat, and Miss Amy maybe go there first. I do not know what to tell you."

"Could you at least give me Pastor Jim's phone number? And please have your church pray for Amy. She is in danger."

He went on to explain the situation to the young pastor. Crutchfield also now heard the full story. Pastor Sokhon gave Lynch the phone number and agreed to ask his members to pray for protection over Miss Amy. They said goodbye, and Lynch headed for the car. Crutchfield rushed to keep up.

Lynch pulled out his cell phone, feeling glad he had purchased his carrier's 30-day plan to include all international calls. He dialed the number given him . . . and was directed on the first ring to voicemail where he was informed the user's mailbox was full and to please call again.

CHAPTER FIFTEEN

Amy glanced about at the people now surrounding her. Other members of the small congregation had joined the three couples. A handful of the newly arrived women took the infants and children and led them away, while others, including James, Felix, and Sokham, encircled the parents of the stolen children, laid hands on them, and prayed . . . in languages other than Khmer and English. Languages. Plural. Each person spoke in a different tongue, but they shared the same fervor as they prayed.

In Amy's safe, Southern Baptist upbringing and church experience she had heard of speaking in tongues, but had never encountered it. She had once been taught that such charismatic gifts of the Holy Spirit had ended with Jesus' apostles and the early church, but she had always suspected otherwise. The Bible taught her that God was the same yesterday, today, and forevermore. To say that these gifts had ended seemed counter to that scripture.

Yes, this was as foreign to her as the culture she now encountered, and she watched in amazement. Not only did these tongues flow with ease from their mouths, but they were fluent. It wasn't just gibberish. She was no linguist, but what they spoke had structure and words she recognized as being repeated. These were clearly languages, with all the components one would expect of such.

At that moment, one of the young Cambodian women raised her bowed head and looked straight at Amy. What she said next hit Amy like a bucket of warm water. No, something thicker than water. Oil, like olive oil.

"You are not here by accident. I have heard *your* prayers and have destined you to a greater calling. Do not fight against the goads, but embrace what I have for you."

The woman again bowed her head and continued on in the tongue she had been speaking.

Amy's brow shot up in surprise, and she blinked her eyes. Had she imagined what she just saw and heard? She turned to find Jim, but he was pacing some distance away, holding his phone up and in different positions as if trying to find reception. She made a quarter turn to her right and saw Pat staring at her, mouth open and eyes wide in surprise. She took three steps toward the older woman.

"Pat, did you hear that?"

The woman nodded in slow motion. "Uh-huh. And with a British accent to boot. Girl, God has got something special in store for you, and you'd better hold on for the ride."

Pat came up to her and gave her a hug. Amy shot back from her as something akin to an electrical jolt hit her body as soon as Pat enveloped her.

"What?"

"You shocked me."

Pat shook her head. "I didn't feel anything, and the way you jumped back, it involved a lot more than some static electricity. Which, by the way, we never see in this humidity. Yes'm, girl, I'm looking forward to seeing what God has in store for you."

Jim approached, looking at them with a puzzled countenance.

Pat smiled, and said, "Our young friend here just had an experience with the Holy Spirit."

"Oh?" He smiled, too, in a knowing sort of gesture.

Pat took his arm and began to lead him away. "Let's give her a minute. I'll tell you what just happened."

Amy appreciated being given some space and time to process what had happened to her. Besides, she couldn't move. She tried to take a step, but it was as if her feet had been anchored in concrete. From her medical perspective, that electrical jolt must have affected her nervous system and muscles. And yet, her arms moved freely. She could turn her head and twist her shoulders. What was going on here?

She tried to take a step a minute later and still found herself planted in place. The words spoken to her echoed in her mind—"Do not fight against the goads, but embrace what I have for you." She realized she was doing just that, fighting it, not wanting to believe she'd just had a supernatural encounter with the living God.

She took a deep breath and tried to relax. She recalled the words of Mary after Gabriel informed her that she, a virgin, was to expect a son and to call him Jesus. "I am the Lord's servant. May Your word to me be fulfilled." *Wait a minute*, she thought. *Mary was told she was pregnant. There's no way. Uh-uh. Not this girl.*

She took another deep breath and calmed her anxiety. A

sense, maybe an understanding, came to mind that this had nothing to do with being with child. So, in a whisper, she said, "Lord, I accept what You have for me."

At that moment, her legs became free. She walked over to the step leading to the church doorway and sat down. ". . . hold on for the ride" Pat had said. What *was* she to expect? Yet, she found herself surprised as she realized she felt no hesitation, no anxiety or concern over that expectation. Instead, she felt a giddy anticipation. Bring it on!

"You okay?"

She looked up to see Felix standing over her. She glanced back to where the group had been praying and saw that they had dispersed into smaller sets. The children had returned to their parents.

She nodded. "More than okay." She stood as Jim and Pat approached them.

Jim held up his phone. "For some reason, I'm not getting any reception here. I need to call our base and let them know what's going on and where we are. You ready to go?"

Amy nodded again. "Sure. Um, whatever we need to do."

Felix raised his hand as if to stop them.

"Jim, could you spare Amy for a day? I'll bring her along either tonight or tomorrow morning."

Jim gave the man an inquisitive look.

"Something she said earlier . . . and her question about that CIC facility up the road. I'd like to make some inquiries, and her medical experience would be a great help."

Jim looked at Pat and gave a subtle shrug. Pat returned the gesture. Amy, however, felt a bit unsettled. A man she had met only an hour earlier wanted her to go with him . . . in a foreign country . . . where she didn't know the language . . . and had no other means of transportation. She didn't know anything about this guy. Not in a real sense anyway. Within a moment, however, her concern gave way to a sense of peace. Was this part of what God had in store for her?

"I'm okay with that," she said. "I just need to get my small bag from your van. It has my passport and things, plus a change of clothes. The rest I won't need for such a short time."

Lynch nursed another Coke™ as he watched Reggie Crutchfield pace along the sidewalk outside the Arunras Restaurant, his phone to his ear. He appeared to be listening more than talking. Five minutes earlier, it had been Lynch walking a groove in the pavement in his sixth unsuccessful attempt to reach Pastor Jim by phone.

During their time in the car, he and Reggie had moved past the formalities that had dominated their meeting at the airport and short trip to the City Centre Hotel. In fact, they had discovered like interests in books—Lee Child and Brad Thor—and music. Who would have guessed that a diplomat in Cambodia liked Christian rock groups such as Skillet and We Are Leo, of all things? They shared a penchant for White Castle™ belly bombers as well, something Lynch could never get Amy to eat.

Lynch had also learned that the man was ex-military, or as Reggie had put it, "Once a Marine, always a Marine." That explained some of the man's questions for Lynch, but not all of them. Those remaining questions gave Lynch cause to think that this man's role at the embassy was more than that of being the first secretary. And with that thought, Lynch realized that the man's willingness to accompany and assist him might have deeper implications than those of simply wanting to gain favor from a new President-elect.

Reggie looked grim as he returned to their table inside the restaurant.

"Staff problems at the office?" asked Lynch, suspecting otherwise.

Reggie leaned toward Lynch and spoke in a hushed voice. "Not really. Let's just say I have a shared interest in finding Abdullah Said Abdi. A friend in the Cambodian military informed me that one of their navy's fast patrol boats out of Ream Naval Base intercepted a Somali fishing trawler working just outside Cambodia's recognized territorial waters. Everything was on the up-and-up, so they couldn't detain them. But it was unusual in that the Somalis don't fish this far from Africa's coast. You confirmed that Adbi was seen in Phenom Penh. We suspect this boat assisted him in getting here."

"How? It would take a trawler like that, what, three weeks at least to travel from the U.S. I was told our Coast Guard was tracking what they thought was a Somali trawler several days ago off the California coast. We thought maybe it had come to retrieve Abdi, but it ended up being a ghost."

Reggie scrunched his eyes, questioning. "What do you mean, a ghost?"

"Something transmitted a signal designed to fool a ship's radar, make it look like a trawler. A perfect decoy.

Homeland Security focused on that fake trawler in its search for Abdi and had folks along the coast on alert to find him. When the Coast Guard moved in to intercept, there was nothing. Nada. Even the radar signature suddenly vanished. While our people focused on that fake trawler, he probably slipped out of the country via Mexico. Canada would have been harder for him to use."

Reggie nodded. "True. The Canucks have much tighter security. With what I know about Abdi, he probably used an associate in Mexico's drug underworld to get out. Since he's already here, he had to have flown. If it had been me trying to enter this country on the sly, I would have used a private charter to fly under the radar to one of the islands off the coast here and then used a boat to go the rest of the way."

Lynch studied the man's face. Yes, there was more to this man than being an office manager. Why else would he know such things about a Somali terrorist and warlord?

"You speak as if you have experience in such things." He gave Reggie a knowing wink.

Reggie returned the gesture with a slight, off-center nod of the head. "Eh. Marine Corps training and all that."

"Right." Lynch suspected it was the "all that" portion of training the man must have received somewhere along the line.

Lynch started to ask another question but was interrupted by his phone ringing and vibrating in his pocket. He fumbled it as he tried to retrieve it from his cargo pants and was too late to answer the call. He checked his phone's log to discover that the call came from the pastor's phone. "Gotta return this one. That was Pastor Jim." He jumped up and hurried outside, both for better reception and privacy.

"Hello."

"Is this Pastor Jim?"

"Who is this? This is like the seventh or eighth time you've called my number."

"Yes, sir. I know. I've been desperately trying to reach you. My name is Lynch Cully, and . . ." He went on to explain the reason for his calls and the danger facing Amy.

"Lynch, I'm . . . I'm sorry. We were . . . in an area without reception. Just a minute. We need to pull off to the side of the road. Atith, pull over, please."

Lynch could hear someone else in the car asking questions and distracting the man. He hoped it was Amy.

"My wife and I are just outside Krakor, but Amy's not with us. She's with another pastor friend from the States, about 15 kilometers south of Krakor. Where are you?"

"Kampong Thom, at the Arunras Hotel."

"Ah. One of our favorites. Well, just stay put. We'll backtrack, get her, and head straight to you."

Lynch heard shouting in the background, followed by pounding on the vehicle and glass shattering. He motioned for Reggie to come outside quickly. "Pastor Jim, what's happening?" More muffled speech came through the phone.

"What are you—"

"Atith, get . . . Don't hurt him!" That was a woman's voice.

There were sounds of a scuffle.

"The woman! Where is the woman?"

Lynch had never heard Abdullah Said Abdi, but this voice had a distinctive accent, most likely African. Then the phone call ended. Where was this Cracker? Lynch had to get there. Now. Abdi had found them.

Abdi was tired of sitting and had no desire to wait in the car for his incompetent guide. He got out and gazed about the compound. He had seen the brochure used by Khay Oudom to entice parents into giving up their children. He had no doubt the children might receive an education here, the first lesson of which was not to be duped. This place bore no similarity to the one in the brochure's photos. A little gasoline and a match would improve the appearance of most of the buildings he saw about him.

Oudom and the boys had disappeared into the larger, two-story building only to emerge several minutes later. Leaning against the car, he watched as Oudom marched the children to another building. In passing, Oudom frowned at him and motioned for him to re-enter the car. Abdi responded by spitting on the ground.

After several more minutes, he wondered how much longer the Cambodian con man would take and became curious as to what the conditions were like inside the building where the boys had been taken. Yes. Perhaps this would give him some leverage. He checked his phone and made note of the GPS coordinates of their current location, so he would have this place's exact location.

He straightened up and pulled away from the car, his phone in hand and its camera active. He took a few steps toward the building and stopped as a Cambodian man exited the building and stood outside the entrance. The man crossed his arms in front of his chest and watched Abdi. Abdi assessed the man as no match for him, should it come to that. Yes, the man appeared far tougher than Oudom, but not one whom Abdi would have trouble taking down.

He took several more steps toward the building only to have his movements answered by a second man emerging from the building. Two against one would be harder, but not impossible from the looks of both men. Yet, within seconds, men came outside from the other buildings and took positions at the heads of the pathways leading to their respective structures. The odds—10:1—were now decidedly against him.

He returned to the car and entered the passenger side to sit and wait. As he did so, the men faded back into their buildings, except the first one, who remained vigilant nearby. Abdi's impatience grew with each minute that passed.

Finally, Oudom exited the dormitory and approached the car. However, instead of getting in and driving away, the man lifted the front hood and began to fiddle with the engine. Abdi risked the ire of his watchers and stormed out of the car and toward Oudom.

"What is wrong now? We are wasting valuable time."

Oudom glared back at him. "We will lose a lot more time if my car breaks down along the way. It loses water and I must check the radiator every day or two." With radiator cap in hand, he pointed to the opening. "See?"

Abdi looked. "I see nothing."

"Exactly. Unless I see water, I don't know how full it is .. . or how long I can drive until the engine blows up." He marched back into the nearby building and returned a couple of minutes later with a bucket of water. With care, he poured the water into the radiator until it topped off. He replaced the cap, returned the bucket to the man standing at the doorway, and motioned for Abdi to get in as he himself settled behind the wheel.

"I thought I told you to remain in the car."

Abdi did not appreciate the tone of the man's voice. He was not a child to be scolded.

"I was tired of sitting and wished to stretch my legs."

"Well, you did not get far, did you? They do not like strangers here. Even I am limited to one or two buildings when I come here. Even you would not have enjoyed the consequences if you had tried to venture further."

Abdi did not know how to take the man's reference to "Even you . . ."

They left the compound and resumed the journey toward Battambang. Abdi sulked in the passenger's seat, as Oudom drove along in silence. They picked up speed as the road conditions allowed and soon were just a few kilometers south of the main road. As they neared the intersection, Abdi noted Oudom perk up. Something up ahead of them had caught his attention. Yes, the man's mood had brightened considerably.

"*Lok* Abdullah, the white van." He pointed to the vehicle just as it pulled onto the national highway.

"Yes, so what? We have seen a dozen white Mercedes vans today."

"But this is *the* van we search for. I memorized the license tag, and this is the one."

Abdi perked up and began to praise Allah. He now saw their detour and even the need for water in the radiator as Allah's way of assisting him. Without those delays, they never would have encountered the van.

"Quickly, do not let them get away." Abdi grabbed his bag from between his legs on the floor of the car and retrieved two items he would need. One he slipped into his pocket and the other he tucked into his waistband at the small of his back.

Oudom turned onto the highway as soon as traffic allowed and sped up to catch the van. "How will we get them to stop?"

"Run them off the side."

Oudom frowned. "No. I will not damage my car doing such a thing. I need my car and you do not pay enough to replace it. Plus, there are too many witnesses, and they all have cell phones. The police would be called, and we, and my car, would be photographed."

But before Abdi could argue with the man, or even offer him the money for a new car, the van pulled off to the side of the road. *Allah smiles on me*, thought Abdi. Oudom pulled in right behind them.

As Abdi jumped out of the car, he slipped his right hand into his pocket and removed it with brass knuckles in place. He walked along the side of the van and recognized the older man and woman inside as having been with Amy Gibbs at Tuol Sleng. But he did not see the woman he sought.

He pounded on the side of the van to catch the driver's attention. The man saw him but did not open the door, so he used the brass knuckles to shatter the driver's window. He unlocked and opened the door, and pulled the driver out. Following two fast punches, the young Cambodian crumpled to the ground, and Abdi dragged the body around the front of the van to a place where he would not be seen by passersby on the road. He then pulled open the side door of the van.

"The woman. Where is the woman?" he screamed.

He grabbed the older man's phone, dropped it onto the ground, and drove his heel into it. In one swift move he dropped the brass knuckles into his pocket and retrieved a 9mm handgun from behind him. He pointed it at the older woman. "Get out. I want the woman Amy Gibbs. Where is she?"

The older couple, now outside the van, stood in front of him but did not answer. Strangely, they did not appear afraid either. In fact, they appeared calm. He fired a shot into the ground at the man's feet. He did not flinch.

"Where is Amy Gibbs?"

They did not answer, but their lips seemed to move as if quietly talking to themselves. Abdi became unsettled by their silence and the peace they exuded from their faces.

"*Lok* Abdullah, we must go. We will be caught if we stay a minute longer. The gun has drawn attention. Many people are watching us now. The police will not be far behind."

Abdi pointed with the gun. "Get in the car. You . . . " He pointed the gun at the man. ". . . In front seat, and you . . ." He pointed at the woman. ". . . In back seat with me."

The woman smiled and gave him a defiant look. "No. We will not go with you."

"Then you will die here."

She raised her brow and slowly shook her head. The man, too, made no move, but said, "We are ready to meet our Lord. If now is the time, now is the time."

"So be it. *Allahu akbar*." Abdi raised the gun to the woman's head and squeezed the trigger.

CHAPTER SIXTEEN

"If you don't mind sitting in the back, that would be great," said Felix after loading Amy's bag onto the seat behind the driver.

Amy laughed. "You sound just like Pastor Jim."

The man nodded. "He's a great role model. It's not that we like to ride shotgun, it's just that we've seen too many accidents here and don't want to put our visitors at risk. Medical care in this country is awful. Most folks go to Thailand if anything serious happens. Just sayin'."

Amy had no response to that reasoning. At least the two men were consistent.

As Sokham began to pull away from the small church, Amy asked, "So, where are you from in the U.S.?"

"My family is in Florida. From Puerto Rico initially. Personally, you might say I'm from all over."

"I know that feeling. I was an Army brat. My dad was an aviator." For the first time since his death, she felt able to talk about him without choking up. "Pat told me you were Special Forces."

"In the broad sense, yes. But not Army—Navy SEAL. SEAL Team Three, the other guys. We let SEAL Team Six take all the attention while we did the hard work." He laughed.

Amy smiled. "I have a friend who was DEVGRU. He used to say that riding on the back of a submarine in a wet SDV was just kindergarten for the real thing."

Her friend had explained that a wet SDV, or SEAL Delivery Vehicle, was like filming the James Bond movie *Thunderball*, just colder, darker, and more dangerous than what was filmed in the shallow, warm Caribbean. Either way, *she* preferred the beach.

Felix laughed louder. "Sounds like a Team Six member. But, hey, I'm impressed you know that much about Team Three."

Amy noted that the driver had slowed. She saw the CIC facility's sign up ahead.

Felix saw it, too, and pointed toward it. "So, any thoughts on how to approach this?"

Amy shook her head. "All I can think of is winging it. What's the name of that coastal city south of here?"

"Sihanoukville."

"That's the one. We could say we were traveling from there to Krakor and became curious as we saw the sign."

Felix nodded. "Works for me."

Sokham sped up on the paved drive to the facility, which they discovered was more of a drive from the road than they had expected. As Amy suspected, the road crossed the plain before heading into the hills, surrounded by jungle. After almost ten minutes, they rounded a bend and saw a gleaming, two-story, white concrete and glass structure loom into view. Behind that, Amy caught glimpses of another building like the first, plus a number of small, but attractive, structures. Despite the dense foliage, a tall fence could be seen enclosing the entire compound.

They came to the gate in the fence where a small guard shack sat to one side. Two men could be seen inside and Amy thought she heard music from within. She decided to go with her gut and climbed down from the Land Rover to walk to them. One of the two men met her before she got halfway.

"Hi," she said. "My name's Amy, and I'm a nurse from the U.S. We were driving from Sihanoukville to Krakor and saw the sign. I am curious about what the CIC is doing in Cambodia and wondered if they might have a job for me. I want to stay here longer than the 60-day limit for tourists, but I need a work visa. And for that, a job here would fit the need."

That sounded plausible, to her. She hoped her delivery came off right.

"No speak English."

The second man from the guard unit joined them.

"I hope you speak English," she said, feeling a bit let down that her acting skills, for what they were, had been wasted.

"I do, and I hear what you say. I am sorry, but no open job here. You must go."

She acted disappointed, but smiled and continued. "Oh. Bummer. So, I am still curious about what the CIC does here. I'm an infectious disease nurse back home and enjoy reading about the work they do. Can you tell me that much?"

She tried to add just the right amount of innocent

charm as she watched him scan her from head to toe and back again. Which meant he had to look up at her, as she was half a head taller than him.

"This is research center. Study animal. Is not open to public."

"Oh my, I should hope not. That could be dangerous. What do they use animals to study?"

"I not know. Please go now."

The men took on a more menacing stand and the first man reached for something on his side, under his shirt. Amy watched as Felix hurried out of the vehicle to join her. He put a hand on her shoulder. She saw that the man had retrieved a 2-way radio.

"See, dear, I told you not to get your hopes up about a job."

"I know you did. Oh well." She offered a slight pout, but turned back to the guards. "Is there at least someone I could call about a job? Maybe something will come up before I am forced to leave the country."

She saw Felix's eyes flick up and to their right. She followed his gaze and saw a security camera she hadn't noticed at first.

The second man shook his head. "I have no information about job. Please go."

"Okay. Well, thank you for your time."

Together with Felix, they returned to the Land Rover. As she climbed into her seat behind Felix, she saw the first man talking on his radio. He then dashed into the guard shack and came running back out toward them. As Sokham began to back up and turn around, the man knocked on his window. The driver stopped, lowered his window, and took something from the man's hand, which he then offered to Amy before heading on their way. A business card:

Walter Tillson, MD, PhD

Director

CIC Primate Research Center-Cambodia

along with a phone number. She showed it to Felix.

He grinned. "Good job. Angelina Jolie has nothing over you. Nice acting."

She scrunched her brow, questioning. "Angelina Jolie?"

"Yeah. She's a huge celebrity over here. She filmed *Tomb Raider* at the Angkor Wat Archaeological Site, fell in love with the country and its people, and has invested millions of dollars here. She built a huge luxury hotel outside the park, where they pay workers American wages. Or so I'm told. It's like the Holy Grail of jobs in this country. As a result, she's the only westerner in the past 30 years allowed to adopt a Cambodian child. That's kind of a big deal, if you think about it."

Movement to the side of the road caught Amy's eye. "Hey, what's that?" She pointed, but the movement stopped. Then the brush began to move again. "There it is again. It's following the side of the road."

Sokham slowed down, but had not stopped when something darted from the brush and careened into the front corner of the vehicle.

Surprise etched Felix's face. "That's not some*thing*—that's some*one*." He opened his door and jumped to the pavement.

Amy followed right behind him, in time to see a short, balding, middle-aged male—western from his appearance—pick up a pair of black-rimmed glasses, put them on, and pick himself up from the road. He brushed off his shirt and pants, and looked at them both.

"I-I'm sorry. That was clumsy of me. I-I'm fine. All good here."

Amy looked for signs of injury and saw none. *Clumsy or well-timed?* she wondered.

"Who are you and what are you doing here?"

He fiddled with his glasses and looked flustered. In fact, he looked like a cartoon professor, lost in the jungle. With rumpled travel clothes, complete with canvas belt outside his shirt, and a green canvas satchel draped over one shoulder, all he needed was a safari hat to complete the costume.

"My name is Jared, Jared Miller. *Doctor* Jared Miller. And before I answer your last question, who are you and what are *you* doing here?"

"We asked first," replied Felix, raising up erect enough to look a bit imposing.

The man seemed to compose himself. "That you did, but I don't quite know how to answer your question until *you* answer it for *me*."

That seemed an odd position to take. Was his answer going to change depending on what they told him? And why would he need to change it? Amy decided to play along. His presence outside a guarded research center was all that was required to max out her curiosity. But then she thought about the last time that had happened—her curiosity and finding that terrorist's explosives cache—and had second thoughts. This time the thought of her dad brought a tear to her eye, but she felt a wave of resolve flush through her. *Nope. Go for it*, she thought. *Felix has my back.*

"Okay. My name is Amy, and this is Felix. Our driver is Sokham. We were driving along and saw the sign. I'm a nurse in the U.S. and got curious about what the CIC was doing in remote Cambodia."

The man hesitated, but then asked, "Are you really an infectious disease nurse looking for a job? You don't look like someone needing a job."

What? He had been listening to them. Amy became more convinced that the man's collision was a well-timed stunt and not an accident.

Felix glowered at him and took a deep breath. The intimidation proved enough to make the man ease back a step. "You were listening to us at the guard shack?"

The man held up both hands, palms out, in defense. "I admit, I was. I-I had little choice. I came to ask questions as well, but Tillson already knew who I was, and the thugs working for him took my car. That was four days ago. I've been living off the land since, trying to find proof of what I came here for. Or, at least steal my car back. The rental company isn't going to take kindly to my losing their car. I've had no luck, and I'm tired of eating papaya. Until you showed up, no one else has come here. It's as if they knew I was still out here. Do you have any water?"

This man was becoming more and more of an enigma. He looked like a thin Jack Black in the 2017 *Jumanji* remake, and yet he had the skills to live off the Cambodian jungle. Just the fact that he was willing to drive a car himself in this country counted for something—either real chutzpah or insanity. Amy wasn't sure which. Then, he had reasons for concern about the work being done, and the director knew his name by reputation. What kind of reputation? Or did he know the guy personally? Was this guy some kind of crackpot? A journalist, perhaps. No, he said he was a doctor.

"What kind of doctor are you?" asked Amy.

"Medical. My specialty is, uh, was, um, still is, immunology."

"Is? Was? Which is it?" asked Felix.

"That's a long story. The bottom line is that I think something fishy is going on behind that fence, and I want to prove it."

"Reggie, where is a place called Cracker? That was Pastor Jim, and it sounds like Abdi found them while we were talking. The phone went dead. They're in trouble."

Lynch watched as Reggie used his phone, walking away from Lynch. Another "friend" in Cambodia's military? Lynch didn't care who he called if it helped them get to this Cracker place faster.

As he waited on the first secretary, he used his own phone to pull up a map. Using his current location, he set the app to find the quickest way for them to reach the destination. He misspelled it the first time, but the app corrected him with Krakor. His heart dropped and eyes bugged out as he saw the results. *Four and a half hours?*

They would have to retrace their route almost all the way back to Phnom Penh, cut across to National Highway 5, and use that to reach Krakor. Surely there had to be a faster way, but every way he looked at it, that big lake and the river were in his way. Southeast Asia's largest freshwater lake stood between him and Amy.

He saw Reggie walking back toward him. He hoped the man had good news, but his face didn't exude confidence in such.

"I called a friend to see if he could provide assistance."

"Military?"

Reggie shook his head. "You got your passport and anything else you might need if we're gone overnight?"

Lynch thought for a moment. He had his ID and valuables. "Um, sure."

"Good. We'll keep the rooms here for now 'cause we'll be back. Get in the car. Let's move. I have no shortcuts to offer you."

They climbed into Reggie's car, and he pulled away from in front of the restaurant. As traffic allowed, he pressed the pedal and sped as able.

"Nice thing about this car. It's got a diplomatic tag. Police won't stop me, as long as we don't hit anyone."

Lynch's brief experience with Cambodian traffic didn't dismiss the odds of that happening. He was glad Reggie did the driving.

"So, if I can ask, who'd you call? You said 'no' to another military friend. Someone at the embassy?"

"No. Interpol this time. You see, Abdi is on their wanted list for nearly a dozen charges involving drugs, money laundering, assault, weapons, and at least one count of kidnapping. I would personally add murder to that list, but that's a story for another day."

"I *know* I'd add murder to that list, too." Lynch frowned. "Okay, you said something about a shortcut. Looks to me like we have a long drive ahead of us no matter how we go."

The diplomat nodded. "That we do. I had hoped my friend might be able to wrangle a helicopter ride across the lake and a car on the other side. He couldn't, so we have to take the long road. Sorry."

"Hey. Thanks for trying. I sure don't have any connections here . . . except for you. I couldn't even spell the name of the place we're going."

As they crossed a bridge over a muddy river, Lynch glanced about. He didn't recall any of the surroundings from their drive in.

"Um, I realize I don't know my way around here, but isn't the shortest route to Krakor the other way?"

CHAPTER SEVENTEEN

Amy watched as the rumpled doctor guzzled a 16-ounce bottle of water. She then looked back in the direction of the research center. They were beyond a point of being able to see it, or to be seen by it unless they had security cameras along the road. She glanced about and saw no manmade posts or poles of any kind. There were no power or other utility lines. She scrutinized the trees and saw no cameras mounted on those big enough to hold such equipment. Unless a vehicle came along the road, she figured they were about as isolated as anyone could be in any country.

"Could I have another?" The man used his sleeve to wipe his mouth and mustache.

Felix retrieved another water bottle from his cooler and handed it to the man. The guy appeared to pose no threat and was in need of help. How could either of them refuse?

Besides, they might even be on the same side—if it came to choosing sides.

"We need to get moving," said Felix. "If you want a ride to Krakor or Battambang, we can get you there."

"Thank you. Yes, I need a ride. I just hope the hotel in

Krong Pursat hasn't thrown out my luggage and is holding the room for me. And I need to contact the police and the car rental agency. Tillson won't get away with taking my car, even if he is likely getting away with murder."

Amy cocked her head in wonder. Was the man using a cliché or was he serious?

"Let's go," said Felix as he opened the back door, grabbed Amy's bag, and moved it to the far back.

"Oh. One moment, please." Doctor Miller ran back into the brush from where he had emerged and came back with something in his hands that he began to brush off.

Amy rolled her eyes. A pith helmet. The man's ensemble was now complete. She took a deep breath and claimed her seat behind Felix.

As they began to move, Doctor Miller asked, "So, Amy, are you even a real nurse or was that just a ploy? And why are you folks interested in the research center?"

Amy decided that she was not quite ready to play along all the way. He needed to answer some questions first.

"Yes, Doctor Miller, I'm an Emergency Medicine and trauma nurse. I work for a helicopter medical evacuation service in St. Louis, and I'm here on a missions trip. But before I can answer your second question, I need you to answer the same thing."

Doctor Miller looked at both of them and pointed to Felix. "Missions trip, too? Oh, and please just call me Jared. I've never been so pompous as to expect people to address me as doctor outside the professional environment."

Felix turned in his seat to face the back seat as best he could. "Was that question to me?"

Jared nodded. Felix turned to see Amy, who shrugged.

"Okay. Missions, yes. A trip, no. I live here and operate a charitable foundation that helps house, feed, and educate children. We also do disaster relief. I work out of Battambang. Amy is here for a month to work with another relief group that operates north of here. We coordinate our services, and I needed their help with something. I borrowed Amy to go to that CIC center while they went on ahead of us."

Jared looked intrigued. "So, you *do* have a special interest in that facility."

Felix nodded. "But, as Amy said, before I say what that is, you need to tell us what your interest is."

Jared looked off into the distance as he appeared to contemplate his answer. After a minute of silence, he nodded.

"Okay. I am an Ivy League-trained physician and Duke-trained immunologist who now questions the safety of immunizations as we know them. I actually once worked for the CIC, until a study I did validated the idea that immunizations in children really can cause autism. They swept the study under the rug, and when I protested, they canned me. I've been blackballed from doing research at every major medical center in the U.S. as a result."

Amy shook her head. The guy was a quack, an anti-vaxxer. Everybody knew that immunizations saved lives.

"I see you shaking your head. You, like everybody, believe vaccines to be safe and lifesaving, right?"

"Yes. And they don't cause autism in children."

"Ah. And why do you say that?" He didn't give her time

to answer. "You say that because you've been told that by the CIC, the FDA, the press, your nursing school, the doctors you know. The list goes on. Everyone has been told that vaccines are needed. They've become mandated by schools and employers. Everyone has consumed the Kool-Aid."

She had to admit, the guy seemed confident in his assessment. But then, what zealot didn't?

"The link between vaccines and autism has never been proven."

"*I* proved it, while working at the CIC. Did you know there are over 240 studies in the medical literature proving the link between vaccines and neuropsychiatric disorders in children, of which autism is at one end of the spectrum? 240 plus. You can find them all in the literature databases . . . except mine, of course. Oh, and there's not a single study that truly disproves the link. They say there are, but those few studies have been shown to be flawed or actually had different endpoints that didn't disprove the link at all. Another popular tactic is to study one dose of one vaccine, instead of the accumulated impact of multiple vaccinations."

Amy felt annoyed, but the guy's confidence made her wonder.

"Why not yours?"

"Pure and simple, greed. The CIC is the major supplier of our vaccines. It's a thirteen-plus billion-dollar business, of which they make over five billion dollars in sales. If vaccine sales disappear, a major reason for their existence disappears. The most ardent promoters of vaccines—the doctors who have labeled guys like me as anti-vaxxers, called us quacks, and prevented us from doing more research that proves them wrong—are the same guys who hold the patents and make millions in royalties."

"So, why doesn't the government shut this down?"

"Let me ask a different question. If vaccines are safe, why did the government have to indemnify the publicly-owned pharmaceutical companies that make them? Why are those injured by vaccines forced to take their cases to a special vaccine injury court in Washington? That same court has paid out over $4 billion in settlements in the past 20 years, and its caseload grows yearly."

Amy wanted to argue now. The guy had raised her hackles.

"The government took over because the pharmaceutical companies were going to stop making vaccines."

"So, why were they going to stop making them? They weren't going to be able to afford the litigation they saw coming their way. I know. I was on the inside back then. Those companies were going to go bankrupt from lawsuits, and the government needed them to keep making the drugs that actually help people, like antibiotics and heart medications. 'Too big to fail' is how some might put it."

"But, if they saw that there were going to be problems, why would the government do that? Why not just rule them unsafe and remove them from the market? The FDA has done that with over a dozen medications since I started nursing."

Jared nodded. "Why not indeed. Inbreeding. Collusion. Corruption. Give it whatever name you want. The people who make up the FDA's vaccine committee are ex-

executives of the pharmaceutical companies, and when they leave the FDA, they go right back into Big Pharma. It's a giant revolving door. And they tell Congress that vaccines are safe and necessary, so the game continues. What we really need is a totally independent vaccine safety board to investigate all safety issues."

Felix had been listening intently. He asked, "If there's that much corruption, and that's the word I'd use from what you described, why hasn't the press taken it on? Sounds like the makings of a Pulitzer Prize to me."

"It does and it would, but guess where over 70% of advertising dollars for the mainstream press comes from."

"Since you're phrasing it that way, I'd guess Big Pharma," replied Felix.

"Bingo."

Amy could see the logic behind the man's arguments, but he hadn't addressed the actual issues of safety, and she didn't want to encourage him. He had climbed onto a soapbox and could express his passion on the topic well. But was it just sour grapes from a disgruntled, ex-CIC researcher who was really envious of the work going on here? She decided to change the subject.

"So, what brought you to Cambodia? A vacation? Friends?"

Jared shook his head. "I wish. You wouldn't expect it, but the CIC has brought its poisons here, too. Did you know that in 1996, Cambodia had the lowest rate of immunizations in Southeast Asia? And autism was nonexistent. The CIC stepped in, worked with the government on boosting immunization rates, and provided cheap vaccines. Now? I talked with a doctor at the Chey Chumneas Hospital in Kandal province last week. He had never seen a case of autism ten years ago. Now they treat 7,000 children a year and get three to five new cases *every* day. Just at that small provincial hospital. A graph showing the growth of autism here matches the increase in vaccination rates, just like in the U.S."

Amy furrowed her brow. "What do you mean, like the U.S.?"

"Like I said. As a med-evac nurse, you're not likely to see these numbers, but I'm pretty sure you're aware that the rate of autism in the U.S. is growing."

Amy nodded.

"In the 1940s, autism was unheard of. In the 1970s, just ten years after the widespread introduction of the measles vaccines, the autism rate was roughly one in 10,000. In 2016, it was one in 250 and now, it's expected to rise to one in 36. The CIC itself predicts that one in two children will be affected by some aspect of neuropsychiatric disorder, if not outright autism, by 2030. Imagine what society will look like then."

Amy raised her brow. She knew autism worldwide was increasing, but she hadn't paid close attention, and those numbers were startling. She had too much to think about. She needed to change the subject, but didn't know where to head. She felt Sokham braking and knew they must have arrived at the main highway.

"Oh no!" exclaimed Felix. "Over there!" He pointed to the side of the national highway, not far from the intersection. "Sokham, pull over wherever you can there."

Amy looked, and her mouth went dry. Half a dozen police vehicles and an ambulance lined the road, their lights flashing, and a large crowd of onlookers mingled about, oblivious to the traffic trying to pass by. And in the middle of the activity sat Pastor Jim's white van.

With a silent prayer on his lips, Lynch watched the Cambodian countryside slide by as Reggie headed toward Siem Reap, the opposite direction displayed by Lynch's map app. From there, they would head farther west, around the end of the lake, and then southeast to Battambang—a five and a half-hour drive compared to the shorter trip to Krakor.

Reggie had insisted that this might finally get them one step ahead and closer to finding Amy Gibbs. His reasoning? If anyone had been injured, they would be taken to the World Mate Emergency Hospital in Battambang. If the police had questions, or needed to hold someone, again, that city's Provincial Commissariat of the National Police was much better prepared than the smaller administrative police office closer to Krakor. And, had they taken the opposite route, the one suggested by the map app, it would take another two and a half hours to follow them to Battambang. They would save an hour and a half by going the direction Reggie had chosen.

Of course, Lynch had countered with his concern that they might still be in Krakor. Then, they would remain separated by over two hours. And what if no one was injured and the police were satisfied with their investigation? The pastor—along with Amy, had they somehow reunited—might choose to drive to their base in Kampong Thom using the shorter route. Then, he and Reggie would be hours behind, chasing them around the lake. Or what if they hadn't reunited with Amy? Where would she end up in that scenario? Lynch hated playing 'what-if' when it came to her.

But . . . Reggie knew the country. He knew their police and emergency medical procedures. Plus, it was his car and he was driving. What could he say?

Lynch's quiet prayer was interrupted by the ringing of Reggie's cell phone.

"Crutchfield . . . Yes?"

The man listened but said nothing, and Lynch could not hear what was being said.

"Thank you. We're en route to Battambang. I'll contact you there."

Reggie glanced at Lynch before turning his attention back to the road, but his face did not express relief.

"That was a friend. He picked up some chatter on the police radio bandwidths about an assault with at least two gunshots along National Highway 5, at Krakor. That's in line with what you heard on the phone. The police are only now arriving on the scene. The assailant was described as an African man with a scar on his face."

Abdullah Said Abdi. It could be no one else, in Lynch's mind.

"Interpol?"

"No, a different friend. But my friend at Interpol was the one who passed the word on to this friend, who in turn has started paying attention to Cambodian police and military communications."

"And, if I ask who that different friend is, and you tell me, would you have to kill me?"

Reggie smiled. "Anyone but you, yes." He laughed. "I trust your discretion."

"So, who is this friend?"

"I can't tell you."

Lynch shook his head and chuckled. "Let me guess. Need to know."

"Something like that. Or, plausible deniability. I could also cite your security clearance level."

"You know my security level?" Lynch, as Bradley Graham's security chief during the campaign, had achieved a clearance one step above Top Secret. But he could no longer claim that as an active clearance level, as he was no longer employed by the President-elect.

"I know more about you than you know about yourself." He grinned. "If I didn't, I wouldn't be doing my job."

"And just which *job* is that?"

The man's grin morphed into a smirk. "I can give you three guesses, but if you guess right, *then* I'd have to kill you."

Lynch chuckled as he shook his head. He liked this guy, and he had a pretty good idea what his *real* job was in Cambodia. He didn't need to press the issue. Instead, he remained grateful for the man's assistance, even if they weren't really any closer to finding Amy. She could be anywhere in the country now.

Amy, Amy, Amy. Maybe she'd be easier to find wearing a red-and-white striped top with matching beanie. He never had trouble finding Waldo.

CHAPTER EIGHTEEN

Amy had her door open before Sokham came to a stop, beating Felix to the ground as both jumped from the vehicle to rush to the van. They were both stopped by police.

"Those are our friends," Amy said in hope of being allowed past. She saw a body on a stretcher being loaded into the ambulance, but at the distance where she'd been stopped, she couldn't tell who it was. "I am a trauma nurse from the U.S. Can I help?"

The officer had no clue what she'd said. Sokham stepped up next to her to act as her translator. He told the policeman what she had said, and the officer replied, as he held up a hand for her to stay put.

Sokham looked at her. "The captain say to stay here while he ask his superior."

A police captain? Why would he have to ask someone else?

As if he read her mind, Sokham continued. "In my country, police captain not very important. They say police captain sleep on his motorbike."

She watched as the man went first to one officer, then to another, and finally a third.

"Must be serious," said her translator. "Third man is general, head of provincial police."

The captain hurried back to her and motioned for her to follow. He led her toward the ambulance, with Sokham right behind her. She glanced about but could not see Jim or Pat. Were they already in the ambulance?

The officer spoke to Sokham, who said to her, "Please help here."

She climbed into the back of the rig but didn't see either missionary friend. Atith lay on the stretcher and appeared in pain. The left side of his face was swollen and a large gash on his scalp was surrounded by a hematoma the size of a large man's fist. The pattern of discoloration was one she had seen before, suggesting brass knuckles.

As he saw her, he smiled, followed by wincing. That was a good sign.

"Miss Amy, good to see you okay."

Something inside her triggered emotions she typically did not feel when in "clinical mode," where she tried to remain as objective as possible. Here, this man she hardly knew had been beaten, and yet, he remained more concerned about her than himself. She felt convicted and loved at the same time. How often, at home, had she put others ahead of herself? If she was to be honest with herself, she realized that even her trip to Cambodia had been motivated more by wanting to escape the emotional pain of losing her father—and to a lesser extent, losing Richard—than by wanting to help these people. Was she as altruistic as she believed herself to be?

She recognized something else. She had once chastised

herself for comparing Richard to Lynch, but, at first, Richard had repeatedly put himself ahead of others. On the other hand, ever since the attack that had almost killed him, leaving him amnestic for several months, Lynch really had changed. She saw his putting others first in a new light. Yet, altruism wasn't the word that came to mind. *Christian* came to mind, and it caught her off-guard.

Lynch. Now she compared him to Richard. She wondered what he was up to back in the States. It felt strange. Back home, in the back of her mind, she always knew she could call on Lynch in a pinch. She chuckled mentally at that. Lynch in a pinch. But here, he wasn't available and somehow that felt isolating.

She looked at the medical technician and asked, "Do you have a penlight? Flashlight?"

The tech gave her a questioning look, until Atith himself beat Sokham to the translation. The EMT handed her a small flashlight, and she checked his pupils and the wound on his scalp.

"Atith, can you follow my finger with your eyes, without moving your head?"

She placed her finger in front of his face and began to move it around. He moved his head to follow her.

"Please, do not move your head. Just your eyes."

This time he seemed to get it, but she noted that he had difficulty following her finger upward and he seemed uncomfortable as he tried to do so.

"Please stop, Miss Amy. Two vision. Not feel good."

She took that to mean diplopia, or double vision. She glanced into his ears with the light and saw no blood—a good sign that there was probably no basilar skull fracture. She saw no otoscope that would allow her a better inspection. She opened her mouth, and he mimicked her. His teeth were intact and no blood noted. She turned her attention to the rest of his body, with what limited tools she had, and felt his injuries were limited to those inflicted by the blows to his head and face. He was going to require surgery.

She turned to Sokham, as the better translator, and said, "He has what we call an orbital floor fracture. That means the thin bone that makes up the floor of his eye socket has been broken, and he will need surgery. I cannot tell if there is any broken bone under the cut in his scalp." She pointed to that injury.

As Sokham spoke to the medic, Atith looked concerned, but he faced her and said, "Thank you, Miss Amy, for pray."

She took his hand, squeezed it, and nodded. She began to get up, but he pulled her down.

"Please pray now." He took her hand and placed it over the swelling in his face.

Uh. Like speaking in tongues, she had read about the "laying on" of hands but hadn't really seen it in practice in her own church experience. She felt awkward, but kept her hand in place and began to pray out loud.

"Lord, I, uh, we, uh, ask for your healing touch for Atith. The Bible says we will lay hands on the sick and they will recover, and in Isaiah you promised us that by your stripes we are healed. I, um, don't know what else to pray, but I know that you know what is needed, so I leave Atith in your loving hands. Amen."

As she finished, she saw serenity flood Atith's face and felt a warmth in her hand. At that moment, she thought she witnessed the young man look heavenward, with Atith's affected eye moving without limitation. He closed his eyes before she could double-check.

"*Aw-koon*, Miss Amy," he whispered.

She started to ask him to open his eyes, but Sokham tugged on her arm. "Police ask you to come."

She turned and saw the captain beckoning her with his hand. She descended from the ambulance and watched it pull away as she followed the officer. She rounded the back end of the van, dreading what she might find, but there sat Jim and Pat sitting on the step leading into the side door of the van. Pat fanned herself with a sheet of paper.

As she ran up to them, both stood and gave her a hug.

"Are you okay?" she asked.

Jim wavered his head back and forth a bit, as if saying "So-so."

"How is Atith?"

"He should be fine, but he might need surgery for his face."

Jim frowned.

"What happened?"

Before Jim or Pat could answer, Amy heard someone behind her.

"Ms. Gibbs, I am General Khan. I have questions for you."

She offered *som pas* and said, "I am pleased to meet you, sir, but questions for me? I was not here and did not see what happened."

He returned the greeting and continued, "I know that you were not here. May I ask where you were?"

Amy felt flustered. His tone almost insinuated that she had something to do with this assault. "I . . ." She pointed to Felix, who remained some 40 feet away. "My friend and I stopped at the CIC research center to make an inquiry. We expected to catch up with our friends here at the KM Hotel in Krong Pursat."

"What kind of inquiry?"

The man's English was excellent, but his attitude intimidated her. However, she did a quick mental check and decided to stick with her story at the research center. If there was something fishy going on there, and various officials had been paid to look the other way, this man might be at the top of that list.

"We saw the sign for the research center as we drove to a small village south of here. I am a nurse, as I mentioned, and I wondered if they might have a job opening there that would allow me to stay in your beautiful country longer than my tourist visa."

The man seemed to relax, although Amy realized she had made a minor blunder. She had told the guards that they had been driving from Sihanoukville to Krakor. She hoped that wouldn't come back to bite her.

"Do you know of anyone in this country who would have reason to hurt you?"

Now Amy was puzzled. Hurt *her*? She wasn't involved in the assault.

Without hesitation, she answered, "None, sir. I arrived in your country just two days ago. I have met fewer than a dozen people so far."

She saw Jim raise his brow. Something was going on, but she had no clue as to what. He stood again and took a step toward the two.

"General Khan, sir, may I have a few minutes to tell her what is going on? It might be easier for her to hear it from me."

The senior police officer nodded, but when Jim ushered Amy to the van's side door and pointed for her to sit next to Pat, the general was right there with them.

"Amy, do you know a Lynch Cully?"

She nodded, finding it curious that she had just been thinking about him and now Jim mentioned his name.

"Good. Glad that's confirmed, because he's here in Cambodia looking for you."

"What? Why on earth would he be here?" Her next thoughts were *how did he find out where she had gone?* She hadn't even told Macy because she knew Macy couldn't keep a secret for long. The only people who knew she was coming to Cambodia were Jim and Pat, and they were here, in Cambodia, when her plans were made until the time she arrived. Plus, they didn't know Lynch. "You two were the only people who knew I was coming here."

"I have no idea how he found out, but he's been desperate to find you. Do you know an Abdullah Said Abdi?"

Amy blanched at the name of her father's murderer and her heart accelerated. Tears filled her eyes.

"He . . . he's the terrorist who m-murdered my father." Despite the emotional confidence she had felt earlier, this time she could not hold back the tears. Pat's arm encircled her shoulders and embraced her.

"Apparently, he's in Cambodia and looking for you. And somehow, he found us. Lynch Cully and I finally connected by phone, and he was telling me what was going on when I had Atith pull over. Suddenly we were being attacked by a thin black man with a nasty scar down his left cheek. He did that to Atith and threatened us with a gun. But when we stood our ground, he seemed to become confused, and the man with him intervened. As we stood there expecting to die, police sirens grew louder, and he fled with his accomplice."

Oudom had become entangled with insanity in the form of this African terrorist. Indeed, he felt as if he was in between a charging bull elephant and a pouncing tiger, with his foot trapped in the brush. Abdi was the tiger, and Tep Rithisak was the larger pachyderm. Even if freed, he couldn't escape them both.

Civilian gun ownership was outlawed in the kingdom and had been since 1999. Only the police and military possessed firearms. The punishment was swift and severe for those violating these laws. And the consequences for murder, with a firearm or otherwise, would be fatal.

When Abdi pulled that gun from his waistband and threatened the Americans, Oudom saw his days becoming limited. And when the man began to squeeze the trigger as he pointed his weapon at the woman, he could physically feel a noose tightening around his neck. After all, he had been aiding this illegal alien and would also be held accountable for the man's extreme actions.

He had screamed for the man to stop, but had been ignored. Oudom did something he would never have imagined himself doing. He ran forward and knocked the man's hand up and away from the couple just as the gun fired. The shot had called more attention to them, but no one had been injured. Despite the anger glaring from Abdi's face, he knew his action had granted him a reprieve from that noose around his neck. He now hoped Abdi realized it as well.

Thankfully, the African saw fit to escape the coming sirens and fled with Oudom to the car. Also seared in his memory was the American man's comment—"Thank you, Yeshua. Praise you, Lord God."—as Abdi turned away. What did that mean?

Now, they drove in silence toward Battambang. Oudom would need to place his charge in a safe house while he changed to a car that would not fit the description of the one he felt sure was being broadcast across police and military radio channels as one belonging to wanted fugitives. Had he been alone, he might be able to talk his way out of a police stop. With the African on board, that would be impossible. He tested the limits of speed and his driving skills to get to the city and the concealment of its back streets before being spotted.

The man fiddled with his handgun. Oudom felt relief that the man, in his anger, had not chosen to use the weapon on Oudom himself.

"I hope you are not too angry with me, *Lok* Abdullah. Had you shot those people, neither of us would have a chance of escaping with our lives. The police and military both would stop at nothing to find us."

Abdi murmured something in his native tongue, and his tone wasn't pleasant. Instead of addressing Oudom's comment, he asked, "Where are we going now?"

Oudom looked at the man as he spoke for the first time since they had fled the scene of Abdi's assault on that driver. What would his demand be now?

"We are going on to Battambang. I will put you in a safe house, and I need to get a different car. The police will be looking for this one."

"And where is the nearest hospital, where that driver will be taken?"

In the flash of time it took for the thought to form in his head, Oudom saw a glimmer of reason behind the assault on the driver. The man was intended as bait. Despite Oudom's disagreement with the man's action, perhaps there was a tincture of sense within the man's mental illness.

"Is that why you beat him? That wasn't really necessary, and it now has the police looking for us. That and your gun."

Abdi nodded but did not become quarrelsome. That surprised Oudom. He had been contentious every other time Oudom had questioned him.

"I know how these peoples think. They will have concern about the driver and will come see him in the hospital. That is where I will wait."

"Maybe the woman you seek will not come. You made it clear that you are after her. They will keep her away."

Abdi shook his head. "No. No. She is nurse. She will

come. She will want to know what is wrong."

Oudom had to concede that the idea made sense. But that would require a small change in plans. He grabbed his phone and made a call to Tep Rithisak's top lieutenant.

CHAPTER NINETEEN

Tillson paced in his office, like a wild animal at a zoo wanting freedom but being caged. The new children at the home required his attention. They still had not had their assessments, but he had to avoid going to the home and giving away its location. Only those who worked there and those who "recruited" new "students" knew its location. Yes, and a few government officials, as well.

But Jared Miller had arrived at his figurative doorstep. How had the man found the facility? Even the CIC kept its location secure—from fear of terrorists learning of it and taking control over it. Its remote location had been chosen as part of that security plan.

Doctor Miller had been discredited in the eyes of the current puppet masters, but had gained "rock star" status among the anti-vaxxer crowd, a group growing larger by the day. With heavyweights like Robert F. Kennedy Jr. and his Children's Health Defense Initiative working hard to expose what they saw as the true dangers of mercury and aluminum and of immunizations that contained those metals, the truth as those people saw it was reaching more and more people hourly. And social media didn't help. The mainstream media could only spin the information so far, and they didn't control social media as much as Tillson would like to see.

And to add to his concern, someone else had shown up at the gate just days after Miller. She had claimed to be a nurse looking for work who had simply stumbled across their sign as she traveled. He returned to his computer and reviewed the security video.

"My name's Amy and I'm a nurse from the U.S. We were driving from Sihanoukville to Krakor and saw the sign. I am curious . . ."

She *looked* sincere, but really, driving from Sihanoukville? Sure, you could get to Krakor from the coastal town using back roads, but who in their right mind would do so? There were no inns or hotels, no restaurants, no gas stations—not even a rest stop for a squatty potty break. Surely, she wouldn't be naive enough to eat from local food stands along the road, not that there were many of those either. The roads were too rarely traveled to make such a home business worthwhile.

". . . saw the sign . . ."

He shook his head. That bloody sign. He had protested it saying their security plan opposed it. However, the Cambodian regime had insisted. Something about the prestige of having such a CIC facility within their borders. When the sign had been erected, a dozen provincial and federal government leaders were on hand for the photo op. Since then, the paint continued to fade, and the weather took its toll. With some luck it might not survive the year, and he could "fail" to request a replacement.

He resumed pacing. If indeed she was a nurse, her skills could actually be helpful. He needed a better qualified caregiver for the children. But, would she have reservations about using the kids as test subjects? True, laws were different here, but most would argue that medical ethics knew no boundaries.

He should have invited her in. Now he could only wait to see if she would call him. He gave that a low probability score. Even if she was serious about a job, the greeting at the gate was likely to deter her from seeking one out.

He shook his head. He had not handled that as he should. Miller's arrival in the area had shaken him up.

Amy sat in the van's open side door and stared into the vegetation beyond the side of the road, her mind lost in the ramifications of what she'd been told. She had fled the U.S. to escape the ghosts, only to have the devil himself follow her here. Now, Jim, Pat, Felix, and all those she encountered here were in danger. Even Lynch.

And then there was this anti-vaxxer doctor. If even half of what he'd told them was true, then a new and different menace faced them all in the form of influence, money, and greed. How could she possibly fight a war on two fronts?

"You don't."

Pat's voice interrupted her thoughts.

"What?"

"You were talking to yourself. You *don't* fight a war on two fronts. You turn it over to God."

"I was talking to myself? Really? I never talk . . ." Amy

never talked to herself or expressed her thoughts out loud like that. She remained convinced she hadn't spoken this time either. And yet, Pat knew what she'd been thinking.

"You have to let go and put your trust in the Lord."

The image of serenity on Atith's face after her clumsy prayer came to mind. He trusted Him.

"Amy, Jim didn't tell you the whole story. When we wouldn't divulge where you were, that man threatened us with a gun. He had the gun pointed at my head, and the rage evident in him was truly from hell. But Jim and I both released the situation into our Father's hands. We told the man that we were ready to go home if it was really that time for us. We both had complete peace at the thought of finally meeting our Lord face-to-face. And that both confused the man and fueled his anger even more. He tried to squeeze the trigger of his gun and shoot me, but the man he was with knocked his arm away, and they fled."

Amy stared at Pat, her mouth wide open in surprised shock. Her trouble had almost cost them their lives. But her shock became amazement. Would she have been able to turn her life over to God? She had often thought that, as a Christian, she could. But push come to shove, would she?

"I have no doubt whatsoever, that had Jim or I put up a fight, tried to do something *our* way, we'd both be dead now."

"And it would have been my fault."

Pat shook her head. "No, Amy, his fault, not yours. It wasn't your finger on that trigger."

Amy noticed Jim and Felix approaching. Jim had gone to the younger pastor to explain what had happened. Amy watched as General Khan stopped Jim and they exchanged a few words, as well as business cards. As soon as that conversation ended, the police began to depart the area. And with that, Jared apparently saw that he was free to join them and hustled to catch up with Jim. Amy closed her eyes. She wasn't quite ready for another encounter with the "good" doctor.

Jim's face was smothered in concern. "Amy, I think you need to reconsider your time here. If this Abdullah guy could find us traveling along this highway, he'll find you at our place. You'd be much safer back home."

Amy thought about that. Would she be safer at home? But then, she also had the children and workers here to consider. She hated to think about turning around and heading home. She had just arrived. But putting the children at risk? Her mind wavered. Too much had happened today. She had difficulty processing it all.

"Wait a minute!"

Everybody turned to face Jared.

"Sorry. Look, I realize I'm just a straggler you picked up on your little side trip to the CIC, but you haven't answered my question, and I think there's something more going on here that you're not telling me. Why were you at the CIC?"

Felix proceeded to enlighten the man about the missing children, many of them being twins. "And Amy here wondered what the CIC center was doing here in Cambodia. But now that you bring it up, she never really told us *why* she was curious."

All eyes turned toward her, but it was Jared who spoke. "I knew it, I knew it, I knew it. You suspect they're using the children for medical testing, too. That old fox Tillson is back at it."

Jim and Pat could not contain their alarm at the concept of "their" children as guinea pigs. It emanated from their faces.

"Medical testing?"

"On our children?"

Spoken in unison, Amy couldn't quite figure who said what, but the sentiment was clear. She nodded. "Twin testing is like the ideal option for many tests. The thought kept niggling at the back of my mind, but I couldn't really believe the CIC could be involved in that. Here or anywhere. There are all kinds of protocols and approvals you have to go through for human testing. Even more so with kids. Medical ethics—"

"Medical ethics?" interrupted Jared. "I doubt Tillson has the least bit of concern about ethics. That's probably why he's here. He's been trying to prove the safety of thimerosal and aluminum in vaccines for years. Here, with relatively little money, he can pay for heads to look the other way and 'buy' children from unsuspecting parents."

Amy had to admit that even with as little as she had learned about the country so far, Cambodia seemed a likely spot to perform illegal testing. A culture with no concept of sin, with impoverished parents willing to give up their children under whatever ruse worked to offer them money. Child traffickers willing to take kids, even cripple them for life, in order to make money. Topped off with government corruption at the highest levels. Perhaps this was all true for many third-world countries, but she was now in Cambodia, and all the pieces seemed to come together.

Jim stood there shaking his head. "Amy, right now, we need to be concerned about *your* safety. Knowing what we're up against with our missing children—assuming all of this speculation is correct—we can use other avenues to find them. We should make plans to get you together with Lynch Cully and get you home."

Jared appeared agitated. "No, please stay. You can help."

Felix appeared caught in the middle. Amy held no doubt that he understood the danger facing her, but there were children from his flock who were among the missing. Plus, the longer they did nothing, the greater the risk of others in his churches falling prey to the traffickers.

"Jim, can you call this guy Lynch and set up our meeting someplace? Maybe he'll have some ideas."

Amy wanted to say "You have no idea" regarding Lynch but held her tongue. This was a decision *she* needed to make.

"No can do. The only way we had to communicate was through my phone, and our attacker made a point of taking and destroying it." He pointed to the smashed phone in the dirt a few feet away. "That reminds me, I need to see if the SIM card is okay." Jim walked over to the crumpled electronics, stooped down, and picked up the mess. A moment later, he held up the card . . . in two pieces.

"So much for using it in someone else's phone," said Felix.

They looked at Amy. She shrugged. "I don't have his number memorized, and I didn't bring my phone with me, on purpose." They looked at her in a sense of apparent amazement. "I didn't want anyone to be able to track me by it, and I didn't want to be distracted by it. So, I decided to simply leave it at home."

Pat rolled her eyes, while Jim offered a subtle wag of the head in agreement.

Jared continued. "Look, I-I don't want to downplay any danger you might be in, Amy. I don't know that whole story, but this vaccine issue is a big one, and if we can get proof of what I think is going on here, it could save thousands of lives. Maybe even improve millions of lives."

Something inside Amy told her to take time to listen. "Jim, Pat, if it's okay with you, why don't we head back to the hotel we stayed in last night, and give Doctor Miller a chance to speak his mind. We might even be able to get you a new phone and get ahold of Lynch."

Pat nodded and looked at her husband. "Fair enough."

Jim seemed less certain, but after a moment, he, too, nodded in agreement.

Felix looked at his driver. "Sokham, would you please drive Jim and Pat in their van? I'll drive the Rover. You two can go in the van or the Rover." He nodded toward Amy and Jared in succession. "I'll follow the van."

Amy took another look inside the van, and then eyed the Rover 40 feet away. "Nothing personal, Jim, but the Rover has much better air conditioning. And its windows are intact." She turned to walk toward the distant vehicle.

"Better air conditioning? I'm in for the Rover, too."

Jared started a brisk walk toward it, but as he caught up with Amy, she looked at him and said, "Uh-uh, doctor. I call shotgun."

*　*　*

Tillson had not been able to focus on his work. Even the antics of the family of monkeys outside the windows of his office offered no entertainment. He sat at his desk drumming his fingers. Jared Miller was after him personally. That's the only thing that made sense. Somehow the man had learned that he had played a dominant role in getting Miller fired and spreading the word to discredit him. And now he sought payback.

One other idea bothered him. Who provided Miller's funding? Miller hadn't been independently wealthy. He hadn't found work with any academic centers. Of that Tillson was sure. Other major research centers had also rebuffed him, to the best of Tillson's knowledge.

But there were new players all the time. Another pesky adversary to his work, a female PhD at M.I.T. whose work focused on biology, environmental toxins, and computation science, had found funding from a Taiwanese computer company. Her work highlighted not only the "dangers," as she saw them, of vaccines but also of glyphosate and GMO foods. Her funding would have been pulled had it come from the U.S. pharmaceutical or agricultural industries.

So, where were Miller's funds coming from? Someone had to provide the capital for his anti-vaccine crusade.

The phone interrupted his thoughts.

"Tillson here."

"Doctor, this is General Khan."

"Good afternoon, General. This is an unexpected but pleasant surprise. How might I help you?"

"It's more that I can help you. You had alerted me to a certain doctor who arrived at your center. Well, he was rescued by two people who arrived at the scene of an incident on National Highway 5. One of the two was a young woman, a nurse. I had the opportunity to talk with her as she also figured into the case I was investigating."

"A nurse? Tall, light hair, fairly attractive?"

"Sounds about right."

"Did you ask her about her companions? The doctor in particular."

"No. Unfortunately, I did not see him there until we had dismissed her."

"Did it look like they were together?"

"Actually, no. She was with the couple who were assaulted, but had been following in a different vehicle. The couple had no idea who that man was." He went on to explain some of the details of the incident.

"Thank you, General. That is intriguing. I will have to think about how this fits together."

"You're welcome, Doctor. You have my account number."

They agreed upon the worth of his information, but more so on the worth of information he might yet come across.

"There is one other thing, Doctor. The doctor you are concerned about has filed a complaint about his rental car being stolen by men in your employ . . . Just a minute."

Tillson heard some chatter in Khmer through the phone.

"Doctor?"

"Still here."

"I was just informed of two things. First, he assured my

captain that the nurse and her friend found him hitchhiking and offered him a ride to his hotel. That would seem to confirm that they have no previous relationship. Second, your doctor 'friend' has actually provided photographs of the car being held inside your compound. Very unfortunate that your men weren't more discreet. With these images, my men are duty-bound to act. I can delay them for a while, but I suggest you return the car to the doctor at his hotel, and that you do so quickly. You might also wish to fill the gas tank. The rental car agency is co-owned by a nephew of the Prime Minister."

Tillson had no trouble picking up the hidden meaning in those last sentences. The last thing he needed was political heat from the central government. Miller presented a big enough concern for him.

He made the call, and within a minute he saw the rental car, followed by another, leaving through the main gate. He could only hope that the two drivers had the smarts to leave the car at the hotel in Krong Pursat and avoid getting caught.

With that issue settled, his pacing continued where he'd left off earlier, even more concerned than before. Miller's arrival. That nurse's inquiry. The coincidental meeting of the two. Or was it? But the nurse was also the target of some African terrorist. He had no idea how the information given him fit together, much less how Miller might fit into it. He hoped she would call him. He had an idea.

CHAPTER TWENTY

For the first time since his arrival in Cambodia, Abdi held a glimmer of appreciation for the Khmer man tasked with assisting him. For the past three days, he had considered Khay Oudom incompetent. In Somalia, the man would have been beaten severely for his poor performance. And yet, somehow the man had rediscovered their target, thanks to memorizing the license plate. Well, those associated with her anyway, placing them one step closer to finding her.

Plus, the man's knowledge of his country and its police had saved him. He had been so angry at the woman not being present in the van that he hadn't heard the imminent sirens at first. It was Khay Oudom whose persistence had prevailed and prevented him from being apprehended. That would have not gone well.

Now, as they entered the outskirts of Battambang, Abdi reflected on the incident. He had allowed anger to rule. From now on, he would remain calmer, use common sense, and listen more to *Lok* Oudom's suggestions. After all, the man knew this country, its peoples, its prejudices, and its authorities. He also had access to resources that Abdi required for a successful mission. Yes, Abdi resolved to take a more measured approach.

They had found common ground in heading toward Battambang. For Khay Oudom, the city provided the means of switching to a vehicle for which the police would not be looking. For Abdi, his plan to lie in wait at the hospital for the woman to visit required heading to the city and staying nearby. Had he been more reasonable with *Lok* Oudom, he would have communicated his plan to the man in the first place so they could coordinate their logistics for finding the woman. But he hadn't done so, and still the man's plan fit his own. That alone was a clear sign from Allah, a signal that he would succeed.

He mental meanderings were jarred by a sudden right turn.

"Trouble, *Lok* Oudom?"

"Perhaps, *Lok* Abdullah. Get down."

Abdi didn't like the tone of being ordered to do so, but reminded himself . . . a more measured approach. Without complaint, he ducked low in his seat.

The car stopped and backed into a shaded drive, or perhaps just a pullout. Lush foliage seemed to enclose them on both sides. *Lok* Oudom, too, dipped low in his seat. Abdi heard a vehicle drive past. It did not sound as if it had slowed. *Lok* Oudom eased upright and gazed beyond them to the right and to the left. In the time it took Abdi to blink, the driver plunged even lower into his seat. Another vehicle passed by, or perhaps it was the same one. This time it seemed to slow down, maybe even stop, before moving on. A light flashed above them, sweeping back and forth.

Abdi expected the worst and found himself holding his breath. Police! That had to be *Lok* Oudom's reason for his sudden actions.

The light disappeared, and Abdi now heard the faint thrum of an engine. A moment later, the sound of a car door slamming found its way to them. Only then did *Lok* Oudom ease his head up to take a look about. A moment later, the man appeared to relax and sat fully upright.

"You may sit up now, *Lok* Abdullah."

Abdi complied and looked about. He saw nothing of note. In fact, he saw nothing but what looked to be palm leaves. "Police?"

Lok Oudom nodded. "They were coming down the street toward us. I had a choice of turning or the risk of being identified and caught. I think my sudden turn caught their attention, but this spot served us well, to keep us hidden."

"Praise Allah for providing this cover."

Lok Oudom shrugged. "I will thank Tep Rithisak. This turnout was created for such a purpose as we needed. We are in his, and my, home territory now. We have several such hiding places."

The man emerged from the car and pushed his way through the foliage. Abdi could see only his head as he turned side to side and gazed along the road.

Upon re-entering the car, he said, "The road is clear. I will use the back alleys now to be safe. We are less than a kilometer from a garage where we can exchange cars. From there, I will take you to a safe place a block away from the hospital. Once there, I will get us some food and confirm that the man you assaulted is in that hospital. I can think of no other hospital capable of such care nearby, but you never know. I go to Thailand for all of my medical care."

An hour later, his belly full, Abdi wished to scope out the hospital. The sun was going down and the shadows would be his ally.

"*Lok* Abdullah, I might suggest waiting a little longer, for the darkness. Here is a sketch of the hospital grounds and surrounding area, plus what I consider the safest route for you to get there. The compound has a tall wall and two gates with guards. Here and here." He pointed to his map. "It will not be easy to get in, but you do not need to get in, only to watch for the woman. Visitors are supposed to use this gate." He pointed again.

Abdi studied the drawing and then folded it up and placed it into his pocket.

"I will go with you."

Within minutes, however, Abdi found the man asleep and snoring in the chair. He would not wake him. If there was trouble, he could fend for himself . . . and pity the person who stood in his way.

At first, Lynch watched in amazement as they entered the city of Battambang. With its heritage first dating to Siam, now Thailand, in the late 18th century, followed by its French influence when Cambodia was unified as a French protectorate, the city housed a diverse population of Thai, Khmer, and Chinese. And with that, he witnessed a transition from rural Cambodian architecture through that with a Buddhist influence and some with a Chinese flavor to buildings of the classic French Provincial style. It seemed surreal.

"I realize Cambodia was a French colony at one time, but these French-styled buildings seem so out of place."

Reggie nodded. "It stands out here even more than in Phnom Penh where there's been a lot more new construction going on. The Chinese introduced the shophouse concept in Cambodia about a hundred years ago, so what you'll see the most of are narrow-but-deep homes with the family's shop occupying the bottom floor and their living quarters on the top floor. Even the old French buildings have been converted to that style."

With that bit of information, Lynch now saw exactly what Reggie described. Other buildings, however, sat unoccupied and crumbling into nonexistence. He wondered how long before new structures would be built that would alter the architectural "feel" of the city.

"So, your call on this one. We can find a hotel first or we can check out the hospitals first."

The sun sat low in the western sky, but Lynch had no desire to delay further his search for Amy. He could sleep in the car if that was what it would take.

"Hospitals first. Then the police headquarters. If they aren't here, we need to head back to that last town."

"Kampong Thom."

"Yeah, that one, where we left our things and where this pastor is based." Lynch paused as he considered having to turn around and return. "I just hope this wasn't some wild goose chase." Goose chase or not, at least he felt as if he was doing something, not sitting idle.

Lynch sat quietly watching the people as they passed by. The Khmer seemed to be a gentle people, but the poverty he noticed as Reggie turned down one street and the next made everyone in the U.S. appear wealthy in comparison. Everyone. He understood now why friends at church back home always said that going on a missions trip would change his life. And he hadn't yet interacted with any of the people of this country. He had no doubt that he would not see life in the U.S. in the same way as he had before coming after Amy.

"Here's the first one."

Reggie's comment broke Lynch's reverie. He glanced about and saw more of the same.

"First what?"

"Hospital."

"Where? I don't see anything close to resembling a hospital."

Reggie pointed to a single-story building with a sign over it written in Khmer and English. Lynch could barely make out the faded red cross at the top of the sign.

"That?"

"I know. Not at all like what we expect. In much of Cambodia, what they call a hospital is more like a small clinic or medical office to us. I honestly wouldn't expect them to come here, but it was the closest, and I didn't think we should discount it. If someone's injuries were minor, he might come here."

"Really? It doesn't look like it could even handle a sprained ankle."

"You might be closer to the truth than you know. Many doctors here are nothing more than herbalists, and those who advertise a degree might have gotten it by mail. If you get hurt or sick, trust me, you don't want to seek medical care here."

Reggie parked, but left the car running. "Sit tight. I'll check it out."

Lynch watched as his guide walked to the front door, found it locked, and walked back to the car. He shrugged as he walked.

Back in the car, he said, "As I thought. Locked tight and nothing to suggest anyone is there."

"So, where to next? Another locked hospital?"

Reggie shrugged again. "Like I said, it was the closest. The place I expect they would have gone is across town, so, to save time, that's next."

"Across town" required less than ten minutes, but at their destination, the building looked more like a small hospital that Lynch might expect. The name, World Mate Emergency Hospital, topped the sign in English, with what Lynch suspected was the Khmer name underneath. There were a handful of one-story buildings comprising the complex. Still, the grounds were dry dirt and littered like much of the area surrounding the hospital.

"This place was built and is funded by a group of Japanese businessmen to provide free emergency care to any Cambodian. I honestly don't know if they provide other care, such as routine surgeries, but I figure anyone involved in an assault or car accident would be brought here. Since it's late in the day, we'll have to circle around the block to the other side of the compound to get in."

A minute later, Reggie pulled into a dirt area outside a security gate, between the street and a tall, plastered wall which Lynch had noticed surrounding the center. The sign here said "Emergency. Surgical care for war victims." Another announced that this entrance was for staff and visitors. Lynch marveled at what he saw. Surrounding the parking area were food carts and semi-permanent booths catering to hospital visitors, even at this time of day. They occupied even the smallest spots of available dirt, while taking care not to intrude into the area marked for parking.

"I have to give these people kudos for industriousness. They seem to stake out the most unlikely places to do business."

" 'Stake out' is probably the wrong term. These folks pay a premium to the hospital for these slots. I'll check in at the security hut to see if anyone has been brought in from the Krakor area. Sit tight. And remember, don't risk eating anything from these vendors. I shouldn't be long."

Lynch watched as Reggie walked behind the several cars between them and the entrance. He debated getting out of the car. Reggie had turned it off and taken the keys, and it began to get hot and stuffy inside. Perhaps there was a breeze outside. But would he be accosted by vendors wanting to sell to someone who so obviously was American?

The climate inside the vehicle became unbearable. He decided to take his chances outside, but would stay with the car. He walked far enough behind the car to see the security hut. Reggie was not there. *He must have had to go inside to find the answer they sought*, thought Lynch.

He glanced around and noticed a gated facility across the street, with the drive leading to a three-story structure of the Khmer style that shouted "government." As he scanned the well-maintained fence to the left of the guard shack, he saw its sign—the Battambang Police Commissariat. *That could be convenient,* he thought.

He returned to the car and leaned against the trunk. Sweat began to bead up on his forehead. The breeze he had hoped for must not have gotten the memo and failed to show up. As he wiped his forehead with the back of his hand, he saw a slim figure walking across the street and looking for a place to remain secluded. After a few stops, the man—an assumption on Lynch's part based only on the person's walk—found a spot where he blended into the shadows created by the setting sun and hospital's lights. That alone seemed suspicious to the ex-cop in Lynch, but what really caught his attention was the man's being bundled in a long-sleeved hoodie. *Who could possibly be cold in this environment?* he wondered.

Lynch shifted his own position so that he could watch the person more closely. As the man reached up to adjust his hoodie, Lynch noticed the person's skin tone. While all of the Cambodians he had seen were darker skinned, he compared their skin tone more to a latte heavy on the milk. This person was darker, blacker, more like that of an African.

The hair on Lynch's arms bristled and gooseflesh arose . . . and not because a cold wind had materialized. An African!

He needed to somehow see the man's face, to search out that distinctive scar. But he was in a foreign land, unfamiliar with its customs and how its law enforcement might respond should he stir up trouble. He couldn't afford to be deported because he saw a ghoul where only a concerned family member might be.

He left the car behind and ventured toward the security guard, thinking the man might be of assistance. However, a family of four beat him to the entrance, and the man became occupied with them. Reggie remained absent.

It was up to him.

He sauntered closer to the hidden figure, glancing about and looking to the ground as if looking for something. A moment later, he saw the figure shift position, pulling deeper into the shadows. But at one point, a ray of light from the entrance gate caught the man's face.

That scar! It was him!

"Abdullah Said Abdi!" Lynch moved toward the man, but the figure took off running. "Stop!" Out of habit, Lynch took off after him. "Stop that man! He's a killer! Wanted for murder in the U.S!"

Lynch chased him down a few streets, but lost him. Nobody seemed willing to help but instead avoided Lynch as if he was a crazy man. Then it hit Lynch, that no one understood what he was yelling, and he probably did appear crazed.

He backtracked, making one wrong turn in the process, but eventually found himself back at the hospital's parking area. Reggie stood next to the car, and two police cars, lights flashing, sat nearby, while multiple officers stood at the ready at the entrance gate to the police headquarters. The diplomat rushed to him.

"What happened? I thought something had happened to you and called for assistance."

Lynch pulled his sweaty shirt away from his chest in attempt to cool down.

"Abdi. He was here, standing right over there. I chased him but lost him somewhere in that direction." He pointed toward the area where the fugitive had headed. "I got a little lost coming back."

"Abdi was here?"

Lynch nodded. "He was wearing a black hoodie, which is what I found suspicious. I moved closer to get a better look, and it was him all right. He took off as soon as I called his name." As he said that, Lynch realized he should never have called out. He should have fallen back to observe and called on the police for assistance. He was fatigued and anxious to get the man. He would react differently in the future.

Reggie motioned for the police officers to come closer. As they grouped together, Lynch caught only a few words as the officers were briefed. A few minutes later, both police cars sped off in the direction indicated by Lynch.

"Give me a minute," said Reggie. He pulled out his phone and made a call. Upon hanging up, he added, "My friend at Interpol. Word will be out to every officer in the province shortly."

Lynch found some paper and began to fan himself. Running in this heat and humidity was as bad as St. Louis at midday in mid-August, and Lynch could no longer say he was in good enough shape for running in either locale under such conditions. As if reading his mind, Reggie handed him a bottle of cold water.

After taking a drink, which seemed to go straight to his pores in the form of new sweat, Lynch asked, "So, what'd you find out?"

"Yes, a man named Atith, who works for some Americans as a driver, was brought here earlier. But the Americans are not here, and the people inside have no idea whether they will come to visit the man or not. Visiting hours are over, so they certainly won't be here tonight."

"Do we know if these Americans are the pastor and his wife? They could be anyone."

Reggie shrugged. "No idea, but I've already asked for help in locating the pastor. As you've already experienced, you have to provide a copy of your passport at any hotel where you stay. I have people canvassing the hotels in the province trying to find them. They have to be somewhere close by."

"Or not. Pastor Jim knows that Amy is a target. They could be taking her far away as we speak."

The first secretary appeared contemplative. "True. Guess we'll know in a couple of hours. In the meantime, I could use a shower and some shut-eye. Let's find a hotel, take a break, and get an early start. By then, I should know which direction to head."

Lynch gave in and nodded. At least he'd have an opportunity to wash out his clothes and let them dry as he slept. Yes, the "miracle" of travel clothing for the tropics, being able to dry in this humidity.

* * *

Abdi slammed the door behind him as he rushed into the apartment one block away from the hospital. He had spent the last 30 minutes weaving a trail around the location, intent on spotting anyone tailing or looking for him. Only after calming his fear of discovery had he decided to return to the safety of the dwelling.

"You went out without me, *Lok* Abdullah. I am not sure that was wise."

Abdi gave him a look that he hoped would make the man desist. Instead, Khay furrowed his brow and gave him closer scrutiny.

"From the look on your face, I should say you have already learned that. What happened?"

Abdi grabbed a bottle of water from the kitchenette and took several long drinks while deciding on his next course of action. Would that include disclosing what had happened to him? He reminded himself of his earlier commitment to rely more on his Cambodian "escort."

As he thought about what to say, he shook his head. He still found it surreal that he had been identified. And by someone who so clearly was an American. An American he had never seen before . . . and on Cambodian soil. What were the odds?

"I made my way to the hospital, just as you had outlined on your map, and found a place in the shadows where I could watch the visitors' entrance." He proceeded to inform his companion of what happened next. "I made sure no one followed me and that I was unnoticed before coming back here."

Khay Oudom stood and began to pace the length of the

room. Abdi could not say the man looked fearful, but his concern about this chain of events jumped out.

"This is not good, not good at all, *Lok* Abdullah. Not only do the authorities know you are in the country, they have guessed your whereabouts. This area will be littered with police very shortly." The man grabbed his belongings. "We must leave now before they gain strength in numbers and set up checkpoints."

Abdi started to nod in agreement but stopped. The man spoke the obvious. But, would fleeing now really help? He changed the nod to a negative shaking of his head.

"Perhaps it would be best to ride it out here. Lay low. In a day or two, they will stop looking here."

Khay's negative reaction intensified.

"No. Once they close down the area, they will search door-to-door. You are a hunted man, on Interpol's list of most wanted, and the government will take great pride in announcing when they have found you. We must leave at once."

Abdi reminded himself once again that he had sworn to listen to this man who had the better understanding of this country's ways. He, too, grabbed his belongings.

"Then we must go."

Khay stopped in his tracks and stared at him. He appeared incredulous that Abdi had agreed so quickly.

"I . . . I . . . I am surprised that you . . . well, that you do not put up more of a fight. I thank you for seeing it my way. I will not disappoint you."

Abdi would be the judge of that, but he recognized that he saw this man in a different light. Perhaps cooperation truly would prove to be the best route.

"You understand the police here. I do not." He started to open the door to the apartment.

Khay stopped him. "Not that way. Follow me."

The man first led Abdi to one of the bedrooms where he rolled up the sleeping mats, set them next to a wall, and followed that action by sliding the small rug aside. Curiously, the rug moved as one stiff unit rather than bunching up as he expected. Beneath it was the subtle outline of an opening—a trap door, which Khay opened. He pointed for Abdi to proceed ahead of him. As Khay reached the bottom of the stairs behind Abdi, he flipped a switch and a lone light bulb illuminated a large room with sleeping mats, shelves stocked with various foods, and more.

"One moment."

The man then swept his hand back and forth near the wall adjacent to the steps. He stopped when he found what appeared to be a thin filament, like fishing line, which he pulled until it became taut.

"I had to move the rug back into position, in case the police break into the apartment and search it. They will see nothing but an empty room and not think to inspect it more closely."

He then turned and beckoned Abdi to follow. Soon they exited the building just a few feet from the car. Abdi turned back to inspect where they had emerged. He could not see the hidden doorway even though he knew where to look. The work was that of a master craftsman. He would keep this in mind for his own operations, both in Somalia and the U.S.

"I am sure you can think of many ways Tep Rithisak might use this place. He has likely used it all those ways, and more. I thought we should take this route to reduce the chance of being seen by others in the building or along the way to the car, which I parked here just for such an escape if needed. A habit of mine."

As Abdi entered the car, he wondered about their next move. The injured driver was his best opportunity for finding the woman. Leaving this area was not to his benefit.

Khay Oudom started the car and proceeded cautiously. To Abdi, they appeared to be moving away from the hospital in a zigzag fashion, but the waning light challenged his sense of direction.

"Lok Abdullah, I know you think watching the hospital for this woman is best move. Until this evening, I would agree. But I told you I not wish to disappoint you. While you gone, I call many contacts see if they make progress with information I ask them about yesterday. My effort was rewarded."

Abdi perked up. *Good news?* he wondered.

"The white van is registered to a relief agency that operates from the city of Kampong Thom. The American man and woman in the van are known to the government as the heads of that agency. Whether it is tomorrow or next week, I do not know, but at some point, the woman will be there with them."

The idea of having to remain in Cambodia for another week or more was not one Abdi wished to embrace. And yet, to date, his aspirations for revenge had been thwarted at every turn, and now, the woman no doubt was aware that he was on her trail, whether from the older couple or from the authorities. He would have to become a tiger, slowly stalking its prey until the right time to pounce from the brush. Yes, he liked that analogy. The embryo of a smile actually formed on Abdi's mouth.

"Are we heading there now?"

"That is my plan . . . unless you wish differently. It is a five to six-hour drive."

"*Lok* Oudom, you have not disappointed me," he lied.

CHAPTER TWENTY-ONE

"Amy, you are in danger. With my phone destroyed, I can't get ahold of Lynch Cully, and vice versa. I *really* think we should head to our base in Kampong Thom. I believe that without direct communication, Lynch Cully will head back there, too."

The disquieted look on Pastor Jim's face revealed his worry. Amy knew he, and Pat, had only her best interests at heart. Still, a different concern filled her.

The waitress appeared at their table. Amy hadn't so much as glanced at the menu. She wanted to talk with Lynch, too, but as she had told the others, she had left her cell phone in St. Louis hoping to stay off the grid. She would have borrowed another phone, but Lynch's numbers had changed when he became employed by the Graham campaign, and she had had no reason to memorize them at the time.

"Pat, would you order for me, please? I haven't the foggiest idea of what to get."

The woman nodded. "We've not eaten here before, so I can't vouch for anything we get. But you can't go wrong with the lemon grass chicken soup. I've yet to eat at a restaurant in this country that hasn't mastered that traditional dish.

The water here is probably okay, for hot tea, but to be safe, stick with a canned soda or bottled water."

Amy looked at the waitress. "The lemon grass chicken soup and a Coke™, please. Oh, and bread, too. I've heard the bread in this country is wonderful."

The waitress nodded.

"*Aw-koon*," said Amy.

The waitress smiled and took the others' orders. As she left for the kitchen, Amy looked at Felix. For some reason, she valued his opinion. She had only met the man that day, but there was something about the guy that made her trust his instincts. Nothing romantic. That hadn't even crossed her mind, and she wasn't ready for anything like that. No, he was a man of character, who had seen the good and bad that people can do to each other, and now tried to better the lives of those he came into contact with. Like her father. And as she thought about it, like Lynch.

"Felix, what do you think?"

The man downed the last of the bottled water he had brought in with him and looked at her. He took his time answering.

"Amy, what Jim says has merit. Your friend Cully is likely to head back there, and it sounds like you'd be safer with him around."

"I'd feel safe with you around, too."

The man smiled. "Well, thanks. I can assure you I would do my best to keep you safe, or Jim, or Pat. But you didn't let me finish." He took a swig from the can of cola—the first of two the waitress just delivered to him. "My worry is that you really won't be safe wherever you go in this country. That goon found you . . . well, the van anyway, in the middle of nowhere. He's bound to have the contacts and resources to find you in Kampong Thom."

Jim leaned forward over the table. "So, you don't think she should go there?" His tone told them all that he didn't agree.

Felix shook his head. "I'm not saying that exactly, but I think that might be the first place he'll go looking for you. All it takes is a phone call and the promise of $10 or $20, and that guy will know where your van is registered. He's likely to beat you there. You still need to be on guard wherever you go, but especially there."

The older pastor sat back in his chair and looked thoughtful.

"Actually, I was thinking that a delay in going to Kampong Thom, for Amy anyway, might throw the guy off. Plus, I'm being a little selfish. I want to find these children, and I think she can help."

Amy smiled, and a weight lifted from her shoulders.

"Jim, I know I came here to help you, and I plan on doing so. But I'm worried about these kids, too. After hearing that doctor, Miller, I think they're being used in human testing by the folks at that CIC facility."

"Speak of the devil. There's the errant doctor himself. Should we invite him to join us?" Felix nodded toward the main door to the restaurant.

Amy wanted to duck and hide, but she saw that the man had already spotted them and now advanced toward them. She glanced around the table only to see that there was more than enough room for one more—maybe even three or four more. The excuse of not having a place for him rocketed out the window.

"May I join you all?"

Felix was the first to agree and pointed to the seat closest to Amy. *Thanks, Felix*, she thought.

The man sat down and flagged the waitress, who sprinted to their table. He said something to her in Khmer, which surprised Amy. All she recognized was "Bud Light" and *aw-koon*. Did the man have other surprises for them?

"You speak Khmer?" she asked.

He shrugged. "Some. They probably get a good laugh at how I butcher their language, and I get some puzzled looks on occasion. Once I was corrected and told that I had just ordered chicken brain in soapy dishwater. But I keep trying. It's the only way to gain proficiency."

Amy couldn't disagree with that. She had learned Italian the same way when her father had been stationed in northern Italy.

His beer arrived in an instant. "It also helps that I tip *very* well. Compared to the States, it might seem like small change, but here, it's a small fortune." He took a swig of beer and seemed to relax.

"I had the most unusual thing happen this evening. My rental car showed up here at the hotel before we did and the keys were waiting at the desk. I checked it out and not a scratch on it. The gas tank was even full."

Jim smiled and asked, "What rental agency?"

"Angkor National."

Jim laughed. "I suspected as much. It's owned by the prime minister's nephew. The thieves probably learned that and decided to take the high road."

"Of course, they took my papers and sunglasses, but those are all replaceable."

Silence ensued as their food arrived and the waitstaff set it about the table. Pastor Jim gave thanks for the nourishment, and everyone tucked into their supper.

A couple of minutes into eating, Felix spoke up. "Doctor Miller, um, Jared, why do you say vaccines aren't safe?"

Amy glared at Felix. She didn't want to get the man back onto his soapbox, but Felix had just offered him a hand in stepping up to it.

"Many reasons," replied the doctor. "Lots of nasty contaminants, but foremost is the inclusion of metals into their formulations. Specifically, mercury and aluminum, although they've made great strides in removing the mercury, the thimerosal, thanks to the anti-vaxx protests." He turned toward Amy, as if she was the only one he thought needed convincing. "What are our bodies' two main barriers to environmental dangers?" he asked her.

Amy swallowed and said, "Our skin . . ." She couldn't think of another barrier against the environment. The lungs could be easily damaged by inhaling toxic gases or fumes.

"Right. Maybe I should rephrase the question for the second one. What are our two first lines of defense against things from outside the body? The skin and . . ."

That did make a difference. The gut was a primary component of the immune system. Some said that 80% of the human immune response came from the gut. Amy felt confident in her answer. "The gut and its role in our immune system." And as she said it, she realized that vaccines bypassed the gut and its role in immunity.

The doctor nodded. "Yes, and it's the liver that detoxifies potential poisons. Which of these defenses play a role in defending against possible poisons in a vaccine?"

Amy saw where he was going with this. "Neither one. When you inject something into a muscle, you bypass both. But the microgram amounts of aluminum aren't a problem, and likewise the ethyl mercury of thimerosal. It's not as damaging as the methyl mercury folks get concerned about when fish and other foods are contaminated with it."

Jared finished the mouthful he was eating, and said, "*Are* they safe? Who's telling us this? Studies on aluminum have looked at the amount you get with one dose of vaccine, not 50-plus doses by high school, or with ongoing flu shots and other booster shots. Like most metals, the aluminum doesn't all disappear from the body, it accumulates. On autopsies, both autistic and Alzheimer patients' brains are full of aluminum in the damaged areas. As for ethyl mercury, it passes through the blood-brain barrier 50 times faster than methyl mercury, and, once in the brain, it's just as damaging as other forms of mercury."

Felix leaned forward and spoke. "Amy, he's beginning to convince me. I mean, the EPA is so concerned about mercury they require special disposal of CFL lightbulbs because of the small amounts of the metal in them."

The doctor nodded. "Exactly. We have way too much exposure to some of these very toxic metals just in things we use. Why are we injecting them right into our bodies? Vaccines are just one part of a multi-factorial problem that also includes environmental toxins, but I won't get into that."

Amy realized she had much to think about. The man's arguments were persuasive.

Jim, who had been following the conversation with a glazed look on his face, took a turn. "Amy is worried that the CIC facility is using Cambodian children as test subjects."

A smoldering anger became evident on the immunologist's face. "Is that why you were there, why you're curious about the lab?"

Amy nodded, but it was Pat who gave the answer that Amy and Felix had denied the doctor.

"We've had a number of children disappear from the communities Felix serves. Three sets of twins so far. Our organization serves an area in the north, farther away from the CIC, and so far, we've not heard of anything like that there. We worry they'll be heading our way."

The smoldering anger flared into ignition. "I . . . I . . . that . . . that son of . . ." The doctor stopped. "Sorry, I need to watch my tongue, particularly in present company. But if this is really true, then Tillson is breaking every ethical standard known. He must be stopped."

Felix raised his brow. "Ethics is one thing, but how about breaking the law and endangering these children?"

Jared turned red from blushing, not anger, this time. "Oh yes, definitely. I-I didn't mean to imply otherwise. I hate to think what might be happening to those kids. There's only one way to find out what's happening there."

Amy felt as if all eyes had turned to her. She had a pretty good idea what that "one way" entailed. Now, she had to put her own faith to the test. Right?

CHAPTER TWENTY-TWO

"Coast clear, Doctor. No one see that doctor again."

Darany made *som pas* and turned away from the door to Tillson's office. *Finally*, thought the researcher. That no-good Miller had not come back, even though he had his car again. Tillson no longer felt restricted from going to the "school" where his subjects resided.

As he packed his things for the visit, a tinge of concern about Miller's contact with that nurse and her friend moved front and center in his thinking. The general had noted no relationship between them, other than two people picking up a stranded person along the road. Although he should have thought of it sooner, he had dispatched a man to the hotel after dinner to watch Miller and make sure there was no other contact between the two parties. Now was a good time for an update.

He pulled out his phone and dialed.

"Vannak, what is your report?"

The man's English was lacking but adequate enough to tell Tillson what he needed to know.

"Last night find doctor in bar. Go room. Stay room. Not see with woman."

"Good, good. Anything else?"

"Today, doctor go car with bags. I not know English word. Um, pay money to leave. "

"Do you mean he's checking out of the hotel? He has paid his bill and is leaving?"

"Yes, checking out. I follow?"

"Make sure he does not meet the woman, but you do not need to follow him. Understand?"

"Yes. Understand. Woman still in room."

So far, it appeared the general's impression was the correct one. The two had not met at the hotel, even though they stayed at the same one. That could be explained by the lack of quality lodgings nearby.

But they had been in a car together and had time to talk. Had Miller accused him of taking the rental car? Had he made accusations toward the CIC and Tillson in particular? If so, the likelihood of the nurse calling him back was remote at best, and he had decided she could be of good service to him—provided she met his "morality" litmus test. He was, after all, bending all known ethics regarding human subjects. The ends warranted the means. The benefits to humanity would be well worth it.

If she did call, should he consider that a good sign? He now waffled about hiring her, knowing that she and Miller had met. The man had no doubt bent her ear with his anti-vax propaganda. However, he could use her clinical expertise to help the children. With his knowledge that an international terrorist was on her trail, he felt that his offer of a refuge, as well as a wage and work visa, might entice her to "look the other way" and join his work. If not, well, her fate then would depend on how much she had learned. He could always get word out to a certain crime lord that she was a hunted woman with a price on her head.

He finished gathering his things, ducked out the back door, and met his driver at the car by his quarters. He didn't require a driver for such a short distance, but he had learned there were certain issues of prestige and image he needed to maintain. He was, after all, the director of a major U.S. lab facility. He couldn't be seen driving himself.

A few minutes later, they pulled up in front of the two-story building that held Duong Chea's office, as well as a number of classrooms. He grabbed his bag and papers from the back seat and met Duong inside.

"Good morning, *Lok* Walter. It good that you now able come in person." The headmaster made *som pas*.

Tillson, his hands full, returned the gesture with a subtle bow. "Good morning, *Lok* Chea. I am happy to be here. Where are the children?"

Duong moved his hand in a sweeping gesture to point down the hallway to his right. "I sorry to say children you plan see are not well. New boys, however, are well-fed, strong, and ready for you. They are twin come yesterday from Me Sang."

Tillson had no requirement that the children be tested in the order of arrival at the school. His only mandate was that the students meet certain health standards before testing.

He followed the man down the hall to their usual room used for testing. As he entered, Duong hurried to the two boys seated cross-legged on mats on the floor and scolded them in Khmer. The boys jumped to their feet and stood at attention for a second or two before making *som pas*. Tillson walked slowly around them, scrutinizing them. Yes, they appeared healthier than the previous three sets of twins who had arrived at the school prior to the arrival of Jared Miller. Those children, found in villages within the local province, had not met the height-weight guidelines he had given Duong and, as such, were receiving extra nourishment to bring up their weights. They were also resisting efforts at testing and crying to go home. Perhaps they would be ready in another week.

Duong handed some papers to Tillson—the neuropsychiatric and IQ tests. The boys' names were Phirum and Ponleak, and their test scores showed them to be a year or two behind their age group. This was not an uncommon finding among the children they tested who came from rural backgrounds.

"Have you explained to them what I am going to do, that I must use a needle to take blood samples?"

Duong nodded. "I have. They never get shots before, but we show them pictures of soldiers getting shots. They wish to be brave, like soldiers."

Tillson smiled. Drawing blood samples was a little different than "getting a shot" but a needle was required for both. The "soldier ploy" had worked before with boys. With the girls, they had often used a different incentive—to show up and be braver than the boys, who always cried.

He prepared his Vacutainers™ for the venipuncture.

"Who's first?"

Duong translated, and both boys' right hands shot into

the air. Tillson chuckled. *Brave, like soldiers*, he thought. In the end, both were. Not a whimper, although Ponleak's lower lip quivered as the needle penetrated his arm.

"*Lok* Chea, do we have a reward for these brave boys?" Tillson, of course, knew he did. Both boys' eyes widened in delight as an ice cream treat was offered to each of them.

Tillson nodded at Duong. The headmaster dismissed both boys to eat their treats and return to their building, accompanied by an "aide." Meanwhile, Tillson secured the blood tubes in his bag. He would run a battery of tests on them that day and return the next day, if all was well.

He glanced back at Duong. "How are the others?"

The man shook his head. "Kaliyanei, she die last night."

That was not the news Tillson wanted to hear. He wanted to hear of success with this program, not its failures.

"And Kunthea?"

"She still not good."

The girls had been among the first sets of twins in his latest study protocol. Each had developed a high fever within 36 hours of their immunization set. By the time the fever cleared, both had become non-communicative and withdrawn. Not just one, but both. And now, one had died.

"You know what to do, right?"

Duong nodded and proceeded to retrieve several tubes of blood, which he handed to Tillson. Kaliyanei's final donation to his work.

Tillson's budget could not afford to bribe various officials to ignore such deaths. He paid a pile of hush money for various reasons already.

CHAPTER TWENTY-THREE

Amy had been awake for over an hour. Well, that was not really accurate. She had barely slept after about two a.m. True, she had come to Cambodia to help Jim and Pat, but as importantly to her, she came to escape what she saw as the demons of her life. Disaster seemed to find her wherever she went. Now, her most recent demon had apparently followed her halfway around the world. Even her close friends called her a . . . well, she would just leave it at a "magnet for something unpleasant."

In her mind, the key always had been that trouble *found her*. Now? Was she actually seeking it out? Had she lost her mind? To purposefully walk into the proverbial lion's den.

And yet, it was the leonine lair that had awakened her in the middle of the night. She'd had the strangest dream. In it, she had replaced Daniel, as King Darius threw her to a certain, gruesome death. Fear and nausea rose up inside as she saw the beasts snarling and licking their lips while the alpha male took two steps toward her. And then a voice called out to her, "Do you trust me?" She looked about for the source of that question and saw no one. Twice more, as the alpha male crept closer, she was asked, "Do you trust me?" The third time, as the male began to leap, she answered, "Yes." Her fear dissipated, and she awoke in her bed.

She had witnessed the child-like faith of those parents earlier the day before. They trusted that God would restore their children back to them. As for being an instrument of God, Amy felt more like Gideon than Daniel. She looked about the room for a fleece, but found nothing suitable.

She needed her morning cup of coffee.

Fingering the CIC director's business card as she walked toward the hotel's restaurant, she began a mental debate as to how best to approach the man. Upon entering the dining area, she discovered that the rest of her team had preceded her there. She glanced about—no sign of Jack Black's Professor Shelly Oberon doppelgänger. His dissertation on vaccines the night before had contributed to her lack of sleep.

"Good morning, sunshine," said Jim, with a wide grin on his face. "Did burning ears wake you up? We've been talking about you."

She was too tired to smile but managed to reply, "And here I just thought it was the Cambodian heat." She looked about the table. "Where's the coffee?"

Pat produced a carafe that was hidden from Amy by the upright menu holder in the middle of the table. Amy grabbed the closest clean coffee cup and filled it—no cream or sugar, just black caffeine.

"Looks like you could use more than one cup. Trouble sleeping?" asked the older woman.

Amy nodded and, after several sips, told them of her

dream. Jim looked concerned, while Felix's poker face remained unchanged. After a moment, he spoke up.

"I've had a few dreams like that. They always seem to be dreams of warning . . . and to date they've held 100% true. One of them spared the lives of me and my recon team in Afghanistan, but that's another story—one I can't legally share yet. I call them my close encounters of the Godly kind."

Pat rolled her eyes. "Who says the charismatic gifts died out with the first apostles? God *is* the same yesterday, today, and forever."

Amy noted that Jim had been staring at her since hearing about her dream. After a couple of minutes, he found his tongue. "I had hoped to convince you to come back to Kampong Thom with us and not do anything foolhardy. Who am I to lead someone down a path that God hasn't chosen for them? But is this the case?"

The conversation had taken on a *Twilight Zone* feel. Amy changed the subject.

"Anyone seen Doctor Miller? I have another question or two for him."

"I saw him check out and leave," said Pat.

"That's odd," replied Amy. *Why would he up and leave?* she wondered. He had her 98% convinced and would be invaluable to any effort she might make to expose what was happening at that compound. He knew what to look for, what questions to ask, and in what ways to ask them so that she wasn't obvious.

"My doing." Felix raised his hand to shoulder height as he sat there. "I saw him go to the bar last night after dinner, so I followed and had a short talk with him. I asked him to check out and leave at first light this morning."

"Why?" That, too, seemed strange. Felix was set on finding the kids and Miller could be instrumental in helping there.

Felix looked pensive for a moment and replied, "I started thinking about his car being delivered here. That means the folks at the CIC knew he was staying here, and they might be watching him. Might not be, too, but who knows how paranoid this CIC guy might be. If he is being watched, we might have blown any and all opportunities to get you inside just by having him join us for dinner last night. If they somehow missed that, having him around increases the risk of our being seen with him. If it looks like we're in cahoots with him in any way, you won't get inside, and we won't find the kids if they're there."

"Or, if they let you in and have reason to believe you're working with him, you'll be in *real* danger." Jim shook his head as he said that. Amy could see he was not in favor of her taking such risks. Not at all. Dream or no dream.

Twelve hours earlier, Amy would have agreed with him. Yet, after her dream—it was so real—she had put her trust in the Lord. She had made that commitment.

"Jim, this has all been so foreign to me. Speaking in tongues, dreams, visions. I know it's all in the Bible, but I'm a Southern Baptist girl. If I hadn't had these two experiences personally, I don't know what I'd be thinking right now. I've seen my share of trouble, too, back in the States. I'm not exactly excited to jump into the lion's den, so to speak, and yet I-I can't just abandon those kids. I saw the faith those parents had. Yes, I know God could deliver them back to their parents in any one of a zillion ways, but I think He wants *me* to step out and become that conduit. I don't know how to explain it except that I feel safe in His hands."

Pat raised her brow and looked at her husband. "Hmmmm. Sounds like someone I know."

Jim looked back at her and had no answer.

Amy had heard stories of Jim's encounters—clandestine traveling for two to three hours to reach a remote home church in hostile territory where the participants could face death, facing bandits on motorbikes in remote Nepal, risking disease pulling corpses from trees and buildings after that deadly typhoon in the Philippines, likewise after the 2004 tsunami in Indonesia, and more. He had stepped out in faith into the face of danger on multiple occasions.

"Let's not forget that a certain African terrorist is also hunting you."

He had no need to remind Amy of that. Abdullah Said Abdi was but one of the many lions facing her.

"I won't leave her by herself. I'll be watching her closely, and I can extract her from their compound at any time. You have my word on that." The look on Felix's face revealed his sincerity and dedication to that statement.

Jim's concern appeared somewhat assuaged, and a wry smile found its way to his lips. "I have to assume you learned a few things with 20 years in Special Forces."

Felix smiled. "A few things, and I've already contacted a friend to get me some special supplies."

"I guess we shouldn't ask what those supplies are."

"It's best you don't. Thanks."

Pat laughed. "So, what can *we* do?"

"I've been thinking about that, too," answered Felix. "And, Amy, feel free to chime in if you want to."

He paused, but Amy could think of nothing at that point. She was curious to hear what he had in mind. Then, maybe, she'd have some thoughts to add.

"Jim, Pat, I think you should head back to your base. If folks ask about Amy, you can tell them the truth—that the terrorist who murdered her father followed her here and that a friend of hers from the States came over to warn her and take her home. You don't have to say that he *did* take her home. Let people make their own conclusion. If this Abdi jerk is already in Kampong Thom, and tries to get info from your people, that's what he'll hear. He might give up and leave the country."

"And if he isn't there, or doesn't leave? I mean, he's not going to be leaving on a commercial flight that might give the authorities a chance to confirm his itinerary."

"True. We'll have no way of knowing if he's left the country or not. We'll have to be vigilant. In the meantime, what better place to be than an isolated CIC lab enclosed with high fences and barbed wire, and patrolled by its own security?"

"And what about me?" asked Amy.

"As I see it, you have the hardest part. You'll have to act like a cold-hearted witch who is an ardent vaccine supporter, someone who doesn't mind looking the other way concerning ethics if the end result is a good one. You have to gain this guy's trust. That might mean having to look the other way on an occasion or two."

"Like an undercover cop?"

Felix nodded. "Exactly. If his target is the drug lord, he'll ignore the lesser infractions and keep his eyes on the goal."

Amy took a deep breath. Clearly, Felix had thought this through more thoroughly than she. Could she look the other way if the medical ethics she so strongly believed in were being ignored? Would God expect that of her?

With all that was on his mind, Lynch felt surprise to awaken to the alarm on his phone. He had slept soundly, as if he had no worries at all. That simply went to prove how tired he had been. Jet lag, emotional distress, and the chase—all had taken their toll on his body. Not to mention the heat and humidity that seemed to drain his energy levels all on their own. Maybe when this was all over, he would leave St. Louis, with its own high summer heat and humidity, for a cooler climate. He'd been to Wisconsin a few times—a beautiful state and not that far from his family.

That musing would be held for a future time. He needed to get moving. Reggie would be waiting in the restaurant.

He grabbed a quick shave and shower and found that his clothing had dried in the closet overnight. Within minutes he was dressed, out the door, and walking toward the hotel restaurant. Reggie intercepted him in the lobby and handed him a paper bag.

"Here. I hope this will suffice for your breakfast."

Lynch peeked into the bag to see an assortment of pastries.

"We need to get on the road."

Lynch looked up at his new friend with optimism.

"Did your contacts find them?"

Reggie nodded. "They're at a hotel in Krong Pursat. Less than two hours from here, if the highway isn't jam-packed. They could check out at any time, so we need to move."

Lynch took a deep breath. "And Amy?"

"She's there, too."

Lynch pumped his fist in the air once. "Yes! Hey, I need to grab a coffee to go."

Reggie pointed to a nearby table where two large, covered foam cups sat. "Grab one, and let's get going."

Lynch did just that and beat Reggie to the car. As they left the Battambang city limits on National Highway 5, both men sat silently as they devoured the bakery goods and washed them down with coffee. Lynch would have preferred a hot meal, but not at the expense of missing Amy. Yet, he had another concern.

Finished with eating, he asked, "Any sightings of Abdi?"

The diplomat shook his head. "None, but then, I didn't expect anything so soon. After the scare you gave him, I'm sure he went to ground. We can only hope that the Cambodian police will keep watch and spot him when he surfaces."

Lynch mulled that over for a minute. "And the odds of that happening are? They don't seem well equipped to me."

Reggie shrugged. "True. By American standards, they sure don't have our technology or communications. However, what they lack in equipment, they make up for in numbers. Cambodia is about the size of your home state, Missouri. Missouri has what, 10 to 12,000 police officers?"

"Almost 15,000."

"And its population is?"

"Just over six million people."

"Well, Cambodia has two and a half times the population, 15-plus million, but 64,000 National Police officers."

Lynch pulled out his phone to use the calculator. "Actually, they equal about the same based on population, about one officer for every 240 or so people."

Reggie frowned. "Okay. I guess I just figured 64,000 officers was a lot for the size of the place. I guess I was off."

Lynch shook his head. "Not really. We should look at it from a land mass perspective instead." Lynch ran some more numbers. "In Missouri, on average, one officer has to cover 5 square miles. Here, each officer covers one square mile. That's five times as many officers based on land mass. And with more officers concentrated in cities and the national highways, there are even more eyes available to spot this guy. I like those odds."

Lynch was glad he did the math. Had he not done so, he would have worried even more than he now did that Abdi would move about unseen, ready to strike. Still, he would not be comfortable until he was with Amy himself.

His mental meandering was interrupted by the slowing of the car. He looked ahead to see a cluster of flashing lights and traffic at a standstill. A small flatbed truck sped by going the other direction with two dead cows on the flatbed.

Reggie shook his head. "Some kind of accident, and it looks like there were bovine casualties. They'll race them to a slaughterhouse to salvage what meat they can."

Lynch thought about that for a moment. Eating "roadkill" at home was something of a running joke. Eating it here was a reality.

"If someone just hit a couple of cows, won't the traffic be moving again soon?" asked Lynch.

Reggie sighed. "I wish. There will be arguing over whose fault it was, followed by demands for payment for damages. They might settle the matter in minutes, or in an hour, but it will all take place right here on the road, not in the nearest police station miles from here."

Lynch sank low into the seat at the thought of being stuck here for an hour . . . an additional hour that might result in missing Amy.

CHAPTER TWENTY-FOUR

After much discussion, bordering on argument, Jim agreed to leave Amy in the capable hands of Felix. Amy couldn't fault his position—to apply subtle pressure on the police to find the children, without involving Amy—and appreciated his concern for her. Part of her still felt anguished about voluntarily stepping into a potential vipers' pit. For the fourth time that morning, she whispered a quiet prayer asking for faith and guidance.

"Here, Pat. Let me carry that," said Felix as the couple emerged from the elevator. He reached for her suitcase.

Amy followed the others as Jim led the way to the van. Without a single item in her hands, she felt a little useless. Pat dropped her bag into the front passenger seat and turned back to face Amy.

"I know I haven't said much about this, but I don't like this idea of your trying to find these kids, either. And yet, I know we serve a great God and know that He'll watch over you."

She reached out and gave Amy a hug, holding her a little longer than Amy anticipated.

"I also don't like being so far away in case you need us."

Amy offered half a smile for encouragement. "I understand. I kinda wish you would be closer, too, but I'm in good hands, both earthly and heavenly."

Pat nodded. "That you are, or we wouldn't be having this conversation."

Jim walked around the front of the van and up to Amy. "Well, you already know how I feel about this, so I won't say anything more." He placed his hand on Amy's shoulder and offered a prayer for protection, which Pat joined. He gave her a quick hug and stepped back. "We hope to see you sooner, not later. Find those kids and stay safe."

"I will."

The older couple entered the van and, a minute later, pulled away from the parking lot. As they slowly drove away, Amy felt alone. Sure, Felix was there, but she'd only met him a day earlier.

Felix finished waving goodbye and turned to Amy. "We still have an hour until check-out. I didn't want to add more fuel to Jim's fire by suggesting we leave this hotel, too, but I think it might be best. I know of a very pleasant inn, more like a B&B in the States, on the Pursat River not far from here. It's owned by an Australian couple I've gotten to know—Roy and Diana. He's a retired commando who helped form the country's Special Operations Command. We hit it off right away."

The mention of this couple reminded Amy of her friends in Ferguson—Mike and Mary Southworth. He had retired from the Army as a colonel, and their beautiful Ferguson home held the potential to be transformed into an amazing B&B. She still found it incredible that by pure serendipity they had hosted the current king of England and his family just two years earlier.

"Whatever you think is best," she replied. In truth, a small inn sounded delightful, particularly if she would be staying there for the duration.

"Good. I've already arranged it with them."

That caught Amy off-guard. She would have preferred being part of the decision. Then again, she had been, as soon as she agreed to whatever he thought best.

"Can you be ready in 15 minutes?"

Amy wanted to take a shower, so she answered, "Can we make it 25, 30 minutes?"

"As long as we're out by 11 a.m., we're good."

True to Reggie's experience with such, the incident tied up the highway for nearly an hour. Lynch visualized the farmer arguing for restitution for his dead cows, while the driver of whatever vehicle hit them would fight for payment to repair his vehicle. Of course, he remained amazed that they allowed cattle to be herded along such a main artery.

As a multitude of small motorbikes continued to speed by, Lynch daydreamed that he, too, had such mobility and could zip past the obstruction to get to Amy faster. He wondered if he could step out of the car and convince one of the owners speeding by to sell his bike.

"How much do these motorbikes run here?"

"Most of them are 125cc bikes and cost about $2,500 new."

Lynch didn't have anywhere near that amount of cash

on him. Plus, he had no idea where he was going. His daydream was an idle one.

A police van sped past them in the opposite direction.

"That's a good sign. Maybe the haggling is over, and we'll get moving again," said Reggie.

Almost before he completed his sentence, the truck in front of them began to inch forward. A few minutes later, they were moving along near the speed limit of 90 km/hr, although for Lynch, the U.S. equivalent of 55 mph seemed fast for the road's condition and traffic level. Once again, he appreciated Reggie's willingness to drive.

He glanced at the clock on his cell phone: 10:05 a.m.

"How long till we get there?"

"About an hour, maybe less if we can stay at the speed limit."

Amy, please still be there, he thought.

For Amy, the shower had been a relaxing solution to her "problem"—how to steel herself against what she might find if she would be hired by the CIC. The tension in her muscles from the stress seemed to float down the drain with the water, while her choice of a cool temperature for the water brought temporary relief from the outside climate.

Of course, she had to keep her lips clamped shut to prevent even a single drop of water from entering her body. She was determined to remain healthy throughout her trip and that was one precaution she had no difficulty taking— along with using bottled water to brush her teeth and clean her toothbrush.

She used her towel to dry her hair first and then combed it out. She saw no use in attempting to style it. The humidity would take its vengeance on whatever style she selected. Wavy hair was in her immediate future.

She checked the time and realized she needed to hurry. Fortunately, she had her smaller overnight bag—her "go" bag, as Felix had called it. Lynch would call it that as well, and she wondered where he was at the moment. She still found it hard to fathom that he had come to Cambodia to warn her, and wondered when their paths would finally meet. She found herself looking forward to that occasion. Putting those thoughts aside, she finished packing in minutes.

She met Felix in the lobby, where he pointed to the main desk.

"Just drop off your key. I've already covered the bill and checked us both out."

The clock on the wall behind the desk showed she had ten minutes to spare.

Felix nodded toward the main door. "The Rover is unlocked, if you want to stow your bag inside. I'm going to get a coffee to go. Want one?"

Amy could feel the burden of heat waft through the front door every time someone opened it. The idea of hot coffee did not tempt her at the moment. Besides, she'd had her two-cup limit at breakfast. Something cold sounded more appealing.

"Cold water sounds better."

"I've got water bottles on ice in the cooler in the car. Don't know that they're very cold yet."

"Then how about a cold Coke™?"

"You got it." He tossed her the keys. "Go ahead and start the Rover and get the AC going. I'll be out in a minute."

She nodded and complied. By the time Felix joined her, the AC began to feel cool. They buckled up, and he eased away from the curb. Amy noticed the clock on the dash— 10:58. She bent down to grab something from her bag, which was on the floor at her feet.

Lynch felt a rise of anxiety as he watched the car's digital clock count closer to 11 a.m.

"What's the typical check-out time for hotels here?"

Reggie glanced at him and replied, "Eleven a.m. is the most common, but some are earlier. Rarely are they later."

Lynch did not want to hear the word "earlier." That increased the odds that he would miss Amy if the group planned on checking out that morning. Of course, the closer they got to 11 a.m. put him in that same predicament. He held onto his hope that the police had required them to stick around one more day because of the incident, of which Reggie had heard only vague details.

He had discovered that he had no way to reach the pastor anymore. His calls were directed right to voicemail, as if it was turned off. Having learned there had been an incident involving the man, he made the assumption that something might have happened to the phone itself.

"The turn to the hotel should be just up ahead. We're three, maybe four, minutes away."

Lynch nodded. *Please be there, please be there, please be*

there, he thought.

Reggie made the turn and a moment later, pointed to a tall structure that appeared new and stood tall above the buildings surrounding it. "There's the hotel."

As Reggie turned into the lot in front of the building, they passed an old Land Rover pulling out. Lynch saw only a man, not Cambodian, driving. There appeared to be no one else in the vehicle. He glanced at the other cars in the lot— no white vans, which they had been informed was what was registered to Pastor Jim's relief agency. But then, the van could have been damaged in "the incident." Lynch wished he knew more about what had happened.

Lynch beat Reggie out of the car and into the hotel lobby. He hurried to the desk and asked for Amy.

The clerk shook his head. "She not here. Just left, five minute ago."

CHAPTER TWENTY-FIVE

Shortly after noon, Tillson received the first of the test results for the twin boys, as well as Kaliyanei, or subject ITWG19A, as he referred to her in the lab reports. The boys were referenced as ITWB16A and B. The blood counts and chemistry panels showed that the boys were healthy with regards to the most basic tests. They weren't anemic, nor did they have leukemia. Their white cell differentials, with its normal eosinophil counts, showed no signs of atopy or allergies. Likewise, they had good kidney function, normal blood sugars, and no signs of liver abnormalities. Additional tests results would become available later that afternoon.

After scanning the printouts for Kaliyanei, he began a frenetic pacing around his office. Shaking his head as he walked, he mentally searched for a reason for those results.

Kaliyanei's blood showed evidence of a cascade of organ failure. Why? She had received nothing outside the test regimen. Her white cell differential hinted at a massive inflammatory reaction. Additional testing would prove or disprove that. But again, why? He prepared his test vaccines according to CIC standards. He knew the levels of both mercury and aluminum in the active immunizations—as opposed to the placebo preparations used for the double-blind aspects of the study. There were a number of academic studies that detailed foreign genetic material and proteins, even a simian virus, being introduced into the vaccine solutions simply through the process of incubating the target virus. A few of those studies even suggested that such foreign genetic material held the risk of altering the patient's own genetics in ways technology could not even study—much like the process of a virus altering the RNA in a patient.

Kaliyanei's blood would be tested in every way possible to him. And when those results were in, her status in the double-blind study would be revealed. He didn't want to know which preparation she had received prior to analyzing her results for fear that knowing would taint his analysis. His fear was that she, too, would be in the group who received the real vaccine, as had all but one of the others who had died. Each death had led to a slight tweaking of the formulation. At some point, he was bound to hit upon the correct one.

He stopped and stared out the window, looking for the macaque family in the nearby papaya grove. He hoped the antics of the little ones could lighten his mood, but he failed to spot them.

Unlike the comical behavior of the immature monkeys, other children at the home had developed depressing behavioral changes—signs of neuropsychiatric injury. The anti-vaxxers would label such alterations as placing the child on the autism spectrum, but he would never say such a thing. He blamed the altered function on the culture's diet, or some as-yet-unknown genetic difference that they would need to account for in future vaccine formulations.

But Kaliyanei was one more, the latest, in a string of deaths, not just a change in behavior. These deaths could never be known, much less be attributed to his work. He paid Duong Chea well to make sure they weren't. The anti-vaccination crowd would have a field day if these results saw the light of day. Thus, the need for secrecy.

And that brought his thoughts to the nurse. He turned back toward his desk, staring at his phone. Had she been serious about wanting a job? Was she truly qualified? Would she call? He longed for someone with American training and experience, as well as the ability to hold an intelligent conversation in English for more than a few minutes. Darany and a couple of the other techs were well-trained, but he sought someone of a higher standard.

Besides, Darany spooked him a little. He always seemed to be watching, as if noting his movements. He had mentioned this to his colleague, Eric Gilroy, but Eric had had no trouble with Darany. He suggested that the tech might be seeking to learn from Tillson's actions. Tillson liked that idea, of being a mentor.

And yet, while he looked forward to such a colleague joining him, even if just a nurse and not a doctor, he had reservations about bringing anyone new, someone unknown to him, into the protocol's inner circle. Even Gilroy knew nothing of it. That person would have to share not only his vision for defeating communicable illness through vaccines, but the willingness to find such cures through whatever means were necessary—even at the expense of some impoverished, third-world children whose hungry mouths the world would never miss.

He returned to his chair and drummed his fingers on the top of his desk. He decided she would need at least a week's worth of "testing" before being allowed to see the children. Yes, a test. She would work with him at the main facility where he would task her with designing a study protocol. He could think of no better way to see where her morals and allegiances lay. If she was willing to take shortcuts, to ignore certain ethical standards, and to agree to suggestions he might make as she designed the study, *then* he would decide if she was "trustworthy" enough to work directly with the children.

And if not, well, there was a certain African terrorist looking for her. He felt confident that Duong Chea's connections would be able to find and contact the man.

Lok Oudom had told him the nicer accommodations were because they might have to stay there a while as they awaited the arrival of the woman, but Abdi could not help but believe his strategy of being nicer, calmer, and more cooperative played a role as well. This dwelling was like one that a person could find on Airbnb with two clean, spacious bedrooms; a nice kitchen; and a large central living space opening onto a garden-like lanai—all overlooking the Stung Sen, or Snake River. The home represented a level of luxury that he hadn't had even in the U.S., where his money could buy not only loyalty and obedience, but many nice things.

As the ceiling fans stirred the air of the main room, he

knew he could get used to such a home—as long as he could remain under the radar of the authorities. Being wanted by police worldwide did have significant drawbacks, and there were always those he could not bribe.

"Here. Enjoy a cold beer."

Abdi looked up to see *Lok* Oudom extending a sweating bottle of Angkor Beer toward him. Beer was not prohibited within Buddhism, although Abdi had seen little evidence that his companion followed its tenets. Alcohol in all forms *was* prohibited by Islam, but Abdi knew without doubt that anyone watching *him* would see that he didn't follow its teachings, except for those convenient for his own welfare. He grabbed the beer and nodded after taking a drink.

"What is word I want? Um, refreshing."

"*Lok* Abdullah, I wish to be up front. I do not much work north of lake. My connections here are few, but I talk with each. I am promise they contact me if they find information on this woman."

Abdi nodded. "I understand. Can Tep Rithisak help? I can call him to work something out."

Khay Oudom shook his head. "His contacts are my contacts, too. But this is good. I need to work this area of country more. This will help me do so. This afternoon I meet someone new to help me find children for someone who pays me well for them. That was my business with two boys you saw."

Abdi had resented having his affairs subjugated to those of the two boys in Khay's possession, but he saw now the monetary drive behind it. He had also been wrong not to cover more of Khay's expenses. Perhaps then the man would have been more responsive to Abdi's needs. That, too, he would change. He reached into his pocket and pulled out a roll of U.S. dollars. He thumbed through them and handed Khay a $100 bill.

"Here. This is for gas and food."

The man's eyes lit up and a smile stretched across his face. "Thank you, *Lok* Abdullah. Thank you. This will much help with expenses. Tomorrow, after meeting, I get more food, and beer. I do not know how long we stay here until woman show up."

Abdi understood that, too. He would help Khay Oudom make the contacts he needed in this province because the more connections the man had, the sooner he would learn of the woman's arrival in town.

CHAPTER TWENTY-SIX

"Do your friends live far from here?" asked Amy.

Felix shook his head.

"Not far at all, actually, but don't be shocked by the neighborhood."

They followed the river back to National Highway 5, turned east over the Pursat River, and took the first right turn onto the road that headed south along the river. The road remained paved, unlike Amy's experience with the roads the day before. That didn't prevent livestock, chickens, dogs, and kids playing soccer from becoming recurrent obstacles in their path. The buildings along both sides were crudely built, with rough-cut lumber or galvanized metal sheets siding them. All had metal roofs. All were surrounded by garbage and debris. To call the area a slum was being kind. The poverty made Amy's heart ache.

Small motorbikes appeared to be the local vehicle of choice, but Amy was most intrigued by the variety of metal trailers that had been fashioned to carry various loads behind said motorbikes. She was startled to see a young man on his motorbike with three poles lashed across the back end. On both sides of each pole, where they extended two feet beyond the sides of the back wheel, were tied five or six live chickens. They did not appear happy with their current mode of transportation.

As she glanced ahead along the road, her attention shot to a nearly fluorescent patch of coral pink in the distance. It stood in bright contrast to its drab, colorless neighbors. Not only did the color shout out to any passerby, but as they approached, she noted the painted, mud brick wall was well maintained, tall enough to deter intruders, and held quality, black metal gates leading inside the enclosure. She also spotted at least one security camera mounted to a tall palm just inside the wall.

Felix's slowing down and preparing to stop at the gate told her they had reached their destination. They waited but a moment before the gate automatically opened for them.

"They know my Rover," Felix said. "Others have to use the intercom." He pointed to a panel of electronics on the gate post.

Within the walls, Amy thought she had entered paradise. Tall palms provided a canopy for a botanical garden of tropical plantings—anthuriums, bird-of-paradise, bananas, lobster claws, red ginger, and many more she did not know the names of. Dozens of orchids hung in planters from trees, posts, and a pergola that doubled as a carport. The lush grass seemed foreign to the dry dirt that the properties she had seen so far used as an excuse for a yard. Even the previous night's hotel, as new and western as it was, had no grass around it. She opened the door, and the scent of jasmine overwhelmed her nose.

"This . . . this is beautiful," exclaimed Amy.

"It is, isn't it. Whenever I need a retreat, I come here, and Roy and Diana pamper me. Yet, I can never stay long. It makes it harder to go back into the poverty and rubble where I work. It's kind of like what Jim talks about. He never encourages his Cambodian workers to go the U.S., whether to just visit or for education. Unless they have a real heart for their own people, they never want to come back. Actually, most don't."

Amy saw a couple emerge from the two-story "inn" that she hadn't taken time yet to visually inspect. It, too, appeared as immaculate as the grounds. The couple greeted Felix with hugs and turned to Amy.

"Roy, Diana, this is Amy Gibbs. Amy, this is Roy and Diana Smith."

Amy suppressed a giggle. Smith? Really? She had expected something much more . . . well, much more what? Exotic? Royal?

Diana reached for Amy and hugged her as well.

As if reading her mind, Felix said, "Smith might be the most common surname in Oceania, but these two are far from common ex-pats here in Cambodia. You are about to experience Aussie hospitality with a Khmer flare." He laughed.

"Wow. Felix gave me no hint of what I should expect. This place is beautiful. It's like a patch of heaven."

Roy nodded in thanks. "Diana has the green thumb. I just do what she tells me to do." He suddenly waved his hand around between them.

Diana smiled. "Don't mind his Aussie salute, dear. He hates the bugs this time of year. Let's go inside and leave the mozzies out here."

The couple insisted on taking Amy's luggage and led the way to the house.

Amy leaned toward Felix and whispered, "Aussie salute? Mozzies?"

Felix chuckled. "You'll catch on. Waving to scare off the bugs and mosquitoes."

Roy held the door for Amy, as he waved his arm about. "C'mon in. We're going to throw some burgers on the barbie in a bit. I can offer you a cuppa or a coldie, if you like."

Amy had watched enough Australian dramas to understand that. Somehow having a cold beer on a missions trip didn't seem kosher. She would follow Felix's lead on that one. As for a cup of tea, hot tea held no appeal in the Cambodian heat. "Would you be offended if I asked for iced tea? With all the precautions about water here, I haven't had a glass of it since arriving here."

Diana smiled. "No worries. You yanks and iced tea. Five years ago, Roy would throw fits if a guest asked for iced tea. Now? He won't admit it, but he favors it, too. Fair dinkum. Don't worry about the water while you're here, except for showering. That comes from the local water supply, and we don't filter it. But every drop from a faucet is safe. State-of-the-art reverse osmosis filtration and separate plumbing. Roy helped develop the system for the military."

Diana showed Amy to a ground floor room in a nearby guest house, walking along pathways lined with orchids and bromeliads to get there.

"Here you go. You can close the doors to the patio if you wish and turn on the air conditioning. If you leave them open, there's usually a nice breeze off the river and the netting keeps the mozzies out. I'll leave you to freshen up if you want. We'll be on the patio of the main house. Felix has asked to talk with Roy there, and I believe you're to be included."

Amy looked about. The room was as gorgeous as the grounds. "If I leave the doors open, are my valuables safe here? Or, is there a place to safeguard them?"

Diana smiled. "Perfectly safe. Right now, you and Felix are our only guests. We're not open to the public, and you won't find us listed on Airbnb or any travel websites. We cater to a, shall I say, special clientele. They value the privacy and security as much as anyone and would do nothing to disrupt that for themselves or other guests. See you shortly."

Diana excused herself, and Amy plopped down on the bed. Just as she liked it—firm and supportive. She arose and explored the room's amenities. There was a small refrigerator stocked with soda and bottled water. A basket on top held a variety of snack crackers and cookies. She found a folding suitcase rack, which she set up and placed her "go" bag upon.

Freshen up? What did she need to do? Maybe 20 minutes had passed since checking out of the hotel. She opted to head over to the main patio.

Lynch and Reggie talked with three members of the hotel staff, hoping to glean some information about Amy's whereabouts. None knew where she had headed, but Lynch did catch one detail that made him think.

"Reggie, the desk clerk said that Jim and his wife left earlier and on their own. If Amy was going back to Kampong Thom with them, why didn't she go with *them?* Instead, she left with some guy named *Lok* Felix."

"Yeah, I caught that, too. *Lok*, by the way, is like our 'mister' in English. And they use the first name, not the last, so it would be Mr. Felix in English." He paused and looked contemplative. "Give me a minute to make a couple of calls."

Lynch watched his friend walk a short distance away with his cell phone to his ear. He wondered about this Felix character. Why had Amy teamed up with him? He wasn't the jealous sort, but he had lost Amy to Richard Nichols in the past. He didn't want to lose his opportunity to win her heart this time. He did have one concern, though—that he was approaching her too soon after Richard's murder. He would have to tread lightly if they finally caught up to her. No, not if, when . . . when they caught up to her.

He looked up to see Reggie walking his way.

"Well, only took one call. I think I've found her, and she's not far away."

"How's that?"

"I haven't met the guy, but I've heard of an American relief worker named Felix Castañeda working out of Battambang. He's an ex-Navy SEAL. That made me think of a friend in these parts who owns an inn of sorts. He's an ex-Aussie Commando, and his inn caters to a Special Forces kind of clientele. I called him, and, sure enough, Felix and 'a lass named Amy,' as he put it, arrived a short while ago. I told him we're on our way."

Yes! Lynch wanted to run to the car.

Amy found the main patio without difficulty and once again marveled at the botanical display. Diana had to have a collection of orchids numbering in the hundreds. She imagined caring for them to be a full-time job. And who took care of the guests' rooms and meals?

And the barbie Roy had mentioned? There was no simple kettle grill here. The outdoor kitchen matched anything Amy had ever seen on HGTV. The Smiths could feed an army here, and maybe at times they did. Diana's veiled reference to their "special" clientele had not been lost on Amy. She felt honored to be included inside this enclave.

Roy was already at the grill. He looked up as Amy approached and nodded in greeting before pointing to a counter to his right. Amy followed his gesture and saw a large pitcher of iced tea, along with six tall glasses. *Six?* she wondered. Diana had told her that she and Felix were the only guests. A slight Cambodian girl came out of the house carrying a platter of hamburgers and a bag of buns. There had to be a dozen burgers there. Who else was eating with them?

"Amy, this is Champei. She's one of our current trainees in the kitchen, helping Diana. Champei, this is Amy."

The girl set the food on the counter, turned to Amy, and made *som pas*. Amy returned the greeting.

"G'day, Miss Amy. I am please to meet you."

"And I am pleased to meet you, too." Amy held back her amusement at hearing a distinctly Australian "G'day" come from the young Cambodian.

"I will be back with more, *Lok* Roy." At that, Champei headed back into the house.

"Champei is a pretty name."

Roy nodded. "It means frangipani flowers. She has been a fast learner. I'm sure you saw the poverty surrounding us here. To some, we stick out like a sore thumb, an example of 'white privilege' as some bone-headed liberals would call it. But to the people here, we are a beacon of hope. We take promising young people from the area and train them in the hospitality industry. We also teach English to many, whether they work for us or not."

"That's wonderful. Is it working? I mean, do they find jobs?"

He smiled. "Not meant as a boast, but we have a 100% success rate with our trainees. And as they move up in their careers, they come back to us and ask for new employees. Sadly, we can only train a dozen or so a year."

Amy could understand his chagrin. She would feel frustrated, too, at being able to make such a difference in people's lives and not being able to expand upon such a successful program.

"Hi."

Amy turned to find Felix walking up behind them.

"Roy, it's been months since I had a good, home-grilled burger. And iced tea, too. You're a saint."

Roy nodded toward Amy. "Give her the credit for the tea. A special request I was told."

Felix poured a glass and handed it to Amy before claiming one for himself.

"He imports his beef from Australia. Right, Roy?"

"Deadset. Cows raised here just aren't the same."

Amy must have looked confused.

"More Aussie slang, Amy. Deadset means true. As I said, you'll catch on." Felix winked. "Roy, do I look that hungry? That's a lot of burgers for four of us."

"Well, looks to be we'll have two more guests joining us. They should arrive any moment. Diana's out front waiting for them."

A slight frown crossed Felix's mouth. "Hmmm, guess we can have our discussion later."

Roy's face was poker straight. "Deadset. Or, maybe not."

Felix gave Roy a quizzical look, but Amy felt certain that her own questioning glance made his appear pale. Two mysterious guests? Had Roy called in favors of some old Special Forces comrades? If so, what in the world was Felix planning? And, what exactly was she stepping into? A sense of trepidation filled her.

"Ah. A car." Roy looked toward the front of the house.

Amy followed his gaze, even though she couldn't see the area where cars parked. She hadn't heard a car, but then, she could always tell when someone pulled into her own driveway back home without seeing them. The brain became accustomed and alert to some sounds, while blocking out a great majority of them.

Two men came into view. She had no idea who the first man was and the second man's face was obscured at the moment. Still, that gait seemed familiar. Lynch?

They rounded the corner and yes, Lynch approached her, as broad a smile on his face as she had ever seen. Seeing him gave her a peace and confidence she hadn't experienced since making the decision to come to Cambodia. She wanted to run to him. Yet, that seemed awkward. True, Richard's death occurred months ago, but the fact remained that she had been engaged to the man, had chosen him over Lynch. Also true, she had thought Lynch dead at the time.

Her brain went into a tizzy. She wanted to rush to him and embrace him, but her feet remained planted where she stood.

Amy! She was actually there, right in front of him, just 40 feet away. Lynch felt the grin stretch across his face. Never had he been so happy to see someone. The "when they caught up" had become reality. Seventy thousand square miles. Fifteen million people. The odds were far and away against his finding her, but . . .

God had delivered him to his needle in the needle stack.

He desired to race to her and sweep her into his arms, but that seemed awkward. They were not a couple. She hadn't so much as confided in him about coming to Cambodia. He'd pulled strings with the State Department and Homeland Security to track down her travel itinerary. No, he would never regret that minor abuse of the authority granted him as part of the President-elect's team. He had taken on the task of finding her because her life was in danger. Yet, he would give his life for hers any day. Maybe they weren't a couple, but they remained friends—a status he hoped would elevate to something more.

He maintained his normal pace and reached her soon

enough. He reached out to hug her, and she allowed it, but the embrace seemed strained—like far-right conservative and far-left liberal cousins embracing at a family reunion.

"I am *sooo* glad I've caught up to you."

"I-I heard from Pastor Jim that you were in country looking for me. I know about Abdi looking for me, too."

Lynch didn't want to talk about that subject right now, but his mission took precedence. "Yeah, I almost caught him in Battambang yesterday, but he got away. We can talk about that later."

"Ahemmm." Lynch looked to his right to see Reggie standing there.

"Amy, this is Reggie Crutchfield. He's the first secretary extraordinaire from the embassy here. Reggie, this is Amy Gibbs."

"Miss Gibbs, I am so glad we've caught up with you. It's been quite an eventful chase."

"Sorry. I didn't mean to be an elusive target."

"Well, I'm glad you were, for your sake."

Roy reached out his hand. "Reggie, good to see you again, mate. It's been far too long. I have some other matters to discuss with you, if you have the time later."

Reggie nodded. "Of course. And this must be Felix Castañeda." He reached to shake Felix's hand, as did Lynch. "I am pleased to finally meet you. I have heard many good things about you, and thank you for your service."

Felix shrugged. "Welcome, and thank you for yours. Another time. Another life."

"Compared to you, I might as well have been a unit clerk. SEAL Team 3, two Purple Hearts, and more ribbons than most admirals. Then, the Navy Cross to top it off."

The man shrugged again. "Just doing my job."

Lynch could see that Amy was both surprised and impressed. He knew he was. At that moment, he knew that Amy had been in good hands prior to his arrival.

"And Lynch, just so you know what company we're keeping here, Roy had an equally distinguished career with the Aussie Special Operations Command. The 2nd Commando Regiment, right?"

Roy nodded. "Right, mate."

Lynch felt like a lightweight in this crowd. He couldn't claim any military service, although his police training had a para-military feel to it.

"And gentlemen, Lynch, here, deserves recognition, too. He has taken down serial killers, human traffickers, drug smugglers, and more, in a very distinguished police career. Plus, he saved the King of England from an assassination plot designed to take down the monarchy, for which he is actually now *Sir* Lynch, Knight Commander of the Royal Victorian Order."

Lynch blushed as Roy offered a slight bow. It had taken months to get his fellow transition team members to stop calling him Sir Lynch. They ended their teasing only because they had tired of it, not because of his protests. Either way, he was happy to just be Lynch again.

Amy elbowed him and smiled. "That should get the ladies interested," she said.

He only wanted the interest of one, and she stood next to him. How was he to take her comment?

CHAPTER TWENTY-SEVEN

Oudom left right after their noon meal to keep his appointment. As he had told *Lok* Abdullah, he had few contacts in that north-central city of Kampong Thom. He hoped to remedy that situation at this meeting.

He drove a short distance north along the river before the road turned back toward the heart of the city. At National Highway 6 he waited for a steady stream of traffic to pass until enough of an opening appeared that he could dodge the coming vehicles and cross to the opposite side of the main road. The Arunras Hotel and Guest House sat to his left as he entered a street lined with double and single-story shops offering a variety of goods but all having the same drab look—the dirty street, garbage-filled gutter, and rusting sheet metal awnings covering the open storefronts, which offered electronics, clothing, toys, canned foods, and pretty much anything else someone might need to buy. Certain "services" could also be obtained discreetly. The street led to the city's central market where dried meats and fish, fresh fruits, limp produce, and a plethora of fried tarantulas, crickets, snakes, scorpions, and more were available for sale. Westerners came here only to take pictures.

He found a place to park and took out on foot from there. Turning right at the next intersection, he moved deeper into the market and counted the fruit stands to his right. At the fifth stand, he entered the storefront and asked for the man he planned to meet. He was ushered to a back room where greetings were made, hot tea was offered, and business arrangements were discussed.

Half an hour later, money was exchanged and Oudom left, not only with several new contacts, but with information on two additional sets of twins within the age group he sought. The children in question were not of Buddhist families, nor of families with too many mouths to feed. He would not be able to "buy" these children, as they were from Christian families. One set participated in a preschool and feeding program about 25 minutes east of the town in a village named Roka, after the Kok Roka temple ruins, and the others lived in a children's home west of town in Tnolbail Village.

On the walk back to his car, he stopped and purchased some candy and four toys. He would need these to lure the children to his car. He regretted moving into outright kidnapping, but beggars can't be choosers, and his survival instincts told him to become competitive. More to the point, he refused to become the beggar.

The first self-closing door of his biosafety level three lab closed behind Tillson as he emerged from the lab itself. His superiors expected him to work on an effective immunization against both the West Nile and Zika viruses, in addition to the H1N1 and H1N3 strains of flu. Both were RNA flaviviruses closely related to dengue and yellow fever. His work focused on creating a plasmid, or circular piece of DNA, that would express the proteins of the viral envelope and trigger an immune response without having to use the virus itself in the vaccine. Such a vaccine held zero potential of causing disease, although some naysayers, like Miller, argued that science could not predict how such foreign DNA material might affect our own. Worrywarts!

One advantage to his location in Cambodia was that the macaque monkey was a good study animal for his research, and a multitude of test subjects surrounded his facility. Initially, he had seen the main disadvantage of his assignment as being in Cambodia. That changed with time as he discovered a second advantage: lax laws on medical— make that human—testing, with a multitude of those test subjects as well. While the laws had been tightened since the beginning of his human tests, the corruption of government officials had not. In a land of abject poverty, his outlay of cash to "blind" those officials had remained nominal.

In reality, he relished his work and expected his results to save tens of thousands, if not millions, of lives worldwide. Why couldn't the Jared Millers of the world see and accept the value of what he did?

After disinfecting his protective gown and disposing of other gear, he emerged through the second self-closing door into an isolated hallway near the back of the facility's main building. Windows there overlooked the separate living quarters of the higher-level employees who lived on the grounds and were treated to a level of accommodation—in housing, food, and entertainment—intended to make up for the remoteness of their work assignment, much like the military's remote bases.

He stopped for a moment to watch workers at one of the living quarters. They were cleaning and repairing it on his orders to prepare for a certain nurse. He couldn't understand why, but he'd had a strong premonition that she would call soon. And when she did, he wanted to be prepared to offer her the full benefits of working there. Or did he? He continued to vacillate on that decision.

As he retrieved his cell phone among the things he'd left in his locker outside the lab, he saw that he had missed a phone call marked urgent. The name of the caller was blocked, but he had no need for Caller ID with this number. He quickly called Duong Chea at the school.

"*Lok* Walter, thank you for fast call. I afraid I have, how you say, bad news, more bad news."

Tillson's heart rate accelerated. He did not know what to expect. The worse news could be disastrous, the stuff of his worst nightmare, on the level of a government raid and the discovery of his clandestine work there. The loss of a generation to Pol Pot's reign of terror had made the government highly protective of its children. Westerners were not even granted permission to adopt orphans from the country—short of the exception made for Angelina Jolie. Should his work become transparent, along with the unreported deaths that had occurred, all involved would face the death penalty with no appeals and the expedient dispensing of judgment.

"Yes, *Lok* Chea, what is it?"

"Kunthea have seizures. She die like sister."

While Tillson disliked hearing the news, her death, as well as her sister's, would not be in vain when he finally overcame the obstacles he faced in completing his research. He would need her blood samples as soon as possible.

"I have her blood for you. I send it to you now."

"I'm sorry to hear that she died. I will expect her samples shortly. Is this the bad news or the worse news, the more bad news?"

"More bad news is that twin boy, Ponleak and Phirum, escape, run away. My men look for them now."

Tillson took a deep breath and fought to calm his thoughts. The only good news would be that Duong Chea's men found them quickly and unharmed. From there, the gamut of bad news played out like a long list from Murphy's Law—the kids getting lost and never found, being killed by tigers or venomous snakes, dying of starvation, being picked up by provincial police, telling the police about the school, blaming Tillson for the deaths of children. Why did the list keep circling back to Tillson's death by firing squad?

"Do you need more men to look for them?"

"I do not think so. They cannot go far."

That much Tillson could agree with. His thoughts turned to his tests. If they weren't found before morning, his protocol would have to start over upon their return. His testing of antibody titers required a strict timetable, starting with the baseline labs that he had drawn that morning.

"What about the other twins?"

"They still sick."

That was a setback he didn't want to hear. Too many such delays were crippling his study.

"Put the word out, *Lok* Chea. We need more sets of twins."

CHAPTER TWENTY-EIGHT

Lynch had asked for and received a room close to Amy's. He wanted to be nearby for many reasons, not least of which was his hope to get time with her alone, to convince her to go home. He had no luggage—just the clothes on his back, his passport, and valuables—and, as such, no need to get situated in his room, but he used that excuse to check the layout regarding his room, her room, and other security issues. Only then did he return to join the others on the main patio.

He saw the small refrigerator built into the outdoor kitchen, and asked, "You wouldn't happen to have a coldie, would you?"

Amy gave him an odd look. Their hosts were Australian. Certainly, Roy knew what a coldie was, but how did Lynch?

"Aye, mate. Comin' right up." Roy reached into the fridge and pulled out two cans, a Little Creatures Pale Ale and a James Squire Nine Tails Amber Ale. "I import these two from Oz. Or, I have Angkor, Himawari Apsara Gold, and Siem Reap Dark Ale for a taste of Cambodia."

He took the can of Nine Tails and sat down. "Thanks." Upon looking about, he saw everyone else had iced tea, and he felt like he'd just gone to lunch with friends after church and had made a social faux pas.

Roy downed his tea and popped the top on the can of Little Creatures before returning to the barbie. Felix stood up with his empty glass, which he set on the countertop before reaching into the fridge and retrieving an Apsara Gold. Lynch had broken the ice. Or was it a case of bad morals corrupting good company? Nope. The Bible admonished against getting drunk, not the imbibing of alcohol per se.

"So, have I missed anything conversation-wise?" asked Lynch.

"A little," said Reggie. "Maybe Amy and Felix can fill you in, as well as tell us all more."

The two looked at each other.

"Felix, you start. I'm just along for the ride."

"I'd hardly say that, but . . ." Felix provided background info about twins being kidnapped from three families in his congregations, their stumbling onto the location of the CIC facility, and of Amy's concern about twins being used for medical studies. He also informed them that Amy had asked about a job at the CIC center in hopes of discovering whether or not her fears were founded.

Reggie's eyes widened about the same time as Lynch choked on his beer.

"You mean you suspect the CIC, *our* United States CIC, of trafficking in children?" Reggie appeared aghast at the thought.

In unison, Lynch protested. "You want to do what? Haven't you learned not to step into harm's way yet?"

Immediately, Lynch wished he'd phrased his comment differently, but the whole idea had caught him off-guard. Amy had a Somali terrorist chasing her, and she now wanted to infiltrate a possible child trafficking ring? Did she somehow now have an entire battalion of guardian angels watching over her? She had earned such. One surely couldn't keep up.

Amy gave him a look of displeasure before answering Reggie. "At first, I thought the whole idea ludicrous, but we met a Doctor Jared Miller. He's a Duke-trained immunologist who has serious concerns about our vaccines and their roles in autism, auto-immune disorders, SIDS, and such. He knows Doctor Walter Tillson, the director of the facility here, and wouldn't put it past Tillson to ignore all medical ethics to use children as human subjects. He's actually here in country trying to find out more himself." She went on to provide additional details of Miller's incident at the CIC facility and of their discussions with the man.

Reggie shook his head. "I think I need to inform the ambassador about this. This could be a major international incident, particularly if we, the U.S., aren't the ones to shut this down and turn the guy over to justice." He stood up and pulled his cell phone from his pocket.

Felix held up one hand as if to stop the diplomat. "Reggie, look, we need proof first. It would also be a major embarrassment if you go charging in and find nothing wrong going on. Amy's in a position to do that for us, and—"

Lynch interrupted, shaking his head with such vehemence he thought he'd pull a muscle. "But she'll be walking into harm's way. It's too dangerous."

This time Amy stood. "I fully understand that. And I'm willing to take the risk if it will save these kids. Plus, what if I get there and find everything on the up and up? I can bow out as soon as I know for sure, tell them it really wasn't working out as I thought it might. I won't be signing a contract for long-term employment. Plus, Felix will take me to work each morning and pick me up in the evening. It's up to you guys to figure out a way to keep me safe in the hours in between. I'm confident you can do that. Right? I mean, look around, the U.S. Embassy, Navy SEALS, Aussie Special Command, and Knights of the Royal Victorian Order are all represented here. Surely you guys can keep one damsel from getting into distress, can't you?"

When it came to Amy, Lynch wasn't so sure.

Oudom stopped at several other storefronts to purchase food and beer. As he lowered the case of Angkor beer into the car's trunk, his cell rang. Caller ID revealed the person on the other end to be Duong Chea. Had a problem arisen with the boys he had delivered a day earlier? If so, that was not his problem. Duong Chea took responsibility as soon as Oudom left the boys in his care.

"Khay Oudom," he answered.

The voice on the other end did not hesitate. In Khmer, Duong informed Oudom that the boys had run away and were being hunted, but the man did not try to blame Oudom. More importantly, the call was to inform Oudom that more twins were needed, and that they would offer 50% more if the children were delivered within 48 hours. Details were sparse, but all Oudom heard was "more money."

Oudom rushed back to the guest house and delivered the food and beer.

"*Lok* Abdullah, I must attend to my other business. Will you be okay here?"

The man nodded. "You provide well. I will be satisfied."

"Good. Please not go far outside. Police will be look for you. If they catch, I cannot help. Tep Rithisak cannot help."

Again, the man acknowledged Oudom's concern.

"At this place, I feel no need to get out. I will be good."

"*Aw-koon, Lok* Abdullah. I gone one, two hour at most. I bring food prepare for evening meal."

Satisfied that the man planned to stay put and out of view, Oudom hurried to his car and headed back to the heart of Kampong Thom. He had two choices—east to Roka or west to Tnolbail. East it would be. The twins at the children's home to the west would be surrounded by other children, many of them older . . . and wiser, wary of any stranger. That made the children in Roka the easier target. They were more likely to be found along the road outside their home. Also, he had paid good money for the names of contacts in both villages who would know where to find the children. Sadly, neither man had a cell phone, so Oudom would have to locate the man in Roka personally, negotiate a price for the information he needed, and then search out the children.

With luck, he would have that information within the hour. With greater luck, he will have located and identified the children, so that he could return the next day, prepared to lure them to his car and grab them.

CHAPTER TWENTY-NINE

After an hour of discussion, Amy succumbed to the need for a beer, just one, hoping it would not only quench her thirst but also help her relax. To say that tension was rising was an understatement. Lynch clearly did not want her to do this. Reggie, too, voiced his concern about "allowing" a U.S. citizen to place herself into potential danger now that he knew about the issues.

"I still think we should ask the ambassador to authorize a visit to the facility in order to investigate this. It is, after all, a U.S. research center. We *have* the jurisdiction and authority to do so."

Felix spoke up. "I've been thinking about that. As much as I would love to avoid putting Amy into this spot, and would prefer to let you take this ball and run with it, I keep asking myself, is this Tillson guy stupid? He would have to be, to keep children on-site at the facility. He has to have another place set up for the children, *if* he has them. I'm sure there are workers there who would not agree with his methods. And, he must have various government officials stopping by from time to time. He can't have them all in his pocket."

"I agree with Felix," said Amy. Roy nodded in agreement, too.

Diana, who had joined the group after her time with Champei and the other trainees had concluded, spoke. "That's true. I've seen photos of a number of government leaders touring that facility. It's a prestige thing for them to be associated with the CIC."

Felix continued. "So, the ambassador calls for an investigation. The inspector general or whoever from the CIC comes in and all they find is a research facility and its director completely on the up and up. We're seen as crying wolf and everything continues as is, no change . . . except anything we might say in the future falls on deaf ears. Not to mention that the corrupt officials helping to hide this racket would then target us and make our work more difficult, if not impossible."

Amy watched Reggie through this exchange. While she preferred his option, which would get her back to the reason she came to Cambodia, she agreed with Felix. The best and fastest way to get to the truth would be to infiltrate the organization and gain the trust of its director, Doctor Tillson. For those twins, speed was critical.

Reggie still looked unsettled, and she imagined his disquiet as being secondary to finding himself between the proverbial rock and hard place. As a diplomat he had standards to meet, laws to keep, and U.S. citizens to protect. In all likelihood, protecting *his* citizens trumped the protection of Cambodian citizens. But children? How could he ignore the trafficking of children to be used as medical guinea pigs?

Amy couldn't. That was her reason for being here—to work with Jim and Pat in their mission of helping the children of the Khmer Kingdom.

Therein lay the rub. She would have to ignore her most basic instincts for helping people if she wanted to gain the trust of Doctor Tillson.

"Amy, I'm here to help *you.* If this is something you feel that strongly about, I'm in there with you. I'll help any way I can."

Amy turned in surprise toward the voice that spoke those words. Had Lynch really said that, or was she imagining it? He had spent the better part of lunch trying to talk her into going home.

"Do you mean that, Lynch? I thought you were against my walking into harm's way, as you've put it several times."

"I'm against anyone purposefully walking into harm's way, but sometimes we have to do that." He looked about the group of people sitting there. "Soldiers, SEALS, police . . . we all selected paths for our lives that put us on a collision course with danger. Nurses, not so much. *But* . . . everyone here knows that truly helping others can sometimes require risk. I know you well enough to know you've already set your mind to doing this, so I want to make sure we minimize that risk." He paused. "But I have one big question for you. Can you really pull this off?"

That was the big question, the central one. If she couldn't pull it off, she would be putting herself at risk with no hope of helping those children.

"I-I think so."

"Lynch is right, sheila. There is no 'I think so.' You have to *know* so. Fair dinkum."

Amy was about to correct Roy about her name being Amy, when she recalled that sheila was the Aussie equivalent to lass or girl.

They spent the next two hours discussing the role she would *have* to play—a hardcore vaccine advocate dead set on saving lives, by whatever means. And if sacrificing a few Cambodian children would be required, she could look the other way. Maybe not be complicit in harming those children firsthand, but certainly willing to bend a few rules. After all, strict medical ethics were for first-world countries, right?

And she couldn't come on too strong with these "convictions" because Tillson was an unknown to her. She would have to appear as if she was testing his beliefs to see if they matched hers. No doubt he would be testing her as well.

As each individual on the patio contributed a new thought or potential pitfall, Amy added a new character trait to the person she would have to be. At times, she began to doubt her ability to play the role, only to see a mental image of scared children being subjected to needles and tests and strong men forcing them to do what they demanded of them. She thought of the pedophile child sex camp that had been discovered outside Tucson not long ago and steeled herself to do whatever it took to save the children. True, these children might not be imprisoned for the pleasure of perverts, but the consequences were the same—a child robbed of innocence and scarred for life. And if Doctor Jared

Miller was correct, the consequences could be worse—being trapped in a body unable to interact with those who really loved them . . . or robbed of life itself.

A lull in the discussion told her that no one had anything new to add. She glanced at the clock on her phone. She couldn't put off the call any longer. She dialed the number on Doctor Tillson's business card.

"Doctor Tillson."

"Yes, Doctor, this is Amy Gibbs. I'm the nurse who showed up on your doorstep, so to speak, yesterday. I had hoped to call you earlier, but I misplaced your card. Is now a good time to talk?"

"Why, yes, it is. I'm glad you called. I've been thinking about your inquiry about a job. Can you tell me more about yourself, please?"

Amy told him of her education and recent professional positions. "I was also a member of the hospital's infectious disease surveillance committee, representing the Emergency Department. I became heavily involved in our immunization program for employees. I find that aspect of medicine fascinating, to be able to prevent so many communicable diseases so easily. But, to be honest, I've not had any experience in research. I am a quick learner, though."

Out of the corner of her eye, she saw Lynch give her a thumb up. She took that to mean she had come across with the right mix of professionalism, interest, and honesty about her abilities.

"And what brought you to Cambodia?"

"After . . ." She hadn't intended to mention this, and she

fought her emotions to do so. "After a family death, I needed some time off. I came here as a tourist, but when I saw the condition of the medical care here, I wondered if there was someplace where I could work to make a difference. I've contacted a couple of medical relief organizations, and they talked of working to boost immunization rates. Then my friend and I literally stumbled across your facility, and it was like fate shouting out to me."

"Well, if it works out, I can get you a work visa, and I don't think you'll find working here a hardship. I have a specific project that I could use help on from someone with the training and experience you say you have."

"Do I have to apply through the CIC for the job?"

"Well, let's cross that bridge when we get to it. Can you come in for an interview? If things seem like a fit for both of us, I do have the leeway to hire short-term employees here. For something more permanent, yes, you'd have to go through the CIC back in Atlanta."

"Interview. Um, when? To be honest, I didn't really come with clothing or anything for a work interview. That was the farthest thing from my mind when I left the U.S."

Tillson laughed. "Trust me. I don't expect you to arrive in a skirted suit and heels. That might be apropos in Atlanta, but not here. Whatever you have is fine. Really."

"Thank you. I could come by tomorrow. Is there a good time for you?"

There was a pause on the other end.

"Would ten a.m. work for you, Ms. Gibbs?"

"Please, Doctor, call me Amy. Yes, my friend said he would keep his schedule free all day tomorrow to drive me there and bring me back. I'm staying at a guest house in Krong Pursat. I understand that's about a 40, 45-minute drive from you."

"Sounds about right. Very good then. I will expect you at ten and will inform the security team at the gate. Have a good evening."

"Thank you, sir. You as well."

Amy inhaled deeply and let the breath out slowly. She couldn't tell if her sweating was from nerves or simply the Cambodian climate. *So far, so good*, she thought.

She turned back to the group on the patio to subtle but unanimous applause.

"I really liked the bit about clothing for the interview. That should be a bit disarming," said Diana. She laughed.

She related his side of the conversation. "Ten a.m. is okay for you, right Felix?"

He nodded. "Plan to leave here at nine."

"What about me?" asked Lynch. "How can I get involved?"

Reggie sighed. "I guess I know what I'm doing tomorrow. I need to drive back to Kampong Thom, check us out of the hotel, and bring your stuff here. You can come with me."

Amy saw Lynch bristle at that idea. He surprised her again when he agreed to go.

"Sure. Hadn't thought about needing to do that, but you're right. I, um, we shouldn't be needed tomorrow, right? It's just an interview, right?"

"Can't see your needing to be here," said Felix. "I'll be on-site at the facility for her interview, so I can't see any problems arising. After that, though, if he hires her, we'll need to work out some kind of security plan for her. Roy, you know this part of the country better than any of us. Maybe you and I can put together something while Reggie and Lynch go get their stuff."

"Right, mate, but I don't know *that* area well. Sounds like a reconnaissance mission is in order."

Amy watched Lynch during this part of the conversation. Tillson's comment about not finding work there a hardship had her thinking she was going to have the easy part of this mission. Lynch, on the other hand, would be a fish out of water. If he'd thought it challenging to work in the Oregon wilderness, how was he going to manage in a Cambodian jungle?

Tillson had been surprised when his phone rang, and Caller ID didn't recognize the caller. He almost didn't answer the call, but misdialed numbers were a rarity for him in Cambodia. He thought the idea of answering an errant call amusing, only to find the nurse on the other end. This call just made his day.

Amy Gibbs, RN, sounded promising. Excellent educational background, assuming he could take her word for it. He had no validation of those credentials. Work with a hospital infectious disease committee. Again, no proof. And yet, she sounded sincere and honest. Why would she make up such credentials? She would know that he needed only to call HR at the CIC in Atlanta to have them verify her story.

But he wouldn't need to utilize the resources back

home. He would be able to tell from a handful of questions at the interview whether or not she knew her stuff. He made a mental note to take time that evening to put together a list of questions so he wouldn't forget them.

She had sounded eager for the interview. Perhaps too eager? However, she did say her friend was keeping his schedule clear to act as her driver. Maybe he wasn't able to do so on later days, and she didn't wish to inconvenience him further. That would explain her desire for the interview to take place the next day.

He needed to make two calls.

"Vannak, do you have more to report?"

"No, Doctor. The woman is at guest house. I not see that doctor at all."

Tillson nodded. The woman had told the truth about being at a guest house. That was good.

"Good. Okay, you can come back here. You do not need to follow the woman anymore."

"Yes, Doctor. I head home. See you in morning."

The second call went unanswered. He glanced at the clock and saw that it was after five p.m. Those workers would have left for the day already. He would have to check on the progress of her living quarters in the morning.

CHAPTER THIRTY

As Felix approached the gate of the CIC facility, Amy's heart began to race. She took a deep breath and steeled her nerves to get into "character." She had rehearsed . . . and rehearsed, and rehearsed.

"We're there," said Felix as the gate came into view.

Amy nodded. "I see that. You did a good job driving here, by the way. Did you practice by riding amusement park bumper cars and learning to avoid everyone else?"

He grinned. "That, and by driving in the Middle East on my missions. You know, avoiding pot holes, camels, and potential IEDs. I just think of every motorbike being a camel and every car as an IED, and I get through unscathed."

"Gee, you're going to put Sokham out of work."

Shaking his head, he replied, "Not as long as he speaks both Khmer and English, and can get me cheaper insurance."

He lowered his window as a guard emerged from the security hut and walked toward them. The guard, a different man from their encounter two days earlier, pointed toward Amy.

"You Amy Gibb?"

"Yes, I am Amy Gibbs."

He checked off something on the paper on his clipboard. "And you?" He pointed to Felix.

"This is my friend, Felix. I have no car in Cambodia, and he drove me here."

"Spell please."

Felix rolled his eyes. "F-e-l-i-x."

"Last name. Spell please."

"N-o-t-i-m-p-o-r-t-a-n-t," which he pronounced as "No-*tim*-por-tant," with the emphasis on the second syl*lab*le.

The guard seemed satisfied and didn't catch Amy's punch to Felix's arm. The gate began to slide open.

"Go please to main building. Is first building with two level. Park on right. Driver must stay with car."

Felix pulled through the gate and eased up the drive toward the main building.

"Cute, Mr. Not Important."

"Well, it wasn't . . . isn't. What do they need my name for?"

"It's a U.S. government facility. What did you expect? What would happen if you pulled that stunt at a naval base?"

"I wouldn't be able to pull that stunt at a naval base. Their protocol is to ask for photo ID."

She shook her head. "Never mind. I hope they don't catch it and throw us out of here."

"Hey, I'm just the driver and have to stay with the car." He paused and looked toward the back seat. "Glad I packed some bottled water and ice."

For that Amy was sorry. Even in the shade of the jungle canopy it was hot, and gasoline was too expensive to simply let the Rover idle with the AC on while she met with Tillson.

Amy checked her makeup in the sun visor's mirror. It was minimal but better than none at all. She still felt awkward about going to a job interview in tropical-weight travel clothes . . . and without having a printed CV and credentials in hand.

After exiting the vehicle, she walked toward what appeared to be the main entrance, a set of double glass doors with a canopy extending out over the walk leading up to them. Unlike other U.S. government buildings, there was no abundance of signs pointing you to each department and office. There were no signs at all.

As she walked under the protection of the canopy, a tall, slim man—likely in his early fifties—opened the door. His close-cropped, light brown hair showed a tint of gray at the temples, and he looked fit. Clearly this was Doctor Tillson— as it so stated on the nametag on his white coat. He looked harmless enough. Was Jared Miller simply paranoid? She wondered where he'd gone off to.

"Doctor Tillson."

"Ms. Gibbs. Amy."

They spoke in unison, as each reached out to shake the other's hand. He chuckled, and she smiled, feeling awkward. She should have allowed him to speak first.

"Come in, come in. Get out of the heat." He nodded his head back toward the car. "Your friend doesn't have to wait out there. It's not much of a waiting area, but I'm sure he'd be more comfortable in here."

"Thank you. I know he'd appreciate it."

She hurried back to the car, invited Felix inside, and introduced him to Doctor Tillson. They made small talk for a minute or two, and then the doctor ushered Amy to his office. She sat in a chair opposite his desk.

"I'm sorry I don't have a less formal place to talk. It's pretty utilitarian around here. So, I have an initial question. At the gate, when you first came here, you mentioned being an infectious disease nurse, but in your verbal resume yesterday, you didn't mention that. You talked about being an ER-trauma nurse."

The question threw Amy off. She hadn't recalled making the statement, but if she hadn't, why would he mention it? She had to think fast. That was not a question her friends had prepped her to answer.

"Sorry for the misperception. I wasn't sure what your guard understood, and I didn't know the gate conversations were recorded." Now she really worried about Felix's stunt at the gate upon their arrival. "I apologize for overstating my experience about being an infectious disease nurse. I never held such a position, in the strict sense, but, as I stated, I was on the infectious disease committee representing the Emergency Department."

She watched his face for a reaction. He seemed nonplussed. *Good,* she thought. *Honesty is once again the best policy.* But how many little white lies would she have to tell from this point on? *Lord, forgive me.*

"Now, you said you don't have any research experience. Your primary care nursing skills could definitely come to use, but the research thing could be an issue here. We are, after all, a research facility."

Thank you, Diana, for thinking of this question and asking it during our preparations.

"By no experience, I mean I've never worked in a research capacity. I have, however, been involved in research protocols, both in college and in nursing school. I understand how to design a study, and I'm very detail oriented."

"Do you have any problems using animals for testing?"

"None, whatsoever. I'm definitely not into the PETA thing, unless you define PETA as 'people eating tasty animals'." She smiled. He didn't. "And I strongly feel that level of testing needs to be done before ever testing something on a person."

She saw his brow furrow. The facial gesture was subtle and short-lived, but he hadn't liked some part of her answer. He shifted about in his seat.

"And human testing? How do you feel about that?"

"Well, that, too, has to be done. That is the end point—safety and efficacy for human use. Right?"

He nodded but did not smile.

"Do you think you could design and monitor a human use test protocol? We're pretty far along in our testing on monkeys, and I'd like to move to the next stage."

She needed to sound positive.

"I'm sure I could. I might need a little help tweaking the protocol, but I'd have no trouble monitoring it. What are you testing? I mean, I assume it's an immunization of some sort, but I would need to know what endpoints you're hoping to achieve."

"We can discuss that later, should this arrangement work out."

Amy struggled with a few of his subsequent questions,

wondering why they were part of her job interview. And then it hit her. He was testing her moral standards with old questions like a boat is sinking with 12 passengers aboard but only 11 life jackets. After describing the passengers, to whom would she withhold giving a life jacket? Under the usual circumstances she would be the one to give up the preserver, but what should her undercover character answer?

"Well, Amy, I'm done with my questions. Do you have any?"

Amy wondered how she had done. His demeanor gave her no answer, and she would hate to play poker with the man. Not that she ever played poker. The only sure bet in gambling was that you would lose money.

"A few. Should you decide to offer me the job, when would I start, and how much would you pay?"

The man looked pensive. "We can discuss that if I decide to offer you the position. Even though I said I had the leeway to hire short-term employees, I do have some hoops I have to jump through to do so, and I have to revisit our budget. Would you like to take a tour of the facility? You can ask questions as we walk. The lab isn't very big, so this won't take long."

He led the way, first taking in the labs on the second floor of the building. Amy saw nothing extraordinary about them. They were equipped much like any hospital lab. Next, they exited into a breezeway that led to the second two-story building. In it were the animal and veterinary facilities along the first floor, while the upper floor housed the biosafety level two and three labs. Amy had only seen photos of such facilities. To see one up close was both fascinating and scary when she thought about what viruses or bacteria might be on the other side of the windows.

As they walked back along the bright corridor leading to the labs, she felt a sense of uneasiness. The man seemed to walk too close to her and invade her space. Maybe he was simply socially awkward. Maybe it was a local culture thing that he had taken on unknowingly. After inching away to a more comfortable distance, another question came to mind.

"One more question. Would the lab have a car I could borrow, or some other transportation? And do I need a Cambodian driver's license?"

He smiled. "Oh, we offer one better." He turned toward the large windows lining the passage. "Over there, the third building from the left. If this works out, that would be your quarters. We would expect you to stay on-site. They're very nice, and the larger building in the middle is the cafeteria, which doubles as a community center. We have a gourmet chef on staff and first-run entertainment on weekends. It's really quite pleasant working here."

Amy's gut hit the floor at the realization that she would be there alone . . . inside a secure fenced perimeter . . . with no car, no way to escape should the need arise . . . and no cell service to call the cavalry. Maybe Lynch was right. Again.

As Tillson opened the main door to greet the nurse, his first impression surprised him. She was taller and much more attractive than he had gleaned from the grainy images afforded by the security system's cameras at the main gate.

That he had such a thought surprised him because he felt he was a progressive man, one who prided himself for *not* using physical attributes to guide his assessment of a person, male or female, but especially women. He did not consider himself chauvinistic, paternal, or dominating in any fashion.

And yet . . . he'd been there for so long without female company.

He put that thought out of mind as she returned to the car for her friend, only to wonder just what kind of friend the man was to her. He subjugated that thought as well.

Prior to her arrival he had reviewed the video footage of her visit to the main gate two days earlier. He noticed that she presented herself as an infectious disease nurse then, but had made no mention of that when he talked with her the previous afternoon. Should he be concerned about the discrepancy?

As they sat down in his office, he decided to address that concern head-on. ". . . At the gate, when you first came here, you mentioned being an infectious disease nurse, but in your verbal resume yesterday . . ."

He absorbed her reply and processed through it. Her answer satisfied him.

He began to ask questions from his list. Animal testing. He wasn't particularly amused at the definition of PETA. It was an old line.

". . . before ever testing something on a person."

Did he sense something else behind her answer? Something about her suggested she had rehearsed that response. Or was he reading more into it than he should? He still couldn't shake the thought that she had talked with Jared Miller, and that Miller was using her somehow to gather information. Yet, his man had not seen them talking at the hotel and Miller had departed for parts unknown. Yes, he was likely reading too much into her tone and body language.

". . . That is the end point—safety and efficacy for human use . . ."

There it was again. The words were on target, but the way she said it was as if she was trying to draw out information from *him*.

After questions about research protocols and the like, he believed her capable of doing such. He believed her to be capable of many things. Again, he surprised himself as he forced his mind to subjugate the fantasy that had arisen in it.

As he moved into questions he hoped would provide some gauge as to her moral and ethical character, her replies had been a mixed bag until the life jacket question. He had expected her to say she would give up the jacket. That had been his impression of her character to that point. It was also the answer most people would give in an interview, hoping to look altruistic and morally superior. When she said she would allow the disabled 80-year-old great-grandmother to go down with the ship, he had been both shocked and pleased. Most people gave interviewers the answer they thought the interviewer wanted to hear. She had given the same answer he would have given. Forget the moral high ground. Go with saving those who could be most productive in society.

As they walked throughout the facility, he found himself

admiring her physical form. And as he pointed out the living quarters, he realized that subconsciously he'd had the workers prepare the lodging right next to his own.

They returned to the lobby and her friend, Felix, stood as they approached.

"I think we're done for the day. I hope you weren't too bored sitting here by yourself," Tillson said to the man.

"Not at all. I hadn't read that particular National Geographic when it came out in 2005." The man grinned, but Tillson found the 'joke' unamusing.

Well, Amy, I need to check a few things, as I said earlier. Can I reach you at the number you called me from yesterday?"

"Yes, sir. That will work. Do you have any idea how long you might take to get back with me? I don't want to tie up my friend for any longer than I need to."

Tillson bobbed his head back and forth a bit. "Shouldn't be long. A day, maybe two at the most."

The man, Felix, nodded. "Not a problem on my end, Amy. Don't worry about me."

"Okay. Then I will be at the guest house until I hear from you. Thank you, Doctor Tillson."

"Thank you, Amy. I will be in touch." They all shook hands, which he found refreshing compared to all the *som pas* he received all day, every day. He watched as they walked to the man's car.

Tillson wanted to offer her the job right then and there, but something made him step back and wait. He needed to mull this over.

CHAPTER THIRTY-ONE

Oudom returned to Roka and found a place to park near the trail to a preschool there. He had been informed that the seven-year-old twin girls he sought would be attending a class there, as well as participating in a feeding program at noon. He pondered whether or not to walk the trail to the school, but decided that he would be too easily spotted. Villagers were a close-knit group. Strangers were quickly noticed and often questioned.

Only a few minutes of waiting lapsed before he saw a handful of kids walking his way. Some were older, ten to twelve, and appeared almost to be directing the younger ones as if herding the family's cattle. The youngest seemed to be about three and struggled to keep up.

Another family joined that one. Then a few older boys arrived on bicycles. Pretty soon a dozen other children converged on the trailhead opposite to where he had parked along the dirt road. All were carrying their own bowls and spoons.

A couple of the older boys scrutinized his car but seemed to pay little attention to him. However, a girl in a school uniform, who appeared to be the oldest of the bunch, watched him closely. He, in turn, paid attention to her as well. If she continued to be too attentive, he would have to change his tactics. However, once she had moved her siblings onto the trail and away from the road, her attention returned to them and away from him.

He continued to scrutinize the children as they filed past. He'd lost count upon turning his attention to the girl, but estimated at least 30 or so children had arrived.

But no twins!

By the time they arrived at the Arunras Hotel in Kampong Thom, Lynch had his fill of riding in a car. And yet, they faced one more daunting trip around the lake to get back to the guest house where Amy was staying.

"Meet me back here as quickly as you can," said Reggie.

"I'm on it."

Lynch didn't wait for the slow elevator but trotted up the four flights of steps to the fifth floor and to his room. By the time he opened the door his shirt was drenched with sweat. Because they had missed the checkout time, he would be paying for the room for that night as well as the two previous nights. He had yet to sleep in the bed or use the bathroom, and he was tempted to take a quick shower before changing from the clothes he had now worn for three days.

Did he have time? Reggie had asked him to be fast.

Yes, he had time for a quick rinse. Following that with a change of clothes would make him feel like a new man.

He opened the door and felt relief to find his luggage there, intact. He walked next to the bed and turned on the air-conditioner to its coldest setting. He then secured the door, stripped, and entered the open shower. The water coursing over his body felt wonderful. He let the stream beat over the top of his head and flow over his face and shoulders. He spit out the small amount of water that collected in his mouth and turned down the temperature of the water to the point of turning off the hot water altogether. The slightly cooler water invigorated him, but he knew he had no time to dawdle.

He quickly toweled off and dressed in a fresh set of clothing. His used travel clothes had dried adequately enough that he had no qualms placing them into a pocket of his suitcase. He would clean and dry them later at the guest house.

Glancing at his phone, he saw that only eleven minutes had passed. Not too bad. He decided to use the elevator with his luggage, so as not to sweat out his clean clothes. He found Reggie sitting in the lobby and talking on his phone. The man pointed to the front desk, so Lynch took that to mean he should go ahead and check out.

With his bill paid in full, he turned back to his guide, who was now off the phone. "Hope that wasn't too long. I really needed a shower and change of clothes."

Reggie shook his head. "Not at all. Hey, look, I know you want to get back as soon as you can, but I just got off the phone with the embassy. They want me to talk with this American pastor here. So, I need to find him and clear up a couple of things. Shouldn't delay us by more than an hour. Maybe less."

Lynch wanted to protest, but realized he had no ground

to do so. The man had been more than accommodating to him.

Finding a children's home in a rural village in Cambodia would seem like an easy task, once you identified the village and its location. After all, a structure capable of housing over 30 children should stick out among the ramshackle structures Lynch had witnessed in their travels. *Au contraire*, he thought, as they retraced their path along Highway 6 back toward Kampong Thom.

Their first mistake was in assuming such a place as Tnolbail Village officially existed. The community was certainly nonexistent as far as Google Maps was concerned.

"The pastor at the church did say to bear left at the fork where Highway 6 heads toward Siem Reap, right? Not to go right onto Highway 62 and head north, right?"

Lynch looked at Reggie in surprise. To this point, the man had been on target with his directions and driving.

Lynch shook his head. "No, I'm pretty sure he said to bear right onto 62 and begin counting side streets. Take the third dirt road to the right and then the second left. The children's home is about 5-600 feet down the road on the right."

"Okay, let's try this again."

Reggie turned around and headed toward the split in the roads, this time taking the right fork onto Highway 62. With the confusion of traffic and the impatience of drivers around them, Lynch found it hard to help navigate. Was that a road or just a dirt drive to a home or business, using the word 'business' loosely? The roadside stands in front of many homes held a variety of items, from steamed bamboo rice to gasoline in used Coca-Cola™ bottles. At some point, at Reggie's suggestion, Lynch wanted to try the rice with raisins packed into a bamboo shoot and steamed to create a soft rice cake that you found upon cracking open the shoot.

"There!" Lynch pointed. "Turn there."

Reggie shook his head. "I think that's just the second road to the right."

A quarter mile later, Reggie made a sharp turn to the right, almost clipping a man on a motorbike on the shoulder carrying enough pots and pans on the back of the bike to outfit the concession stands of an NFL stadium. The peddler drove on past them without a second glance their way, as if nothing had happened.

Now off the main thoroughfare, Lynch found it easier to delineate roads from driveways, even though all were dirt. The second left was a cinch to find. And sure enough, a short way along that rutted path they came across a two-story building with a large, blue 'carport' in front. The open-air structure teamed with kids. He glanced 50 feet ahead and to the left and saw a church. Only a cross atop its main door revealed its role in the neighborhood.

Reggie eased into a spot at the side of the short driveway into the carport and stopped. The children stopped playing in unison, and a young Cambodian man looked up from a bicycle he appeared to be repairing. He stood, wiped off his hands, and approached them. The grin on his face showed true delight in greeting us.

As both men emerged from the car, the young man

made *som pas*, and said, "Ah, you find us. Pastor Sokhon call, say you come. I am Samuel. I get Pastor Jim."

Without waiting for a reply, he turned and ran into the building. A minute later, a man in his early sixties, standing at about five-foot-seven and stocky, exited the home and approached them at the table where they now sat. A bushy, sandy brown mustache filled his upper lip, which curled into a smile. He made *som pas* and then extended his hand to shake theirs.

"Welcome to the Tnolbail Children's Home. I'm Jim."

Lynch extended his hand first. "I'm Lynch and this is Reggie Crutchfield, from the embassy. He's been kind enough to play host, chauffeur, translator, intercessor, and all-around travel guide for me."

Reggie and Jim shook hands. The diplomat laughed as he looked back toward Lynch. "Don't assume all of that service is because Lynch here is such a good guy—"

"Or because I have direct access to the President-elect."

"Well, that did help, at the beginning. Now? We have bigger concerns and those involve you, too, Pastor Jim. By the way, I'm surprised we've never met, your being an American citizen and all."

"Fortunately, God has blessed my work here and given us favor with the authorities. I've really had no need for assistance from the embassy, but now that I know someone there, maybe I'll have to find something you can help me with." His countenance became serious. "I'm concerned about Amy, as I know you are, too. How can I help?"

"It's more than about Amy. We left her in good hands."

Jim raised his brow in surprise. "So, you caught up with

her, and met Felix Castañeda?"

Lynch nodded. "She's staying with Felix at a guest house south of Krong Pursat, if I have my bearings and town names correct." He went on to describe the Smiths, their "special" clientele, and Amy's desire to infiltrate the laboratory in hopes of finding the children.

Jim frowned at this idea. "I offered my opinion about that when we were last together."

Reggie added his two cents here and there as Lynch spoke. He then talked about his concerns that an American government entity might be trafficking in children for medical research.

Jim shook his head. His disgust openly showed itself. "Back home, child protective services in several states have trafficked in children for years. Why should I be surprised that the CIC does it here where children are seen more as commodities than as gifts from God?"

Lynch nodded as he noted that the comment took Reggie by surprise. He thought about Sinead O'Malley and her family, and Amy's stint in jail for harboring the fugitive mother and child, but he didn't want to change the subject and give chase along that rabbit trail. "That's a story for another time." *And Cambodia is a vastly different culture*, he thought.

As they talked, a four-wheel-drive Jeep drove up next to Reggie's car. A middle-age man dressed as a cartoonish jungle explorer stepped out and walked toward them. Jim acknowledged the man with a nod, and all three men stood.

"Reinforcements, Pastor?"

"Doctor Miller, I didn't expect you here." Jim turned

back toward Lynch and Reggie. "Gentlemen, this is Doctor Jared Miller. Amy might have mentioned him."

The men shook hands, but Reggie took special interest in this serendipitous meeting. He began to pepper the man with questions about his suspicions as to what might be going on at the CIC facility, for info on the facility's director, and finally, about himself and what led him to come to Cambodia. The latter questions seemed to come about as Reggie appeared to realize he needed to validate the man he was using for information.

"I once worked for the CIC and directed a study on the safety of vaccines and their link to autism spectrum disorders. When my results countered their politically expedient talking points and widely-known public stand on vaccines being safe and effective, they refused to publish the work, instead of being intellectually and academically honest. I asked for permission to seek publication in other journals and was refused. Suddenly, I found my funding cut from all of my other projects. Without any research in progress, it didn't take long to get my first, and only, negative work review. Soon after that I was asked to leave. When I applied for positions at other academic centers, I wasn't even afforded the courtesy of a response to my application."

"So, is this just a case of sour grapes? Was Doctor Tillson directly involved in your career's nosedive?"

"I suspected Tillson had his hand in it, but I have no proof, and at this point, I don't care. Sour grapes? Not at all. What I care about is the future of our children."

"How so?" asked Lynch.

"Look, until several years ago, I followed nose-to-tail the long line of vaccine scientists who touted vaccines as safe and effective, the party line of vaccines being the single best way to prevent the scourge of infectious diseases that killed children and many adults, too. I ignored the studies showing otherwise, called those researchers anti-vaxxers in its most derogatory sense. Then I did my own study and was shocked that it supported their findings. I was like an atheist out to disprove Christianity once and for all, only to see the light and have my own Road-to-Damascus experience. After leaving the CIC, I had plenty of spare time to read their studies."

"Vaccines haven't really affected the death rates of these illnesses at all. True, the number of cases has dropped, but that's due to better sanitation, nutrition, and improved general hygiene, not vaccines."

"And at what cost? A child born today has a one in 36 chance of becoming autistic or developing Asperger's Syndrome or an attention deficit disorder. Over half of the kids in the U.S. are overweight or have a chronic illness. One in 20 has a seizure disorder. One in six has a learning disability. One in 12 has food allergies. The list goes on. And the growth curve of these problems over the past 50 years matches the rise in immunization use. I know several pediatricians back in the States who will tell you unequivocally that their healthiest kids are the non-immunized."

Lynch didn't know what to say to that. He had always dutifully accepted his annual flu shot as a police officer, and every year he caught a case of the flu, often following on the heels of the shot itself. He had to admit he felt better now that he'd stopped taking the shots.

"So, at dinner the other night, you mentioned there was only one way to catch this guy, Tillson, if he was using our kids as guinea pigs. What did you mean?" asked Pastor Jim.

Jared nodded. "Someone needs to put him under surveillance, collect evidence that he's ignoring standard medical ethics, and raid the lab to put him out of business."

Lynch gave him a quizzical look. "And by someone, who do you mean?"

"Either the Khmer or U.S. authorities, of course."

Lynch groaned, and Reggie gave him a wide-eyed stare.

"What?" Jared looked concerned.

"Amy's planning to take a job there, if offered, and collect the evidence you mention."

Jared's concerned look turned anxious.

"No, no. You need to stop her. Don't let her do that."

"I knew I didn't like that idea," said Jim.

"I don't know if I can get ahold of her in time. The phone reception where she is, is spotty at best. Is she in physical danger?"

Jared nodded again. "Maybe not for her life. Tillson wouldn't go that far, but I don't know about whomever he's working with."

"But she is in danger, you say?"

"Let's just say, the Hollywood elites and political power mongers have an equal in Walter Tillson. When it comes to sexual misconduct, Tillson is at the #methree, #mefour category, not just the #metoo level."

CHAPTER THIRTY-TWO

Amy stared out the window of the Land Rover as Felix drove down the winding drive of the lab back to route 53B. Not a word had been spoken since leaving the CIC compound, and she remained lost in thought. They turned north onto the Cambodian road and continued toward the guest house—with Amy glaring off into the distance.

"Okay, I give up. What's up?"

Felix's voice interrupted her mental gymnastics.

"What's up?" she replied.

"Yeah, what's up? You haven't spoken a word since we got into the car. I don't have a degree in mind reading, so are you going to tell me what happened? Clearly, something is bothering you."

Amy sighed. *That's an understatement*, she thought. She didn't reply right away, but as she glanced at him, she saw that he appeared anxious, wanting to know what she was thinking.

"Soooo . . ." She took a deep breath. "I think the interview went okay. He caught me on my little indiscretion about being an infectious disease nurse when I only participated on that hospital committee as the E.D.'s representative. I think I smoothed that over well enough. And he seemed satisfied that I could handle a research protocol, with a little guidance. But . . . "

Her mind drifted away again. Silence again engulfed the vehicle, but not for long.

"But what?"

"He gave me a tour of the lab. Pretty impressive for being in the literal middle of nowhere. But there's no place at all where kids might be housed."

Felix shrugged. "Well, we anticipated that, right? None of us expected him to actually have the children on the grounds . . . if he has them at all."

She nodded. "True."

"You didn't answer my question, but what?"

"He seemed a bit too eager to provide personal guidance on whatever research protocol he cooks up for me to develop."

Felix stopped the car and took that moment to scrutinize her.

"Something more is bothering you. I can feel it, and we don't even know each other that well."

"We don't know each other at all."

He gave her a look she couldn't quite interpret.

"Something else is bothering you, and I get the impression it's not a minor concern."

"I have to live on the grounds."

He shook his head as if he hadn't heard that correctly. "Did you say—"

"I have to live there, if I take the job. All the main staff have housing there, with a cafeteria, a common area with entertainment, the works."

The man emitted a low whistle, while shaking his head. He resumed driving.

"I don't like that idea one bit. If something bad happens, how do we get to you?"

"You're asking me? I dislike the prospect of being imprisoned there more than you do. Plus, the guy just seemed creepy. I don't know how to explain it. Bad vibes, or something. Like I said, too eager to provide personal, make that hands-on, guidance. I don't know."

"I think you do. Go on."

She paused and thought about how she wanted to phrase her next statements. How much did she want Felix to know about her?

"Okay. Like you said, we don't know each other. So, here's my first 'gee-you-might-want-to-know-this-about-me' revelation. I was once kidnapped by a human trafficker in St. Louis. It's a long story, but in a nutshell, the guy was an absolute sleaze-bag and sexual pervert. Nothing happened to me; Lynch and my ex-fiancé came to my rescue. But I'm getting the same sort of vibes from this guy. He didn't do anything inappropriate while I was there. It's just more of a feeling, an intuition, that I got. I can't explain it any better."

"No further explanation needed. I get those vibes, as you called it, frequently, and it's usually God behind them. If I listen to them, things go okay. If I don't, there's typically trouble."

He shook his head and pounded the steering wheel.

"That does it. We're pulling the plug on this operation. We'll find some other way to find those kids if he has them."

She placed her hand on his arm. "No. We're not. Because I also got this sense that I would be just fine, that nothing is going to happen to me. That's part of what I was struggling with. I couldn't figure out why I was so torn between anxiety over living at the lab compound and this sense of assurance I was feeling. You just told me what I couldn't understand. God is indeed behind my going undercover to find these kids, His kids."

Felix sighed. "I should have been more specific in my prayers, like asking for direct revelation about where the children are. You know, like a flashing neon arrow pointing in their direction."

Reggie glanced at his watch and stood up. "Gentlemen, Lynch and I need to get going. We have an appointment to keep."

Lynch gave the first secretary a quizzical look. No mention had been made of any appointment.

Reggie then nodded toward Jared Miller. "Doctor Miller, it's been a pleasure, and informative. Will we see you again?"

Lynch stood as the doctor replied, "Perhaps. I have more data to collect from regional hospitals, but I might have to change that schedule now that I know what's going on."

Pastor Jim also stood and extended his hand toward the two departing men. "I'm glad I got to know you two a bit better. Please keep me in the loop. Pat and I will do anything we can to help."

Lynch nodded. "We most certainly will. Right now, the best thing you can do is spread the word among your pastors and other NGOs that twins are being targeted for kidnapping."

"Oh, we've already started that. Word has gone out to the small churches in the immediate area, but it might take a few days to reach our outlying groups. I know two sets of twins in the area personally, one set right here in the children's home. They are going nowhere without staff or a group of older children to protect them."

"Good move, Jim," added Reggie.

Lynch followed Reggie to his car, still puzzling over what appointment they had to keep. As they pulled away from the home, he asked, "What appointment are we keeping? You never mentioned anything, and I thought we would be heading straight back to the Smith's guest house."

"We are, and I just received the text about the appointment I'm referring to while we were talking back there. I think you'll want to keep this one."

A moment later, they left the children's home, with Reggie hitting the gas a little harder than usual. As they reached Highway 62, Reggie turned right, not left which would take them in the direction they needed to go.

"Hey, you turned the wrong way again. National Highway 6 is the other direction."

"Not this time. Our meeting is a few miles up the road this way." He grinned. "You're going to like this one."

A few minutes later, Reggie slowed down and turned left into a field where cattle grazed. To their left was a sign that appeared ready to topple, its letters faded and unreadable. Up ahead, Lynch could see several buildings. Well, the ruins of several buildings. They had partial walls and no roofs. He counted nearly two dozen scrawny cows feeding on the lush grass as they neared what appeared to be an old grass landing strip. Despite the abundance of vegetation everywhere Lynch had been in the country, the cattle seemed malnourished. *What's with that?* he wondered.

The car came to a stop, but Reggie didn't turn it off or make any move to get out of the vehicle. He simply checked his watch once more.

"What are—"

Reggie interrupted by holding up his hand with one finger pointing upward. Less than two minutes later, Lynch could feel it before he heard it—the low frequency beat of helicopter blades. Reggie smiled.

"Right on time. If we'd been late, they wouldn't have waited."

The chopper was the biggest that Lynch had ever seen, and painted in the white and blue of the Royal Cambodian Air Force, it looked like a huge cloud settling to the earth. The car began to shake as it neared the ground.

"Eight blades. It's a Mil Mi-26 Russian transport helicopter. It's on record as being the heaviest lifting rotary aircraft in the world."

"And we're going on that thing?"

Reggie nodded. "Unless you want to drive all the way around the lake again."

Lynch could barely hear his friend over the beat of the blades, even as they slowed after landing 50 yards away.

"How in the world did you manage this?" he yelled.

"Friend of a friend of a friend. They're on a routine training flight and agreed to pick us up here, take us to Battambang."

"But your car."

Reggie pointed out the window at a man, an American, running from the aircraft toward them. "One of my guys. He left an embassy car in Battambang and will drive this one back for me. Get your stuff."

Lynch didn't need to be told twice. This would shorten their trip by hours. He just hoped the pilot didn't like doing aerobatics like Amy did in her Cessna. But then, he doubted this monster helicopter could even do such stunts.

Did they just take pictures of me and this car? wondered Oudom. Three of the older children in the group had cell phones and appeared to have just photographed him. That was not a good thing.

He had waited the remainder of the day for the school children to return from their lessons and walk home. He had discovered that he was at the correct place to watch them walk to and from the small village preschool.

The term 'preschool' was something of a misnomer he had also learned. Although the teacher definitely worked with younger children, the school also provided basic English lessons to older children. He knew that knowing English offered a distinct advantage . . . and was something of a bragging point. He personally had used his own skill in the language to further his career.

In addition, the school held no reservations about teaching any child who came there. Age was not a determining factor. In the Khmer Kingdom, a public-school education had one limiting requirement. The student must attend school in uniform. Period. No uniform, no classes. For many rural families, this meant no formal education because they could not afford the clothing. That this school, run by Christians, would accept any child had not been lost on Oudom.

Unlike earlier in the day as they walked to school in groups of two or three, or alone, the kids now seemed to walk in small packs of six or more. It was as if they sensed danger and found safety in numbers.

He glanced down the path toward the school and saw his target—the twins. And yet, as they neared his car, more children joined their group, including a few boys in their early to mid-teens. That was unusual. These older boys were expected to be working on the family farm. By the time the twins reached his car, they were literally surrounded by over a dozen others. What was going on?

The entire group walked by him, but not without making their displeasure of his presence there known. How could he nonchalantly entice the twins to his car with treats when every child in the group stared at him while walking past. One of the older boys turned and started to approach him, but the others pulled him back. Anger beamed from the lad's face.

What is going on? Oudom asked himself again. The display by these children was one of disrespect for an elder. Part of him wanted to launch into a tirade about traditions and respect, but he caught himself short from doing so. All it would take was one or two of the children to run home and tell their fathers, and Oudom might not leave the village without a beating.

The thought of such unnerved him. He started his car and waited for the herd of children to pass by. He slowly backed into a nearby turnout, and left the village by the road he came in on. Once on the national highway again, he began to mull over the incident.

Lost in thought, he drove as if on autopilot and found himself at the house where he'd left *Lok* Abdullah. He had forgotten to get more food, but that did not concern him as much as the strange encounter he'd just left.

"Ah, *Lok* Oudom. You are back. But no children?"

"No. No children, *Lok* Abdullah. It was the strangest thing." He proceeded to tell Abdi about what had happened thirty minutes earlier.

The African offered him a warm beer. He guzzled down half of it before stopping for air.

"It sounds to me that someone has warned the children of what Americans call the bogeyman."

Oudom nodded. "I know that phrase. You may be right." That possibility had crossed his mind on the drive back to the house. But how? Who would have known to warn the children?

Then it hit him. That man and his wife, the ones he had saved Abdi from shooting. They lived or worked in this region. That's why he had brought Abdi here, for the woman who appeared to be working with them. But again, it stymied him. How? How could this man have known that

Oudom was seeking to abduct twins?

He retrieved his cell phone and made a call. Friends working directly with Tep Rithisak would have resources he didn't. He needed to learn more about this man and his wife.

CHAPTER THIRTY-THREE

Upon returning to the Smith's guest house, Amy retired straightaway to her room. She needed to think through what might happen, to play Lynch's favorite game of 'what if,' before facing the others. She wondered when he might return to the guest house. Now that she had seen him here, in Cambodia, she found herself wanting his presence and the connection he gave her to "home" in St. Louis. She felt a level of assurance with him around. He had covered her back on more than one occasion, rescued her from more than one predicament. Felix, Roy, and Reggie were no doubt highly skilled men in a variety of areas, but they weren't Lynch. She had no history with them.

She refocused her musing on the problem at hand, make that plural, problems. To work at the lab and return to the comfort and companionship of this place each evening, despite the lengthy commute, was one thing. Staying there, at the lab, behind tall fences and guarded by a security team, was quite another.

Her mind strayed back to the thought that had just crossed it—the lengthy commute. Forty-five minutes each way was not so much the problem; her having to obtain a car and learn to drive in crazy Cambodian traffic was.

The whole idea was another con in her mental list of pros and cons. So far, the cons were winning.

Her thoughts went back two days. Had it really been only *two* days? The faith she had witnessed in those parents who had lost their children spoke to her. Why didn't she possess such commitment?

"God, I believe, please help my unbelief," she said to the empty room, paraphrasing the scriptural voice of the father who had brought his young, epileptic son to Jesus for healing.

A soft voice spoke clearly inside her head, "The faith is there. Just grab hold and claim it."

The words seemed so real, almost audible, she turned around to see if someone else had entered the room. No one else was there. At least physically anyway. And with that she realized that God was indeed with her wherever she went. He wasn't some obtuse, figurative concept. He *was there,* at that very moment, with her. And He would be with her at the lab.

A knock at the door disrupted her moment with God. She opened the door to find Diana standing there.

"Amy, hey. I thought I'd check to see if you need anything. The men are gathering at the patio around the grill, and dinner should be ready in half an hour. Can I get you anything?"

"I'm fine. Thanks, Diana. Give me a sec, and I'll walk back to the house with you."

She double-checked her appearance in the mirror, stashed her valuables in her luggage, and returned to Diana who waited just outside.

"Ready." She closed and locked the door behind her. As they walked, she could sense the other woman wanted to talk. "What's on your mind?" she asked.

"I was thinking the same thing of you," replied the innkeeper. "You're about to get another overt dose of testosterone-fueled thinking, and I wondered if you needed to talk with another woman first."

Amy thought about that for a moment. "Actually, I might need that afterward, to balance out the men. Like most guys, they'll no doubt tell me what I *need* to do and how to do it."

She laughed. "Oh, that much in tandem. We're talking two alpha males here, with enough skill and firepower to take down a small army if it came to that. And if Reggie and Lynch get here, make that in quadruple." She gave Amy a curious look. "Actually, that Lynch seems like a good bloke. And I hear he came all the way from the U.S. to warn you about trouble, to look out for you. That's, well, extraordinary. Fair dinkum. He must really care for you."

Amy pondered that. She knew it to be true. But she now recognized a difference. In the past, before his brief disappearance from her life, he had voiced his love for her, but his actions revealed a different set of priorities, preferences where work and career came ahead of their relationship. Now? His actions spoke what he would not confess to her after she had accepted Richard's proposal. He really had flown halfway around the world for her. That spoke more than any words he could offer to her.

"Yes, he did. He really is a good bloke. I just, uh . . . I

don't know." She proceeded to tell Diana a brief synopsis of her on-off relationship with Lynch, of her engagement to Richard and of his murder.

"Ah, so now you think your having chosen Richard at the time has created a barrier between you and Lynch."

Amy looked at the woman. She hadn't said as much to her, but that was precisely how she felt. How could she go back to Lynch now? Would he feel like he was her second choice? How could she do that to him? Yes, he had changed. Yes, she liked that change. And true, she had cut off her engagement to Richard just prior to his death . . . but not because of Lynch.

"How . . . how . . . I didn't say that, but yes, that's exactly how I feel. How could you know that?"

"Because you're telling me my own life, with a few minor alterations. I could be you and Roy could be Lynch. Roy chose the military life that I really didn't want to be part of. I became engaged to another, but he was killed in a car accident months before the wedding. Roy came back into my life much like Lynch has in yours. He didn't have to fly around the world or anything to show he cared. I put off his advances for the same reason you are, but his persistence won me over. Fair dinkum. Been married just over 35 years now."

"Amy, Diana! Come join us. There's a coldie waiting for you."

Amy looked ahead to see Roy waving at them from the patio just ten yards away. She turned to Diana and took her hand. "Thank you. You've given me something to think about, but right now, I could use a beer."

Lynch had flown in med-evac and police helicopters before, but never a military bird. Now he could boast of having flown in a Russian-made Mil Mi-26 transport helicopter, even though his first thoughts upon entering the cavernous belly of the aircraft was that it had seen much better days and would they survive the flight.

Yet, the flight was smooth and uneventful. So far. Lynch wanted to ask questions of Reggie, but the machine was so loud he didn't dare remove his helmet and earphones to try to converse. He wanted to be able to hear things other than ringing after the flight. He'd once been told that helicopters could only fly because they were so noisy the earth rejected them. This bird gave proof to that saying.

It seemed as if they began to descend for landing just minutes after taking off. Lynch glanced at his phone—40 minutes. He smiled. Their five-and-a-half-hour drive had been cut by almost 90%. He wanted to give Reggie a hug for arranging this, but knew that would be strangely awkward.

He doffed his head gear, grabbed his luggage, and exited the chopper as quickly as he could to avoid the noise. Reggie was right behind him and tapped him on the shoulder.

"This way." He nodded to their right. "The car should be next to the terminal."

Lynch glanced about. At least this airport had a paved strip and three small hangers. Behind them, he noted the Mil Mi-26 lifting off and skirting the pavement as it moved just ten feet or so above the ground toward the fuel depot—a sole tanker truck parked 100 feet from one of the small hangers. The terminal ahead of them consisted of a single-story, long, white rectangular building with large windows overlooking the runway. It appeared empty. He saw no vehicles on the single runway's side of the structure, save the fuel tanker in the distance.

Reggie led him around the end of the building, as they had no need to go through it even if, by chance, they found it unlocked. He saw no vehicles there either, at first. As Reggie dropped his luggage and groaned, he saw what the first secretary had reacted to: a lone white sedan with embassy markings, jacked up onto cinder blocks and missing all four wheels.

Tillson left his quarters and made his way toward the canteen building and cafeteria. He paused briefly outside the residence next to his. The workers had completed their task of refurbishing the building and preparing it for its next occupant. He shook his head. He had found himself fantasizing about having the American nurse living there and working with him, but it wasn't to be.

The remainder of his afternoon, after Amy Gibbs had left the facility, had been unproductive. She had convinced him of her abilities and intellect, but he had remained unsettled about hiring her. He couldn't pin it down, but her appearance at the same time as Jared Miller simply could not be coincidence. He had no evidence of their being complicit partners in trying to destroy his work. In fact, all of the "evidence" seemed to say otherwise.

Unable to focus on his work, he had absentmindedly

reviewed paperwork. The autopsies on their two most recent deaths at the children's home revealed larger than expected amounts of aluminum in their brains, but he glossed over that information as his mind contemplated yet again whether or not to employ Ms. Gibbs.

By four o'clock, he realized that he was rereading a paper he'd already completed two days earlier when he turned the page and saw his own annotations in the margins. Yes, his mind was preoccupied. Yes, she was qualified. But no, he would not hire her. He made up his mind. To hire her would leave him looking over his shoulder at every turn, rob him of sleep at night, and possibly cause the return of his peptic ulcer. That was settled.

Still, as he looked at the quarters where she would have stayed, he wondered if he'd made the correct decision.

"So, are you hiring that nurse?"

Startled by the question, he turned to find Eric Gilroy approaching as he, too, was likely heading to dinner. The younger virologist, unaware of the children's home and Tillson's extracurricular project there, had questioned the need for her services earlier that day. After all, he argued, they needed another vet tech to handle the primates, not an RN. Gilroy would remain unaware. Tillson was not so vain as to think he could escape the wrath of his superiors should they find out about his "shortcuts" in studying vaccine responses in children.

Tillson shook his head. "No, not at this point. Like you pointed out, we would be better served by another vet tech. Still, I could have used her to start developing a phase 2 and phase 3 study for me."

Gilroy shrugged. "Phase 2 and 3 studies? Why bother? We all know vaccines work. We don't need more studies. You're sounding like an anti-vaxxer."

Tillson held open the door for the younger man. "Hardly. You know me better than that."

He grabbed a tray and prepared to fill his plate from the self-serve salad bar when his private cell phone rang. It was a Cambodian number he did not recognize. He set things aside and moved to a quieter corner of the room.

"Hello."

"Doctor Tillson." The accented greeting by a gruff male voice he did not recognize held an ominous tone.

"W-who is this, and how did you get my number?"

"Ah, Doctor, is that how you greet, um, benefactor I think is right word."

"Benefactor?" Now Tillson was puzzled.

"I am Tep Rithisak, and how I get your number is important not."

Tillson blanched at the man's mention of his name. The man was indeed a benefactor and one which Tillson had hoped never to encounter personally. To Tillson, the obvious source for the man getting his private number was Duong Chea. Even though the children in the school were obtained by less than honest means, Tillson had never really considered the children's home as a criminal enterprise. True, the children were most often procured by Tep's men, but they were paid well by Tillson, not Tep. Why would his work there concern the notorious crime boss?

"Sir, I am surprised by your call. *Lok* Chea should have forewarned me."

"Not if he value life, his life. I tell him I want to surprise you, as you say. But I do not call about children."

Tillson felt a chill of fear trickle through him. Not about the children? They had nothing else in common, and Tillson was an American, the head of a distinguished American laboratory, a man with connections to the prime minister himself. Surely, Tillson would be above any threats by this man.

"Little bird tell me you want to hire American nurse who come here recent."

Now Tillson was truly puzzled. What could Tep possibly want with one Amy Gibbs?

"I had considered it, but decided not to hire her."

"Wrong answer. You will pretend hire and take to children home. I have financial interest in her."

"Financial interests? I don't understand what you could possibly want—"

"Is of no business to you. You do not question Tep Rithisak. Take her to children home, and my men keep her there until my business done with her."

An undertone of snarling could be heard in the voice. Duong Chea had once told Tillson that Tep Rithisak might one day ask a favor in return for the use of his men. Tillson had brushed that comment aside. But now, he recalled something else Duong Chea had said. You do not question Tep Rithisak, and you do not say no.

"Y-yes, sir. I will call and make the offer. But what if she says no?"

"You will convince her say yes."

CHAPTER THIRTY-FOUR

Amy glanced about the guest home grounds as she carried her "go" bag from the room to Felix's Land Rover. Lynch and Reggie had failed to show up last night for dinner, a fact that had her mildly concerned. They had already encountered Abdullah Said Abdi once by chance. She worried that the terrorist had somehow tracked them in order to get to her. Such a scenario would give Abdi the upper hand and element of surprise. She hoped Lynch and Reggie were okay.

She stashed her luggage in the back seat of the vehicle and looked back toward the main house. Felix had told her that he'd get them both some coffee and meet her at the Rover. The "cool" of the morning—however relative that phrase was in Southeast Asia—was now giving way to the heat of the day, and yet, the time was not quite eight a.m.

A moment later, all three new friends—Felix, Roy, and Diana—exited the main door and headed her way. Diana reached her first and extended her hand holding a paper sack.

"Some snacks. You know, in case the food there doesn't agree with you."

Amy claimed the bag and peeked inside. Diana's wonderful macadamia nut brownies, raisin-rice cakes, and more tempted her from within.

"Thank you so much. These look delicious."

"They are," said Roy in response. "By the way, we heard from Reggie this morning after breakfast. They hope to be here within the hour. Someone stole the wheels off the embassy car. They couldn't get a replacement car until this morning. Lynch asked that you not leave until he gets here. He sounds as if he's of like mind with the rest of us."

"Fair dinkum," said Diana. "Amy, we really wish you'd reconsider going there."

Their discussion the previous evening had started with the coldies on the patio, extended through dinner—when the call came from Doctor Tillson offering her a two-month position, and lasted much later than she had planned. The more they talked, the more Roy and Diana favored taking any other means possible to surveil the laboratory, to discover the whereabouts of the children—if they were there at all, and to send in the authorities to rescue the children. And the more entrenched Amy became about saving time by doing it herself. After all, time was not in the favor of the children.

Amy nodded. "I know you do. I have nothing to add to last night's discussion. I still really think my going there will be the fastest way to find the children."

Felix had been quiet the night before, which Amy found a bit odd. Even now, he seemed content with letting the Smiths take point to her counterpoint. She followed him around the side of the vehicle.

"Felix, you haven't said much either way. What do you think?" she asked.

He appeared pensive for a moment, glanced at the Smiths and then back to her. "What I think is that nothing I say will sway you one way or the other. I happen to agree with you that time is critical, and simple surveillance might take too long. But I don't like your putting yourself in harm's way, and that's what you'll be doing. Tillson isn't in this alone. Someone's kidnapping those kids, and they're not going to play nice like some CIC research scientist. You'll be dealing with those people, too. Also, we learned this morning through Reggie that this Tillson character is a big-time sexual predator. The CIC handled their PR problem and disposed of their problem child by sending him to Cambodia."

Amy stepped back at that new revelation but realized it really didn't faze her. She'd dealt with sexual harassment in the workplace on more than one occasion, and she'd handled being kidnapped by a human trafficker and placed in the pervert's "harem." Being forewarned now was being forearmed.

"That explains the weird vibes I kept getting from him when we toured the lab. I knew something was off about him, but now that I know that, I can handle him okay. Trust me, I won't accept any drinks from him."

Roy extended a small canvas bag to her. "These are *my* treats." He opened the bag to show her its contents and pointed to two items in particular. "These two I'd try to keep handy at all times."

* * *

Oudom reflected on the good mood *Lok* Abdullah had been in since their move to the house along the river in Kampong Thom. What he didn't understand was why? Why the dramatic change from the aggressive, domineering warlord he'd first met along the shore of the Sre Ambel River? Was it simply offering the man pleasant housing, adequate food, and plenty of beer?

Oudom drove west on National Highway 6 and continued northwest on Highway 62. To his right lay Tnolbail Village, a loose collection of lower class and farm homes sitting along narrow dirt roads northeast of the highway. His contact here had given him explicit directions to the children's home where he would find the twins he sought.

However, after the previous day's experience in Roka, he had little hope of catching the twins, and the children's home staff, off-guard. He headed there hoping for a little luck . . . and because just sitting in that house waiting to hear that the woman had arrived in town would drive him stir crazy.

As he made the turn onto the third dirt road to the right, his cell phone chimed. He smiled as he saw the number on Caller ID for one of Tep Rithisak's top lieutenants, a man with whom he had favor and got along well. He pulled as far to the side of the road as he could and stopped.

"Khay here," he answered in Khmer. Although conversing with *Lok* Abdullah in English had been good exercise, he looked forward to talking in Khmer with a fellow citizen.

"Hello, my friend. I hope your day has started productively."

"Too soon to tell, *Lok* Sangha, too soon to tell. I am curious about why you call."

"Ahhh, straight to the point. As always. Tep Rithisak sends his greeting and has a present for you. Your inquiries about an American nurse have paid off, but she is not on her way to Kampong Thom as expected." He continued to explain.

As quickly as he could without drawing the attention of police, Oudom backtracked to the house where Abdi hid. They had a lengthy drive ahead of them . . . back to the children's home. He would soon be rid of his foreign charge.

CHAPTER THIRTY-FIVE

Amy took a deep breath as Felix neared the security gate outside the laboratory. She bowed her head and said, "Lord, I'm about to enter the lion's den. Please protect me as you did Daniel. And please give me discernment and direction."

"Amen," said Felix.

She looked at the man, surprised that he'd completed her short prayer.

"I couldn't have said it any better. Like you, I'm trusting in Him for your protection. But also know that either I or Roy will be minutes away. The disposable cell phone he gave you may or may not work, depending on where you are. Keep the pepper spray handy, and that pen he gave you will—"

"I know, I know. It will signal you that I'm in trouble if I twist the top the way you both showed me—multiple times. I feel like Jane Bond with a new toy from Q."

He grinned. "Hey. The Lord allowed man to invent technology. I think he expects us to use it sometimes. Anyway, trigger the signal and the cavalry will come running."

"Yeah, the Lord's cavalry of one."

"With Jesus as the troop commander, that's all you need." He slowed even further as the gate came into view. "We're here. You know, it's not too late. I can turn around."

She shook her head. "He's *my* troop commander as well."

The guard at the gate must have seen Amy through the windshield as he motioned to his companion to open the gate and allow them to pass. Both men nodded to them in greeting as the Rover passed by.

Felix frowned. "They seem a bit too eager to feed the lions."

Amy poked him in the arm. She then took the pen and clipped it into the breast pocket of her travel shirt. From that point on, she would keep it with her at all times. The pepper spray sat in her bag, but she would put it someplace with easy access in her quarters.

Felix pulled into the parking area of the main building. Before he could turn off the vehicle, a smiling Cambodian man came rushing from the building. Amy stepped out of the car and greeted him with *som pas*. She remembered him as Sok Darany, Doctor Tillson's lead technician.

"Hello, Nurse Amy. Is good see you again. Doctor Tillson ask I show you to quarters and let you get settle. He is in isolation lab, and I will come get you when he ready for you."

"*Aw-koon, Lok* Darany."

He smiled at her use of their traditional greeting. "Please, Nurse Amy, is just Darany."

"And I am just Amy. Nurse Amy is not needed."

The young man furrowed his brow. "Doctor Tillson not like. He expect us call you Nurse."

"Well, if he's not with us, then you can call me Amy, without the nurse."

His smile returned even wider. "May I?" He pointed to the back seat of the Rover. "We drive to back, where houses are. I show you."

Less than a minute later, Darany pointed to a structure to their left. "There is. That one for you. On left is Doctor Tillson house. On right is Doctor Gilroy house. My house farther on street. You learn soon who live where. That building is common area and dining place."

He pointed to the larger building between the labs and the residences. Amy remembered it from her tour.

As Felix stopped in front of the quarters, Darany jumped out first. "I help with luggage. Where is?"

Amy pointed to the small bag on the back seat next to where Darany had sat.

"That all? You travel light."

"Most of my luggage is in Kampong Thom. I will have to arrange for it to come here."

"I can do that," replied Felix. "Be happy to do it."

She regretted not having thought of asking Lynch and Reggie to pick it up for her. Of course, she hadn't been offered the job at that point. Now, Felix would spend hours in the car to get her things. Yet, as Darany nodded, Amy could see the gears in Felix's mind working. Bringing her luggage in a couple of days would give him an opportunity to check on her directly.

The dwelling was larger and more luxurious than she

had anticipated. The main living area was spacious enough for entertaining, and a small kitchenette extended from one end. There was one bedroom with a private bath and large walk-in shower. The closet was adequately sized considering someone's clothing needs in the middle of a jungle. The bed and other furnishings were top quality.

A third room branched off from the living area opposite from the main bedroom. It was furnished as a study but held a queen-sized futon for overnight guests. Amy assumed such guests would normally be family members or friends visiting from the States. She foresaw no potential guests to make use of the room. When Doctor Tillson had mentioned that they had finer amenities than most, he hadn't been understating it.

"Very nice, Amy," exclaimed Felix. "I guess I no longer have to worry about your roughing it in the Cambodian jungle. Well, I should get going and let you settle in. Can I do anything else for you beside arrange for your luggage?"

Amy shook her head. "Don't think so, but I have your number. Thank you so much for all you've done already."

She assumed she would have access to a phone in the lab, should the burner phone provided by Roy not have service. She watched Felix head back toward the main gate, with Darany in the front seat to be dropped off where they had picked him up. She looked about and listened for the roar of lions. Quiet.

Lynch had a bad feeling about things. He got off the phone with Roy Smith who had informed him that Amy had already left for the lab and should be there by now. He tried to reach Felix directly, but the calls kept going to voicemail. That meant the man was in that no-signal zone between the lab and National Highway 5. He did not like the fact that Amy had gone ahead.

But more urgently, he just plain felt bad, and his gut was roiling.

"Reggie, pull over."

"Huh?"

"Yeah, pull over. Like, right now."

Reggie found a place to pull off the road, and Lynch had the door open and was outside before they had even stopped rolling. He doubled over and retched his guts out along the side of the road. People on motorbikes and bicycles sped right past them without so much as a double-take.

Reggie leaned over into the passenger seat and said, "Uh-oh. What did you eat? Did you try something I warned you against?"

Lynch took a deep breath and during a spell when his stomach seemed settled, answered, "No. I've only eaten what you saw me eat. Honest." His gut rebelled, and he leaned into the roadside weeds once again to recycle his stomach contents.

"Water? Did you drink any water, or even just get a little bit in your mouth?"

"No, just bottled . . ." And then he recalled the small amount of water he'd gotten into his mouth while showering the day before. He groaned. "Rats. Yesterday, when I showered. It couldn't have been more than a tablespoon, and I spit it right out."

Reggie sighed. "That's all it takes here. Shoot, I need to get you to the guest house. You're going to be laid up for two, three days at best, maybe longer."

Lynch stopped vomiting long enough to protest. "No, I-I need to see Amy. Go to the lab, not the guest house."

"They're not going to let you in there. You might be . . ." The man started to chuckle. "Oh, the irony. They're not going to let you in because . . . because you might be *contagious*."

Lynch felt the wave of nausea subside enough to feel comfortable getting back into the car. How long that would last was anyone's guess.

"Funny man. Drive."

CHAPTER THIRTY-SIX

Amy paced in the living space of her new quarters, bored. How long did it take someone to settle in when she only had two extra changes of underwear, one change of clothing, toiletries, and her valuables and ID? She had plopped onto the bed and given it her approval. She tested the hot water—it arrived within seconds from its in-line heater—but she hesitated to taste the tap water. She recalled being told it was filtered and safe. Or was that just in the canteen? Wisdom told her to confirm that before drinking anything other than the bottled water she had in her bag.

She had checked out the kitchenette. The microwave worked, the refrigerator was cold and stocked with bottled water and soft drinks, and she found an inexpensive—make that cheap—place setting for four in the cabinets. Curiously, or not, there were more wine and cocktail glasses than anything else. Did that speak to the previous occupant's dependencies or to the lack of entertainment at the facility? The electric cooktop's coils glowed within seconds, but cookware was absent, so she did not expect to do any of her own cooking. Besides, the foods were different enough and with the water being questionable, why would she attempt it?

Within the extra room, the desk and accompanying chair were quite nice, and she believed the chair would suffice as her new reading spot. Rooting through the desk she discovered several spiral-bound notebooks, one of which she selected to become her new journal. Taking the pen from her shirt, she took care not to activate it and found that it wrote smoothly and fit her hand well. That made her think of the pepper spray. Where would be a good place to keep that? She would look for a spot after finishing with her journal entry.

She required a moment to recall the correct date and then jotted down her first journal note:

> Having arrived at the CIC Laboratory in Cambodia at 10 a.m., I was first escorted to my new quarters.

She continued with her impressions of the living area and Sok Darany, a man she found pleasant and eager to please.

> It's now 10:20 and my "settling in" is complete. I'm pacing the floor waiting to be summoned by the boss. I hope the demands of my new position begin to fill up the days quickly or I am likely to be utilizing the wine glasses I found.

Her next entry:

> It's now 10:45 and I've explored the commons building and dining area. Very nice as well. I am eager to get to work, but right now, waiting, I wish I had packed my tablet into my "go" bag so I could kill time reading.

By 11:30 she debated simply heading back to the main building and finding Darany, but in glancing out the window, she saw the man walking her way in no particular hurry. She double-checked her valuables, making sure they were secure, and headed out the door to meet him. He smiled when he saw her coming toward him.

"Amy, you are settle in I hope."

"Darany, you saw my bag. I was settled in within ten minutes." She laughed, but he looked a bit unsettled himself. "I also took time to explore the commons building and dining room. I hope that's okay."

"Is most fine. Is almost lunch. I will show you how—what is English? —how chow line work." He turned slightly and pointed to the main building. "Doctor Tillson out of quarantine lab and in his office. We go see him now."

Amy followed Darany back to the main building, but he used a back door closer to the living quarters to get into the building. She noted that he used his employee ID as an electronic key to open the door.

As he shut the door behind them, he said, "You will get badge to do same. Much less walk in the heat."

Moments later, he ushered her into the doctor's office

and excused himself. Doctor Tillson was not there, so she sat down in the sole empty chair across from his desk. This time her wait was not long.

"Ah, Miss Gibbs, Amy. Welcome. I am glad you decided to take me up on my offer. There will be some paperwork to complete, of course. There's always paperwork. But it might take a few days to get it all together. This was kind of a spur-of-the-moment thing. Hiring you, that is. What I do need to get you is an ID badge. It's necessary to get you into the office where you'll work, to unlock various doors like the back door near the quarters, to get you into the commons building after dark, and the like. Places where you aren't cleared to go will not open, such as the quarantine labs and veterinary facility. It's a lot like in the U.S., although not as strict since we're a secure facility in the middle of a jungle."

Fifteen minutes later, with her new ID badge in hand, she followed the doctor from office to office, being introduced to the other employees. Darany joined them for this. The Americans were outgoing and seemed happy to have another fellow westerner among them. The Cambodians made *som pas* and seemed distant, until Darany said something to them in Khmer that made them relax and smile.

"Well, it's lunchtime. Darany will show you the ropes in the dining room. I'll join you shortly."

"See you there, Doctor," she replied.

As they walked, Amy looked at Darany and asked, "What did you say to your fellow Cambodians? They seemed to relax after whatever you told them."

He smiled. "I tell them you very nice lady and that you

show them respect like you show me. To be honest, Doctor Tillson and Doctor Gilroy not always nice to Cambodian. You will see." He seemed eager to push ahead. "Come now. Time to eat and get to know others on more people level."

Tillson watched as the nurse and Darany walked down the hall toward the back door. Yes, indeed, that nurse was one tall drink of water in his dry and thirsty land. Yet, he needed to be a good boy. His assignment to Cambodia had not been without candid explanation. His best behavior was expected if he hoped to be reassigned to the main labs in Georgia. Still, his libido had not been broken by the heat and humidity.

However, even more chilling than a cold shower or what his superiors expected of him was what Tep Rithisak expected of him. In light of that request, he would have no trouble steering clear of any and all sexual harassment claims. The nurse would not be around long enough to tempt him.

He smiled as he reflected on their meeting. Nurse Gibbs appeared accepting of his explanation that the paperwork would take a few days to come together. In reality, he needed to stall because he wanted no paper trail of her having been there. The ID badge was handled locally on their computer system and all reference to her could be removed with a simple keyboard stroke. Employment records and payroll were a much different matter, as was the promised work visa. Yes, he would need to stall those requirements until Tep Rithisak dealt with her.

*　　*　　*

Abdi watched as Oudom stood at the head of the driveway leading to the home where they had been hiding. He felt anxious to get on the road. The woman was finally his to mete his vengeance upon, and yet they remained stuck where they were.

Oudom returned to the front of the house where Abdi sat in the car hoping to depart at the first opportunity.

"*Lok* Abdullah, I am sorry for the delay, but we still cannot leave. The road block continues. I will make a few calls to see what I can find out."

Abdi watched the man disappear into the house. He fought to keep his emotions in check. When Khay had told him the good news about finding the woman and that Tep Rithisak had intervened to make sure she remained in reach, he had experienced an emotional high not unlike when he chewed khat back in Somalia. Even the news that they would have to return to the children's home six hours away had not brought him down.

Sitting in the car for the past two hours, however, had been like withdrawal from the drug. He needed to move on, deal with the woman, and leave the country before getting caught there. Beside his illegal entry into the country, he would face gun charges, assault, and more. He could feel the blindfold hiding his eyes and hear the firing squad's rifles chambering their rounds as he sat in that car unable to move on.

Khay returned from the house.

"*Lok* Abdullah, we might as well get comfortable inside the house. We will not be leaving right now."

Abdi glared at the man, forgetting at that moment his need to comply with and rely upon his Cambodian guide.

"I am sorry, but it is not something I can influence. Or Tep Rithisak, I am afraid. Someone reported seeing a black man in the area, and we know that you have been identified inside the country. I do not think it was you, but the result is the same. They are looking for you. They have set up several road blocks in the city to screen every passing vehicle. Even if we got past this one, we might run into others.

Abdi did not wish to admit that it might have been him who had been seen. He had wandered out of the house and the high walls bordering the property to walk across the road to the riverbank. Just once, for five minutes or less, and near dark. He did not see anyone else, but that did not guarantee that no one else saw him.

Khay had warned him not to stray, and he had assured the man that he wouldn't. Now, Allah made good his retribution for Abdi's not honoring his own word. He could not blame Khay.

At Khay's suggestion, he moved back inside the home and retrieved a beer from the kitchen.

CHAPTER THIRTY-SEVEN

"You don't look so hot. You sure you want to do this? It would be a whole lot faster to go on the mend at Roy's guest house."

Lynch couldn't argue with Reggie's thinking, but he needed to see Amy, to be there if she needed him. Still, he had no idea what to expect at the lab facility. Amy had said nothing to him about living at the facility, which made him all the more determined to go there, sick or not. It was Reggie who informed him that medical staff had separate quarters there. Lynch did not like that arrangement one bit.

He glanced at his watch. She would be there already. He simply had to try to connect with her. But would he be welcomed, especially if she was seen as being distracted by nursing him to health? Would they even have a place where he could crash while recovering, or would the lab be required to turn him away? It was a secure facility, after all.

He had played the 'what if' game continuously since leaving Kampong Thom, interrupted only by answering nature's call as it tried to turn him inside out. What if he went to the lab? Would he be too much of a distraction? Would he even be able to help should some negative event unfold? If not, he could become a liability. Plus, what were the odds that she'd find out anything within a week's time? He'd be healed by then. And what then? He would no longer have an excuse to extend his stay at the lab, if the director allowed him to stay at all.

And what if he went to the guest house as Reggie suggested? He had no doubts that they would care for him, nurse him back to health. But if something happened at the lab, he'd be nearly an hour away. He'd be of no help that way.

During these mental gymnastics, though, he found himself asking, *why* was he doing this? He had convinced himself that, even though it was unplanned, this was a good ploy to watch over her for a limited time. As he thought it through over and over again, he wondered if he had subconsciously taken that mouthful of water in hope of having *her,* just her, nurse him back to health. Wouldn't that force her to confront her feelings for him? He knew he needed to move on with life, with or without her. While he preferred a future *with* her, if that wasn't going to happen, he would be better off knowing that now, not at some undefined point in the days or years to come.

"I know you're right, but I need to talk with Amy. My whole reason for coming to Cambodia was to find and protect her. I just can't see myself sitting in a room 45 minutes away, sipping on soda in between retching my guts out. I wouldn't be able to rest, knowing she's on her own in potentially hostile country with a known terrorist and murderer on the loose looking for her."

"Okay, okay. We're not far away. Still not convinced this

story you've concocted is going to fly."

"What? It's not a story; it's the truth. I flew halfway around the world to see her, and I got sick on my way to the lab. So, I'm embellishing it a bit."

"Yeah. Being her boyfriend. Wanting to surprise her. Only trust her to help you get better. Geesh. Sounds like the making of a hokey Hallmark movie."

"With a murdering terrorist thrown in. Sure, I could pitch that plot to Hallmark . . . and get thrown out of the building."

"What if she doesn't take the cue and denies your being her boyfriend or something. Maybe deny she knows you at all. Right now, I think I would."

"She's quick. She'll catch on right away. Look, you just need to play your part. The embassy car will help. Just wait, you'll see."

Reggie rolled his eyes, just as if Amy had taught him how to do it. Exaggerated, with an accompanying sigh.

"Here's the turnoff. Almost showtime."

Reggie turned left onto a paved road heading into the jungle. The sign for the CIC -Cambodia facility had seen better days. Lynch found it curious that such a secure, advanced bio-lab would announce its location to everybody and anybody driving by. But then, they hadn't passed another living soul for the past 15 miles. Maybe it was a moot issue.

"Reggie, pull over."

The car stopped on a dime, and Lynch dove out the door. The dry heaves had ensued. He had little left to offer.

A moment later, he returned to his seat. "There. I-I

should be good for a little while."

Reggie shook his head and resumed their course into the wilds. Lynch sipped on a cold lemon-lime soda, letting his gut settle between sips. He couldn't afford to get dehydrated, but he had noticed a slight, lightheaded feeling upon entering the car. He didn't dare say anything to Reggie for fear the man would turn around and head straight to the guest house. Moments later, a tall chain-link fence came into view with a wide gate and guard shack. Two men emerged from the structure. Reggie lowered his window.

"ពេលរសៀលខ្ញុំជាលេខាធិការទី1Crutchfield មកពីស្ថានទូតអាមេរិក។"

If he was holding true to their plan, Reggie had just introduced himself as the first secretary from the U.S. Embassy. He would next ask for Amy Gibbs and state why they were there.

"ខ្ញុំត្រូវបានគេប្រាប់ថា   Amy   Gibbs គិនុប្បមកពីសហរដ្ឋអាមេរិកគឺជានៅទីនេះ។ បុរសម្នាក់ដែលនៅជាមួយខ្ញុំបាននហោះហើរពីសហរដ្ឋអាមេរិកដើម្បីមកជួបនាងហើយឯកអគ្គរដ្ឋទូតបានសុំខ្ញុំជួយគាត់។"

Lynch was impressed. The man sounded like a native speaker. This was beyond being Greek to Lynch.

The man went into the shack, spoke into a phone, and proceeded to open the gate.

"Don't have a clue what you said, but it worked."

"So far. I just told him we understood that an American nurse, Amy Gibbs, was here, and that the ambassador asked me to help you find her."

The guard said something in Khmer, and Reggie nodded.

"I'm to drive to the main building ahead."

Reggie pulled into a parking spot outside the building, and they both exited the car and headed to the main doors. Before they could reach them, a slim Cambodian man greeted them with *som pas.*

"Hello, I am Sok Darany. I am Doctor Tillson's top technician. How can I help you?"

Both men returned the greeting.

"I am First Secretary Reginald Crutchfield, of the U.S. Embassy in Phnom Penh. This is Lynch Cully. He has flown around the world to surprise his girlfriend, Amy Gibbs, and we've been told she is here."

The tech pointed to the doors. "Please, please, come in. Have seat. I find Amy Gibbs and Doctor Tillson."

Lynch controlled the urge to heave into the grass next to the sidewalk. Instead, he said, "*Aw-koon,*" and followed Reggie into the building. He welcomed the cool air conditioning.

A few minutes later, a man he assumed to be the doctor walked into the reception area.

"I am Doctor Tillson."

The two men stood. Reggie extended his hand first. "Yes, Doctor, we've met once before. I'm Reginald Crutchfield, with the embassy. This is Lynch Cully. He's with President-elect Graham's transition team, but he also happens to be Amy Gibbs' boyfriend. He's flown halfway around the world to surprise her. Passport control led us to a guest house where she was staying, and they directed us here."

The doctor gave them both a strange look, before he

directed his scrutiny to Lynch. Lynch wanted to return the inspection, but despite knowing the man's history, he played it cool. He heard Sok Darany's voice, followed by Amy saying, "My boyfriend? I don't—"

She stopped short upon rounding the corner and seeing Lynch. "Lynch? Wh-what are you doing here?"

She didn't look happy to see him. Lynch took a step toward her, intending to give her a hug, but his stomach recoiled. He lurched for a nearby trash can and proceeded to empty what little soda remained in his stomach into it.

Then everything went black.

Doctor Tillson had called Amy and asked that she meet him in the reception area. She thought she'd heard him say she had a visitor. Puzzled, she headed toward the main doors where she had personally been received upon arrival. She knew of no other reception area.

As she neared the location, Darany intercepted her. "Boyfriend here. Fly around world to see you."

Her boyfriend? What in the world?

She had started to deny having a boyfriend when she saw Lynch and Reggie. What was going on?

"Lynch? Wh-what are you doing here?"

Then she looked at Reggie and saw him wink, then point outside with his eyes. She knew better than to acknowledge knowing him and realized she needed to play along. But, at that moment, Lynch lurched forward toward a waste can and began to vomit. And then he was out.

She rushed to his side and knelt next to him. Cradling

his head in her hands, she helped lay him flat on the floor. She checked for a carotid pulse. Strong. His breathing was even. But his skin was pale. She pinched the skin on the back of his hand. It tented easily and did not flatten as expected. He was severely dehydrated.

"Lynch? Can you hear me? Open your eyes for me."

She sensed Reggie kneeling next to her, but quickly glanced at Tillson. He looked aghast, ashen, almost as pale as Lynch. She had just shown up to work for him a handful of hours earlier. What must he be thinking? Was he angry? No, she didn't see anger. It was fear. Fear? Why?

"He said he was feeling a little off when we left the guest house, but he insisted on coming here to surprise you. He mentioned getting a mouthful of water while showering yesterday morning, but spit it out right away. I've seen westerners get sick on such a small amount of water, but not so quickly."

"He had to have been vomiting a lot already. He's badly dehydrated."

"Can you give him IV fluids here? I don't know how I could possibly get him to Battambang like this in my car."

Amy looked at Doctor Tillson, who seemed to have regained his composure. "Doctor? I could start an IV to get him back on his feet faster. Can we?"

"I, uh, I guess so. But where can he stay? We don't really have a sick bay here."

Amy didn't hesitate with her answer. "The futon in my quarters will work. I can start my project work there just as easily as in the office you gave me. I can work on getting up to speed on testing protocols, etc., and still keep an eye on him."

"I-I guess that could work. But how long will it take?"

Reggie stood and faced the doctor. "In my experience, 3 or 4 days usually does it, but IV fluids should work faster."

"Okay, take him to your quarters, Amy. Darany, help them get him there."

Amy noticed Tillson wringing his hands, despite his voice sounding calm. Something about this situation was agitating him. But what?

Tillson had always thought of himself as a man in control. He had done well in school, achieved a life of scholarly and medical commendation with all of the perquisites that came with that, and quickly rose to leadership in the academic and medical circles he had chosen as his destiny. His progress toward the CIC directorship position had been steady, until some shortsighted female staffers had failed to see in him the greatness that was there, that he wished to share with them.

Their claims of sexual harassment had shown them to be unworthy of his attention. His colleagues' support of their claims had been out of professional jealousy. And yet, he found himself sent into "exile" in Cambodia, not recognized for his contributions in immunology for which he had anticipated an assistant director's position. Instead of working in an oversized closet overlooking the domain of a monkey family, he should be sitting in a prestigious office suite in Atlanta.

Some saw his reassignment to Cambodia as a demotion.

Yet, all successful men had experiences that others saw as failures. What made those men truly great had been their ability to learn from those encounters, to push beyond the obstacles, and to achieve bigger and better things as a result. That's what Cambodia offered to Tillson—the opportunity to produce groundbreaking research that would launch him to the top of his chosen specialty.

With his assignment to Cambodia he had experienced his first sense of having lost control of his life. But that feeling had been little more than a fleeting emotion, a fist-sized rock on a gravel road that barely disturbed his tire as he rode over it.

Why did he now feel as if the road had just disappeared beneath him?

Darany had knocked on his door post with a look of surprise on his face. At least the usual *som pas* had been forgotten.

"Doctor Tillson, we have visitor in reception area. Nurse Gibbs' boyfriend fly around world to surprise her. He here with man from U.S. Embassy. I go find Nurse Gibbs."

A boyfriend? That won't do, he thought. *Not at all.* As he walked toward their small reception area, he pondered what he would do. He needed to get rid of them, but how? Perhaps a straight forward approach—she was just hired to do a job and won't have time to play. And according to their policies, he wouldn't be allowed to stay with her.

He turned the corner into the main entry and saw two men. Both were over six-foot and appeared in good shape. Well, one didn't look so good, pale with dark shadows under both eyes.

"I am Doctor Tillson."

The two men stood. The healthier-looking man extended his hand first. "Yes, Doctor, we've met once before. I'm Reginald Crutchfield, with the embassy. This is Lynch Cully. He's with President-elect Graham's transition team, but he also happens to be Amy Gibbs' boyfriend. He's flown halfway around the world to surprise her. Passport control led us to a guest house where she was staying, and they directed us here."

And then things happened too fast. Amy arrived. The other man, her boyfriend, stepped forward only to lurch toward the nearby trash can, vomit, and pass out. Amy and Crutchfield going to the man's side to help him. Amy commenting on the man being dehydrated and asking to give him IV fluids.

In that instant, Tillson realized he wasn't between the proverbial rock and a hard place, he was in a car compactor with the sides moving quickly to crush him. Tep Rithisak was not a man to toy with. He would not accept any excuse for a delay in handing over "the woman," as he called Amy. And yet, now there were two men here—Crutchfield, whom he remembered from the embassy, and this boyfriend who was on the transition team of the newly elected President. Crutchfield, as he recalled, wasn't some lower staff member. He was fourth man on the totem pole, or whatever culturally appropriate analogy could be found for the Khmer. His knowledge of Amy being at the lab complicated her pending disappearance. And this other guy? Did he have the ear of the President-elect? One wrong move could crush any and all aspirations Tillson had to become CIC Director.

Amy glanced up at him, asking about IV fluids and could they help him.

"I, uh, I guess so. But where can he stay? We don't really have a sick bay here."

The ensuing conversation seemed a blur as Tillson agreed to letting the man stay at Amy's quarters. But, several days? Tep Rithisak expected Amy to be delivered to the thugs at the school upon request, sometime within the next few days. How could he say no?

"Okay, take him to your quarters, Amy. Darany, help them get him there."

As Darany called for assistance in moving the man, Tillson turned to leave. "I'll get the fluids and an IV set for you."

He left the area and headed for his office. He needed time to think. By the time he collected his keys to the supply rooms in the veterinary wing—where the IV supplies were kept—he began to see this as possibly a good turn of events. The man would be housed in Amy's quarters where not only she, but he, could keep a close eye on him. The embassy man would leave. When the time came to deliver Amy, he could dispose of the boyfriend, too. And if the embassy staffer asked, he could just inform them that Amy had changed her mind about the job, now that her boyfriend was here, and the two left.

Only one loose end came to mind. The man who had brought Amy to the lab was supposed to be bringing her luggage there. He would expect to see her. Tillson decided that he could deal with that problem easily enough. Yes. As he thought it through, he decided he could even reason with

Tep Rithisak to wait a day or two, if need be, in order to avoid suspicions and the curiosity of the U.S. Embassy.

He unlocked the door to the supply room, entered, and found a bag of normal saline, along with the IV set to administer it. He grabbed some alcohol pads, tape, and other needed items, then left and locked the room.

But instead of heading toward Amy's quarters, he moved to a nearby room where they kept their pharmaceuticals for the animals. Once inside, he found what he wanted. There were a number of acceptable protocols for use in preanesthetic sedation in rhesus macaques, but only two drugs were acceptable in human use. Use of the other drugs might cause a reaction that could alert Amy to trouble, so he decided to stick with those two—midazolam and ketamine.

He calculated the man's weight and drew up appropriate doses of both into syringes. These he added to the IV fluid. The man's dehydration might resolve with the fluids, but he wasn't going to be any trouble for them. Not as long as Tillson provided the fluids.

He took a moment to look for one other item. Yes, there was an adequate supply of morphine as well. When the time came to eliminate this boyfriend, an overdose would make it painless.

CHAPTER THIRTY-EIGHT

Darany and another tech had carried Lynch to Reggie's car and then from the car to Amy's quarters. Reggie followed them inside with Lynch's luggage.

"Ms. Gibbs, I'm sorry. I knew he wasn't feeling well, but I had no idea he was this bad. I feel like I'm dumping him on you folks."

Darany shook his head. "Is okay, Mr. Crutchfield. We have saline and medicine. Is Nurse Amy's boyfriend. Only right she take care of him."

"Well, I . . ."

Amy looked from Reggie to Darany and back again. If this was some ploy on Lynch's part to gain admittance to the lab facility, it had worked. But he appeared to play his part too well. He clearly had been dead weight when the techs tried to lift him. Even now, stretched out on the futon, he didn't budge.

"I think Doctor Tillson get the IV, but I go check."

With that Darany and the second tech both left the building. Amy watched Lynch, expecting him to open his eyes and wink. He didn't.

"Amy, I really am sorry to bring him to you like this. He

insisted. I wanted to take him to the Smith's place. Oh, and thanks for playing along. He said you'd catch on right away."

"Reggie, what happened?"

"Just like I said. He took a quick shower before we checked out of the hotel in Kampong Thom yesterday and got the water in his mouth. To save time, I arranged for us to fly into Battambang and pick up the car, only to find someone had taken all four wheels. By the time we got that fixed and on the road, he had already started to vomit. I've seen lots of westerners get sick on the water, but I've never seen it happen so fast. His body must have been depleted from sweating, too, and this only compounded it. I—"

A knock at the front door interrupted him. Doctor Tillson appeared.

"He's in here, Doctor."

"Ah, yes. Well, here are the supplies you'll likely need. Do you need help?"

She met him at the front door. The man seemed antsy. Was he squeamish about needles, or blood?

"Not at all. I can handle the IV."

"Good. I, um, need to finish some things in my office. Mr. Crutchfield, can I talk with you?"

Reggie nodded. "Of course. Ms. Gibbs, again, I am so sorry to deliver him to you like this, but I believe I'm leaving him in quite capable hands."

He walked out with the doctor, and the two men left in the embassy car. When Amy saw that they were out of sight, she returned to the study.

"Okay, Lynch, they're all gone. You can wake up now."

Nothing. Not even a flit of an eyelid. He really was in

bad shape.

After starting the IV fluids on Lynch, Amy settled into the chair at the desk opposite the futon and, using the lab-provided laptop, began to review a number of the studies suggested by Doctor Tillson as models for the study he wanted her to develop. She found it curious that all of the studies involved human subjects, while the lab only handled primates like the macaques that lived around the facility. Was his study going to be a human trial? If so, where did he plan to recruit his subjects? Or did he have them already?

Amy felt a strong confirmation that the latter was the case. But where?

As she read, she repeatedly cast her gaze upon Lynch. He "slept" soundly. His breathing was regular and normal, as best she could determine without a stethoscope. An hour into the fluids, she checked his skin. Its turgor had not yet improved. It remained tented when she pinched it. Maybe for a second less than when she had first checked, but still . . . And he didn't stir or even flinch when she pinched him.

She debated increasing the rate of the fluids. In the E.D. they would have emptied that first bag of saline into him over a two-hour period. But there they had the full support of a top trauma center and physicians of every specialty as backup. Here? Two research immunologists—MDs who had not spent a day in clinical medicine since medical school—in the middle of a jungle hours away from what at best could be considered third-world care. No, she chose the conservative route and kept the drip rate at a moderate level.

Two hours later, her stomach grumbling, she called it a

day with regards to reading. Lynch remained as still as a large rock sitting on the futon. As she prepared to examine Lynch yet again, a knock at her front door interrupted her.

"Doctor Tillson."

The man stood at her door holding another bag of normal saline in his hands. He extended it toward her.

"Here, Amy. Thought you might be getting close to needing another one."

"Thank you. Yes, the first bag should still have an hour or so to go. I was going to contact you about needing a new bag when it got a little closer to empty." She took the plastic container from him.

"May I?" asked the doctor as he pointed inside the quarters.

Amy stepped back and ushered him inside. Being alone, she wasn't fully comfortable allowing him into the building—like a hen opening the gate for the fox, but she couldn't let on that she knew about his past indiscretions.

"How's he doing?"

"He seems to be doing well, but he must have been dangerously low on fluids. He's had nearly the whole first liter of saline and hasn't stirred. Not even so much as moved on the bed."

"Well, hopefully another round of saline will change that. How are your quarters?"

She nodded. "I hope so. And yes, the quarters are quite nice. Much bigger than I expected, or really need. Thank you."

He smiled. "Tell you what. If you wish, I'll stay here and watch over your boyfriend, so you can grab some dinner.

The canteen is open, and you can meet some of the others, too."

Amy wanted to correct him about her relationship with Lynch, but the ruse had worked to allow him to stay there, so she wasn't about to ruin that. She didn't want to think about what kind of care Lynch might receive should Tillson insist that he be taken elsewhere. She knew that she could give him the attention required to get him back on his feet quickly.

"I, uh, well, okay. Thanks. He's . . ." Amy pointed to the room that doubled as guest room and study. "Oh. I guess you already know he's in there."

Tillson smiled and nodded. "Yes. All of our quarters are pretty much the same."

She looked at Lynch as they entered the room. He still hadn't moved an inch on the futon, but his breathing remained even. She took his wrist and timed his pulse. He was still tachycardic, but his heart rate had decreased. That was a good sign. She inspected the first bag of fluid. Her estimate of having about an hour remaining didn't change.

"You don't have to watch him. I have some snack foods here. I'll be okay."

"Nonsense. I might not be a primary care doctor, but I can at least babysit while you get a good meal and he continues getting juiced up." He smiled.

Amy hesitated. "Okay, I guess. I just hate to leave him. You know, if he wakes up and I'm not here. That sort of thing."

"Go. Get some dinner. Meet some of the other personnel. I can handle this."

*　*　*

Tillson watched as Amy wandered toward the canteen. Even the condemned deserved a good final meal. He could understand her hesitancy. After all, a clinician he was not. But then, he didn't have to be. A day or two more and he could give up the masquerade. Neither of them would be his problem any further.

He stood next to the futon and gazed down at the man. Amy's boyfriend. Not much there to consider, thanks to the drugs in the saline. Still, he wondered what he was like and what she saw in him.

He took the book he had brought with him and retired to the main room. He had enough serious study and technical reading throughout the day. He enjoyed his evenings as a time dedicated to fiction and light reading, when not involved in some form of entertainment at the dining hall. He settled into one of the chairs and resumed where he had left off the previous day.

He'd only read a page or two when his cell phone rang. He groaned as he saw the number that came up on his screen.

"This is Doctor Tillson."

"I expected no one else. The woman is there. Yes?"

"Yes, she is here."

"Good, you bring her to school tomorrow afternoon. My client expect her arrive there at that time."

"I will do my best."

"Not good enough! She *will* be there or else."

"She is not here alone." He went on to explain the sequence of events that had occurred that day. "The boyfriend can be dealt with, but she must still be here when the man with her luggage comes. If he does not see her, he will get suspicious. And since the embassy now knows she is here, we must avoid such suspicions."

There was silence on the other end. Tillson began to get nervous. Had he overstepped his bounds?

"You say this boyfriend work for new American president?"

"Yes, and the woman knows the new American president, too." Tillson didn't know that for a fact but extrapolated that tidbit from what he had been told by the embassy staffer. "It will be bad enough for Cambodia-U.S. relations when they disappear without explanation. If it is discovered that Tep Rithisak had a hand in it, even the most powerful of friends will be of no help."

Okay, yes, he was playing his hand more like a sleight of hand entertainer than a pro poker competitor. But, sometimes, with nothing in your hand to play, smoke and mirrors were needed, not a good bluff.

"I will inform Duong Chea. But do not delay long."

"Amy! Amy! Come, come. I show you how to get food."

She saw Darany waving from across the room as he stood from the table where he'd been sitting with others. He rushed over to her and pointed for her to follow.

"This way. Is different from lunch. Not so much sandwich and salad bar. Start here."

She had expected the food service to be cafeteria-style as at lunch, but the starting point held no trays, dinnerware, or cutlery. Instead, Darany gave her a tablet device.

"This list tonight menu. You choose by tap-tap on screen. You want to see what food look like, you go over here."

He led her to where the lunchtime sandwich bar had been, but now the food choices appeared behind the glass windows looking into the kitchen. Darany tapped on the glass and motioned for the workers within the enclosure to approach.

"These the cook. Tall man in back is chef. He too busy to meet you. Maybe later."

He started to talk to them but she only understood when her name was mentioned. Each of the three cooks in turn smiled and made *som pas* to her. She returned the gesture to each.

"You look at food. You like what you see, you tap-tap on tablet to pick. When you done, you go over here for drink. As I say at lunch, all ice, all water is safe here, but not in quarters."

He led her to the beverage bar, but in addition to the water, teas, coffee, and sodas she had as selections at lunch, she now found a selection of beers, wine, and top-shelf liquors as well. Happy hour was self-serve.

"You leave tablet here. The cook bring you food and collect tablet for other to use."

"*Aw-koon*, Darany. I'll go back to order my food. May I join you and your friends?"

"Yes, please, Amy. They look forward to meet you."

Amy liked this system, a hybrid of cafeteria and full-service restaurant. Tillson had told her that their food service was one of the premiere benefits of working there. Lunch had been good, but from the aromas wafting from the back, as well as the food's delicious appearance, she suspected dinner would prove him right by being exceptional.

At the beverage bar she decided to stick with a soft drink. After embarrassing herself in front of Richard a few years back, when they started dating, she had resolved to restrict her wine imbibing to special occasions. Besides, she had to care for Lynch. She carried her glass to the table where Darany sat and faced a barrage of names and *som pas* from around the table. The levels of English literacy varied, so Darany did his best to interpret.

The food arrived and exceeded her expectations. The chicken was perfectly cooked, the lemon sauce, sublime, and the steamed vegetables had just the right level of a*l dente*. The accompanying French bread could rival that of her favorite restaurant back home, *La Bonne Bouche* in St. Louis.

She thought about the last time she'd been there. It had been with Lynch, not Richard. Not even with her dad. Lynch. And he had indeed come halfway around the world for her. And it had been a surprise, despite the ominous message he had brought with him. In that moment she felt much loved. Tears welled up in her eyes, but she quickly wiped them away.

The meal was so good that halfway through, she excused herself, arose from the table, and went to the window overlooking the kitchen. She tapped on it, and when all three cooks looked her way, she said "*Aw-koon*, delicious." As if in Italy, she kissed the fingertips of her right hand and flipped them away from her mouth. Then, realizing cooks in Cambodia might not know that sign, she held up both thumbs. The cooks laughed and said something she couldn't understand, probably that they thought she was crazy.

She returned to the table and finished eating. The techs were talking in Khmer. It was at this point that she noticed the American techs seemed to sit off by themselves. Doctor Gilroy sat by himself.

"Darany, can I ask a question?"

"Yes, Amy."

"Do the American technicians ever join you for meals, or the doctors?"

"Only when want to talk business. You are first to join us just to be social. For that, my friend say they really like you. Also, you show thanks to cook. You quickly become favorite." He laughed. "Careful, they fatten you up if favorite." He laughed again.

She thought about the situation. Was it simply having common backgrounds and interests that led to the division, or was there implied racism involved? She held to her Christian tenets of showing respect to all men, as well as giving thanks where thanks was due. Maybe she was there to set an example.

"So, how is mister boyfriend?"

"Doctor Tillson agreed to watch over him while I eat."

Darany's brow rose in apparent surprise.

"Does that surprise you? What is Tillson like?

Darany fidgeted in his seat. He clearly seemed uncertain as to how to answer her.

"Yes, I am surprise. He is not most friendly man. Very strict. By book, I think is term. But he have funny side."

"A funny side?" Amy had had minimal contact with the man so far, but a humorous side had not been evident.

"Not funny, ha ha. Funny like, I don't know word, different, maybe strange."

"We have a word, quirky. It can mean peculiar or strange behavior or mannerisms."

"I not know word peculiar, but strange, yes, that word fit. For example, he name all macaques. The vet, he simply assign number to test animals. Tillson give name, like Kaliyanei and Kunthea, as well as number. He give me blood sample from both, say he euthanize them. I do not understand because vet is usual one to euthanize, so I just do what he say and run tests for him."

Amy thought using names unusual for a lab that did only animal testing. On the other hand, if the man was testing on children as they feared, names might be used. But assigning numbers, too? There would be labels that wouldn't match up with those used by the veterinary resources, should an audit take place. Could this be an unexpected paper trail of evidence? However, she almost blanched at the word 'euthanize.' Had two children died in his care? Certainly, the man wouldn't euthanize children, would he? The idea left her with a queasy stomach.

"So, again, how is mister boyfriend?"

Yes, just what is going on with Lynch? she wondered. "His name is Lynch Cully, and I believe he's getting better. His heart rate is down and his skin is beginning to show that his body fluids are improving. But he isn't waking up. In fact, he hasn't moved an inch on that bed. He doesn't even flinch when I pinch his skin."

"What is flinch?"

"Oh, sorry. It's like a little jerk." She demonstrated with her arm.

She noticed a slight frown cross Darany's face. "Like being anesthetized? Did I say that right?"

"Yes, you did, and yes, like he was anesthetized."

The frown deepened. "After you go back, I go check something. I hope I am wrong."

CHAPTER THIRTY-NINE

"*Lok* Abdullah, we have a choice to make."

Abdi looked at Oudom Khay as if the man had just told him that water is wet. Of course, they had a choice. His patience waned. The woman was at hand.

"My contacts say the police checkpoints will continue for at least a few days. We can stay put, out of sight, until they end. Or we can try to move past them in the dark. I think it best to avoid them by staying here. The woman will not be leaving."

Abdi refrained from scowling at the man. It would do no good. Oudom thought only of his own hide. He did not wish to be caught.

Nor did Abdi when it came down to reality. His desire was to seek his revenge, leave the country, and flee to Somalia where his influence remained great. To get caught in Cambodia would result in prison at best, the death penalty at worst. Perhaps the right payments to the right people would change that to deportation to Somalia. Of one thing he could be sure, getting caught would not lead to his return to the U.S. to face murder charges. Cambodia had no extradition treaties with the U.S.

His biggest fear in getting caught was that it might happen *before* he had subjugated that woman and sold her into sexual slavery. That had been his *raison d'être* for coming into Cambodia. Some might think him blinded by a need for revenge. He preferred to think of it as being focused and goal oriented. Plus, the sale of a woman like her into the slave market would more than make up his costs for this entire operation.

"No, the woman awaits judgment. You will see, I will blend into the night as we approach any police."

He stood and donned his dark hoodie.

"Starting now. I will meet you by the bridge over the river."

With that he walked off into the dark. If Oudom got caught now, it would be for his own wrongdoings. And if that were to happen, money talks. Abdi would still make his way back to the school and the revenge he was due.

Amy rushed through the remainder of her meal and picked up a plate of tiramisu for a late evening snack. She hurried back to her cottage, but upon arriving, stopped and regained her composure. She had to act normally, even though the alarm in Darany's voice produced a torrent of anxiety about Lynch's well-being. If Tillson was capable of using children as vaccine test subjects, would he see Lynch as a possible threat?

She tapped on her door as she proceeded to open it. The doctor looked up from the chair where she found him sitting and reading. He stood to meet her.

"How was dinner?"

"You certainly didn't exaggerate when you said the meals were first-class. It was delicious and I probably ate too much. I even brought home a piece of tiramisu for later. I didn't expect to come to Cambodia and gain weight. I'll need to watch myself." She glanced toward the side room. "How is our patient?"

"Snoring a little while ago. I think he'll be much better after a second bag of saline. He's been moving around a little on the bed for the past 15 minutes or so."

Amy smiled, and hoped he didn't see it as being as fake as she felt it to be. "Well, thank you, Doctor Tillson. I'll take over from here and let you get some dinner now."

The man nodded. "I will do that. If you need anything, I won't be long at the canteen. I'll be in my quarters after that. Oh, and when we're not around the other staff members, please call me Walt. No need for formality outside the lab itself."

Amy caught herself taking a deep breath and stopped. In normal circumstances, such a request would be normal among co-workers. With what she knew of his past, however, she saw that as his opening salvo to gain familiarity.

"Thank you, Walt. I'll see you in the morning."

She watched him leave and locked her door behind him. She walked into the study and saw that Lynch's position *had* changed, but it didn't look natural. He looked as if someone else had posed him. The next thing she noticed was that his fluids were almost gone. She gathered up the second bag of saline and examined it. Darany's comment about anesthesia had made her wonder. Had Lynch been drugged? She could find no evidence of the bag being tampered.

As the drip stopped, she took down the empty bag and switched it out with the new one. She adjusted the flow to continue through the night, and hoped she would find Lynch awake by morning.

She sat down next to him on the futon and took his hand. This man in her care had shown her more love over the past few years than she deserved. Even after she had chosen someone else, he watched out for her and made her happiness a priority over his own. He had said that he'd changed, and she'd ignored him. With her father's and Richard's deaths, he'd been there for her. And now, with the potential danger she faced from that Somali terrorist, he had flown around the world to protect her.

Tears welled up in her eyes as she recalled her last conversation with her dad. He had asked her if she was truly "over" Lynch and wanting to move on. Was she? Maybe not. She leaned over and kissed him on the cheek.

He responded with a snort and brief apneic spell. She watched and listened. His breathing wasn't the even, regular respirations she had noted throughout the afternoon. His uneven breaths were interspersed with more apneic periods. She took his hand again and checked his pulse at the wrist. Bradycardic? His heart rate shouldn't be so slow if he's dehydrated.

She felt an edge of panic ruffle her. What could she do? Maybe she could reach Reggie. He would know how to handle a medical emergency. But they were so far away from any of the acute care hospitals Cambodia had to offer.

Too far away?

A knock at her door caught her attention. She rushed to find Darany standing there.

"Darany, something's wrong. Lynch shouldn't be like he is. He should be getting better with the fluids, not worse."

The man's countenance was one of serious concern. He hurried to Lynch's side and knelt next to the bed. Amy watched as he, too, checked Lynch's pulse and noted his breathing pattern. He opened Lynch's eyelids and looked at his pupils. Darany's appearance of concern became one of anger.

"I go to check IV supply and medicines. Two bags of saline were used, and they are both here. But I also find supply of midazolam and ketamine does not match record. Vet track both when use on macaques. I find no record of use."

Midazolam and ketamine? Amy knew both were used for sedation, but not for long term. Midazolam was used in intermittent doses, not in an IV drip. Ketamine could be used in a drip, but only in small bags—250 to 500 milliliter bags—for short periods, not in a full liter bag meant for rehydration over hours. The bradycardia. The hypersomnia. The apnea. All could be effects of the drugs, particularly in combination.

"Amy, his low heart rate, sleeping all the time and not moving, and time when breathing stop, all could be from drug."

Darany had just confirmed her diagnosis.

"Doctor Tillson gave me the first bag of saline, as well as this one I just now plugged into Lynch's IV line. What if?"

Darany shook his head. "I work with doctor for over year. I do not see him able to do such a thing. Maybe someone else."

Amy wanted to straighten out Darany about his boss but could not afford to blow her cover. She liked Darany, but she did not know where his allegiance lay.

"I go get new bag of fluid, but must be careful not to be notice. Also, people out and about in cooler evening hour. I think it best I not be seen entering your cottage. I will put new bag outside your door. Check for it in 20, 30 minute."

"What do you mean, it is best that you not be seen in my cottage?"

Darany sighed. "Is one thing that you will eat with us and be friend with Khmer. But others here not like that. For me to be seen entering your cottage is possible big-time problem. Fraternization, I think is right word. I take extra precaution this time. Not good to take risk second time."

So, her concern about an undercurrent of racism at the lab was real. In this day and age, especially among highly educated technicians and scientists, she found that dismaying. She determined that she would set a better example.

He started for the door, but she stopped him. She went to her desk, collected some of the journal articles and notes she had reviewed over the course of the afternoon, and handed them to him.

"Now, if anyone sees you leave and asks why you were here, you can tell them I called you to collect this paperwork for me. You can put them in my office in the morning."

"Thank you, Amy, for being friend, showing respect."

"No, thank you, Darany, for helping me. I will look for that bag of fluids in a little while."

Darany looked in all directions before leaving her cottage and ran toward the main building. He did not look back, and Amy shut the door after glancing about the area herself. The coast seemed clear.

But now she faced a dilemma. She had no way to prove that Lynch had been drugged. Did she stop the fluids and allow some time for the drugs to clear his system? If he began to wake up, would that prove he'd been drugged? Or just that the fluids had finally benefited him? But if his current condition was related to dehydration, he still required the fluids. Should she continue the current flow of saline?

Darany said he'd deliver the saline within half an hour. She decided to keep the fluids going. Assuming the drugs to be present in the saline, another 30 minutes under the influence of midazolam, ketamine, or maybe both, might not be disastrous. She would keep a close eye on him.

Tillson had prepared two additional syringes, one to bolster the sedation of Amy's boyfriend should he start to arouse and the other with a lethal dose of morphine for the time when he wished to guarantee that he never aroused. The timing was not yet right for the latter to be used. He first had to deliver Amy to Tep Rithisak at the school and then return to clean up the loose end that was her friend.

He hadn't informed Amy that he planned to take dinner in his quarters. One of the cooks had delivered it to him shortly after he called the kitchen to request it. He savored it, eating in his front room rather than the kitchenette, with the lights dimmed so he could watch the nurse's dwelling.

As he sipped his wine, he felt surprise to see Darany approach her door and more so when she allowed him inside. He frowned upon fraternization but recognized that he had not discussed such with her. What was the point, when she would not be around to make it an issue?

The tech left the building just minutes later. Tillson's curiosity was piqued. He wanted to let it go, knowing what the next day or so had in store, but something about the man's visit bothered him. Why would he have gone there? He had a pile of papers in his hands upon leaving. What was that about?

Instead of retiring to a better-lit area to read, Tillson continued to sit in the dark near the front window. He saw a few techs and the facility's vet walking outside, as they often did in the cooler evening temperatures. Gradually, they disappeared into their quarters or back into the canteen for the evening's diversions. He thought for a moment about the entertainment schedule. Was it some recently-released, first-run superhero movie or casino night for tonight's recreation?

With the grounds appearing empty, he stood and prepared to move to his reading chair, but a figure emerging from the nearby door to the labs caught his attention. The person moved hesitantly at first and then made a beeline to Amy's dwelling. Was it Darany again? In the dark of night, he could not be sure.

However, as the individual neared Amy's door, he

recognized the gait and silhouette as that of his lead tech. His hands held what appeared to be a bag of IV fluids. Had the nurse become suspicious? Had she called Darany for a fresh bag of saline? That would be the logical way to test her suspicions.

Darany left the item outside her door and sped away toward his own quarters. Tillson realized he had but a brief window of opportunity to "correct" the situation.

He jumped up from his chair and grabbed the syringe for sedation. He flipped out the lights in his main room so no light would appear from his door, opened the door, and slipped into the dark. He headed for Amy's door, prepared to jump into the shadows at the first hint of her opening the door.

So far, so good. He took ahold of the bag and fingered the syringe in his pocket.

"Hey, Walt."

Startled, he looked up to see Eric Gilroy walking to his own dwelling next door.

"I heard about the boyfriend. How's he doing?"

Tillson placed the bag of saline back where he'd found it. He then took several steps toward his colleague.

"Still out of it at dinnertime. Just leaving another bag of fluids for him."

"Well, I hope he's better by morning, as I guess you do, too. I know you're not fond of visitors on the grounds."

"That I'm not. Too many risks around here. I hate being liable should anything go wrong."

Gilroy laughed. "I hear you. Glad that's on your shoulders, not mine."

"Gee, thanks. I'll keep that in mind next time you request a visit from your daughter." He, too, laughed, trying to make it seem like a joke. The two did have a friendly rivalry going, much like fans of two competing sports teams. But sometimes their jests took on a serious edge to them.

He watched Gilroy enter his quarters and turned back to retrieve the saline and complete his task. The bag was gone.

CHAPTER FORTY

"Where's the bathroom? I *really* have to pee!"

Amy startled awake at the sound of Lynch's voice and jumped forward in the chair at the desk where she'd fallen asleep. At the same time, her heart leapt in joy at hearing his voice again. She had been so worried.

"Lynch! Finally, you're awake. I—"

"Where's the bathroom? We might need a mop if I don't get there ASAP."

Amy pointed out the door. "Across the main room, just off the main bedroom."

Holding his IV bag in one hand, he scurried out the door. Amy followed him as far as the main room, where she debated making a cup of coffee, getting a glass of juice from the bottle in the fridge, or settling for bottled water, also in the refrigerator. She opened the appliance's door to see that she only had three bottles of water left—liquids that Lynch might need. Coffee would consume one of those, as would drinking the water plain, so she opted for a glass of juice. After pouring it, she glanced at her phone to see that it was four a.m.

Moments later, she heard the flush of the toilet. Lynch

emerged into the main room and sat down on the nearest chair. He appeared so much better, but still not his usual self. Of course, any color at all in his face was 50 shades better than the ghostly pale he had exhibited 12 hours earlier.

"Are you thirsty? I have bottled water and commercial OJ. I'll need to stock up the fridge later."

He gave her a 'are you kidding?' kind of stare. "I just peed enough to float the Queen Mary, and you ask if I'm thirsty? Not really, but my mouth tastes like the Gobi Desert, and my throat is just as parched. So, how about a bottle of water?"

She retrieved one and walked it over to him.

"You had me worried. You weren't moving at all. You didn't even flinch when I started the IV, and then your breathing and heart rate started getting all weird, like, the opposite of what I expected."

The previous evening, she had thought that his waking up would settle her quandary about his being drugged or only dehydrated. Four a.m. meant he had received the saline supplied by Darany for approximately the previous six hours. Now he was awake. Was it due to the fluids only? Or if drugs had been present, had they finally worn off? She couldn't recall details about the pharmacology of midazolam and ketamine, but in her experience a typical IV bolus of midazolam would clear his system within an hour or two. A thought at the back of her mind told her that six hours was not out of the question, though. She had less experience with ketamine, but seemed to recall that its duration was much shorter than that of midazolam. Of course, that assumed the normal administration of both drugs. She had no idea how receiving them in an IV drip might affect the body's clearance of them.

"It was strange for me, too. I seemed to be half awake at times. Totally out of it at others. I even dreamed someone kissed me on the cheek at some point."

Amy felt a blush come to her cheeks and hoped he didn't notice. Not that she regretted doing so, she simply wasn't ready to confront her feelings about him, or for him, or whatever. She didn't know what she felt, and she sure wasn't ready to talk with him about *that*.

The dilemma hadn't left, however. Fluids or drugs? Did she accuse Tillson of drugging him despite having no firsthand knowledge of such, no proof? No, she would be with Lynch throughout the day and could watch him, and his interactions with Tillson, closely.

Lynch unscrewed the top of the water bottle and took a cautious sip.

"Yeah. Good. Take it slow. Just a sip, let it settle, and then another."

He nodded. "Thank you, doctor. I do recall the drill." He took a second sip and followed that with a deep breath and closing his eyes. "Wow. Yep, I still need to take it slow. You wouldn't happen to have any wonder drug for nausea, would you?"

Amy shook her head. "Sorry, I don't, but I can ask later. Why don't you go lie down again, take it easy."

He nodded. "Yep. I think I will. What about this IV? Can I get rid of it?"

She shook her head. "I think we should keep it in for

now. Maybe if you have to pee again soon, we can get rid of it. As long as you're keeping oral fluids down. Go lie down, and I'll slow down the rate. I'll ask Darany for another bag, though, just in case. Also, I don't know if whatever is getting you down might relapse. I should have asked Reggie. I'd hate to have you getting better, remove the IV, and then have you get worse again."

"You and me both."

Amy followed Lynch into her study and watched as he stretched back out on the futon. He sat up long enough to take another sip of water and lay down again.

"You know, this futon is actually pretty comfortable."

"Good," said Amy as she adjusted the rate of flow for his fluids. "Rest up. I'll be in the other bedroom. I want to see if I can get another hour or so of sleep. Falling asleep in that chair didn't really cut it for me, and now that I know you're improving, I can sleep better."

He grinned. "See, you *do* care."

The tease she remembered was back in his voice. She didn't reply, but she found herself acknowledging his comment in her mind. Yes, she really did care. But how much, and in what way? Maybe father really did know best.

Tillson readied himself for the day . . . as best he could. He wanted a shot of something, anything, to calm his nerves. The deaths of test subjects were easy to compartmentalize, much like those of the macaques he sometimes euthanized. He only dealt with these deaths from a distance, and they weren't the healthiest of subjects to begin with. Their deaths, while unfortunate, were not his direct doing.

But today? Or maybe tomorrow, if circumstances forced a delay, death would be upon his doorstep. Maybe he could get one of Rithisak's thugs to do the dirty work. He hadn't signed up for murder, but survival was a masterful motivator.

Anticipation contributed to his anxiety. He wanted this situation behind him. If forced into a 24-hour delay, he wondered if he could cope.

His mind rushed from one problem to the next. The recent scrutiny by Jared Miller had started his troubles. Then came Tep Rithisak's "request" to deliver the nurse, forcing him to hire her against his better judgment. And on her very first day, a sick boyfriend appeared. What were the odds that this was all coincidence?

The man's presence in the compound had complicated his problem in so many ways, he wanted to crawl back into bed and pretend the day hadn't started yet. Delivering the nurse into the hands of Rithisak and not knowing her fate was easy to place into its own neat little box. The boyfriend's presence, however, required actions that Tillson wished he could avoid. Add to that his being a friend of the incoming president and the involvement of the embassy, Tillson couldn't begin to count the potential cost. Even the other friend of Amy's, the man bringing her luggage, posed as a major unknown. Who was he really?

He paced as he considered the options set before him, only to realize he had no options. He certainly had no out. He'd passed the clichéd "point of no return" long ago. He also held no delusion that this would be a one-and-done deal. Rithisak, not him, would hold all the bargaining chips.

He tried to force the day ahead out of his mind.

The canteen opened for breakfast in 10 minutes, and he liked being among the first there. To be late might be noticed as a break in his routine. Yet, he needed to stop next door and see how "their" patient fared.

He rushed to finish dressing, collected the papers he needed to take to his office, and headed out the door. A short walk later, he knocked on Amy's door.

"Just a minute!"

He imagined her half-dressed and hurrying to make herself presentable. He realized that his past problems facing sexual harassment allegations were minuscule compared to the challenge he faced that day.

A couple of minutes later, Amy unlocked and opened the door. "Doctor Tillson, um, Walt. Good morning."

"I'm heading to the canteen for breakfast, but wanted to stop in and check on your friend. How's he doing?"

He suspected that the man had improved. After all, the chance was better than good that the medications Tillson had injected into the two bags of saline had been discontinued. But had she suspected him of tampering with the bags? He would likely have no answer to that nagging question.

"He finally woke up early this morning and feels much better. Not back to normal, but better. He still has nausea, and I was wondering if the lab had any anti-emetics to ease that."

"You know, I think we do, but I'd have to check. I've not had any need for such personally."

"Oh, by the way, I hope this isn't an issue. I had Darany pick up some papers and bring me another bag of saline. I fumbled the second bag you gave me and accidentally stepped on it and broke it open. Sorry."

A sense of relief flooded through him. He hadn't been suspected after all.

"Not a problem. I'm glad he's feeling better. Might we see you at breakfast then?"

"Um, maybe. I guess that will depend on how he's doing now. I haven't checked on him this morning. But if you don't mind, could I work from here again today?"

"I, uh . . . I don't see any problem with that."

How could he say no without it seeming out of place? He wanted to head back to his quarters for antacids. What else could happen to complicate his day?

One of the things Amy thought she excelled at was reading people. And when Tillson appeared at her door, the chapter on anxiety opened up in large print. In considering why he might be anxious, she decided to test her observation by lying about the second bag of saline. She reasoned that if his anxiety existed out of fear of it being discovered that he had tampered with the fluids, her ruse might put him at ease.

But it hadn't, and she felt more confusion. Maybe *she* was the paranoid one.

She saw no point in telling Lynch of her suspicions about Tillson. That's all they were, suspicions. No proof. Lynch needed to focus on healing. Plus, she would be around to keep an eye on things.

"So, that's the guy, eh?"

She again startled at his voice from behind her. She turned to face him.

"Quit doing that."

"Quit doing what?"

"Startling me, that's what."

She took a deep breath and calmed herself. She, too, felt anxious and hoped Tillson was blind to that fact. Of course, she had a plausible explanation, should she be asked. She had started a new job, with expectations that were new to her. She saw no need to mention that she was actually there to investigate Tillson and look for missing children.

"So, hey, can we get rid of this IV now?"

"Have you peed again?"

"No."

"Are you still nauseated?"

"Yeah, I guess. A little."

At least he was being honest with her. That was another sign of change. The "old" Lynch, in his bravado, would have claimed being back to his 100% self.

"Then, no. Let's keep the IV a while longer, just to be sure. Since you're up and about, I'm going to go to the canteen to grab some breakfast and see if Darany can get me another bag of fluids. You know, just in case. I'll pick up some apple juice and cereal for you. We'll see how you handle that."

He waggled his head. "So, I guess that means a couple of fried eggs, bacon, hash browns, and coffee are out of the question."

She was about to reply when she saw his smirk. He knew the drill.

"I'll be back."

"Hey, I need to write some things down, make a few notes. I found some paper in your study but nothing to write with."

Without a second thought, she slipped the pen from her shirt pocket and handed it to him.

"Here. I'll be back in a bit."

CHAPTER FORTY-ONE

Oudom reflected upon their departure from Kampong Thom. When Abdi left the house and disappeared into the night, he had expected he might never see the man again. That had been a pleasant thought, although one that he tempered with the reality that he had never been a lucky one. He had also considered simply abandoning the man and letting him go it alone. Of course, that thought was short-lived. He would have to face Tep Rithisak for such an action.

Crossing through the checkpoint took little time. A single vehicle preceded him, and while it was a truck loaded with various home goods—pots, pans, water containers, and the like, the police spent little time searching it. From the laughter he heard, it sounded as if the policemen and the driver knew each other. The search of his own car took as much time, even though it was clearly empty save for Oudom.

As he neared the bridge where National Highway 6 crossed the Stung Sen a hooded figure appeared by the side of the road. Oudom had to admit that had Abdi not revealed himself, he would never have seen him. Fortunately, other traffic was nearly nonexistent due to the late hour.

They repeated the scene at a second checkpoint west of the city, where the national highway veered northwest toward Siem Reap and Highway 62 headed due north. Again, the man slipped into the night, and Oudom could not discern him, even knowing the direction the man took. Then, half a mile past the police barrier, the man appeared at the roadside waiting for Oudom.

The remainder of the trip had been uneventful, although they had stopped at a safe house in Battambang for a brief rest and nourishment. As soon as the sun rose over the horizon, Abdi had insisted they resume their travels.

Now, two hours later, Oudom made the turn south onto road 53B and smiled. The proverbial light at the end of the tunnel shone brightly ahead of him. Soon, this Abdullah Said Abdi, this arrogant African, would be his responsibility no more.

Amy sat in her main room reading another study while allowing Lynch to sleep some more in the other room. He had been able to hold down the cereal and juice, but at the expense of a roiling gut that did its best to repel the onslaught of food entering its domain. As he neared the end of the second bag of saline, he still hadn't urinated again. He gave no argument when she plugged in the third bag.

Her phone rang—Tillson.

"Yes, sir. What's up?"

"Just thought you'd want to know that your luggage is here." He began to whisper. "Look, I don't know if this guy is another boyfriend or what. So, why don't you come up here to talk with him."

She rolled her eyes. "No, Walt, he's just a friend. But Lynch is sleeping again, so rather than wake him up with a visitor here, I'll be there in a minute."

Amy set aside her reading, stood, and walked to the doorway of the study. Lynch appeared sound asleep, which was good. He would heal faster with rest. She headed out the door and hurried to the back door of the lab building. Within a few minutes of the call, she walked into the reception area to find Tillson and Felix, along with the bags she had left in the care of Pastor Jim.

"Felix, thank you so much. You've really gone above the call to get these for me."

She walked up to him and gave him a hug.

"No problem. Happy to help. Do you want me to take these to your quarters?"

Amy pondered the question. Surely, he knew that Lynch was here. That was a given. Reggie had headed back to the guest house to coordinate support with the Smiths and Felix. But had Tillson said anything? Unless he had, Felix shouldn't know anything about Lynch.

"Thanks, but I can get it. I had a surprise visit from a friend, but he's a little under the weather. I don't want to disturb him."

"Oh. Right. Doctor Tillson said your boyfriend from the States had shown up unannounced. Made the mistake of ingesting some water. I hope he's okay."

"He's on the mend. I think by evening he'll be back on his feet. Thanks. I look forward to introducing him to you at some point. Are you going to be in the area for much longer?"

"A few more days, probably. Visiting those friends I told you about in Pursat. Maybe we can get you there for dinner before I leave. I know you'd like them."

Amy relished the idea of dinner with them all. She could brief them on her current situation, and with some luck, she might even convince Lynch to stay with them. She was convinced that his presence at the lab hindered her ability to dig deeper into those test subjects that Darany said had names, as well as numbers.

She noted that Tillson had stepped just outside the reception area to talk on his phone. Yet, he remained in earshot, and she remained on alert regarding what she could say.

"I'm sure I would. We'll play it by ear. Thanks again for playing courier. I really appreciate it. Let's link up again when I get some time off. You can show us some of the sights in Cambodia."

"We'll plan on it. You have my number, right?"

Amy nodded.

"Then I'll be off. Looking forward to hearing from you again."

With that, Felix gave her an exasperated look and exited the building. She watched as he walked to his Land Rover without a glance back. She wished she could have communicated more freely with him.

As his vehicle pulled away and headed toward the main gate, she heard Tillson behind her.

"Why don't we put your things in my car? We can—" His phone interrupted.

"This is Doctor Tillson. Um, yes, Chef . . . What

happened? . . ."

He stepped away again, and Amy could only hear bits and pieces of his end of the conversation. A moment later he returned.

"Amy, I could use your help. Our chef's wife has not been well for the last few months. Evidently, she passed out, fell, and cut her arm on some broken glass. Could you ask Darany for our first aid kit and then could you join me at my car? I'll put your luggage in the back while you get it."

"Uh, sure. Okay. I'll track down Darany and meet you there."

She could hear the doctor dealing with her large suitcase as she left the area. A minute later, she found Darany and explained the situation. He gave her a puzzled look as he retrieved and handed her a hard-shelled aid kit the size of a carry-on bag. She had seen these before. The commercially-produced kit could handle most situations short of a major medical event such as a heart attack or major trauma. A few stitches, if needed, would be no problem.

She found Tillson in his car, the AC already cooling the interior. A minute later, they headed down the drive toward the main road.

"Doesn't the chef live on the grounds?"

Tillson shook his head. "We, uh, only have room for the main scientific and medical staff. The others live in Krakor, Pursat, or in the countryside around the lab. He, uh, lives in a home just minutes from here."

Despite the air conditioning, the man continued to sweat profusely. His anxiety level seemed off the charts.

What was going on?

Just a short distance from the CIC drive's merge with the main road, he turned to the east. Just past a banana grove Amy saw the tall fence and several buildings. Her anxiety now matched his.

As they pulled up in front of the sole two-story building, she saw another car. From it a figure emerged, a male. The man turned toward them and she blanched as she recognized the dark, scarred face of the man who stood there waiting for her—Abdullah Said Abdi.

She patted her breast pocket to find her pen. Nada. She had failed to take it back from Lynch.

CHAPTER FORTY-TWO

Amy's words echoed through Tillson's mind as he drove back to the compound.

"How could you do this?"

"You're supposed to be a man of medicine, helping people!"

"You might as well kill me yourself!"

Her tears had had no effect on him. He had seen many women shedding tears over what they alleged he had done to them. *Had* done to them, if he was forced to admit it.

You might as well kill me yourself! Those words swirled through his head. He had indeed left her to the wiles of a Somali terrorist, out for her blood for reasons he did not even know. He tried to shut her screams from his mind because they added to the difficulty of the task immediately before him.

He entered the compound and drove directly to his quarters. Inside, he retrieved the syringe he had prepared for this moment. He knew that the boyfriend—he refused to acknowledge his name because it humanized him—might be awake, but now he had a ploy. Amy had asked about an anti-emetic for the man's nausea. In his hand he held the ultimate anti-emetic.

He walked as casually as he could to Amy's quarters, slid open the front door, and slipped into the main room. He stopped and listened. Nothing. He walked to the doorway of the study and saw the man sleeping on the futon. He eased up to the bedside, trying not to alert the man, and picked up the IV line with his left hand. As he slid the needle into the injection port, the man's eyes opened in surprise.

"For the nausea." Tillson's tone reflected a sense of guilt as he pushed the morphine into the line.

The man's hand reached up to stop him. "I don't need anything . . ."

The hand moved from Tillson toward the IV catheter inserted into a vein in the other arm, trying to pull it out. But the man fumbled. He couldn't coordinate his movement to remove the IV. A moment later, the hand dropped to the bed, and the man's breathing slowed.

Tillson did not wait to confirm his "kill." He couldn't stand there and watch the man die by his hand. The man had done nothing to him. His only mistake was being in the wrong place at the wrong time.

He rushed to his own quarters to place a call. Rithisak's men, previously hired to guard the front gate at the crime lord's "request," would soon come to remove the body, luggage, and all traces of both people. There would be no need for a burial. The jungle would recycle the body, from dust back to dust.

"So, this is the woman who shamed me before my

people."

Abdi circled around her, eyeing her from head to toe. He held no weapon, but she had no chance of escape. A small circle of men corralled them both to a small plot of hard-packed dirt. Any attempt by her to run would result in one or more of them stopping her.

The car from which he had emerged sat there, running. If only she could get to it. But then it stopped, and a Cambodian man exited from the driver's seat. He stood there, leaning against the car, watching them over its roof. That option had disappeared.

"I didn't shame you. You did that all on your own, and then you murdered my father, shooting him through a window because you're a coward."

Her defiance surprised them both. A surge of boldness rose up within her. As the man returned to a spot in front of her, she spat at him. And, at the moment he looked down at the spittle on his chest, she lunged for him. She had a height advantage on him, maybe even the weight advantage, but she didn't have his strength . . . or half a dozen men to defend him.

Abdi pushed her away with relevant ease and with a flick of his wrist, commanded the men to take her.

"Take her away. The auction will be soon, at noon."

The Cambodian man by the car translated his statements into Khmer, and the men responded.

"Auction?" The comment puzzled Amy.

Abdi glared at her. "You think I kill you? Ha! Slow death maybe." He laughed. "They tell me Siem Reap is top three for sex vacation. Man, woman, boy, girl. All desire fulfilled.

American woman like you bring good price. I see you at auction."

With that Abdi strolled away toward the two-story building.

Two men held Amy by the arms and led her to one of the smaller buildings nearby. Two other men followed. She tried to look for a way out, but saw none. And then the reality of Abdi's plan for her settled in. She had experienced but a taste of it when she had been kidnapped by Darko Komarčić for his personal harem in St. Louis. The reality of sex trafficking in Cambodia was far worse, involving drugs, rape, violence, and more. His mention of a slow death rang true.

CHAPTER FORTY-THREE

Upon entering the door of the building, the scent of urine and feces assaulted Amy's senses. A few bare bulbs provided scant light to the long hallway, and a second door could be seen at the other end. As her eyes adjusted to the gloom, she saw a dozen or so doorways leading to rooms on both sides of the hall. She heard occasional grunts and groans coming from those rooms. Music from a radio farther down the hall added to the cacophony.

The men ushered Amy into a windowless room the size of a large walk-in closet at home. A sole light bulb barely illuminated the space. She noted six decrepit sleeping pads on the filthy floor and two five-gallon buckets in separate corners of the room. The stench of human waste from those buckets made her want to vomit. The men left her there and departed.

After the men were gone from sight, Amy rushed to the doorway, as much for fresher air than anything. There was no door. The men had retreated to the doorway where they had entered the building. The doorway at the far end appeared open and empty.

With as much stealth as she could muster, she headed

that direction and soon found herself outside . . . but inside a chain-link cage. Twelve-foot fencing surrounded the three sides not enclosed by the building, and chain-link covered the top, from fence to fence. She rattled the fence. Solid. Spot welding held it to the posts, and the four-foot-wide rolls of fence that made up the walls were welded to each other. There would be no dividing the rolls to create an opening.

She gazed around the pen and spied a few broken toys, a deflated kickball, and, curiously, a pile of clothing or something in one corner. Upon closer inspection, she saw that tattered blankets and linens, torn clothing, and what appeared to be soiled cloth diapers comprised the pile. In fact, all of the items appeared soiled, and not from the dirt of the enclosure. At least in the open air, the stink had abated.

Diapers? Broken toys? She cautiously lifted a torn shirt from the pile. It was a child's size. Had she found the missing children, or at least where they were being held?

She walked back into the building. The men at the doorway at the far end hadn't moved. Clearly, they had no concern about her escaping. She entered the first room to her right. Although larger than the room she had been taken into, it was no different, except the buckets were apparently empty. Odor-free, anyway. The room opposite that one was similar but held one large window, with bars, designed not to keep people out but to keep them in. The next two rooms matched the first two.

In that second windowed room she thought to test the bars. Secure. She returned to the first window and repeated her test. Also secure. But as she looked outside, she saw children playing in the "cage" behind the adjacent building, although a couple of them seemed to wander aimlessly about the enclosure.

As she headed toward the third, presumably windowed room, she realized it was the source of the music. Inside, sitting on the sleeping mats, were two young children, rocking forward and backward to the music. Their eyes stared straight ahead, and they did not recognize her entering the room. Bowls of rice and vegetables covered with flies sat in front of them.

Amy had seen such children before—the worst of the autism cases she had encountered as a nurse. Tears welled up in her eyes. These kids deserved better care. No, they deserved some care, any care at all. Instead they had been tossed away into this place like the soiled linens on the pile in the back.

The next room revealed other children, all withdrawn. As she passed one doorway, she was surprised by a young voice. It sounded like "chom-reap-sur." Amy had learned that "hello" in Khmer was pronounced that way. She entered the room to find two sets of twins. They seemed excited to see her. All four children were restrained by ropes tied to the wall, but the rope allowed them to sit or sleep on their respective mats.

"Chom-reap-sur," she whispered back and then held her finger to her lips, hoping they understood that meant to stay quiet.

She inspected the ropes and found each looped through rings on the wall and ultimately secured to the wall by a pin at the far end of the room, too far for the children to reach because the rings restricted the length of rope tethering them. But there was no lock. Releasing the pin would allow the rope to be removed. Once the pin was freed, the children could be easily freed.

But now was not the time. She had no way to escape with them should she free them.

She returned to the doorway, and the children began to cry. How could she communicate with the kids? She tried crude sign language, using two fingers to point to her eyes and then down the hall. And then to herself, pointing down the hall and back again. Would they get it?

She started to leave, but something held her back. She looked over the children. They appeared to be the right ages and sexes of four of the children missing from Felix's congregations—three boys, two identical, and the other a fraternal twin to the one girl. An idea came to mind to determine if these were those kids.

She returned to their sides and whispered, "Do you know Pastor Felix?" She realized they wouldn't understand the English, but maybe Felix would be called 'pastor' in either language. "Pastor Felix. Do you understand?"

The one boy who had said "hello" nodded his head. "Pastor Felix, good."

Amy smiled. "Yes, he is. Pastor Felix good." All four children nodded. She again tried her rough sign language to assure them, get them to stay quiet, and that she would be back.

At that moment, it seemed to be a promise she wouldn't be able to keep. And where were the other two kids?

CHAPTER FORTY-FOUR

Lynch felt his brain swirling, but this was different. He had been drugged once before and that felt as if the whirlpool was taking him down a drain into blackness. This time he seemed to be emerging into the light as if the whirlpool was about to cough him up onto the floor, or bed, or chair. What was he on?

His blurred vision quickly sharpened, and he found himself in the study of Amy's quarters. What had happened? He recalled that doctor, Tillson, saying he was giving him something for nausea. Instead, he blacked out.

He glanced up and saw a Cambodian man. He recognized the man, but could not recall his name.

The man breathed a sigh of relief. "Good, good. I not too late."

Lynch felt himself recovering from whatever he had been given. He even noted that his nausea was gone, although he could not claim his strength, nor his stamina, to be back to normal.

"W-who are you again?"

"I am Sok Darany. Darany is first name. I am lead technician here."

"What are you doing here. Where's Amy?"

The man sat on the floor next to the futon. "I worry Doctor Tillson drug you. I tell Amy that and give her new bag of fluid to give you. Then, you wake up."

"Drugged me? Why?"

"I know of Doctor Tillson past. I asked by, not remember words, man high up CIC who watch for wrong."

"Inspector General?"

"Yes, that. His office ask that I keep eye on doctor if woman ever hired by CIC to work here. Doctor know you are Amy boyfriend, so I worry he drug you to get you out of way."

To Lynch, who also knew of Tillson's past, that made sense.

"So, why are you here and not Amy?"

"Amy luggage come, and doctor get phone call. Do not know who call. Next thing I know, Amy ask me for first aid kit and say doctor take her to see chef wife who fall and cut arm. But chef not have wife so I get suspicious."

Amy went somewhere with Tillson? Lynch did not like what he heard.

"I watch for return, but only doctor come back, and he come straight here. I get to back door in time to see him come inside, then leave minute later. I rush here. Find you unconscious, breathing slow, not well. Pupils small, like pin."

The man used his fingers to exaggerate the comment. *Wait a minute*, thought Lynch. Pinpoint pupils? Tillson didn't give him something for nausea. He gave him an opiate overdose. Tillson tried to kill him.

"Opiates."

Darany nodded. "Yes. I run and find morphine missing from pharmacy. I grab Narcan and come right back. Happy to be in time."

"Thank you, Darany. I'm happy you were in time, too. I-I can't believe the man tried to kill me."

"I not believe, too. I not ever suspect doctor able do such a thing."

Lynch didn't hesitate in peeling back the tape and removing the IV catheter from his arm. He'd had enough of that. He stood . . . too quickly. Darany caught and steadied him.

"Where's Tillson now? He has to tell us where Amy is. If he did this to me, she's in trouble."

"Last I see, he go to quarters."

With Darany's assistance, Lynch headed toward the doctor's quarters next door. The door was unlocked. Feeling stronger, Lynch didn't wait for an invitation to come in. He opened the door and walked into the main room. No one was there. He checked the study. No one. But on the bed in the main bedroom, Tillson lay supine, his eyes open, not breathing. A rubber tourniquet remained wrapped around his left upper arm. An empty syringe sat in the linens next to him.

Lynch checked for a pulse. Was there one? He repositioned his fingers. Yes, it was weak and unsteady, but there was a pulse.

"Call for help."

Darany edged in next to Lynch and also checked the doctor. "I do not think so. Look, not breathe."

The tech took the bedside lamp and held it over the

doctor's face. He turned the light on and off, and repeated. Tillson's pupils were fixed and dilated.

Lynch checked again for a pulse, but did not find one this time.

"Okay. Call whoever you need to call. I need to find Amy."

Lynch hurried back to Amy's study. On the wall he had spotted a framed map of Cambodia earlier. He pulled it down and laid it on the desk. He traced the roads until he determined where they were at the lab and marked the map. Darany had said that Tillson hadn't been gone long. But how long? A 30-minute trip represented a much larger search area than a five or ten-minute trip.

He tried to flip the pen Amy had given him between his fingers. He couldn't do it. He had yet to find a pen he couldn't manipulate around his fingers. This pen was off-balance somehow.

He examined the writing instrument more closely. Exposing and retracting the pen tip posed no problem, but the top of the pen did not seem to want to open. Then he saw it. A small button or release of some kind that would allow him to twist the top. He smiled at the discovery. Roy had not left Amy without a way to call for help. His smile was short-lived, however. What good was the emergency call button when it was held in Lynch's hand?

Amy had not ventured to the rooms closest to the front door of the building. She had no desire to face the men there guarding her. To do so might stir up trouble not just for her but for the twins as well.

The phone Roy had provided had been confiscated and destroyed. Its pieces lay in the dirt just outside the building. Outside the lab, she doubted she would have enough signal strength to call for help even if she'd had an opportunity to use it. Even with no signal, she couldn't blame them for taking it. If she were in their shoes, not that she ever would be, she would have done the same. Why risk a potential phone call or having someone trace the location of the phone?

In her immediate situation, she wanted to know the time. She guessed it to be nearing noon but had no way to confirm that without the phone.

The other rooms of what appeared to be an old barracks revealed more damaged children. While the adjacent building appeared to hold healthier kids, this one held those too damaged to interact, except for the twins. She didn't understand that.

She retreated to the outdoor pen for the fresh air. She took that opportunity to look beyond the immediate vicinity of the building. Another tall fence topped with razor wire closed them in about 100 yards away. If it was built with the same precision as her current cage, then the only way out that she had seen to that point was the main gate. It had appeared unguarded when Tillson drove through, but that might only have been the appearance they wanted the outside world to see.

She heard yelling from inside and rushed to the door. The two men roamed from room to room until one of them saw her and informed the other. Together they came to get her. She saw little hope in putting up a fight, so she let them guide her along the hall and out the main door. They led her to the main building and into a brightly lit room filled with men.

She refused to show fear, but to her surprise, she felt none. The anger and defiance she had shown earlier had also disappeared. In their place, she felt peace, and she knew that God was in control, even here.

The two men led her to a raised platform and pushed her roughly up onto it. They stepped up next to her and stood one on each side of her. She tried to stand facing away from the men, but her guards pushed her around where the men could scrutinize her. Someone in the back talked to her "bidders" in Khmer. Several of the men nodded. Others looked disinterested. As she watched them, she became aware that while the room was filled, only six of the men were in control. These were the ones with the money.

"Turn. Face to your left."

She refused. A command in Khmer followed, and her guards forced her to turn to her left.

"Face behind you."

Again, she balked and was manhandled into position. Each time they touched her, they became more brutal.

The bidders became more animated and their chattering more vocal. One would speak out, only to be followed by another, and back and forth. From the look on Abdi's face, he not only enjoyed what he watched but that her price kept increasing.

"Take off your clothes!"

"No!"

"Take off your clothes!"

She wrapped her arms around her chest and dropped to a sitting position. She was not going to make it easy for them to strip her, although she felt certain that was next.

Two other men from the side of the room joined her guards. The four men each grabbed an extremity and began to spread her apart. A fifth man joined them and began to pull her shirt up. She struggled to get free.

An explosion from outside surprised all of the men in the room, and her guards dropped her. The men began to run from the room and toward the outside. Several of them pulled handguns from the waistbands of their pants. Soon, one sole guard remained with her as she pulled her clothing back together. When she saw that his attention seemed focused on the ruckus outside as well, she gave him a hard elbow to the chin, and he collapsed to the floor.

Amy sped out the door, but once in the hallway, she had no idea where to go. She knew the cars were parked outside the main door through which she had been led inside. To go that way was without a doubt the wrong move. But where?

A tug at her pants leg surprised her. She looked down to find a young boy, maybe six years old, pulling at her clothing and pointing the opposite direction from the main door. He ran ahead of her and motioned for her to follow. She did without hesitation, although she had no idea what she might find.

The boy led her through another large room that appeared to be a classroom and into a small antechamber. The window there was wide open, and he climbed up and through it as if he was a macaque climbing a papaya tree.

She followed suit, although the window presented a bit of a squeeze for her.

Once outside, she was surprised to find a twin boy. They each grabbed one of her hands and ran for the nearby fence. Upon arriving there, she discovered they had managed to find a hole in the chain-link. They eased through it without difficulty, but this presented a bigger challenge for Amy than the window.

"Here, let me help."

A pair of hands appeared to help widen the opening. She knew that voice from somewhere. As she stood up outside the fence, she looked up to find Doctor Jared Miller.

"Doctor Miller?" She was shocked to see him.

"Quick, away from the fence. Into the foliage where they can't see us."

Once the compound was out of easy view, he stopped, and the boys looked to him, smiling. He laughed.

"ការងារក្មេងប្រុសល្អ."

To Amy, it sounded like he said, "karngear kmengobrosa." She would never get the hang of the Khmer language.

"I told them, good job, boys." He handed each of them a packet of beef jerky. "I have yet to meet a boy who didn't like jerky."

"What are you doing here?"

"I should ask you the same thing, Ms. Gibbs. You're going undercover wasn't the wisest move."

"How did you know I was here?"

He explained how he had run into Reggie and Lynch at the children's home outside Kampong Thom and knew he had to help. He called upon some friends to help him get here by crossing Tonle Sap Lake straight into Krakor.

"I had discovered this place from drone footage before Tillson stole my rental car, but I thought it was abandoned. I staked out the drive to the lab again, like I had when I first ran into you. First, I discovered these two young urchins. Meet Ponleak and Phirum."

At the mention of their names, the boys stopped chewing and made *som pas* to Amy. She returned the gesture, saying "*Aw-koon*" to each in turn. They resumed chewing.

"From the best I could translate, they were taken from their home in an eastern province and brought here, but managed to escape a day and a half ago. They didn't know where to go, so they stuck around and stole food from the kitchen, while watching the road for someone they thought they could trust to help. I think that when they saw me spying from the side of the road, they knew I wasn't in league with the kidnappers. So, they revealed themselves to me, and we've watched the place together since. That's when I saw Tillson with you in the car. I suspected he was up to no good and followed you here."

"They showed me this hole in the fence. We saw the men take you inside the main building, and I knew it couldn't be good. We created a little diversion. The boys pointed out the man who brought them here. I couldn't understand everything they said but he appears to make his living taking children. So, with a grease-soaked rag we found, we lit up his car. *That* got their attention."

Jared's mention of the boys coming from an eastern

province meant that these two were not from Felix's congregations. Were even more twins involved?

"Yes, but my absence and the loss of that car will really anger them. They won't stop looking for me, and there are two other sets of twins tied up in the building where they held me. Plus, a third set I didn't find in that building. They all could be in danger, too."

"Not as long as Tillson wants twins for his devilish experiments. They won't harm them. Tell me, Ms. Gibbs, what did you see in that building?"

She gave him a detailed account of children she had found there.

"Do you still question my concerns about vaccines? I think we'll discover those children were used in Tillson's quest to exonerate his vaccine theories."

"And I think we'll find one or more children died. His lead tech mentioned two names that Tillson passed off as macaques."

"Oh dear. C'mon, let's see what we can do to get those twins."

He motioned to the twins. He placed his hand on each one's shoulder, and then held up six fingers and pointed to each of them again. They nodded.

"កូនប្រាំមួយនាក់?"

"I recognize the number six, but I'm not sure of the rest." He smiled and held up one hand to stop them. He pulled out his phone. "I should have thought of this earlier." He spoke into the phone, "There are six other children we need to find." He hit a button on the phone and Khmer came out of the speaker.

The boys' eyes widened. Each grabbed for the phone as if it was magical, but Ponleak prevailed. He handled the phone like it was a treasure, and spoke into it, "តើពួកគេនៅឯណា?"

Jared hit the correct button, and the phone said, "Where are they?"

Amy held up four fingers, for the four kids she had found, and pointed to the building where she had been held. The boys nodded and waved for the adults to follow them. In silence the four crept back into the compound where the boys took them the long way around to the barrack. The men remained occupied with putting out the car fire, having moved the vehicles nearby. Amy kept a close eye on them whenever they came into view between buildings. Soon they hid in some shrubs behind the cage.

Phirum pointed to the cage and asked for the phone. His words translated to "Follow me."

Follow me? Amy wondered. She had found no way out. How would they get the children without going through the front door just 20 yards from the thugs who wished them harm?

Phirum scurried straight to the corner of the fence where the rag pile sat, wormed his way under the fence, and emerged from underneath the pile on the other side. Ponleak began to follow but Amy held him back.

"I need to go. I know how to free them from the ropes."

Jared looked relieved. "Glad you're volunteering because I would never fit under there."

Amy ran to the fence and inspected the hole. There was ample evidence that small hands had cleared the dirt to create the opening. She inspected it more intently. Another tight squeeze.

She began to worm her way under, only to come to a complete stop halfway. The fence had snagged her clothing. She tried to back out but got nowhere. She tried again, forward and backward. Phirum came back under the laundry and tugged on her to no avail. She was stuck.

And then she heard the commotion. Men yelling. Feet running. Above them all, Abdi's voice stood out. "Find her!"

CHAPTER FORTY-FIVE

The CIC facility had shut down all but essential work activities as the news of Tillson's apparent suicide spread. Doctor Gilroy, as the deputy director, had contacted the authorities, both U.S. and Cambodian, and the embassy stated that representatives would be on their way to the lab. Cambodian police were also in route.

Lynch, desperate to find Amy, had spent no time discussing details with the doctor. He and Darany now sat in the tech's cubicle with access to the lab's landline phone system. He tried calling for help, but the number he dialed for Roy Smith rang and rang without going to voicemail. He tried Reggie's number with the same results.

"Darany, I'm not getting anywhere. The phones just keep ringing."

Darany frowned. "Sometime lab phone do this. Result of Cambodian phone system. Doctor Tillson always rely on cell phone."

Lynch had considered taking the doctor's cell phone from his residence, but recognized that it would be considered evidence in whatever crimes the man had committed. He would not tamper with that evidence. And yet, his own cell phone had no service. Thus, his attempt to use the lab's phones.

With Darany's assistance and feedback, Lynch fell back to the "old ways." He drew a radius around the lab consistent with the time period covering Tillson's absence from the facility. That was a lot of territory to cover.

"Darany, do you know of any place inside this circle where he might have taken her?"

The man shook his head. "Only see one, two house along main road. Maybe there?"

Lynch didn't think so. The houses he had seen sat right along the road. There was no seclusion, no place to keep her. And why had he taken her? Only one thought made sense. If the man was involved in trafficking children for his research, he would require resources, criminal resources. And that element would find an attractive American woman valuable in their sex trades. Or worse, Abdi had connected with that underworld and worked with them to get to Amy.

That latter idea seemed more and more plausible as Lynch contemplated it. Criminal connections could have been instrumental in Abdi's finding Pastor Jim along the highway. Police officers on the dole could easily use their positions to find a vehicle registered anywhere within the country.

"Well, we need to get busy. Is there a vehicle we can use?"

"Doctor's car at his quarters."

Lynch shook his head. "No, can't use that. Since he's dead, that becomes evidence, too. Anything else?"

"Electric cart? We use around the ground."

Lynch wanted to laugh—electric would offer stealth, but a golf cart? Still, the seriousness of the situation snuffed that thought out before a lip could curl. A golf cart would have to do.

"Let's go."

They passed through the front gate which sat wide open. Not a single guard in sight. Lynch became more convinced that a criminal group was involved, and that it likely provided the "guards" as well.

"Darany, who hired the guards?"

"Doctor Tillson. Say recommended to him, but I always wonder about them. Rough. Not professional."

The thought that Tillson's death might not be a suicide crossed his mind. He would have to take a closer look at the scene. Yet, there was a good chance the FBI might get involved, to assist the Cambodian government, since it was a prominent U.S. research facility.

As they traveled down the long drive to its intersection with the Cambodian road system, Lynch retrieved the pen from his pocket and inspected it again. He knew it functioned as more than a writing device, but what? He flicked it a couple of times. Nothing unusual there. He tried twisting it. It wouldn't budge going clockwise, but in going counter-clockwise, he felt a click.

He waited. Nothing happened.

They reached the main road and stopped. Lynch pulled out the map again and debated as to which way to go. Before he could look both directions, a dozen armed men, all dressed in camouflage, emerged from the scrub foliage surrounding them. And in the middle of the pack he saw Roy

Smith, Felix, and Reggie.

"Wh-where did you guys come from?"

Roy stepped forward first. "We've been camped back in the brush, out of sight. Where's Amy? Why'd you trigger her emergency alert?"

Lynch looked at the pen. "So that's what this was?" He looked at Roy and the others. "I'm trying to find her, too." He went on to explain the short version of what had happened that morning.

Reggie shook his head. "Tillson's dead?"

Lynch replied, "Yep, looked like a suicide, but I have my doubts. My concern is where Tillson took Amy. We came down here to start looking for her. Where was your camp?"

Felix pointed north, just off the main road. "About a hundred yards that way. They didn't go that way. We would've spotted them."

Lynch found that helpful in eliminating almost half of their search zone. "I have this map. Maybe your friends here can help. Umm, just who are they, by the way?"

Roy smiled. "Friends from Cambodia's SF-911 unit, the Counter Terrorist 14 Group, to be precise." He introduced Lynch to their commander. Lynch, in turn, introduced Darany, who looked a bit wary around the group.

The commander asked Roy something in Khmer.

"Lynch, is the lab secure? He doesn't want anyone to take advantage of the situation before the police show up. The lab would be a prime target for terrorists.

"No, it's not. I think the so-called guards there were thugs from whatever crime group had been cooperating with Tillson. I think they might have killed Tillson, too. To prevent him from talking."

The SF-911 commander gave orders to two of his men. They took off running up the drive.

Lynch watched them for a moment, amazed at their stamina in the heat, and then turned to show the others the map. He told them that his search radius had been based on the time during which Tillson had been gone from the lab.

The commander pointed to the southeast and spoke to Roy.

"There's an abandoned military base half a mile that way. At that moment, an explosion rocked the ground and a ball of fire and black smoke billowed up over the palm trees precisely where the man pointed.

Lynch sighed. "Yep. That would be Amy."

Amy felt a pair of stronger hands helping to free her from the fence. From Jared Miller's comical looks, she had expected him to act more like that Professor Shelly Oberon character in the *Jumanji* sequel. But the man had more metal than was obvious. First, he had come looking for Amy when he realized the danger she was in, and now, he didn't hesitate to leave the seclusion where they'd hidden moments before to come to her aid.

"There. You're free. Go get those kids. I'll be right here."

Amy ignored the "stuff" she crawled under and emerged from beneath the pile to follow Phirum to the door into the building. There, she led the way and found the four children as she had left them. They became animated upon seeing her, but Phirum said something that quieted them in a second. Within a minute, with Phirum's help, she had removed the ropes.

The children followed her to the room's doorway. When she stopped, they stopped. When she started sprinting to the back, they ran, although one of the boys said something to Phirum. Amy imagined that he wondered why they were running toward the cage which had no exit. She, too, would have questioned the move 40 minutes earlier.

When Phirum dove under the pile of dirty, feces-stained linens and clothing, the four children followed. Amy stayed behind, making sure they made it through past the barrier first. She heard men yelling from within the building. Had they been seen?

She scrambled into the heap of cloth and wiggled under the fence. Jared was there to help. Together they gathered the children into a tight group.

Two more to go. "Which way?"

Jared seemed uncertain. Men could be seen running between the buildings and fanning out along the perimeter fence. "Back to the shrubs over there."

As they ran the 50 or so feet to the protection of cover, the commotion around them suddenly changed. New sounds, from the direction of the main gate, reached their ears. More shouting. Gun fire. Several sudden flashes of light followed by loud bangs. More yelling. Amy saw three of the "bad guys" trying to climb and escape over the fence, only to face the razor wire at the top and drop to the ground. Men who appeared to be soldiers surrounded them.

"Amy! Amy Gibbs! Where are you?" The voice came from the direction of the main building."

Lynch? She stopped Jared and the kids. "I-I think help has arrived. You stay here with the children, and I'll see if I can figure out what's happened."

With caution, she edged along the side of the building. She still couldn't see Lynch or anyone else she recognized. At the same time, she also didn't see Abdi or any of her captors. She felt something bump into her leg and looked down. All six children huddled behind her and behind them stood Jared with his palms up.

"Don't look at me. They refused to stay with me."

"Amy!"

She looked back toward the main building to see Lynch running toward her. A second later, Felix came running from an adjacent building with two kids in his arms. He headed their way, and the four children they had just rescued bound past her and began running toward the man.

"Pastor Felix," all four squealed in unison. The man lowered the children in his arms and fell to both knees. He reached out for all of them with both arms. The group hug that ensued brought tears to Amy's eyes.

She walked over to Lynch and stretched her arms around him. But something was different. She felt no hesitation. Her guard wasn't just down, it had left. As they embraced, she found her way to his lips. She would no longer resist her attraction, her love, for the man who had flown halfway around the world to protect her.

"Thank you, Lynch," she whispered into his ear.

"I love you, Amy Gibbs. I always have," he whispered back.

*　*　*

Abdullah Said Abdi was no man's fool. He had survived two battles between warlords in Somalia, as well as a challenge to his leadership of their clan. He still bore the scar on his face from that fight. He and his crew of pirates had survived the guns of a U.S. naval ship protecting a cargo ship in international waters off Mogadishu. Not once, but twice.

He had traveled through Mexican drug cartel territory to find a way into the U.S. but had not succeeded unscathed. A bullet wound to his left upper arm took months to heal. Ironically, upon securing his position among the Somali contingent in St. Louis and establishing his own "pharmaceutical" business, that same cartel partnered with him to move their drugs into and throughout the U.S. His "business" matured and with it came the role of terrorist and the plan which that woman had foiled. He had failed to exact his revenge then, but as the noose of American law enforcement tightened, he again escaped.

And now, he managed to escape again.

In America, he had heard the saying that a cat had nine lives. He was the king of cats, a lion among his people. But he still was not satisfied.

He had learned from a near-fatal past mistake that the explosion of a car foretold nothing good. So, when the car outside the building where his auction of the woman was being held shook the building and lit up the sky, he did not wait around to see those men try to extinguish it . . . or what kind of omen the explosion signaled. He used the opportunity to slip out the main gate. Hidden within the brush, he watched as Cambodian military and four white men advanced on the school compound with the precision of a SWAT team. Perhaps that was exactly what those men were trained to be.

Nevertheless, he would not be among those they apprehended. Sadly, Khay Oudom would be, and he would lose his chauffeur. However, as a survivor he had learned to use his ingenuity. He would find his way south, back to the coast. From there, he could signal his crew on the trawler. And, once on board, the three-week trip back to the U.S. would allow time for those hunting him to forget about him. His return to Somalia would not be in his immediate future. The woman still lived.

What was that other English saying, "He who fights and runs away, will live to fight another day?" He would still take his vengeance upon that woman.

CHAPTER FORTY-SIX

Still holding Lynch's hand, Amy backed away and saw Jared Miller with the other twin boys—Ponleak and Phirum—approaching. The excitement and joy that filled her heart a moment earlier fell upon seeing their faces. Something terribly wrong remained.

Lynch walked over to the doctor and extended his hand. "Thank you. You were here in time to save her."

Jared nodded. "I'm glad I was able to help. I only wish we'd been here soon enough to save them all." Sadness filled the man's countenance. "Ponleak and Phirum have been telling me about this place. Follow us."

Amy suspected they would be led to the building where she had been held, to show them the damaged children living there. Instead, the two boys waved with their arms for the adults to follow them, pointing toward the area behind a different building.

Lynch called to Reggie. "Reggie, Commander, you might want to come with us."

The two men rushed to join them.

"What's up?" asked Reggie.

"I'm not sure, but I think we're about to discover

something about this place."

Behind the distant building, and its own cage, the boys stopped and pointed to a clearing. Amy saw nothing out of the ordinary, but this time, the boys spoke to the commander in their native tongue. The man walked into the clearing and knelt onto the ground. With his hands he began to dig into the sandy soil, gently at first and then with more vigor. Five minutes later, with Lynch's help, both men dropped their heads.

Amy walked closer to them to see that they'd found, at the same time fearful of what they'd found. Her heart sank as she caught a glimpse of it—a child's hand and forearm. She gazed around the immediate area. Now she could see the small patches of disturbed dirt. She, Pastor Jim, and Pat had never made it to Choeung Ek, the Buddhist memorial to those lost under Pol Pot. Cambodia had over 20,000 such Killing Fields, and she had had no desire to see it after visiting Prison S-21. Yet now they had found a new killing field. Dozens of small graves surrounded them.

The debriefing seemed to take all day. Military and police vehicles filled the old-military-compound-turned-school-of-torture. A helicopter had delivered the U.S. ambassador himself, along with three top Cambodian ministers. Reggie and the ambassador spent the afternoon trying to prevent a major international incident.

Amy and Lynch, as well as Felix and Jared Miller to a lesser degree, gave testimony to half a dozen officials. They spoke of their suspicions about medical testing being done on the children and how those suspicions came about following the kidnapping of the twins from the villages where Felix provided relief. They all steered clear of mentioning Christianity, or churches, or missions. Communists still ruled Cambodia, and they did not want to risk their work there. General Khan, as the provincial police commander, found himself the subject of questioning when it became known that he had done little to respond to the reports of those kidnappings. He was taken into custody when his phone number was discovered on Tillson's phone. Amy spoke of what had happened to her, while Lynch did the same about Tillson's attempt to kill him.

The afternoon would soon yield to evening and Amy felt exhausted. She needed something to lift her spirits.

Felix walked up to her.

"Hey, I've got something I need your help with. Are you cleared to leave?"

"I think so. Let me ask."

She approached the man who had been tasked with investigating the incident and cleared it with him.

"I'm good to go. What's up?"

"Follow me."

Felix led her to his Land Rover, where the back seat was filled to capacity with children. The short drive south to the small village where she had first met this incredible man was filled with the laughter of children. At seeing the happiness of parents and children being reunited, joy once again found its way into Amy's heart.

"Thank you, Felix, for letting me be part of this."

He smiled. "I know the horrors of what you, we, saw

back there will be forever etched in our minds. But I hope the joy of this reunion will help restore your hope for humanity. I know it does mine." He paused and looked at the four remaining children in his Rover. "C'mon, we have two more families to reunite."

CHAPTER FORTY-SEVEN

"Captain, it's back!"

Captain William Chase looked at his radarman. "What's back?"

He sat in his chair on the bridge of the USCGC Bertholf, as they cruised north ten miles off the Baja Peninsula. Their recent drug interception efforts had paid off again with the seizure of a "rum runner" packed to the gunwales with cocaine as it sped north toward the U.S. coast.

"That weird radar signature we saw a month or so ago, sir. The Somali fishing trawler that suddenly picked up speed to 50 knots and then disappeared."

"What's its location?"

"That's strange, too, sir. It's in almost the same spot— twenty miles offshore, more or less parallel to the Mexican border."

Will thought about that. Had there been something in the water, a buoy perhaps, that gave off computer-generated radar signals to act as a decoy? Had they missed it? And why a Somali trawler? At that time, why not a Somali ship? They had received word to watch out for a fugitive Somali terrorist. If the cartels knew of that, as they likely did, a

Somali ship would be the most obvious decoy. The Bertholf's attention would be drawn there as a high priority target.

"Is it moving?"

"Yes, sir, but this time it's heading due east. We're on an intercept course."

"Don't alter our course or speed. Ensign, send up a UAV. Let's see what we're dealing with but not give away our hand by moving in on it."

A handful of minutes later, the UAV found their target.

"Sir, it actually is a trawler, but they have a cigarette boat on the port davit."

That, in itself, meant they were up to no good. For what purpose would a fishing trawler use a fast boat like that? Only one thing—smuggling, whether people or drugs.

"Take a closer look. How many people on board? Anything out of the ordinary about it?"

"Yes, sir. Closing in. Images are on your screen."

Will gave his attention to the monitor above him. Other than the fast boat, everything above deck seemed on the up and up. He counted three crew members to the stern of the bridge, on the main work deck. There were two men on the bridge, or so it appeared. A glare on the glass made it difficult to get an exact count. Wherever they were headed and whatever their intentions were, they clearly weren't fishing.

At that moment, a man stepped outside the bridge and stood gazing forward. Will had seen that face before.

"Lieutenant, do we have that DHS alert on the Somali they were hunting for last month?"

The younger officer nodded. "One moment, sir." After a

number of keystrokes on the keyboard at his station, he added, "On your screen, sir."

Will pursed his lips and nodded. Abdullah Said Abdi. "Well, I'll be. We've been given a second chance. That dirtball seems to be headed back into the U.S. Move to intercept and board. Full speed ahead."

"Aye-aye, sir. Full speed and moving to intercept." The junior officer picked up a hand mic and announced, "Boarding team, get ready. Fifteen minutes to launch point."

Will directed his attention to alerting his command in California. After consultation with the admiral, he had orders to take the terrorist into custody, as well as permission to use deadly force if required.

Eighteen minutes later, their long-range interceptor deployed from the stern ramp. Its crew of five was fully armed, and its M240 machine guns were manned. They did not expect a compliant welcoming committee.

"LRI deployed, sir."

Will donned his headset and with it was in direct communication with the lieutenant commanding the interceptor.

"Our goal is the arrest of Abdullah Said Abdi, Lieutenant."

"Understood, sir."

Moments later, as the 11-meter, aluminum rigid-hull inflatable neared the target vessel, gunfire could be heard.

"Sir, they're firing on us."

"Return fire."

Will could hear the roar of the M240 as it fired its .30 caliber rounds from disintegrating belts at over 700 rounds per minute. It would shred the cabin of that trawler in minutes.

"Incoming! Hard to port!"

The Bertholf had come into range where its surveillance electronics could home into the action between the LRI and the trawler. Will saw the RPG heading toward the LRI and missing his craft.

"Lieutenant, clear the immediate area." He turned his attention back to the bridge crew. "Weapons control, bring the Bofors to bear. Scuttle that ship."

The Bofors MK 110 was designed for both surface and anti-aircraft warfare. Its 57mm shell had an effective range of over five miles and the Somali ship was less than a mile away. One shot, mid-ship, was all that was required.

"Lieutenant, check for survivors."

"Yes, sir."

Five minutes later, the LRI reported no survivors and returned to the Bertholf. Will Chase hoped he would have the opportunity to tell Lynch Cully personally that they were now even.

CHAPTER FORTY-EIGHT

Lynch wiped the sweat from his brow and took a drink from his water bottle, as he looked back along the 80-foot "sewer" line he had just completed behind the children's home in Tnolbail Village. Connected to five squatty-potties that sat outside, next to the building, the four-inch PVC pipe directed the waste away from the home and into a nearby drainage ditch that served as the "rural sewer district." Clearly not up to American standards, but few things in the Third World were.

Amy handed him a bamboo rice snack.

"Not bad for a city boy," she said. "Nice work. I'm not sure who Jim and Pat are going to miss more, you or me."

"Definitely you," he replied.

Amy smiled. She knew he was being complimentary. During the three weeks following the CIC debacle, they had agreed to remain available for the investigation. In return, the government had granted them extended visas. Between interviews, they had worked together on a variety of projects—a new well, a new house for a single mom of six, feeding kids almost daily, and finally, the latrine for the children's home. Lynch hadn't pulled the short straw when it came to the hard and dirty work—he had volunteered. And he smiled throughout.

Amy felt a new appreciation for him growing day by day. At least she told *him* it was "appreciation." She recognized her feelings as being much deeper. And when she saw him playing with the kids during their lunch break or at the end of a day, she saw a lot more "potential" in him. He had told her he had changed. Well, God had changed her as well.

In fact, God had shown her things about herself she had never recognized. Where once a self-centered nature existed, she was more prone to put others first. Her "Christianity" also had had a lot of "self" in its expression. Pastor Jim called it a "cultural Christianity." She identified as being an evangelical but mostly because her father had been a believer, not because she had her own deep relationship with God. She saw that changing, too. God had started her along a path of deeper relationship, and she eagerly sought Him.

Pastor Jim and Mama Pat, as the kids called her, approached.

"Let's head to the hotel. You can get cleaned up and then we'll treat you to a dinner you won't forget—scorpions, beetles, tarantulas, crickets, snake and an assortment of fruits. We'll top off the meal with durian. Maybe some baby bees."

Amy gagged at the thought. Lynch, too, shook his head. Jim was known to love durian, the world's smelliest fruit. Amy didn't want to be in the same room with it.

"I didn't think the restaurant would let you bring

durian in for fear of chasing out the other customers."

"They let *me* bring it. We just have to sit at the table closest to the open doors." He grinned.

"I think I'll still pass, thank you," said Lynch. At that moment, his phone rang. He furrowed his brow at seeing the Caller ID. "I don't know who this is. Give me a sec." He turned away from the group.

Amy didn't want to eavesdrop, but . . .

"This is Cully . . . Who? . . . Hey, wow, a voice from the past. What are you now, a commander? . . . A captain. Way to go . . . What? Did I hear you correctly?" Lynch started pumping the air with his fist and jumped up and down. "Yes! Will, thanks for the call. Hey, we're flying through San Francisco in four days. You going to be in dock? . . . You're not. Oh man, I would love to treat you to dinner for that news. You have no idea what a relief that is . . . Thanks. God speed."

He returned to the group with a grin from ear to ear. "Talk about God at work. That was a Coast Guard captain that I knew, like, well, years ago when he was a lieutenant JG. He called to tell me we no longer have to worry about Abdullah Said Abdi. They caught him trying to get back to the U.S. and ended up shooting his trawler out of the water. They found no survivors. He's gone to meet his maker."

Amy expected to feel as if a weight had been lifted from her, but in fact, she didn't. Her fear of that man had dissolved weeks earlier.

Jim and Lynch wandered away, and Pat took Amy aside. "Remember that young woman who spoke to you in perfect English? I've been watching you. I think you've taken those words to heart. You *have been* embracing what God has for you."

"I'm trying. It's not easy sometimes."

"I know. That's why God gives us helpmates. I've been watching you two." She pointed to Lynch. "It's really clear how he feels about you. Don't let him get away. He's one of the good ones."

Amy had to agree. But the ball was in his court. He had failed to commit once before, and that part of their past still nagged her. In fact, her history with men so far had been one of their failing to commit. But he *was* one of the good ones . . . and he *had* changed.

Sneak Preview: *Resurrected Trouble*

ONE

As the sun rose for the seventh day, its scorching heat seemed to evaporate away even more of his strength. He was a man comfortable with the sea, but now, with no land in sight, perhaps it would be best to simply let the sea claim him. All he needed to do was let go.

Had he really survived a full week adrift?

The fools. He had told the boat's captain and crew to cooperate. He told them to ditch the fast boat, leaving a GPS locator aboard so they could find it later. He had a suitable and impossible-to-find hiding spot aboard the fishing vessel. Even infrared detection equipment wouldn't find his location surrounded by ice and their plentiful catch. Their paperwork was in order, and their excuse that engine problems had prompted their heading for the nearest port in Mexico was easily backed up. A special governor on the engine could duplicate the problem time and time again, as often as they needed to authenticate their claim to any intervening authority.

He stepped outside the bridge in time to see the drone coming their way. He screamed to the captain to release and move away from the fast boat on their port davit, but the man was attached to his expensive toy, despite the fact that its presence screamed "smugglers." The man's hesitation gave the drone time to come close enough that its markings as U.S. Coast Guard were clearly seen, close enough to see the fast boat. Maybe even close enough to see him.

As he rushed to the access of his hiding place, he heard the crew begin to shoot. The men had a death wish, something Abdullah did not share with his countrymen. As he secured his spot, he heard the splintering of wood as return fire from the Coast Guard began to shred the cabin and bridge of their vessel. Then came the whoosh of an RPG launch. He knew at that moment, should he survive the next ten minutes, he would not be celebrating with the captain and crew. And if he didn't, he would see them in Paradise.

Inside his waterproof cache, surrounded by the metal bins filled with ice and fish, he felt more than heard the boat explode around him. Allah protected him. The bins withstood the attack, and he believed he now floated free of the debris along with those containers. Yet, he couldn't leave his space just yet. The Coast Guard would be searching for survivors. He felt confident that there would be no others, but only by Allah's good will would the sailors not think to inspect the fish holding bins more closely.

He lost track of time inside the dark space where he lay supine. That claustrophobic world began to become more turbulent. The ice had no doubt melted, and the water it left behind began to toss and heave with every swell. With one sudden lurch he found himself upside down and his face planted against what had previously been the top of his hiding space.

Floating with the swells and cursing the sun, he now recalled the sense of panic that had rushed through him at that moment. Panic was a foreign emotion to him. The fish bins no longer acted like their own little boat, displacing the sea and staying afloat. Whether upside down or sideways, they would begin to take on enough water to sink. In fact, it had felt as if they already were. The panic came from the thought of being dragged to a deep watery grave in a metal coffin of his own design.

In another instant, amid creaking and groaning of metal rubbing metal, he sensed his "casket" shooting upward and beginning to bob up and down. The image of a simple cork fishing bobber undulating in the wake of a boat replaced the panic.

But only for a second.

He found himself standing on his head in the rectangular cubicle. That meant the door was underwater. To open it now would flood the space with water. Or would it? Again, Allah's hand had intervened. If he could keep the container in its current position, he could escape, shut the door behind him, and keep the air trapped inside. What might have been his coffin became his flotation device.

Today, on day seven—or was it eight? —of his ordeal, he reconsidered the decisions he had made then. Sinking deep into cold water, he would become hypothermic before succumbing to a lack of oxygen in the chamber. It would have been a peaceful way to die. Of course, the cubicle's breaking away from the fish bins robbed him of that option.

Now, he barely had the strength to hold onto his bobber. His lips were chapped to the point of bleeding, and he had sores and scabs covering his scalp and shoulders. When using his shirt to cover his head, his shoulders burned, and vice versa. Water surrounded him, but he was dying of thirst.

He closed his eyes and focused on saying his *dua*, his prayer to Allah to reach home safely. "*Alw bham a wbaa llrbhanwa tdwhb ab lsha yyghaadr 'llnyana ḥw bwal h alnḥ mld whww 'l a kll shyw'r qd yrsh aybṭwnn twamb wnḍ 'abnd wnr sajadrwny lḥr bmnaa ḥramdwn ṣndqa allahl w'khdyhr whndhṣhr 'bdh w hzm alaahḥlzhab wnḥ'dwh bk mn shrha wshr ahlha wshr ma fyha.*" I have come back, I have come back, I seek forgiveness from Allah with such a repentance that leaves me with no sin.

AFTERWORD—The Vaccine Issue

First and foremost, everything you've ever heard or read stating that "the science on vaccines is settled" is wrong. The statements regarding vaccines within the text of this story are true and verified.

Five years ago, I stood firmly in the pro-vaccine camp. As a physician, we were never taught specifically about vaccines, although we learned about the forms of immunity our bodies possess. We were told that vaccines worked, they were crucial to public health, and that we could trust the CDC, WHO, and other health agencies which had only our "best interests" at heart. Since retiring from practice, I've actually had the time to research the topic and discovered just how naive I was. The afterword I wrote is just a "brief" summary of what I've learned. I could add pages and pages on each vaccine.

Yet, that "brief" summary would add another 45 pages to this book, so I opted to make it available online at my website:

https://www.braxtondegarmo.com/the-vaccine-issue.

I hope you'll take the time to read it and educate yourself on vaccines. It could make a difference to you and your family.

ACKNOWLEDGMENTS

As always, I again want to acknowledge and thank my dear wife, Paula, for her valuable proofreading skills, help and encouragement. Many thanks as well to Lenda Selph for her expert proofreading. I thought I was getting better, but together they keep finding my "goofs."

Many thanks as well to Capt. (Ret) Jerry Underwood, USCG, and William H. Hawley, Class of 1966 USCGA, for their assistance regarding the Coast Guard material within the book.

A big thank you to my editor, Patrick LoBrutto, who has secretly admitted that he's also become a fan of my books and can't wait for the next one. Oops. Not a secret anymore. His feedback always makes my stories better.

And finally, a HUGE thank you to "Pastor Jim" and "Mama Pat." Their unselfish work throughout SE Asia has made an incredible impact on the people they minister to. Sometimes at great personal risk, they work tirelessly behind the scenes in communist and Hindu countries where Christianity is a target for persecution and prosecution. As such, I'm not supposed to reveal their real names, but they know who they are.

ABOUT THE AUTHOR

Braxton can't lay claim to wanting to be a writer all his life, although his mother and seventh grade English teacher were convinced he had what it would take. A bachelor's degree in Bio-Medical Engineering led to medical school and a residency in Emergency Medicine. He served for a decade in the U.S. Army Medical Corps with tours such as the Chief, Emergency Medical Services at Fort Campbell, KY, and as a research Flight Surgeon at Fort Rucker, AL. Who had time to write?

By the 1990s, as a civilian, his professional and family life had settled down, somewhat, and his mother once again took up her mantra, "Write a book. You're a good writer." In 1997, a Valentine's Day writing contest convinced him that maybe he could write fiction. He spent the next fifteen years learning the craft of writing.

Now, twenty-plus years after that first hesitant start, he has sixteen novels published, as well as non-fiction books and a children's book, and can't find enough time to write. As a Christian, he writes "true-life" Christian fiction (suspense and thrillers) that many call "cutting edge," as he's not afraid to take on such issues as human trafficking, racism, and more. His characters are real-life as well, with all the flaws and blemishes real people have. As such, his books are never likely to gain acceptance by the Christian Bookseller Association. But then, he never intended to tell stories just to the choir.

Books by Braxton DeGarmo:

<u>Still Here Series:</u>
The End Begins - 1
The Shaking - 2
The Beasts – 3
The Trumpets – 4
The Mark - 5

<u>Non-fiction Study Guides:</u>
Still Here! Surviving the End Times
Still Here! The Apocalypse is Now
Still Here! Countdown Revelation

<u>MedAir Series:</u>
Looks that Deceive – 1
Rescued and Remembered – 2
The Silenced Shooter – 3
Wrongfully Removed – 4
A Zealot's Destiny – 5
Kidnapped Nation - 6
The Khmer Connection - 7
Resurrected Trouble - 8

<u>Seamus O'Connor Thrillers:</u>
The Militant Genome
Ten Seconds 'Til

<u>Other Books:</u>
Indebted

<u>Children's Books:</u>
The Toucan Who Can Can-can